Science Fiction: The Future

Science Fiction: The Future

Edited by Dick Allen
University of Bridgeport

Harcourt Brace Jovanovich, Inc.
New York / Chicago / San Francisco / Atlanta

ISBN: 0-15-578650-4

LIBRARY OF CONGRESS CATALOG CARD NUMBER: 78-152584

Printed in the United States of America

Copyrights and Acknowledgments

COVER PHOTO courtesy Cutler-Hammer, Inc., Milwaukee, Wisconsin.

ISAAC ASIMOV for permission to reprint his "Social Science Fiction" from Reginald Bretnor, ed., Modern Science Fiction. Copyright 1953 by Coward-McCann, Inc.
LURTON BLASSINGAME for "They" by Robert A. Heinlein, copyright 1941 by Street & Smith Publications, Inc. For "The Green Hills of Earth" by Robert A. Heinlein, copyright 1947 by The Curtis Publishing Co. Both reprinted by permission of the author's agent, Lurton Blassingame.
CITY LIGHTS BOOKS for "Poem Rocket" by Allen Ginsberg from Kaddish and Other Poems, Nineteen Fifty-Eight to Nineteen Sixty. Copyright © 1961 by Allen Ginsberg. Reprinted by permission of City Lights Books.
COMMENTARY for "The Future of Prediction" by John P. Sisk. Reprinted from Commentary by permission. Copyright © 1970 by the American Jewish Committee.
DELACORTE PRESS for "Harrison Bergeron" by Kurt Vonnegut, Jr., from Welcome to the Monkey House by Kurt Vonnegut, Jr., copyright © 1950, 1951, 1953, 1954, 1955, 1958, 1960, 1961, 1962, 1964, 1966, 1968 by Kurt Vonnegut, Jr. A Seymour Lawrence Book / Delacorte Press. Used by permission.

To
Clifford D. Simak
and
Judith Merril
for
their writings, their
friendship, their belief.

Preface

This book assumes that science fiction has become a respectable genre of literature, deserving serious critical and scholarly attention. In the late 1960s and early 1970s, Vladimir Nabokov, Kurt Vonnegut, Jr., Doris Lessing, John Barth, Jorges Luis Borges, John Williams, Andre Voznesensky—to name only a few major contemporary writers—have been involved with science fiction concerns and techniques. Issues that SF writers have traditionally dealt with have become matters of public interest and concern. In 1969, Michael Crichton's *The Andromeda Strain* helped make the American public conscious of biological dangers that might result from a spaceship's return to Earth; books on ecology and "the population problem" are discussed on late-night television shows. Allen Ginsberg says, "We're in science fiction now," and Buckminster Fuller calls this world, "Spaceship Earth." Songs such as *In the Year 2525, Hey, Mr. Spaceman,* and *2000 Light Years from Home* have climbed the best-selling record charts. In the college cafeteria students discuss Robert Heinlein's *Stranger in a Strange Land,* Frank Herbert's *Dune,* the Hobbits of Tolkien, and the Lensman series. In the movie theaters or on television one is confronted with the psychedelic visions of *Barbarella* and *2001,* Rod Steiger with living tattoos, the burning of books in *Fahrenheit 451,* Charly achieving immense intelligence, the invasion of the Green Slime, and a broken Statue of Liberty on the sands of *The Planet of the Apes.* In a world where it is increasingly difficult to tell fantasy from reality, it appears that the age of space has truly arrived, and with it the age of the science fiction writer (or as he would rather be called today, the speculative fiction writer) and the futurist.

Science Fiction: The Future is designed to explore concepts of the future as seen by SF writers. It is a deliberately open-ended book, in keeping with the nature of its subject. For some it may also provide an introduction to fictional and nonfictional treatments of an area that deserves increasing sociological and critical attention.

Virtually all of the selections are from American and British writers, as I have wished to focus the book on concerns of English-speaking peoples, as well as to avoid the obvious problems of treating literature in translation. However, the student should be aware that there is a great body of science fiction in the literature of other countries, particularly in the Soviet Union. Most Soviet science fiction is of the philosophical utopia and "man triumphs against all odds" type. To Western readers, these stories usually seem old-fashioned. Marxism lends itself especially easily to predictions of the future, which, although interesting, seem seriously flawed by a lack of awareness of ecology and of the consequences of an ever-expanding technology. But this short-sightedness is rapidly changing and the student who wishes to sample the Marxist writers might well be referred to Nicolai Amosoff's *Notes from the Future* (1970) and to the discussion of Soviet science fiction in the May 1969 issue of *Extrapolation: A Science-Fiction Newsletter.*

The book at hand is divided into three parts. The fiction has generally been chosen for its literary merit as well as for how it transforms normal reality and represents a variety of perspectives. The first part is meant to lead the reader into the subject without causing extreme disorientation. Richard Wilbur's poem gives needed advice to the futurist, begging him to speak in human terms as he foretells destruction. The *Time* Magazine article *No Way Out, No Way Back* treats the scene of passengers stranded by the February 1969 snowstorm as a prediction of a terrifying future. David Lyle discusses the results of overpopulation; George Mac-Beth constructs a serious parody of the steps leading toward complete nuclear war. Nathaniel Hawthorne's *Earth's Holocaust* is included in this section to show how a sense of perspective can either change or reaffirm the belief in the importance of man's accomplishments.

The second part, *Alternate Futures*, is subdivided into two sections. In *The Present as Future* the word *future* is used to connote a sense of unreality. These strongly allegorical stories concern a future that may have happened or may be happening. All deal with different aspects of reality and might be closer to what is termed speculative fiction or social science fiction than to that which is commonly called science fiction. Isaac Bashevis Singer writes a fantasy in which the Earth is a preordained Hell. Nunez, wandering into H. G. Wells's "country of the blind," confronts the problems of meeting another way of life. *They* concerns a mental patient who may or may not be insane and raises interesting questions: Are aliens already with us? Are we characters in someone's dream? What is the nature of the paranoid? Can the imagination be controlled? Kenneth Koch's *The Artist* and Donald Barthelme's *The Balloon* are both heavily symbolic renderings of events that may happen tomorrow; both ask us to consider how we shall react to the tremendous changes ahead of us.

The section devoted to the future as such is composed of more traditional science fiction. It will be useful for the student to compare and contrast these stories with those in the preceding section, as a method of discovering what formal elements make up a science fiction story. Strong differences in style and emphasis between the stories in the two sections may also be noted. *The Future* includes stories on perfect equality (Vonnegut), utopia (Forster), the artist in the future (Zelazny), war's aftermath (Bradbury), immortality (Thomas), and the end of the world (Clarke, Wells).

The last part, *Theories,* provides basic definitions and discussions of science fiction as a genre, as literature, and as a medium for understanding changes in future religion and society. Kingsley Amis, in *Starting Points,* gives a brief history of the genre. Susan Sontag's essay on the SF film points the way toward a type of pop and archetypal criticism that is useful in understanding the literature. John P. Sisk considers the hidden prejudices and limitations of the "'futurists."

At the end of the book are forty suggestions for critical or research paper topics. A list of term paper titles that may help the student to focus his ideas is also provided. Primary science fiction materials are extremely easy to obtain and since most students will naturally supplement this book with such materials, a selective bibliography closes the book. Most of the works listed are available in paperback.

Dick Allen

Contents

part 3   Theories   243

Science Fiction: The Future

Introduction

I

In the city the noise is constant, terrific. Police cars sit at intersections, waiting for traffic accidents. Sweet young girls, wearing transparent blouses and leather skirts, search for and enter the hidden doorways. Many of the girls have long wires dangling from their ears; expressions change constantly. Neon lights flash. People halt, look around to check if anyone is watching, and then furtively slip small pills into their mouths.

Neil Armstrong has walked on the moon.

The ion drive is in the first stage of what appears to be a successful development.

Public nudity, voyeurism, and exhibitionism are relatively legal.

Robots are beginning to exhibit emotional responses.

In Co-Op City, built in lower New York State, live some people who will not venture out of its boundaries from birth until death.

Ultramicrofiche (UMF) can put two thousand pages on a transparency small as an average book page.

No one seems more at home in this futurist world than the science fiction writer, for in the 1970s fact has at last caught up with his fantasies and predictions. The science fiction writer has found himself to be a person in demand—a writer whose previously cultish genre of literature has become enormously popular, and whose skills of prediction and extrapolation are suddenly very useful.

The old science fiction was a type of literature that stressed the future and made new inventions seem plausible—in some ways it was a literature of translation. The scientists came up with various hypothetical inventions and the SF writers wove stories around these inventions. Science fiction was (a large part of it still is) that genre of literature defined by SF writer and critic Sam Moskowitz as "a branch of fantasy identifiable by the fact that it eases the 'willing suspension of disbelief' on the part of its readers by utilizing an atmosphere of scientific credibility for its imaginative speculations in physical science, space, time, social science, and philosophy."

The key word for the new science fiction is *speculation,* and the key factor in its increased importance may well be how it has moved from a stress on the painless translation of scientific theories toward a stress on the nature of human reactions when encountering "future shock." As we move rapidly toward the year 2000, it appears that our civilization is becoming increasingly, even obsessively future-oriented. This attitude is partly attributable to the sheer excitement of those who realize that they may actually live to see the first years of the next millennium; but more of the future orientation relates to a growing mass popular consciousness that our technological society is determining our futures, rather than we determining the direction in which our burgeoning technology will take us. Futurist articles are no longer confined to the back pages of popular SF magazines. A whole new group of "futurists" has begun to organize and to be written about in such books as Victor C. Ferkiss' *Technological Man: The Myth and the Reality.* The physicist Gerald Feinberg has devoted his book *The Prometheus Project* to an urgent plea that mankind set future goals for itself before it is too late.

SF writers have been dealing with similar concepts and possible futures for most of their writing lives. Will mankind achieve a working symbiotic relationship with the machine, as Samuel R. Delany posits in his novel *Nova?* What would be the result of mass freezing of the dead? Clifford Simak deals with the problem in *Why Bring Them Back From Heaven.* James Blish studied the effects of immortality in a series of novels collectively entitled *Cities in Flight;* Jonathan Swift has presented a picture of the immortals in *Gulliver's Travels.* Philip Wylie has written at length about hydrogen bomb warfare. For almost any possible future we can imagine, an SF writer has postulated the manner in which humans will react to the new environment.

The SF writer often writes with a sense of fear. Afraid of the future he posits, he constructs stories to warn his readers. Two of the most famous classics of mainstream SF writing, Aldous Huxley's *Brave New World* and George Orwell's *1984,* may have helped us avoid taking the direction in which our civilization once seemed headed. The warnings continue, for the SF writer is generally a humanity lover and an individualist. He writes to make his nightmare visions so vivid that they will be discussed and hopefully avoided.

However, a utopia such as that set out in *Brave New World* is not always despaired of in SF writing, and a counter-optimism can provide comfort. Huxley's novel *Island,* written toward the end of his life, offered a transcendent vision of a future utopia. Robert Heinlein's *Stranger in a Strange Land* owes much of its popularity to its attitude of hope, its advocacy of communal living and nudism, and its rebel figures who outsmart the rest of the world. And there is Skinner's *Walden II*—a famous scientist's vision of conditioned happiness.

Stranger in a Strange Land is characteristic of modern science fiction in its strong concern with religion and its attempt to provide a way to believe in an afterlife. For many, God is dead—at least as he has been known in the past—and yet the God-yearning continues unabated. Science fiction provides many patterns of belief, ranging from justifications of the idea of transmigration to pseudo-scientific pictures of the possible heavens that await us all. It often sets up situations that call for new religious and ethical patterns. For instance, a mainstay of SF stories is the situation in which humans are locked on a spaceship bound for another galaxy; they must devise their own society and formulate its rules. In an alternative version, they have landed on an alien planet and must organize a new world structure. By reading this type of story, members of various subcultures can find patterns for their own experimentations in such things as communal living and worship.

Connected with the religious aspect of much of SF writing is the acceptance, among most SF writers, of mind-expanding drugs. Some feel that drugs will lead mankind to develop heretofore unknown powers of comprehension, a merging of the individual with a "universal oneness." Dreams experienced while under the influence of marijuana and mescaline are not laughed at or put down in most science fiction. The images used by SF writers—of wild yearless trips into both inner and outer space—easily merge with the imagery members of the drug culture use to describe their own experiences.

As Kurt Vonnegut and the younger generation have observed, SF writers, both old style and new style, work in one of the few forms of literature that is able to deal cogently with this increasingly incomprehensible world; and they generally do this without bundling their characters up in tight little knots of despair. Science fiction has always been a popular form of epic and romantic literature: its heroes are larger than life; its plots deal with the fate of entire societies; its basic motivations are those of quest and self-discovery; its affirmation is that of the power of the human to adjust to fate. In science fiction, man, the individual man, still makes a difference. The hero may be part of a vast cooperative organization but he finds, like James Bond, ways of expressing his individuality within that organization, generally without feeling a need to either overthrow or escape the organization. The SF hero, in other words, is no anti-hero doomed from the start. His interior struggles are not made the endless subjects of the novels, short stories, and poems that concern him. Strong plot, character, constant amazement, are the important ingredients of his story.

Is it any wonder that a new generation has rediscovered science fiction, rediscovered a form of literature that—aside from its beautiful psychedelic fantasies—argues through its intuitive force that the individual can shape and change and influence and triumph; that man can eliminate both war and poverty; that miracles *are* possible; that love, if given a chance, can become the main driving force of human relationships?

II

Still, it must be admitted that much science fiction is pure escapism. There are only a few ways by which Americans can sublimate their obsession with time. Most of us are not about to strip our wrists of the little faces we consult, or paint over the clocks on the classroom walls, or devise legislation to remove government-regulated on-the-hour and half-hour station breaks. We seek to escape the reminders of our obsession through our counter-obsession with means of escape. We fill in our leisure time, we watch television, we read only lightly challenging books. The reading of historical fiction and futurist fiction are allied. Both types of reading experiences allow us to transcend time, to escape the present, while they concurrently allow us to redeem ourselves from guilt as we maintain they provide us with important or at least interesting facts. Thus we fulfill the need to escape the regulation of our impulses.

Machines cannot be *wild* without being in the process of breaking down, of becoming nonfunctional. Humans can. In our brief moments of irrationality, young SF writers might maintain, we are the most human. It is often noted that animals cannot really laugh; it is less often remembered that machines cannot laugh either—yet. Both animals and machines are depressingly conditioned by their functions.

Humans who function with near perfect smoothness are inevitably present-centered, like animals and machines. Should they be required to move from the confines of their prescribed dimension, they either become outmoded (as the astronauts could be) or are judged unreliable (the scandals that befall many politicians). Those humans who have been careful to retain an element of uncertainty about them, or who subscribe to Emerson's dictum "A foolish consistency is the hobgoblin of little minds" are the most free (if freedom is for the moment defined as the ability to change at will) of all individuals.

Toward the end of his poem "Birches," Robert Frost wrote, "I'd like to get away from earth awhile / And then come back to it and begin over." This ability to escape being time-locked may be encouraged by the achievement of time perspective, getting "away from earth." Imagine yourself in the future, looking back at the present. Large contemporary problems seem insignificant; small problems develop into huge threats. No one who seriously ponders the sense of perspective achieved in H. G. Wells's *The Time Machine* and Arthur Clarke's and Stanley Kubrick's *2001: A Space Odyssey* can remain blind to the terrible psychological results of a present-oriented philosophy of life. The ecological crisis of the planet dooms hedonism, that most present-centered of all philosophies. The future, it can be argued, is one of those very few things left to our consciousness that, when we can control our fear of it, makes us able to acknowledge and rejoice in our humanity. Unlike a future plotted out by a machine, the future plotted by a man remains inexorably subject to change and magic.

Current underground movements in America are not basically present-centered, but future-oriented. Their participants see themselves as vanguards of the years to come, when the technological society will seek desperately for ways to *plan* to be spontaneous. Presently our recreation is time-oriented (fifteen-minute coffee break, three-day weekend, two-week summer vacation). Those who are future-oriented (free enough in the present to easily accept or at least *choose* their future lives) can step away from the schedules and *look back*, as the astronauts may look back from the moon to the tiny spaceship earth, at our current American behavior patterns. From the perspective of the future (of total culture destruction, or of a ruthless technocracy—among millions of possible patterns) we receive or enhance our powers to *abstract* generalities concerning our lives and the lives of those in our society. Unlike J. Alfred Prufrock, who was confined in the narrow city streets of present time, the future-oriented have the ability to create and believe in *absolute* truths or falsehoods— "Make love, not war," for example. The imagined society works on principles not tied to the limited perspectives of the clock-obsessed.

It is uncreated, waiting.

D. A.

part 1

First Perspectives

There is a temptation, particularly in the 1970s, to accept the new simply because it is new. As T. S. Eliot wrote at the end of his essay "Literature and the Modern World,"

> An age of change, and a period of incessant apprehension of war, do not form a favorable environment. There is a temptation to welcome change for its own sake, to sink our minds in some desperate philosophy of action; and several such philosophies are being urged upon us. Contempt for the past, and even ignorance of it, is on the increase, and many are ready for the unlimited experiment. We cannot effect intelligent change unless we hold fast to the permanent essentials; and a clear understanding of what we should hold fast to, and what abandon, should make us all the better prepared to carry out the changes that are needed. Thus we can look back upon the past without regret, and to the future without fear.*

Surely something must be done, and done soon, if we are to save this planet from ourselves; whether we will be able to save it for ourselves is another question. But before we leap into visions of the years to come it might be wise to consider our own past and present; consider, as Richard Wilbur does, how best to convince others that catastrophes seem inevitable. Shall we shout out our warnings, or shall we try to talk humanely, brother to brother? And what is there about the human race worth saving, anyway? If, as in "Earth's Holocaust," we cannot reform the human heart, are we doomed to repeat the same foibles and wars forever, caught in a series of endless rises and falls? The time is short; already a near disaster like that of "No Way Out, No Way Back" is not unexpected. More frightening, it does not even seem unacceptable. If, as David Lyle's article argues, "The Human Race Has, Maybe, Thirty-Five Years Left," is there any real sense in trying to turn things around? George MacBeth's "The Crab-Apple Crisis" is humorous until its terrifying final line.

    T. S. Eliot wrote in "The Wasteland," "Shall I at least set my lands in order?" We must begin somewhere.

---

*American Prefaces, Vol. V, No. 9 (June 1940).

Richard Wilbur has won both the Pulitzer Prize for Poetry and the National Book Award. In 1970, copies of David Lyle's article were distributed nationwide by Planned Parenthood/World Population *as part of an appeal for contributions to this organization. George McBeth, born in Scotland, publishes frequently in the British SF magazine* New Worlds *and is the author of five books of verse. A pioneer study of Nathaniel Hawthorne and his relationship to science fiction can be found in Bruce Franklin's* Future Perfect: American Science Fiction of the Nineteenth Century (*New York: Oxford, 1966*).

Advice to a Prophet

Richard Wilbur

When you come, as you soon must, to the streets of our city,
Mad-eyed from stating the obvious,
Not proclaiming our fall but begging us
In God's name to have self-pity,

Spare us all word of the weapons, their force and range,
The long numbers that rocket the mind;
Our slow, unreckoning hearts will be left behind,
Unable to fear what is too strange.

Nor shall you scare us with talk of the death of the race.
How should we dream of this place without us?—   10
The sun mere fire, the leaves untroubled about us,
A stone look on the stone's face?

Speak of the world's own change. Though we cannot conceive
Of an undreamt thing, we know to our cost
How the dreamt cloud crumbles, the vines are blackened by frost,
How the view alters. We could believe,

If you told us so, that the white-tailed deer will slip
Into perfect shade, grown perfectly shy,
The lark avoid the reaches of our eye,
The jack-pine lose its knuckled grip   20

On the cold ledge, and every torrent burn
As Xanthus once, its gliding trout
Stunned in a twinkling. What should we be without
The dolphin's arc, the dove's return,

These things in which we have seen ourselves and spoken?
Ask us, prophet, how we shall call
Our natures forth when that live tongue is all
Dispelled, that glass obscured or broken

In which we have said the rose of our love and the clean
Horse of our courage, in which beheld   30
The singing locust of the soul unshelled,
And all we mean or wish to mean.

Ask us, ask us whether with the worldless rose
Our hearts shall fail us; come demanding
Whether there shall be lofty or long standing
When the bronze annals of the oak-tree close.

QUESTIONS

1. Discuss what Wilbur means by the phrase, "Unable to fear what is too strange."

2. During the Second World War over 6,115,000 residents of the Soviet Union died. Over 3,250,000 Germans were killed. The United States had more than 1,000,000 casualties. What do you suppose would have been the reaction if a prophet had appeared in 1935 and published these statistics to the world?

3. What explains the power of such phrases as "The Cold War," "The Bamboo Curtain," "The Beat Generation"? Use this poem as a basis for exploring the relationship between concrete language and imagery and successful propaganda.

4. Can the theme of "Advice to a Prophet" be reduced to a basic statement such as "One picture is worth a thousand words"?

5. Read Wallace Stevens' famous poem "Sunday Morning" and compare the attitude toward death expressed there to that conveyed by "Advice to a Prophet."

No Way Out, No Way Back

Time Magazine

What will it be like, at the finish? In *Weekend,* French Film Maker Jean-Luc Godard foresees the end of the world as an immense traffic jam. Stanley Kubrick sees the men of 2001 as murder victims of a machine they have made more clever than themselves.

Or consider this scenario: The people are thrown together against their wills, trapped in colossal, modernistic buildings on a landscape devoid of trees. The lights are always lit. Pavement stretches everywhere. Cars and buses and trains and aircraft are useless; there is no way out. No darkness. No silence. No beds. No escape from an endless series of broadcast announcements, no avoiding the silly, circular games of other people's children. There are queues for food, queues for asking questions, queues for liquor—and finally queues for nothing, because there is nothing left. Then there is only boredom, and the debris of boredom. Dirty glasses, old newspapers, crumpled cigarette packs. Even the people are debris. Women wander aimlessly, their hair frazzled, their makeup so streaked that their faces look as if they are melting. Men in rumpled suits, with three days' growth of beard, slump in chairs staring at the message boards that bear no messages.

Packaged and Shipped

Perhaps it will all begin with a simple and foreseeable act of God—say a heavy snowstorm in New York City. There, last week, at the world's largest international airport, the scenario came true. Even at its best, an airport terminal seems inhuman—a monstrous machine disguised as a building and designed to process people and baggage. To the machine, there is no difference between men, women, children, suitcases, pets. All are collected, screened according to route, classified by status, divided into units of the right size, packaged in aircraft—and shipped. When 17 inches of drifting snow clogged the runways and access roads of John F. Kennedy airport, 6,000 people were forced to exist inside nine broken machines. And, because of the incredible slowness of Mayor John

Lindsay's snow-removal machinery, they were prisoners there for three days.

For Michael Rogers, a student headed back to Georgia's Oglethorpe College, the ordeal began shortly after 10 A.M. Sunday, when he telephoned Eastern Airlines to check on its 11:25 A.M. flight to Atlanta. Assured that the flight would depart with "a slight delay despite the snow," Michael drove to the airport and checked into the Eastern terminal at 11 A.M.—only to discover that the flight had been canceled. He was still there 56 hours later. Thousands of other travelers were similarly misled by the airlines, which, out of either optimism or greed, led them to believe that planes were still taking off. American Airlines waited until 2 P.M. on Sunday to announce the indefinite cancellation of all future flights, although all outgoing planes had officially been grounded since 10 A.M. Eastern waited until 9:30 P.M. Sunday to announce that no flight would leave until at least noon of the next day.

Crash Pad

Passengers kept pouring into all the major terminals, only to find that the snow had left no way out and no way back. Three people never even made it to a terminal; they were found in their car in Parking Lot No. 4, dead of carbon-monoxide poisoning. As the snow kept falling and drifting, it gradually dawned on everyone in the terminals that they were completely stranded. Airline officials struggled to provide minimal creature comforts. That is, some struggled. Trans World Airlines turned out 11,500 meals and 18,500 snacks in two days. TWA's clamshell terminal building, designed by the late Eero Saarinen, proved more adequate than most as a crash pad; the decorative red carpets in its gateway tunnels made comfortable mattresses for weary refugees. The airline also converted one of its planes into a movie theater, showing three films continuously from 10 A.M. to midnight on Monday to 142 passengers at a time.

At the Pan American building, where there are no carpets, passengers stretched out wherever they could—behind ticket counters, on luggage carts, even on the huge steel turntables in the baggage area. "Everybody is taking advantage of us," complained Frank Russomanno, a salesman from San Francisco. "The cafeteria is overcharging. The airline is not considering the people—especially the children. There are 1,000 children here, and they haven't done anything for them. They should have organized games. Or something."

Eastern Airlines had only 500 blankets for 1,500 people; when a father managed to get hold of four—one for each of his children—an Eastern official demanded them back for his agents' use (the father refused). A few passengers found their way to the employees' cafeteria in the basement, and stole food. As they crossed the terminal with loaded trays, they became an increasing source of frustration to 500 others who stood in line for five hours one night, only to be finally turned away. The restaurant manager blamed the foul-up on passengers who refused to give up their seats inside, even when they had finished eating. "Some stayed for three days," he said. "They did their laundry and hung it on chairs. They refused to go." Go where?

More Chaos

A few passengers did have enough pull—or gall—to escape. One with pull was Chris Craft Chairman Herbert J. Siegel, who was stranded at the Eastern terminal while awaiting a flight to Acapulco. Siegel called Manhattan Publicist Tex McCrary, who in turn phoned Pro Football Commissioner Pete Rozelle. They managed to commandeer a helicopter that was originally chartered to CBS-TV news. It took McCrary half an hour to locate Siegel after the helicopter landed on the Eastern runway; by the time they got back to the 'copter, three strangers—with gall—were placidly settled in its seats. They refused to get off, so the pilot had to fly them to Manhattan and return for Siegel three hours later.

Not until almost 10 A.M. Tuesday did planes again fly out of Kennedy. By then, though, an airport access road had been plowed—creating even more chaos: in poured a stream of new travelers with reservations on Tuesday flights, who demanded that their tickets be honored. Airline agents explained that they would have to wait until stranded passengers had been cleared out—perhaps another 24 hours. Whereupon they clumped angrily out of the terminals, hailed cabs to return home, and encountered yet one more annoyance. Never noted for their resistance to temptation, taxi drivers were flagrantly gouging passengers, carrying six to a cab and charging $20 a head for the ride into Manhattan—a total of $120, or about $113 over the legal metered fare. Quite a price to pay to get from one Godard traffic jam to another.

QUESTIONS

1. What other experiences of the sort written about in the *Time* article might also be described as if they were science fiction?

2. Do you think the situation at Kennedy Airport was primarily a result of fate or was it a result of modern society's dependence on machines?

3. Do you feel that the behavior described is characteristic of large numbers of people crowded into small areas? Were the taxicab drivers' actions to be expected in a crisis situation?

The Human Race Has, Maybe, Thirty-Five Years Left

David Lyle

In the seventh century, according to the records of the Church of Mayo, two kings of Erin summoned the principal clergy and laity to a council at Temora, in consequence of a general dearth, the land not being sufficient to support the increasing population. The chiefs . . . decreed that a fast should be observed both by clergy and laity so that they might with one accord solicit God to prayer to remove by some species of pestilence the burthensome multitudes of the inferior people. . . . St. Gerald and his associates suggested that it would be more conformable to the Divine Nature and not more difficult to multiply the fruits of the earth than to destroy its inhabitants. An amendment was accordingly moved "to supplicate the Almighty not to reduce the number of men till it answered the quantity of corn usually produced, but to increase the produce of the land so that it might satisfy the wants of the people." However, the nobles and clergy, headed by St. Fechin, bore down the opposition and called for a pestilence on the lower orders of the people. According to the records a pestilence was given, which included in its ravages the authors of the petition, the two kings who had summoned the convention, with St. Fechin, the King of Ulster and Munster and a third of the nobles concerned. . . .
W. J. Simpson in A TREATISE ON PLAGUE

In a year of poor harvest, the weight of the burthensome multitudes lies heavy upon the shoulders of the affluent. My grandfather had a book that his father gave him, presented upon his reaching young manhood; and whether it was given with a kind word or a black look, I can't say, but the title was *Where to Emigrate and Why*. My grandfather headed West—this at a time when emigration remained plausible for young men found to be surplus upon the home ground.

Today the crowd is global. There is no place to go. There has never been such a crowd, and in no time at all now, it's going to be twice as big. As for man's efforts to cope, the performance of St. Fechin suggests a certain lack of promise. Perhaps the mildest we can hope for is the suggestion of a prominent anthropologist that birth-control agents be applied liberally to the public water supply.

14

The case is this: Fifteen thousand years ago the earth probably held fewer people than New York City does today. The population doubled slowly at that time—say every forty thousand years. Today there are more than three billion people in the world and the rate of increase is almost a thousand times greater. Doubling occurs in less than forty years.

On a graph the human population line now rises almost vertically, which will not continue—there must be leveling off or decline. Leveling seems rational. Decline can be a landslide, as the history of the Irish and the lemming imply. The critical period near a population peak is likely to be a time of anxiety, of extreme unease. Thus President Johnson told the troops in Korea last year: "Don't forget, there are only two hundred million of us in the world of three billion. They want what we've got and we aren't going to give it to them." (Quoted by John Gerassi, in *The New York Review of Books*.)

In the United States a huge majority sees population as infinitely less threatening than crime and communism. Population crisis in America tends to become a cliché—a joke in the newspapers about standing room only in the year 2600. After which the matter may be dismissed—possibly it's something the Chinese are up to.

A few—the ecologically-minded, some Senators and scientists and academicians—cry out that growth and change are tearing the world apart. But on television the audience cheers a father of ten; and in Washington the political leadership continues heavily occupied in the shadows, scuffling with crime and communism, hustling money for defense and space and the war, and plotting ways to insure more growth and change.

Population increase and technological change are immense forces driving the world ahead at an accelerating pace into a turbulent and highly uncertain future. The effect of these forces upon the United States is already profound; no Island of Affluence or Fortress America notions are likely for long to fend off the future, or to make a particle of difference in the logic of vertical increase.

To grasp the implications, look first at the world that remains poor, then at the changes wrought in man and animal by extreme crowding, and finally at the consequences in the U.S.

Begin with India.

I: THE CITY OF THE FUTURE

At Sealdah Station, Calcutta, misery radiates outward . . . dusty streets straggle away in every direction lined with tiny shacks built of metal scraps, pieces of old baskets, strips of wood, and gunnysacks. In the dark interiors of the shacks, small fires glow through the smoke, and dark faces gaze out at children playing in the urinous-smelling, fly-infested streets. In a few years the children who survive . . . will grow taller and thinner and stand in the streets like ragged skeletons, barefoot, hollow-eyed, blinking their apathetic stares out of grey, dusty faces . . . Calcutta today . . . swollen by millions of refugees until the streets are spotted with their sleeping bodies . . . may very well represent the City of the Future.

Philip Appleman in THE SILENT EXPLOSION

In Calcutta six hundred thousand people sleep, eat, live in the streets—lacking even the shacks Appleman saw at Sealdah Station. The American visitor sees these thousands lying upon the ground "like little bundles of rags"; sees "women huddling over little piles of manure, patting it into cakes for fuel; children competing with dogs for refuse"—and reacts with shock and revulsion. A student told Appleman, "I wanted to run away, to weep. I was disgusted, horrified, saddened. . . ."

Calcutta stands for three worldwide forces—burgeoning population; food shortage; a torrent of migration to the cities.

Today there are about five hundred million people in India. In thirty years or so there may well be one billion. Most Indians live in rural villages—but the villages are overflowing. The surrounding lands no longer produce enough food. The excess population drifts into the big coastal cities where there is hope of food; Calcutta has become an immense breadline where the starving from the countryside gather to feed on grain from American ships.

The vision of six hundred thousand people lying in the streets at night —a prostrate breadline waiting for Midwestern grain—must be burned into the mind if the fate of the third world (and of the United States) is to assume reality. Because as the population rises, the supply of grain is running out. This is true not only for India but for two-thirds of the human population. All over the third world the City of the Future is a place where the rural poor gather to await the grain handout from abroad, while it lasts.

From Calcutta, draw the implications for the third (so-called "underdeveloped") world—briefly, as follows:

The 1960 population of the developed world was about 900,000,000; that of the third world ran over 2,000,000,000.

The agricultural land resources of the two parts of the world are approximately equal.

By the year 2000—in less than thirty-three years—the developed world must feed 1,300,000,000 on its half of the world's croplands. The third world will have to feed about 5,000,000,000 people on its half.

The industrial states have moved on to high-yield agriculture, getting maximum production from the land. The third world must make the same transition—but there very well may not be time to make it before mass famine sets in.

The bind is this: There is a desperate need to cut population growth and to raise food production within the next three decades. The most urgent period will be the ten or fifteen years immediately ahead. All right, then, say the hopeful—birth control; but Cora Du Bois, an anthropologist with much experience in India, reports that ". . . any effective reduction of population growth among heavily breeding rural populations is not foreseeable in less than possibly fifty years. I believe this is a question on which it is wise to have no illusions."

Nor is the prospect for rapid increase in food supply much brighter. On the contrary, according to Lester R. Brown, an economist with the U.S. Department of Agriculture: "The food problem emerging in the less-developed regions may be one of the most nearly insoluble problems facing man over the next few decades."

There are, nevertheless, a few optimists. Some talk of farming the sea, eating plankton; but this will not help anyone soon. Anyway, says William Vogt, who is experienced, "Few of the people who advocate this, I am sure, have tasted plankton. . . ."

Recently, an optimist of some renown appeared—Donald J. Bogue, a sociologist at the University of Chicago. He said the United Nations' projections of about six billion people by the year 2000 are exaggerated; Dr. Bogue predicted a rapid decline in growth after 1975. The immediate reaction of his colleagues was disappointing. Dr. Bogue said, "Most were angry. I found no one who agreed with me."

Perhaps the most disturbing thing about the present world-population situation, as Dr. Bogue himself suggested, is the almost uniformly pessimistic outlook of so many very capable people who have examined the matter closely. Lloyd V. Berkner, a leading American scientist, remarked that in the third world, "We are probably already beyond the point at which a sensible solution is possible." Eugene R. Black, when he was president of the World Bank, said, "We are coming to a situation in which the optimist will be the man who thinks that present living standards can be maintained."

Dr. B. R. Sen, Director-General of the United Nations Food and Agriculture Organization, has said, "The next thirty-five years . . . will be a most critical period in man's history. Either we take the fullest measures to raise productivity and to stabilize population growth, or we will face disaster of an unprecedented magnitude. We must be warned . . . of unlimited disaster."

In Pakistan, President Ayub said in 1964, "In ten years' time, human beings will eat human beings in Pakistan."

The third world, then, is in acute danger of entering into a descending spiral where each successive failure reinforces the last in a descent toward chaos. The process may have begun. There is a tendency in the U.S. to believe it will be possible to isolate ourselves from this, retreat into the land of affluence. For a while perhaps.

Consider this: As of 1954 the United States was using about fifty percent of the raw material resources consumed in the world each year. The rate of consumption has been rising and by 1980 the U.S. could be consuming more than eighty-three percent of the total.

Today the U.S. is a net importer of goods. Its reliance on foreign trade grows each year. The third world, in the meantime, sees industrialization as the road to salvation; its demand for raw material can be expected to accelerate. Today we can soothe the hungry by offering a certain amount of food and aid. Tomorrow we will be competing for raw material and there will be no spare food to offer.

The prospect is not bright. As Professor Harold A. Thomas, Jr. of Harvard's Center for Population Studies put it, ". . . unless we engage ourselves today in problems of development of the poor nations, the conditions under which we live during the next two generations may not be attractive. The fuel required to sustain our mammoth technological apparatus may constitute a gross drain on the resources of the earth. Other societies cannot be expected to regard this favorably. A vista of an enclave of privilege in an isolated West is not pleasant to contemplate. Wise and human political institutions do not thrive in beleaguered citadels."

II: THE MOUSE EXPLOSION

Mice were generated and "boiled over" the towns and fields in the midst of that region, and there was a confusion of great death in the land.

Vulgate 1, Kings, v. 6

The periodic, vast increase in numbers of field mice is a peculiar and ancient phenomenon, and men have long feared it. In the cult of Apollo this fear gave rise to religious ceremonies—the keepers of Apollo's temple kept tame mice in the sanctuary and a colony of them beneath the altar.

Aristotle was astounded by the capacity of mice to increase.

The rate of propagation of field mice in country places, and the destruction that they cause, are beyond all telling. In many places their number is so incalculable that but very little of the corn crop is left to the farmer; and so rapid is their mode of proceeding that sometimes a small farmer will one day observe that it is time for reaping, and on the following morning, when he takes his reapers afield, he finds his entire crop devoured. Their disappearance is unaccountable: in a few days not a mouse will be there to be seen. . . .

The mouse horde has for centuries represented a serious problem in Europe. Charles Elton, the director of the Bureau of Animal Population at Oxford, has described one historic outbreak in France:

. . . an impressive picture of insurgent subterranean activity, of devastation breaking like a flood upon the crops. All man's vigilance and care are taxed by the multitude of small, swift, flitting forms that infest the ground and devour all living plants. Poison, plowing, fumigation, trenches, and prayers, all these can scarcely stop the destruction. . . . In [1822] Alsace was absolutely in the power of mice. "It was a living and hideous scourging of the earth, which appeared perforated all over, like a sieve!"

The animal responsible for this devastation is normally quite inconspicuous—a tiny creature, short-legged, short-tailed, broad of face—known commonly as the meadow mouse, or vole. The vole rarely travels more than twenty-five feet from its burrow. It lives less than a year. But during its short life it is absolutely voracious. Each day it consumes its own weight in food. First it takes care of the plants above ground; then it burrows down after roots and tubers. In an orchard, voles may girdle and kill trees.

The vole population follows a typical four-year cycle of rise and fall, proceeding from relative scarcity to a peak of abundance, then declining and beginning the cycle all over again. The remarkable thing about voles is their capacity under certain circumstances to increase to enormous numbers within a single breeding season. On occasion—in Europe this occurs perhaps once in a generation—there is an increase of truly catastrophic proportions, a "scourging of the earth," as in Alsace in 1822.

There have been a good many locally catastrophic mouse population explosions in the United States, the most severe in the far West. Perhaps the most devastating of all was centered in Oregon just a few years ago, and the damage to crops ran into millions of dollars. Wells were polluted because of the numbers of voles that fell into them. In the most heavily infested areas there were two or three thousand mice to the acre and their burrows crisscrossed the ground like a lace network. One man counted twenty-eight thousand burrow entrances in an area a little over two hundred feet square.

The end of a mouse outbreak is always abrupt. At the peak, food begins to run short and crowding leads to tension and fighting. It is as though a tremor of anxiety had begun to run through the whole population—tension, food shortage, the stress of crowding (with demonstrable physical effects), disease, fighting, cannibalism—all these appear and lead into the descending spiral, a rapid decline that ends in mass die-off. Toward the end, predatory birds gather in spectacular numbers to feed on the mouse horde. Only then does the earth begin to recover.

The vole cycle gives a broad picture of population dynamics, of catastrophic increase in numbers. In recent years, studies done by John B. Calhoun have shown in great detail just what happens to social behavior under such circumstances. Dr. Calhoun worked with rats in captivity, and he found that under extreme crowding startling behavioral changes occurred. Among male rats these changes ranged from "sexual deviation to cannibalism and from frenetic overactivity to a pathological withdrawal." Among female rats the number of miscarriages increased, nest-building ability deteriorated, and so did the ability to care for the young.

The female rats built no nests at all under extreme crowding, but bore their young on the floor of the pen where the young rats were easily scattered and few survived. Females lost the ability to transport the young. En route somewhere a female would set a young rat down and then, distracted, wander off and forget it. The scattered young were seldom nursed, finally were left to die.

Dr. Calhoun developed a term for the social deterioration occurring under extreme crowding; he called it the "behavioral sink."

III: CANDELARIA

India gets the publicity; but Latin America is the fastest-growing region of the world and one of the most unstable. The shock of population growth there can be incredible. By one estimate there are a million deaths a year from starvation and malnutrition. A Notre Dame sociologist, Professor Donald N. Barrett, describes a slum where "two or three children [are] dying per week because of the ravenous dogs." Today the populations of Latin America and North America are not far apart; by the end of this century Latin America could easily have as many people as China today—750,000,000, dwarfing the U.S.

The population of India doubles every thirty-one years; in Colombia it doubles in twenty-three years, and there are rural areas doubling in sixteen. In a brief space, it is probably impossible really to convey what this means. A Colombian doctor who has been in the midst of it has said the implications are "almost beyond comprehension." To see, even to a small extent, what this means, look at the village of Candelaria and what Dr. Alfredo Aguirre found there—as he reported it to *The Population Council.*

Candelaria is semi-rural—a village where, quite literally, people are multiplying at such a rate in relation to resources that almost everything has broken down. Big families are crammed into tiny rooms in flimsy shacks; there isn't enough food; what food there is goes mainly to the father because he must work in the nearby cane fields or sugar mills. The children go hungry and, as Dr. Aguirre put it, "undernourishment means early death for many of the children, and if death fails to intervene . . . [there will be] delay in walking, retardation in speech development, difficulties in relating to other people . . . a diminished capacity to adapt."

The adolescent in this world

> may exhibit antisocial tendencies [and] ultimately abandons school without having developed any skills. Finally he joins the mass of unemployed . . . tends to flaunt authority . . . cannot adapt to a social system that involves laws and mores of which he is unaware because nobody has ever taught him, and that apparently deny to him and his family the right of survival.

This is the analytic language of social science; behind it is the reality of Colombia: a country on the edge of revolution, with guerrilla bands in the mountains, disaffection in the cities, extremes of poverty and affluence, and one of the highest homicide rates in the world.

The typical young girl in Candelaria has a child or two in her teens. She is unmarried, illiterate or semiliterate, has no way to support the children. She has, Dr. Aguirre says, two options:

> One is to seek a more or less stable marital relationship, not just out of sexual instinct but from economic necessity, although this means sacrificing her own freedom, since in this type of relationship it is the man who decides how long it shall last, who distributes the family income according to his own convenience (other women, alcoholic beverages, etc.), and who determines the number of children to be conceived.
>
> The other solution to the mother's problems is the death of the child ("masked infanticide") in which children between six months and four years of age are often allowed to die when attacked by any disease. . . . We have even seen mothers who objected to their children being treated and [who] were upset when curative measures were successful. No less rarely, such children are abandoned in the hospital. . . . A frequent indication of "masked infanticide" is apparent when a mother or a couple of very limited means approaches the physician for a "death certificate" for their child without any emotion or anguish. . . .

Candelaria is the human equivalent of Calhoun's behavioral sink.

IV: REUNION AND TIKOPIA

Reunion is an island in the Indian Ocean: "The accounts of the first visitors [sixteenth century] are a description of Eden."

The French geographer Pierre Gourou has described what happened thereafter. First, European settlers set up coffee and sugar plantations on the island and ran them with slave labor. (Islands were favored; the slaves couldn't run off.) By 1848 there were 61,000 slaves and 45,000 free, and in that year the slaves were freed. The planters were unwilling to change their approach—that is, to pay and otherwise treat the blacks as free men. So the ex-slaves tended to move up onto the island's steep interior slopes, where they practiced subsistence farming on small plots. The big planters imported Indian labor to work the plantations. The smaller planters found they could no longer compete. They were forced to abandon their plantations; they moved up onto the slopes with the freed slaves.

Through World War II, the population grew with fair speed and regularity. The island changed—plants and animals native to it were exterminated. Cultivation of the steep slopes caused heavy erosion, threatening the future of the subsistence farmers. And in the course of a century, the quality of the lives of those small planters driven onto the slopes with the former slaves had changed remarkably. "Their ancestors, three to four generations before, had stone houses and fireplaces, and spun and wove wool; but these people live in plank or leaf houses, have no fireplaces, and shiver in their thin cotton clothes."

After World War II modern medicine and sanitation brought a quick drop in the death rate, and the population began shooting upward. There were 310,000 inhabitants in 1957; there may well be 620,000 by 1980. There is no place for the overflow; unemployment is swelling. The situation, as Gourou says, "is really alarming."

Tikopia is an island in the Pacific where the "primitive" people in residence learned to regulate their own numbers by, as Raymond Firth put it, "restraint on the part of the male." The Tikopian recognized that their environment was limited, that the island could support only so many people. They acted accordingly, with a remarkably clear vision of the consequences if they should fail. An islander told Firth,

> Familes by Tikopia custom are made corresponding to orchards in the woods. If children are produced in plenty, then they go and steal because their orchards are few. So families in our land are not made large in truth; they are made small. If the family groups are large, they go and steal, they eat from the orchards, and if this goes on they kill each other.

It may be that the Tikopia were rare among human societies in their acute awareness of cause and effect. But the point is that they did have ways of limiting their numbers, and used them, as have many other premodern peoples. And in this they were typical of animals generally.

All animals produce more young than necessary to maintain their numbers. So if a species is to stay within the limits of its food supply, some check on numbers is essential. Such checks are quite common—predators, disease, the maintenance of territory or of hierarchies or peck orders, etc. The ultimate check of famine operates on a large scale rather rarely, because the other checks have kept population within limits of the food supply.

But all this assumes an undisturbed environment and a complex one. In a disturbed environment peculiar things begin to happen. For example, where man disturbs the plant environment through cultivation, weeds proliferate as they would not ordinarily in the wild. Where man cultivates a single crop over wide acreage, destructive insect populations like the boll weevil multiply as they would not normally in a natural environment. Great mouse plagues occur where man sets up ideal conditions for them. This suggests something about the difference between Reunion and Tikopia.

In Tikopia, over many generations, men have learned to live within the limitations of their world. Every man is in close touch with the essentials of life—with food, water, shelter, education of the young. Every man is aware of outer limits. To put it in computer jargon, there is a daily feedback which tells a man what his situation is, and there is an ancient pattern of tradition which tells him how then to carry on.

Reunion is a disturbed environment, and in this it is typical of most of the modern world. Reunion is peopled with uprooted Europeans, uprooted Africans, uprooted Indians, people for whom all the old patterns and traditions have been smashed by a galaxy of new forces. In the shock of change all the old ways of dealing with the world are forgotten. Or they don't work anymore. Or they are illegal. The uprooted man is at first baffled and disorganized because nothing works anymore. Then, increasingly, he is bitter. The old self-regulating feedback systems will not be restored in a day; if they are restored at all, it will take generations.

In the meantime almost everyone on earth is out of touch with the essentials, with the clear view of outer limits possessed by the Tikopian. Nowhere is the evidence of shattered patterns, of drift away from the awareness of essentials, more apparent today than in the United States.

V: THE AMERICAN ENVIRONMENT

The U.S. birthrate has been declining since 1957. Even if this decline continues, population will grow at an accelerating pace for some decades to come. There were 100,000,000 Americans about fifty years ago. There are 200,000,000 now; there will be 300,000,000 by 2000, assuming the continued *decline* in the birthrate; and there could well be 400,000,000 by 2015 or 2020. Note that each time the population increases by 100,000,000, it takes far less time than it took to add the previous 100,000,000. This is one aspect of acceleration, and today acceleration touches everything.

Today, according to one student of American society, "It takes only a year or two for the exaggerations to come true. Nothing will remain in the next ten years. Or there will be twice as much of it." (Warren G. Bennis, in *Technology Review.*)

To Americans, growth has always been a "good"—growth stocks, the Soaring Sixties, the Baby Boom, the Biggest Little City in the West, etc. India has a population crisis; the U.S. has "growth," the booster philosophy, "Dig We Must for a Growing New York." The dismal side of all this is becoming only too apparent today: in the birth of the city that never ends; in the difficulty of getting anywhere within that city, or of getting out of it, or of finding (once out of it) any place worth getting to that isn't already overrun with other escapees; in the air and water pollution; in the difficulty of finding a doctor; in the evolution of the Kafka-esque bureaucracy, corporate and governmental.

All this is rather well-known. Some aspects of the situation are less well-known. For example:

1. *Water.* A recent writer in *Science* said, "A permanent water shortage affecting our standard of living will occur before the year 2000." This, of course, has all kinds of ramifications. Consider just one. In the Western states forty percent of all agriculture (and much allied enterprise) depends on irrigation. Much of this may have to be abandoned. Gerald W. Thomas, the Dean of Agriculture at Texas Technological College, writes that some of this agriculture "may have to be shifted back to the more humid zones in the next fifty years." This is likely to mean higher costs to consumers. And of course the more humid Eastern zones are precisely the ones now urbanizing most rapidly.

2. *Urbanization.* We are spreading out over the landscape at a phenomenal rate. Highways now cover with concrete an area the size of Massachusetts, Connecticut, Vermont, Rhode Island and Delaware. William Vogt has recorded the fact that the National Golf Foundation desires to cover an area the size of New Hampshire and Rhode Island with new golf courses. In downtown Los Angeles sixty-six percent of the land is taken up by parking lots or streets; in the whole Los Angeles area one-third of the land is paved. The trend is toward the creation of Los Angeles everywhere. We are developing urban complexes so vast that one can travel a hundred and more miles before reaching open country. The leapfrogging, haphazard pattern of development hastens the process of spread; in California, housing that need have covered only twenty-six square miles actually knocked out two hundred square miles of farmland.

3. *Mobility.* Automobiles are multiplying three times faster than people and five times faster than roads necessary to accommodate

them. Freeways are obsolete before completion. If all our registered vehicles were laid end to end, the line would begin to approach in length the total mileage of city streets in the United States. Which suggests why Boston had a traffic jam a few years ago—no special cause—that froze the entire downtown area for five hours. Or why a single New Jersey jam lasted seven hours and tied up a million and a half vehicles. Senator Claiborne Pell of Rhode Island, who put all these facts in a book called *Megalopolis Unbound*, believes that the search for perfect mobility is leading to total immobility.

4. *Farmlands.* The spread of the cities takes at least a million and a half acres of open land every year, fifty percent more than a decade ago. The popular outcry has been minor; after all we have had huge crop surpluses. But now there is some concern. Maurice L. Peterson, Dean of Agriculture for the University of California, has said that "urbanization of prime farmland is one of the most serious problems facing us in agriculture. The population is increasing at a far more rapid rate than our ability to produce food, and farmers are being forced up into the hills, where it costs more to produce." California produces twenty-five percent of the nation's table food, forty-three percent of fresh vegetables, forty-two percent of nut and fruit crops. By conservative estimate, half of California's prime cropland will go to housing and industry in the next thirty-three years; pessimists believe it will be eighty percent.

The U.S. seems unlikely to have a food problem soon; it has enormous capabilities in food production. This capability has a price, however, as two of our ecologists, William Vogt and Raymond F. Dasmann, have made quite clear. American rivers run brown because they are full of earth washed from the fields bordering them. Twenty years ago, Dr. Vogt wrote: "American civilization, founded on nine inches of topsoil, has now lost one third of this soil." Part of the Sahara and much of the barren wasteland of the Middle East is, to a large extent, man-made desert. In the dust-bowl regions of the American Southwest, Dr. Dasmann has said, "What the Bedouin took centuries to achieve, we have almost equaled in decades."

5. *The economics of change.* The biggest public-works project in history, according to President Eisenhower, was the $41,000,000,000 public highway project undertaken during his Administration. (When the American people voted for it through their Congress, said Lewis Mumford, "the most charitable thing to assume . . . is that they hadn't the faintest notion of what they were doing.") But the requirements just ahead make the highway program look like a county supervisors' boondoggle. A Congressional committee recently put the cost of providing clean water at $100,000,000,000. The effort to do something about air pollution is likely to cost at least as much in the next thirty years. Senator Ribicoff says city rehabilitation will require $1,000,000,000,000. A housing expert sees the need for $100,000,000,000 (a popular figure) in Fed-

eral housing aid. The population of the country will double in fifty years. This means—if the living standard is to be maintained or improved—something close to a doubling of facilities, public and private. Will we, then, duplicate in fifty years, and pay for, what has taken much of the nation's history to produce? Or will we balk at the effort and the cost, and suffer a gradual decline in the quality of our lives? The evidence is powerful—in failed school bond issues, deteriorating environment, overburdened public facilities—that we are balking already. Eugene Black's description of the optimist as a man who believes living standards can be maintained takes on new life.

6. *Pollution.* Everybody knows something about air and water pollution today. But there are exotic effects which remain less well known:

a. Pesticides are essential to high-yield agriculture as now practiced in the U.S. Pesticides wash from field to river to sea, where they are concentrated by diatoms. I quote now from Lloyd V. Berkner, who is studying the phenomenon in detail.

> Now the point is this: Our supply of atmospheric oxygen comes largely from these diatoms—they replenish all of the atmospheric oxygen every two thousand years as it is used up. But if our pesticides should be reducing the supply of diatoms or forcing evolution of less productive mutants, we might find ourselves running out of atmospheric oxygen.

b. Agricultural fertilizers are another essential of high-yield agriculture, as now practiced. They are used in ever-greater quantities each year. Nitrates from these fertilizers are getting into water supplies both in the U.S. and Europe. At a certain level of concentration, the water becomes toxic. At least one town, Garden Grove, California, has had to shut down some of the wells providing its public water supply because of nitrate contamination. Other towns scattered around the nation have begun to discover similar problems. In Minnesota, during one three-year period, fourteen infant deaths were attributed to nitrates in well water.

c. Dr. Barry Commoner reported recently (in his book, *Science and Survival*) that the burning of fuels has caused the carbon-dioxide content of the earth's atmosphere to rise fourteen percent in the past century. This has produced a general warming effect on the atmosphere. The President's Science Advisory Committee concludes that this warming may begin melting the Antarctic ice cap by the year 2000 (raising sea levels four feet a decade and, of course, finally inundating huge land areas and major cities, like New York).

d. There is a call for nuclear power today to replace coal or oil-fired electric generating units and thus reduce air pollution. Frank M. Stead, when he was with the California Department of Public Health, concluded that in his state after 1980 "electrical power sources must be progressively replaced with nuclear sources if clean air is to be maintained."

A Congressional subcommittee headed by Representative Emilio Q. Daddario of Connecticut concerns itself specifically with science and the effects of technological change. The subcommittee reported recently:

> There has been little progress in devising a way to get rid of the toxic by-products [of the nuclear power plant]. The best we can do with ra- dioactive waste is what we first thought of—bury it. But someday that system will no longer be feasible. Then what? . . . At this point there is no convincing evidence that anyone really knows.

Yet nuclear power plants are being planned or built countrywide.

The United States, of course, lacks a monopoly on nuclear power. In a recent book, *Inherit the Earth*, the zoologist N. J. Berrill finds that ra- dioactive wastes from atomic-energy plants already constitute a world- wide problem—"country after country is already dumping them into the sea, to contaminate or poison whatever life there be. Our total inherit- ance seems to be at stake if no restraint appears."

e. More on California. Mr. Stead, the environmental health expert, has said: "It is clearly evident . . . that between now and 1980 the gaso- line-powered engine must be phased out [in California] and replaced with an electrical power package. . . . The only realistic way . . . is to demand it by law." The forces working against this—considering many of our largest corporations are based on the auto industry—are vast.

The fundamental question here is this: To what extent today are we threatened by the very technology—and the institutions—we find essen- tial to support a rapidly expanding population? The technology will not be abandoned. It is put to new uses every day, and with almost no thought of ultimate effects.

VI: THE CULTURAL SHOCK FRONT

The point should be clear—change occurs today at a fantastic pace in the U.S. and the pace is accelerating. We have no real idea where it all leads, any more than we know what to do with the hot waste from nuclear power plants. We rocket along, straight into the unknown, treasuring a Panglossian notion that somehow it will all work out for the best. This is true in the technological sense; equally so in the social sense.

For some the strain of contemporary life is already too great. Medi- cine links the stress ailments—heart disease, mental aberration, ulcers (which appear commonly in overcrowded animals)—to the tempo of modern life. Psychiatry recognizes an "automation syndrome" in which older workers, replaced by a machine, may break down, suffer amnesia or commit suicide. One sociologist predicts increasing alcoholism in the automated factory—this in a nation which now has one of the world's most substantial alcoholism problems.

In a sense today you can feel a tremor of anxiety through the whole society—feel it in the city riots, in the war, in the accelerating crime rate, in widespread unrest, unease, disaffection, tendency to drop out, turn on, drink up. You hear it in the cry for more police to "deal with the situation in the cities." You hear it in the shrillness of the extremist—the point being not what is said but the anxiety exhibited and the high decibel count. All this is directly related to population growth, to crowding, movement and swift social and technological change.

Sir Julian Huxley said the "stress effect of overcrowding and frustration . . . is undoubtedly operating on the inhabitants of any city with over a million inhabitants in the world today, and has, to my mind, very serious implications." (This idea was belittled at length recently in a rather strange article by Irving Kristol. My money remains on Sir Julian.)

Keeping in mind the stress effect, the pace of growth and change, consider this: Population will grow by at least fifty percent in the U.S. during the next thirty-three years, barring catastrophe. During the same period U.S. urban population will come close to doubling. Thus in the most congested areas the effects of simple population growth will be doubled by the effects of movement and migration. Urban areas in the U.S. will grow at about the same rate as the population of India. India today we consider to be in a state of population crisis—but in the U.S. the boosters are still in charge. When the population hit 170,000,000 in 1957, Secretary of Commerce Sinclair Weeks said, "I am happy to welcome this vast throng of new customers for America's goods and services. They help insure a rising standard of living. . . ." Four years later the population hit 185,000,000 and Secretary Luther Hodges led a round of cheers at the Commerce Department.

The effects of social and technological change, of growth and movement—these are already great in the United States and they will be compounded in the next thirty years. Some central cities will become highly unstable places, and what we now see in terms of crime, rioting and disaffection is just a preview. Today in the U.S. nearly everyone belongs to the class of the uprooted. The factory worker's daughter moves into the middle class; the commuter migrates daily to the city; the executive living in Louisville develops little concern for the affairs of his town because next year the company will shift him to Des Moines; the rural family migrates to the city and disintegrates; the more affluent flee the city for the suburbs; Easterners go West. Everyone, everything is in motion—as never before, anywhere.

The newspapers are filled with stories of turmoil in the world; factories harbor a new technology that is in the process of antiquating the skills of millions of workers; schools prepare the young for a world, and for jobs, that no longer exist; the accumulation of knowledge is so swift that "a major problem in research is to find out what has been done by others so as to avoid rediscovering the same information." Our institutions were formed for—and mentally and emotionally our political and other leaders exist in—a world that has ceased to be.

"I think," said the biophysicist John R. Platt, "we may be now in the time of most rapid change in the whole evolution of the human race, either past or to come. It is a kind of cultural 'shock front,' like the shock fronts that occur in aerodynamics when the leading edge of an airplane wing moves faster than the speed of sound and generates the sharp pressure wave that causes the . . . sonic boom."

Look at what's coming. The first industrial revolution replaced the pick-and-shovel man. Skilled scientists and administrators may survive the second (cybernetic) revolution, as Norbert Wiener said, but "taking the second revolution as accomplished, the average man of mediocre attainments or less has nothing to sell that is worth anyone's money to buy." In other words, the computer today functions at the high-school graduate level. High-school graduates are becoming industrially superfluous: so is the middle-management echelon.

Automation creates some jobs, of course—there is a demand today for more skilled and educated workers. So it's essential to upgrade education, make everyone skilled. Yet there is evidence that American schools have declined steadily in quality for years now. Considering the pace at which the school system has grown, this will hardly come as a stunning surprise. In a sample study made during an eighteen-month period twenty-five percent of the men who took the Selective Service test failed the mental part of it. There are more than fifty million people in the country who failed to make it through high school, and some time ago the Labor Department estimated that thirty percent of students might be high-school dropouts in the 1960's. Whatever the demand for skills may be or may become, we are turning out masses of young who will be unable to cope in a cybernated world.

It becomes essential, then, to "improve the schools." But the rigidity of the educational bureaucracy is legendary. It would be difficult to change the direction of this bureaucracy in any circumstances. It will inevitably be far harder at a time when the attention of that bureaucracy is focused primarily on problems of growth and change—as it must be for the next thirty years at least.

As recently as 1963, thirty-six percent of all vocational education funds went to what must be the single most rapidly declining major area of employment in the nation—agriculture. An investment, that is, in training for non-jobs. Much of the rest of the vocational-education money went into home economics. All of which says something profound about the relevance of our education efforts, about the intellects in charge, and the capacity for change.

Today the United States has the highest rate of unemployment as well as the highest rate of public dependency and population growth of any modern industrial state. From here on, according to Philip M. Hauser, former chief of the Bureau of the Census, population growth will "worsen the U.S. employment problem, greatly increase the magnitude of juvenile delinquency, exacerbate already dangerous race tensions, inundate the secondary schools and colleges . . . augment urban congestion and further subvert the traditional American Government system."

There are between thirty and forty million people living below the poverty level in the U.S. today. The rural Negro's movement to the city and the middle-class flight to the suburbs is reaching a crescendo. In Washington ninety percent of the schoolchildren are Negro, in Manhattan seventy-five percent are Negro or Puerto Rican—indicating the future city population. In the cities Negro unemployment averages about ten percent—there are areas where it runs much higher, up to twenty-five percent or more. Nor is this likely to be the peak. Commissioner of Labor Statistics Arthur M. Ross of the U.S. Department of Labor has said Negro unemployment could be running three or four times higher within eight years if present trends continue.

This could mean unemployment rates of thirty or forty percent and up for the city Negro. The industries that might hire them are moving to the suburbs. In Chicago in recent years seventy-seven percent of new plants have located outside the main metropolitan area; in Los Angeles eighty-five percent. The newspapers lately have been full of the exodus from New York—the black man reaches the promised land, and the white man packs it up and takes it to Westchester.

The prospect ahead for the thirty-odd millions of poor is more poverty, or the dole, or some form of Federal work project, perhaps all three; and it seems highly likely that even all three will provide no real solution. The crowd, or the mob, seems likely to reappear as a force in politics. Watts was a prelude.

The cultural shock front is an area of extreme turbulence, of buffeting, of exotic and swift currents. The question is whether the society we've known in the U.S. will survive passage through it.

VII: TRANSFORMATION

Dr. Platt is one of a group of people who sees the present as a critical period of transition. A brief composite of the group's view might go like this:

For most of his two million years, man has operated in a fairly stable—slow to change—world. Stone Age. From generation to generation there was almost no social or technological change. There was no gap between generations; father was like son was like grandson; they shared the same world, the same outlook. And every man was in touch with the essentials.

All this began to change with the advent of agriculture about 10,000 years ago. Food surpluses appeared. A few people, then, had time to do something other than hunt and cultivate. The efforts of the few led to civilization and to the accumulation of new knowledge. Knowledge brought innovation, changes in the accumulated human pattern of two million years. The more knowledge accumulated, the more innovation there was, until the process of change accelerated into the dizzy pattern of the present.

Dr. Platt sees the period of accelerating change—civilization—as transitional, the step between the old stability of the Stone Age and some new stability that may last equally long. Either we reach this new stability or, you might say, the whole thing goes belly-up. Because the pace of change can't accelerate indefinitely.

The present is probably the critical period in the transition. Dr. B. R. Sen, you remember, saw the next thirty-five years as decisive in terms of food. A sharp decline in population growth must come soon, or the likelihood is reduction through famine, war and disease. Aside from the population imbalance, the other major obstacle of the transition period is the danger of nuclear war.

Dr. Platt sees a limit here, too, because the big powers are playing nuclear roulette, and in the mathematical sense if you continue to do this,

> It finally, certainly, kills you . . . some have estimated that our "half-life" under these circumstances—that is, the probable number of years before these repeated confrontations add up to a fifty-fifty chance of destroying the human race forever—may be only about ten or twenty years . . . this cannot continue. No one lives very long walking on loose rocks at the edge of a precipice.

Do we make our way into the new stability, or do we not? The class divides into optimists and pessimists. Assume we make it. There is again a division into optimists and pessimists, the question being, this time: Do we emerge into Churchill's sunlit uplands or into Orwell's 1984?

To find an answer you have to consider that:

World population is almost certain to double before any final stability is reached.

The growth of a crowd inevitably restricts freedom. In the packed subway, finally, you are unable to raise your arms.

The crowd must be more highly organized as it grows, to avoid chaos and to permit the technology which supports the crowd to function.

Cybernetics and game theory will inform the actions of government— the process is underway in the United States. This will, very likely, have effects foreseen by Norbert Wiener and the Dominican friar, Père Dubarle. The process is exquisitely simple. In the game with the individual, as Father Dubarle put it, "The *machines à gouverner* will define the State as the best-informed player. . . ."

The players are likely to be cooperative. Because each will be a specialist. Technology demands it, and the specialist is by definition the Dependent Man. He cannot provide the essentials of life for himself. He is dependent upon others to provide, to create opinion, order, to *know what must be done.*

Dependent Man, properly fed and educated, is Acquiescent Man—he who lets others do it. Programmed for conformity. "Orthodoxy means . . . not needing to think. Orthodoxy is unconscious," said George Orwell.

Herein lies the chief danger of the U.S. becoming a beleaguered citadel in a world entering the descending spiral; the already great pressures for conformity would become overwhelming.

Sometimes the elements of the Orwellian world seem remarkably close.

> The control of human behavior by artificial means will have become by the year 2000 a frightening possibility. Government—"big brother"— might use tranquilizers, or hallucinogens like L.S.D., to keep the population from becoming unruly or overindependent. More and more subtle forms of conditioning will lead people to react in predictable ways desired by government or by commercial interests without people quite knowing how they are hoodwinked . . .

—thus H. Bentley Glass, biologist and vice-president of the State University of New York at Stony Brook.

Recently Representative Daddario's subcommittee raised the question whether we may not reach a day when "a magnetic public personality, provided with sufficient funds to place his image electronically before the populace as often as the psychologically programmed computers dictate, will automatically be guaranteed election."

Which sounds like Buck Rogers stuff, until you remember that the gravity belt is here, and so are Senator Murphy and Governor Reagan and now yet another television personality—the Governor of Oregon, Thomas McCall.

QUESTIONS

1. Has the general public's attitude toward the population explosion significantly changed since 1967, when David Lyle's article first appeared in *Esquire* magazine?

2. Discuss this article in terms of Wilbur's "long numbers that rocket the mind."

3. Do you feel it is possible to draw valid parallels between the actions of mice and men?

4. In what way is "culture shock" similar to "future shock"?

5. Why do you think Lyle chooses to leave the American problems until the final paragraphs of his article?

6. Religious objections aside, should human sterilization be made compulsory for males who have fathered two children? How would a program of compulsory sterilization alter the behavior of males and females in a future society?

Crab-Apple Crisis

George MacBeth

*To make this study concrete I have devised a ladder—a metaphorical
ladder—which indicates that there are many continuous paths between a low-level crisis and an all-out war.*
Herman Kahn in ON ESCALATION

LEVEL I: COLD WAR

Rung 1: Ostensible Crisis
                    Is that you, Barnes? Now see here, friend. From
where I am I can see your boy quite
clearly soft-shoeing along towards
my crab-apple tree. And I want you

to know I can't take that.

Rung 2: Political Economic and Diplomatic Gestures
                                If you don't
wipe that smile off your face, I warn you
I shall turn up the screw of my frog
transistor above the whirr of your

lawn-mower.   10

Rung 3: Solemn and Formal Declarations
                        Now I don't want to sound
unreasonable but if that boy
keeps on codding round my apple tree
I shall have to give serious thought

to taking my belt to him.

LEVEL II: DON'T ROCK THE BOAT

Rung 4: Hardening of Positions

I thought

you ought to know that I've let the Crows
walk their Doberman through my stack of
bean canes behind your chrysanthemum

bed.   20

Rung 5: Show of Force

You might like a look at how my
boy John handles his catapult. At
nineteen yards he can hit your green-house
pushing four times out of five.

Rung 6: Significant Mobilisation

I've asked

the wife to call the boy in for his
coffee, get him to look out a good
supply of small stones.

Rung 7: 'Legal' Harassment

Sure fire my lawn

spray is soaking your picnic tea-cloth   30

but I can't be responsible for
how those small drops fall, now can I?

Rung 8: Harassing Acts of Violence

Your

kitten will get a worse clip on her
left ear if she come any nearer

to my rose-bushes, mam.

Rung 9: Dramatic Military Confrontations

Now see here,

sonny, I can see you pretty damn
clearly up here. If you come one step

nearer to that crab-apple tree you'll
get a taste of this strap across your
back.

40

LEVEL III: NUCLEAR WAR IS UNTHINKABLE

Rung 10: Provocative Diplomatic Break
I'm not going to waste my time
gabbing to you any longer, Barnes:
I'm taking this telephone off the
hook.

Rung 11: All Is Ready Status
Margery, bring that new belt of
mine out on the terrace, would you? I
want these crazy coons to see we mean
business.

50

Rung 12: Large Conventional War
Take that, you lousy kraut. My

pop says you're to leave our crab-apple
tree alone. Ouch! Ow! I'll screw you for
that.

Rung 13: Large Compound Escalation
O.K., you've asked for it. The Crows'
dog is coming into your lilac
bushes.

Rung 14: Declaration of Limited Conventional War
Barnes. Can you hear me through this
loud-hailer? O.K. Well, look. I have
no intention of being the first
to use stones. But I will if you do.

60

Apart from this I won't let the dog
go beyond your chrysanthemum bed
unless your son actually starts
to climb the tree.

Rung 15: Barely Nuclear War

Why, no. I never

told the boy to throw a stone. It was
an accident, man.

Rung 16: Nuclear Ultimatum

Now see here. Why

have you wheeled your baby into the   70
tool-shed? We've not thrown stones.

Rung 17: Limited Evacuation

Honey. I

don't want to worry you but their two
girls have gone round to the Jones's.

Rung 18: Spectacular Show of Force

John.

Throw a big stone over the tree, would
you: but make sure you throw wide.

Rung 19: Justifiable Attack

So we

threw a stone at the boy. Because he
put his foot on the tree. I warned you   80
now, Barnes.

Rung 20: Peaceful World-Wide Embargo or Blockade

Listen, Billy, and you too

Marianne, we've got to teach this cod

a lesson. I'm asking your help in
refusing to take their kids in, or
give them any rights of way, or lend
them any missiles until this is

over.

LEVEL IV: NO NUCLEAR USE

Rung 21: Local Nuclear War

John. Give him a small fistful

of bricks. Make sure you hit him, but not   90
enough to hurt.

Rung 22: Declaration of Limited Nuclear War
                                        Hello there. Barnes. Now
get this, man. I propose to go on

throwing stones as long as your boy is
anywhere near my tree. Now I can
see you may start throwing stones back and
I want you to know that we'll take that
without going for your wife or your
windows unless you go for ours.

Rung 23: Local Nuclear War—Military
                                                        We   100

propose to go on confining our
stone-throwing to your boy beside our

tree: but we're going to let him have
it with all the stones we've got.

Rung 24: Evacuation of Cities—About 70%
                                            Sweetie.
Margery. Would you take Peter and
Berenice round to the Switherings?

Things are getting pretty ugly.

LEVEL V: CENTRAL SANCTUARY

Rung 25: Demonstration Attack on Zone of Interior
                                            We'll
start on his cabbage-plot with a strike   110
of bricks and slates. He'll soon see what we
could do if we really let our hands
slip.

Rung 26: Attack On Military Targets
                        You bastards. Sneak in and smash our
crazy paving, would you?

Rung 27: Exemplary Attacks Against Property
                                        We'll go for

their kitchen windows first. Then put a
brace of slates through the skylight.

Rung 28: Attacks on Population

O.K.

120

Unless they pull out, chuck a stone or
two into the baby's pram in the
shed.

Rung 29: Complete Evacuation—95%

They've cleared the whole family, eh,
baby and all. Just Barnes and the boy
left. Best get your mom to go round to
the Switherings.

Rung 30: Reciprocal Reprisals

Well, if they smash the

bay-window we'll take our spunk out on
the conservatory.

LEVEL VI: CENTRAL WAR

Rung 31: Formal Declaration of General War

Now listen, *130*

Barnes. From now on in we're going all
out against you—windows, flowers, the
lot. There's no hauling-off now without
a formal crawling-down.

Rung 32: Slow-Motion Counter-Force War

We're settling

in for a long strong pull, Johnny. We'd
better try and crack their stone stores one
at a time. Pinch the bricks, plaster the
flowers out and smash every last

particle of glass they've got.   *140*

Rung 33: Constrained Reduction

We'll have

to crack that boy's throwing-arm with a
paving-stone. Just the arm, mind. I don't
want him killed or maimed for life.

Rung 34: Constrained Disarming Attack

> Right, son.

We'll break the boy's legs with a strike of
bricks. If that fails it may have to come
to his head next.

Rung 35: Counter Force With Avoidance

> There's nothing else for

it. We'll have to start on the other   150
two up at the Jones's. If the wife
and the baby gets it, too, it can't
be helped.

LEVEL VII: CITY TARGETING

Rung 36: Counter-City War

> So it's come to the crunch. His

Maggie against my Margery. The
kids against the kids.

Rung 37: Civilian Devastation

> We can't afford

holds barred any more. I'm going all
out with the slates, tools, bricks, the whole damn
shooting-match.   160

Rung 38: Spasm or Insensate War

> All right, Barnes. This is it.

Get out the hammer, son: we need our
own walls now. I don't care if the whole
block comes down. I'll get that maniac
if it's the last thing I—Christ. O, Christ.

QUESTIONS

1. Once you have read "Crab-Apple Crisis," does the escalation

of a small conflict into a global war seem somehow natural, even acceptable? Is there something comfortable in taking this perspective? Would it
be easier to begin the steps leading toward final war in an age when most
people owned fallout shelters?

2. Why are we able to laugh at the violence detailed in "Crab-
Apple Crisis"?

3. How believable are the characters portrayed in this poem?
Have they earned your sympathy? Or does the event overshadow the personalities?

Earth's Holocaust

Nathaniel Hawthorne

Once upon a time—but whether in the time past or time to come is a matter of little or no moment—this wide world had become so overburdened with an accumulation of wornout trumpery that the inhabitants determined to rid themselves of it by a general bonfire. The site fixed upon at the representation of the insurance companies, and as being as central a spot as any other on the globe, was one of the broadest prairies of the West, where no human habitation would be endangered by the flames, and where a vast assemblage of spectators might commodiously admire the show. Having a taste for sights of this kind, and imagining, likewise, that the illumination of the bonfire might reveal some profundity of moral truth heretofore hidden in mist or darkness, I made it convenient to journey thither and be present. At my arrival, although the heap of condemned rubbish was as yet comparatively small, the torch had already been applied. Amid that boundless plain, in the dusk of the evening, like a far off star alone in the firmament, there was merely visible one tremulous gleam, whence none could have anticipated so fierce a blaze as was destined to ensue. With every moment, however, there came foot travellers, women holding up their aprons, men on horseback, wheelbarrows, lumbering baggage wagons, and other vehicles, great and small, and from far and near laden with articles that were judged fit for nothing but to be burned.

"What materials have been used to kindle the flame?" inquired I of a by-stander; for I was desirous of knowing the whole process of the affair from beginning to end.

The person whom I addressed was a grave man, fifty years old or thereabout, who had evidently come thither as a looker on. He struck me immediately as having weighed for himself the true value of life and its circumstances, and therefore as feeling little personal interest in whatever judgment the world might form of them. Before answering my question, he looked me in the face by the kindling light of the fire.

"Oh, some very dry combustibles," replied he, "and extremely suitable to the purpose—no other, in fact, than yesterday's newspapers, last month's magazines, and last year's withered leaves. Here now comes some antiquated trash that will take fire like a handful of shavings."

As he spoke some rough-looking men advanced to the verge of the bonfire, and threw in, as it appeared, all the rubbish of the herald's office —the blazonry of coat armor, the crests and devices of illustrious families, pedigrees that extended back, like lines of light, into the mist of the dark ages, together with stars, garters, and embroidered collars, each of which, as paltry a bawble as it might appear to the uninstructed eye, had once possessed vast significance, and was still, in truth, reckoned among the most precious of moral or material facts by the worshippers of the gorgeous past. Mingled with this confused heap, which was tossed into the flames by armfuls at once, were innumerable badges of knighthood, comprising those of all the European sovereignties, and Napoleon's decoration of the Legion of Honor, the ribbons of which were entangled with those of the ancient order of St. Louis. There, too, were the medals of our own society of Cincinnati, by means of which, as history tells us, an order of hereditary knights came near being constituted out of the king quellers of the revolution. And besides, there were the patents of nobility of German counts and barons, Spanish grandees, and English peers, from the worm-eaten instruments signed by William the Conqueror down to the brand new parchment of the latest lord who has received his honors from the fair hand of Victoria.

At sight of the dense volumes of smoke, mingled with vivid jets of flame, that gushed and eddied forth from this immense pile of earthly distinctions, the multitude of plebeian spectators set up a joyous shout, and clapped their hands with an emphasis that made the welkin echo. That was their moment of triumph, achieved, after long ages, over creatures of the same clay and the same spiritual infirmities, who had dared to assume the privileges due only to Heaven's better workmanship. But now there rushed towards the blazing heap a grayhaired man, of stately presence, wearing a coat, from the breast of which a star, or other badge of rank, seemed to have been forcibly wrenched away. He had not the tokens of intellectual power in his face; but still there was the demeanor, the habitual and almost native dignity, of one who had been born to the idea of his own social superiority, and had never felt it questioned till that moment.

"People," cried he, gazing at the ruin of what was dearest to his eyes with grief and wonder, but nevertheless with a degree of stateliness,— "people, what have you done? This fire is consuming all that marked your advance from barbarism, or that could have prevented your relapse thither. We, the men of the privileged orders, were those who kept alive from age to age the old chivalrous spirit; the gentle and generous thought; the higher, the purer, the more refined and delicate life. With the nobles, too, you cast off the poet, the painter, the sculptor—all the beautiful arts; for we were their patrons, and created the atmosphere in which they flourish. In abolishing the majestic distinctions of rank, society loses not only its grace, but its steadfastness"—

More he would doubtless have spoken; but here there arose an outcry, sportive, contemptuous, and indignant, that altogether drowned the appeal of the fallen nobleman, insomuch that, casting one look of despair at his own half-burned pedigree, he shrunk back into the crowd, glad to shelter himself under his new-found insignificance.

"Let him thank his stars that we have not flung him into the same fire!" shouted a rude figure, spurning the embers with his foot. "And henceforth let no man dare to show a piece of musty parchment as his warrant for lording it over his fellows. If he have strength of arm, well and good; it is one species of superiority. If he have wit, wisdom, courage, force of character, let these attributes do for him what they may; but from this day forward no mortal must hope for place and consideration by reckoning up the mouldy bones of his ancestors. That nonsense is done away."

"And in good time," remarked the grave observer by my side, in a low voice, however, "if no worse nonsense comes in its place; but, at all events, this species of nonsense has fairly lived out its life."

There was little space to muse or moralize over the embers of this time-honored rubbish; for, before it was half burned out, there came another multitude from beyond the sea, bearing the purple robes of royalty, and the crowns, globes, and sceptres of emperors and kings. All these had been condemned as useless bawbles, playthings at best, fit only for the infancy of the world or rods to govern and chastise it in its nonage, but with which universal manhood at its full-grown stature could no longer brook to be insulted. Into such contempt had these regal insignia now fallen that the gilded crown and tinselled robes of the player king from Drury Lane Theatre had been thrown in among the rest, doubtless as a mockery of his brother monarchs on the great stage of the world. It was a strange sight to discern the crown jewels of England glowing and flashing in the midst of the fire. Some of them had been delivered down from the time of the Saxon princes; others were purchased with vast revenues, or perchance ravished from the dead brows of the native potentates of Hindostan; and the whole now blazed with a dazzling lustre, as if a star had fallen in that spot and been shattered into fragments. The splendor of the ruined monarchy had no reflection save in those inestimable precious stones. But enough on this subject. It were but tedious to describe how the Emperor of Austria's mantle was converted to tinder, and how the posts and pillars of the French throne became a heap of coals, which it was impossible to distinguish from those of any other wood. Let me add, however, that I noticed one of the exiled Poles stirring up the bonfire with the Czar of Russia's sceptre, which he afterwards flung into the flames.

"The smell of singed garments is quite intolerable here," observed my new acquaintance, as the breeze enveloped us in the smoke of a royal wardrobe. "Let us get to windward and see what they are doing on the other side of the bonfire."

We accordingly passed around, and were just in time to witness the arrival of a vast procession of Washingtonians,—as the votaries of temperance call themselves nowadays,—accompanied by thousands of the Irish disciples of Father Mathew, with that great apostle at their head. They brought a rich contribution to the bonfire—being nothing less than all the hogsheads and barrels of liquor in the world, which they rolled before them across the prairie.

"Now, my children," cried Father Mathew, when they reached the verge of the fire, "one shove more, and the work is done. And now let us stand off and see Satan deal with his own liquor."

Accordingly, having placed their wooden vessels within reach of the flames, the procession stood off at a safe distance, and soon beheld them burst into a blaze that reached the clouds and threatened to set the sky itself on fire. And well it might; for here was the whole world's stock of spirituous liquors, which, instead of kindling a frenzied light in the eyes of individual topers as of yore, soared upwards with a bewildering gleam that startled all mankind. It was the aggregate of that fierce fire which would otherwise have scorched the hearts of millions. Meantime numberless bottles of precious wine were flung into the blaze, which lapped up the contents as if it loved them, and grew, like other drunkards, the merrier and fiercer for what it quaffed. Never again will the insatiable thirst of the fire fiend be so pampered. Here were the treasures of famous bon vivants—liquors that had been tossed on ocean, and mellowed in the sun, and hoarded long in the recesses of the earth—the pale, the gold, the ruddy juice of whatever vineyards were most delicate—the entire vintage of Tokay—all mingling in one stream with the vile fluids of the common pothouse, and contributing to heighten the selfsame blaze. And while it rose in a gigantic spire that seemed to wave against the arch of the firmament and combine itself with the light of stars, the multitude gave a shout as if the broad earth were exulting in its deliverance from the curse of ages.

But the joy was not universal. Many deemed that human life would be gloomier than ever when that brief illumination should sink down. While the reformers were at work, I overheard muttered expostulations from several respectable gentlemen with red noses and wearing gouty shoes; and a ragged worthy, whose face looked like a hearth where the fire is burned out, now expressed his discontent more openly and boldly.

"What is this world good for," said the last toper, "now that we can never be jolly any more? What is to comfort the poor man in sorrow and perplexity? How is he to keep his heart warm against the cold winds of this cheerless earth? And what do you propose to give him in exchange for the solace that you take away? How are old friends to sit together by the fireside without a cheerful glass between them? A plague upon your reformation! It is a sad world, a cold world, a selfish world, a low world, not worth an honest fellow's living in, now that good fellowship is gone forever!"

This harangue excited great mirth among the bystanders; but, preposterous as was the sentiment, I could not help commiserating the forlorn condition of the last toper, whose boon companions had dwindled away from his side, leaving the poor fellow without a soul to countenance him in sipping his liquor, nor indeed any liquor to sip. Not that this was quite the true state of the case; for I had observed him at a critical moment filch a bottle of fourth-proof brandy that fell beside the bonfire and hide it in his pocket.

The spirituous and fermented liquors being thus disposed of, the zeal of the reformers next induced them to replenish the fire with all the boxes of tea and bags of coffee in the world. And now came the planters of Virginia, bringing their crops and tobacco. These, being cast upon the heap of inutility, aggregated it to the size of a mountain, and incensed the atmosphere with such potent fragrance that methought we should never draw pure breath again. The present sacrifice seemed to startle the lovers of the weed more than any that they had hitherto witnessed.

"Well, they've put my pipe out," said an old gentleman flinging it into the flames in a pet. "What is this world coming to? Everything rich and racy—all the spice of life—is to be condemned as useless. Now that they have kindled the bonfire, if these nonsensical reformers would fling themselves into it, all would be well enough!"

"Be patient," responded a stanch conservative; "it will come to that in the end. They will first fling us in, and finally themselves."

From the general and systematic measures of reform I now turned to consider the individual contributions to this memorable bonfire. In many instances these were of a very amusing character. One poor fellow threw in his empty purse, and another a bundle of counterfeit or insolvable bank notes. Fashionable ladies threw in their last season's bonnets, together with heaps of ribbons, yellow lace, and much other half-worn milliner's ware, all of which proved even more evanescent in the fire than it had been in the fashion. A multitude of lovers of both sexes—discarded maids or bachelors and couples mutually weary of one another—tossed in bundles of perfumed letters and enamored sonnets. A hack politician, being deprived of bread by the loss of office, threw in his teeth, which happened to be false ones. The Rev. Sydney Smith—having voyaged across the Atlantic for that sole purpose—came up to the bonfire with a bitter grin and threw in certain repudiated bonds, fortified though they were with the broad seal of a sovereign state. A little boy of five years old, in the premature manliness of the present epoch, threw in his playthings; a college graduate his diploma; an apothecary, ruined by the spread of homœopathy, his whole stock of drugs and medicines; a physician his library; a parson his old sermons; and a fine gentleman of the old school his code of manners, which he had formerly written down for the benefit of the next generation. A widow, resolving on a second marriage, slyly threw in her dead husband's miniature. A young man, jilted by his mistress, would willingly have flung his own desperate heart into the flames, but could find no means to wrench it out of his bosom. An American author, whose works were neglected by the public, threw his pen and paper into the bonfire, and betook himself to some less discouraging occupation. It somewhat startled me to overhear a number of ladies, highly respectable in appearance, proposing to fling their gowns and petticoats into the flames, and assume the garb, together with the manners, duties, offices, and responsibilities, of the opposite sex.

What favor was accorded to this scheme I am unable to say, my attention being suddenly drawn to a poor, deceived, and half-delirious girl, who, exclaiming that she was the most worthless thing alive or dead, attempted to cast herself into the fire amid all that wrecked and broken trumpery of the world. A good man, however, ran to her rescue.

"Patience, my poor girl!" said he, as he drew her back from the fierce embrace of the destroying angel. "Be patient, and abide Heaven's will. So long as you possess a living soul, all may be restored to its first freshness. These things of matter and creations of human fantasy are fit for nothing but to be burned when once they have had their day; but your day is eternity!"

"Yes," said the wretched girl, whose frenzy seemed now to have sunk down into deep despondency,—"yes and the sunshine is blotted out of it!"

It was now rumored among the spectators that all the weapons and munitions of war were to be thrown into the bonfire, with the exception of the world's stock of gunpowder, which, as the safest mode of disposing of it, had already been drowned in the sea. This intelligence seemed to awaken great diversity of opinion. The hopeful philanthropist esteemed it a token that the millennium was already come; while persons of another stamp, in whose view mankind was a breed of bulldogs, prophesied that all the old stoutness, fervor, nobleness, generosity, and magnanimity of the race would disappear,—these qualities, as they affirmed, requiring blood for their nourishment. They comforted themselves, however, in the belief that the proposed abolition of war was impracticable for any length of time together.

Be that as it might, numberless great guns, whose thunder had long been the voice of battle,—the artillery of the Armada, the battering trains of Marlborough, and the adverse cannon of Napoleon and Wellington,—were trundled into the midst of the fire. By the continual addition of dry combustibles, it had now waxed so intense that neither brass nor iron could withstand it. It was wonderful to behold how these terrible instruments of slaughter melted away like playthings of wax. Then the armies of the earth wheeled around the mighty furnace, with their military music playing triumphant marches, and flung in their muskets and swords. The standard-bearers, likewise, cast one look upward at their banners, all tattered with shot holes and inscribed with the names of victorious fields; and, giving them a last flourish on the breeze, they lowered them into the flame, which snatched them upward in its rush towards the clouds. This ceremony being over, the world was left without a single weapon in its hands, except possibly a few old king's arms and rusty swords and other trophies of the Revolution in some of our state armories. And now the drums were beaten and the trumpets brayed all together, as a prelude to the proclamation of universal and eternal peace and the announcement that glory was no longer to be won by blood, but that it would henceforth be the contention of the human race to work out the greatest mutual good, and that beneficence, in the future annals of the earth, would claim the praise of valor. The blessed tidings were accordingly promulgated, and caused infinite rejoicings among those who had stood aghast at the horror and absurdity of war.

But I saw a grim smile pass over the seared visage of a stately old commander,—by his warworn figure and rich military dress, he might have been one of Napoleon's famous marshals,—who, with the rest of the world's soldiery, had just flung away the sword that had been familiar to his right hand for half a century.

"Ay! ay!" grumbled he. "Let them proclaim what they please; but, in the end, we shall find that all this foolery has only made more work for the armorers and cannon founders."

"Why, sir," exclaimed I, in astonishment, "do you imagine that the human race will ever so far return on the steps of its past madness as to weld another sword or cast another cannon?"

"There will be no need," observed, with a sneer, one who neither felt benevolence nor had faith in it. "When Cain wished to slay his brother, he was at no loss for a weapon."

"We shall see," replied the veteran commander. "If I am mistaken, so much the better; but in my opinion, without pretending to philosophize about the matter, the necessity of war lies far deeper than these honest gentlemen suppose. What! is there a field for all the petty disputes of individuals? and shall there be no great law court for the settlement of national difficulties? The battle field is the only court where such suits can be tried."

"You forget, general," rejoined I, "that, in this advanced stage of civilization, Reason and Philanthropy combined will constitute just such a tribunal as is requisite."

"Ah, I had forgotten that, indeed!" said the old warrior, as he limped away.

The fire was now to be replenished with materials that had hitherto been considered of even greater importance to the well being of society than the warlike munitions which we had already seen consumed. A body of reformers had travelled all over the earth in quest of the machinery by which the different nations were accustomed to inflict the punishment of death. A shudder passed through the multitude as these ghastly emblems were dragged forward. Even the flames seemed at first to shrink away, displaying the shape and murderous contrivance of each in a full blaze of light, which of itself was sufficient to convince mankind of the long and deadly error of human law. Those old implements of cruelty; those horrible monsters of mechanism; those inventions which seemed to demand something worse than man's natural heart to contrive, and which had lurked in the dusky nooks of ancient prisons, the subject of terror-stricken legend,—were now brought forth to view. Headsmen's axes, with the rust of noble and royal blood upon them, and a vast collection of halters that had choked the breath of plebeian victims, were thrown in together. A shout greeted the arrival of the guillotine, which was thrust forward on the same wheels that had borne it from one to another of the blood-stained streets of Paris. But the loudest roar of applause went up, telling the distant sky of the triumph of the earth's redemption, when the gallows made its appearance. An ill-looking fellow, however, rushed forward, and, putting himself in the path of the reformers, bellowed hoarsely, and fought with brute fury to stay their progress.

It was little matter of surprise, perhaps, that the executioner should thus do his best to vindicate and uphold the machinery by which he himself had his livelihood and worthier individuals their death; but it deserved special note that men of a far different sphere—even of that consecrated class in whose guardianship the world is apt to trust its benevolence—were found to take the hangman's view of the question.

"Stay, my brethren!" cried one of them. "You are misled by a false philanthropy; you know not what you do. The gallows is a Heaven-ordained instrument. Bear it back, then, reverently, and set it up in its old place, else the world will fall to speedy ruin and desolation!"

"Onward! onward!" shouted a leader in the reform. "Into the flames with the accursed instrument of man's blood policy! How can human law inculcate benevolence and love while it persists in setting up the gallows as its chief symbol? One heave more, good friends, and the world will be redeemed from its greatest error."

A thousand hands, that nevertheless loathed the touch, now lent their assistance, and thrust the ominous burden far, far into the centre of the raging furnace. There its fatal and abhorred image was beheld, first black, then a red coal, then ashes.

"That was well done!" exclaimed I.

"Yes, it was well done," replied, but with less enthusiasm than I expected, the thoughtful observer who was still at my side; "well done, if the world be good enough for the measure. Death, however, is an idea that cannot easily be dispensed with in any condition between the primal innocence and that other purity and perfection which perchance we are destined to attain after travelling round the full circle: but, at all events, it is well that the experiment should now be tried."

"Too cold! too cold!" impatiently exclaimed the young and ardent leader in this triumph. "Let the heart have its voice here as well as the intellect. And as for ripeness, and as for progress, let mankind always do the highest, kindest, noblest thing that, at any given period, it has attained the perception of; and surely that thing cannot be wrong nor wrongly timed."

I know not whether it were the excitement of the scene, or whether the good people around the bonfire were really growing more enlightened every instant; but they now proceeded to measures in the full length of which I was hardly prepared to keep them company. For instance, some threw their marriage certificates into the flames, and declared themselves candidates for a higher, holier, and more comprehensive union than that which had subsisted from the birth of time under the form of the connubial tie. Others hastened to the vaults of banks and to the coffers of the rich,—all of which were open to the first comer on this fated occasion,—and brought entire bales of paper money to enliven the blaze, and tons of coin to be melted down by its intensity. Henceforth, they said, universal benevolence, uncoined and exhaustless, was to be the golden currency of the world. At this intelligence the bankers and speculators in the stocks grew pale, and a pickpocket, who had reaped a rich harvest among the crowd, fell down in a deadly fainting fit. A few men of business burned their daybooks and ledgers, the notes and obligations of their creditors, and all other evidences of debts due to themselves; while perhaps a somewhat larger number satisfied their zeal for reform with the sacrifice of any uncomfortable recollection of their own indebtment. There was then a cry that the period was arrived when the title deeds of landed property should be given to the flames, and the whole soil of the earth revert to the public, from whom it had been wrongfully abstracted and most unequally distributed among individuals. Another party demanded that all written constitutions, set forms of government, legislative acts, statute books, and everything else on which human invention had endeavored to stamp its arbitrary laws, should at once be destroyed, leaving the consummated world as free as the man first created.

Whether any ultimate action was taken with regard to these propositions is beyond my knowledge; for, just then, some matters were in progress that concerned my sympathies more nearly.

"See! see! What heaps of books and pamphlets!" cried a fellow, who did not seem to be a lover of literature. "Now we shall have a glorious blaze!"

"That's just the thing!" said a modern philosopher. "Now we shall get rid of the weight of dead men's thought, which has hitherto pressed so heavily on the living intellect that it has been incompetent to any effectual self-exertion. Well done, my lads! Into the fire with them! Now you are enlightening the world indeed!"

"But what is to become of the trade?" cried a frantic bookseller.

"Oh, by all means, let them accompany their merchandise," coolly observed an author. "It will be a noble funeral pile!"

The truth was, that the human race had now reached a stage of progress so far beyond what the wisest and wittiest men of former ages had ever dreamed of that it would have been a manifest absurdity to allow the earth to be any longer encumbered with their poor achievements in the literary line. Accordingly a thorough and searching investigation had swept the booksellers' shops, hawkers' stands, public, and private libraries, and even the little book-shelf by the country fireside, and had brought the world's entire mass of printed paper, bound or in sheets, to swell the already mountain bulk of our illustrious bonfire. Thick, heavy folios, containing the labors of lexicographers, commentators and encyclopedists, were flung in, and falling among the embers with a leaden thump, smouldered away to ashes like rotten wood. The small, richly gilt French tomes of the last age, with the hundred volumes of Voltaire among them, went off in a brilliant shower of sparkles and little jets of flame; while the current literature of the same nation burned red and blue, and threw an infernal light over the visages of the spectators, converting them all to the aspect of party-colored fiends. A collection of German stories emitted a scent of brimstone. The English standard authors made excellent fuel, generally exhibiting the properties of sound oak logs. Milton's works, in particular, sent up a powerful blaze, gradually reddening into a coal, which promised to endure longer than almost any other material of the pile. From Shakespeare there gushed a flame of such marvellous splendor that men shaded their eyes as against the sun's meridian glory; nor even when the works of his own elucidators were flung upon him did he cease to flash forth a dazzling radiance from beneath the ponderous heap. It is my belief that he is blazing as fervidly as ever.

"Could a poet but light a lamp at that glorious flame," remarked I, "he might then consume the midnight oil to some good purpose."

"That is the very thing which modern poets have been too apt to do, or at least to attempt," answered a critic. "The chief benefit to be expected from this conflagration of past literature undoubtedly is, that writers will henceforth be compelled to light their lamps at the sun or stars."

"If they can reach so high," said I; "but that task requires a giant, who may afterwards distribute the light among inferior men. It is not every one that can steal the fire from heaven like Prometheus; but, when once he had done the deed, a thousand hearths were kindled by it."

It amazed me much to observe how indefinite was the proportion between the physical mass of any given author and the property of brilliant and long-continued combustion. For instance, there was not a quarto volume of the last century—nor, indeed, of the present—that could compete in that particular with a child's little gilt-covered book, containing

Mother Goose's Melodies. The Life and Death of Tom Thumb out-
lasted the biography of Marlborough. An epic, indeed a dozen of them,
was converted to white ashes before the single sheet of an old ballad was
half consumed. In more than one case, too, when volumes of applauded
verse proved incapable of anything better than a stifling smoke, an unre-
garded ditty of some nameless bard—perchance in the corner of a newspaper—soared up among the stars with a flame as brilliant as their own.
Speaking of the properties of flame, methought Shelley's poetry emitted
a purer light than almost any other productions of his day, contrasting
beautifully with the fitful and lurid gleams and gushes of black vapor
that flashed and eddied from the volumes of Lord Byron. As for Tom
Moore, some of his songs diffused an odor like a burning pastil.

I felt particular interest in watching the combustion of American authors, and scrupulously noted by my watch the precise number of moments that changed most of them from shabbily-printed books to indis-
tinguishable ashes. It would be invidious, however, if not perilous, to
betray these awful secrets; so that I shall content myself with observing
that it was not invariably the writer most frequent in the public mouth
that made the most splendid appearance in the bonfire. I especially remember that a great deal of excellent inflammability was exhibited in a
thin volume of poems by Ellery Channing; although, to speak the truth,
there were certain portions that hissed and spluttered in a very disagreeable fashion. A curious phenomenon occurred in reference to several writers, native as well as foreign. Their books, though of highly respectable
figure, instead of bursting into a blaze, or even smouldering out their
substance in smoke, suddenly melted away in a manner that proved them
to be ice.

If it be no lack of modesty to mention my own works, it must here be
confessed that I looked for them with fatherly interest, but in vain. Too
probably they were changed to vapor by the first action of the heat; at
best, I can only hope that, in their quiet way, they contributed a glim-
mering spark or two to the splendor of the evening.

"Alas! and woe is me!" thus bemoaned himself a heavy-looking gentleman in green spectacles. "The world is utterly ruined, and there is nothing to live for any longer. The business of my life is snatched from me.
Not a volume to be had for love or money!"

"This," remarked the sedate observer beside me, "is a bookworm—one
of those men who are born to gnaw dead thoughts. His clothes, you see,
are covered with the dust of libraries. He has no inward fountain of
ideas; and, in good earnest, now that the old stock is abolished, I do not
see what is to become of the poor fellow. Have you no word of comfort
for him?"

"My dear sir," said I to the desperate bookworm, "is not Nature better
than a book? Is not the human heart deeper than any system of philosophy? Is not life replete with more instruction than past observers have

found it possible to write down in maxims? Be of good cheer. The great book of Time is still spread wide open before us; and, if we read it aright, it will be to us a volume of eternal truth."

"Oh, my books, my books, my precious printed books!" reiterated the forlorn bookworm. "My only reality was a bound volume; and now they will not leave me even a shadowy pamphlet!"

In fact, the last remnant of the literature of all the ages was now descending upon the blazing heap in the shape of a cloud of pamphlets from the press of the New World. These likewise were consumed in the twinkling of an eye, leaving the earth, for the first time since the days of Cadmus, free from the plague of letters—an enviable field for the authors of the next generation.

"Well, and does anything remain to be done?" inquired I somewhat anxiously. "Unless we set fire to the earth itself, and then leap boldly off into infinite space, I know not that we can carry reform to any farther point."

"You are vastly mistaken, my good friend," said the observer. "Believe me, the fire will not be allowed to settle down without the addition of fuel that will startle many persons who have lent a willing hand thus far."

Nevertheless there appeared to be a relaxation of effort for a little time, during which, probably, the leaders of the movement were considering what should be done next. In the interval, a philosopher threw his theory into the flames,—a sacrifice which, by those who knew how to estimate it, was pronounced the most remarkable that had yet been made. The combustion, however, was by no means brilliant. Some indefatigable people, scorning to take a moment's ease, now employed themselves in collecting all the withered leaves and fallen boughs of the forest, and thereby recruited the bonfire to a greater height than ever. But this was mere by-play.

"Here comes the fresh fuel that I spoke of," said my companion.

To my astonishment, the persons who now advanced into the vacant space around the mountain fire bore surplices and other priestly garments, mitres, crosiers, and a confusion of Popish and Protestant emblems, with which it seemed their purpose to consummate the great act of faith. Crosses from the spires of old cathedrals were cast upon the heap with as little remorse as if the reverence of centuries, passing in long array beneath the lofty towers, had not looked up to them as the holiest of symbols. The font in which infants were consecrated to God, the sacramental vessels whence piety received the hallowed draught, were given to the same destruction. Perhaps it most nearly touched my heart to see among these devoted relics fragments of the humble communion tables and undecorated pulpits which I recognized as having been torn from the meeting-houses of New England. Those simple edifices might have been permitted to retain all of sacred embellishment that their Puritan founders had bestowed, even though the mighty structure of St. Peter's had sent its spoils to the fire of this terrible sacrifice. Yet I felt that these were but the externals of religion, and might most safely be relinquished by spirits that best knew their deep significance.

"All is well," said I, cheerfully. "The woodpaths shall be the aisles of our cathedral,—the firmament itself shall be its ceiling. What needs an earthly roof between the Deity and his worshippers? Our faith can well afford to lose all the drapery that even the holiest men have thrown around it, and be only the more sublime in its simplicity."

"True," said my companion; "but will they pause here?"

The doubt implied in his question was well founded. In the general destruction of books already described, a holy volume, that stood apart from the catalogue of human literature, and yet, in one sense, was at its head, had been spared. But the Titan of innovation,—angel or fiend, double in his nature, and capable of deeds befitting both characters,—at first shaking down only the old and rotten shapes of things, had now, as it appeared, laid his terrible hand upon the main pillars which supported the whole edifice of our moral and spiritual state. The inhabitants of the earth had grown too enlightened to define their faith within a form of words, or to limit the spiritual by any analogy to our material existence. Truths which the heavens trembled at were now but a fable of the world's infancy. Therefore, as the final sacrifice of human error, what else remained to be thrown upon the embers of that awful pile except the book which, though a celestial revelation to past ages, was but a voice from a lower sphere as regarded the present race of man? It was done! Upon the blazing heap of falsehood and wornout truth—things that the earth had never needed, or had ceased to need, or had grown childishly weary of—fell the ponderous church Bible, the great old volume that had lain so long on the cushion of the pulpit, and whence the pastor's solemn voice had given holy utterance on so many a Sabbath day. There, likewise, fell the family Bible, which the long-buried patriarch had read to his children,—in prosperity or sorrow, by the fireside and in the summer shade of trees,—and had bequeathed downward as the heirloom of generations. There fell the bosom Bible, the little volume that had been the soul's friend of some sorely-tried child of dust, who thence took courage, whether his trial were for life or death, steadfastly confronting both in the strong assurance of immortality.

All these were flung into the fierce and riotous blaze; and then a mighty wind came roaring across the plain with a desolate howl, as if it were the angry lamentation of the earth for the loss of heaven's sunshine; and it shook the gigantic pyramid of flame and scattered the cinders of half-consumed abominations around upon the spectators.

"This is terrible!" said I, feeling that my cheek grew pale, and seeing a like change in the visages about me.

"Be of good courage yet," answered the man with whom I had so often spoken. He continued to gaze steadily at the spectacle with a singular calmness, as if it concerned him merely as an observer. "Be of good courage, nor yet exult too much; for there is far less both of good and evil in the effect of this bonfire than the world might be willing to believe."

"How can that be?" exclaimed I, impatiently. "Has it not consumed everything? Has it not swallowed up or melted down every human or divine appendage of our mortal state that had substance enough to be acted on by fire? Will there be anything left us to-morrow morning better or worse than a heap of embers and ashes?"

"Assuredly there will," said my grave friend. "Come hither to-morrow morning, or whenever the combustible portion of the pile shall be quite burned out, and you will find among the ashes everything really valuable that you have seen cast into the flames. Trust me, the world of to-morrow will again enrich itself with the gold and diamonds which have been cast off by the world of to-day. Not a truth is destroyed nor buried so deep among the ashes but it will be raked up at last."

This was a strange assurance. Yet I felt inclined to credit it, the more especially as I beheld among the wallowing flames a copy of the Holy Scriptures, the pages of which, instead of being blackened into tinder, only assumed a more dazzling whiteness as the finger marks of human imperfection were purified away. Certain marginal notes and commentaries, it is true, yielded to the intensity of the fiery test, but without detriment to the smallest syllable that had flamed from the pen of inspiration.

"Yes; there is the proof of what you say," answered I, turning to the observer; "but if only what is evil can feel the action of the fire, then, surely, the conflagration has been of inestimable utility. Yet, if I understand aright, you intimate a doubt whether the world's expectation of benefit would be realized by it."

"Listen to the talk of these worthies," said he, pointing to a group in front of the blazing pile; "possibly they may teach you something useful without intending it."

The persons whom he indicated consisted of that brutal and most earthy figure who had stood forth so furiously in defence of the gallows, —the hangman, in short,—together with the last thief and the last murderer, all three of whom were clustered about the last toper. The latter was liberally passing the brandy bottle, which he had rescued from the general destruction of wines and spirits. This little convivial party seemed at the lowest pitch of despondency, as considering that the purified world must needs be utterly unlike the sphere that they had hitherto known, and therefore but a strange and desolate abode for gentlemen of their kidney.

"The best counsel for all of us is," remarked the hangman, "that, as soon as we have finished the last drop of liquor, I help you, my three friends, to a comfortable end upon the nearest tree, and then hang myself on the same bough. This is no world for us any longer."

"Poh, poh, my good fellows!" said a dark-complexioned personage, who now joined the group,—his complexion was indeed fearfully dark, and his eyes glowed with a redder light than that of the bonfire; "be not so cast down, my dear friends; you shall see good days yet. There's one thing that these wiseacres have forgotten to throw into the fire, and without which all the rest of the conflagration is just nothing at all; yes, though they had burned the earth itself to a cinder."

"And what may that be?" eagerly demanded the last murderer.

"What but the human heart itself?" said the dark-visaged stranger, with a portentous grin. "And, unless they hit upon some method of purifying that foul cavern, forth from it will reissue all the shapes of wrong and misery—the same old shapes or worse ones—which they have taken such a vast deal of trouble to consume to ashes. I have stood by this live-long night and laughed in my sleeve at the whole business. Oh, take my word for it, it will be the old world yet!"

This brief conversation supplied me with a theme for lengthened thought. How sad a truth, if true it were, that man's agelong endeavor for perfection had served only to render him the mockery of the evil principle, from the fatal circumstance of an error at the very root of the matter! The heart, the heart,—there was the little yet boundless sphere wherein existed the original wrong of which the crime and misery of this outward world were merely types. Purify that inward sphere, and the many shapes of evil that haunt the outward, and which now seem almost our only realities, will turn to shadowy phantoms and vanish of their own accord; but if we go no deeper than the intellect, and strive, with merely that feeble instrument, to discern and rectify what is wrong, our whole accomplishment will be a dream, so unsubstantial that it matters little whether the bonfire, which I have so faithfully described, were what we choose to call a real event and a flame that would scorch the finger, or only a phosphoric radiance and a parable of my own brain.

QUESTIONS

1. Why do people come so willingly to the bonfire Hawthorne describes?

2. Characterize Hawthorne's attitude toward war. Do many of the characters in this story seem to exhibit this same attitude?

3. Explain Hawthorne's concept of going "no deeper than the intellect." What various qualities does he ascribe to "the human heart"?

4. This story is obviously an allegory, as is much of speculative fiction. But can "Earth's Holocaust" be called *science* fiction?

5. Is the story an allegory concerning primarily concepts of anarchy or of revolution?

6. Are some of the references in "Earth's Holocaust" outdated, particularly those to kings and heraldry?

7. Could other Hawthorne stories such as "The Birthmark," "Rappaccini's Daughter," and "The Artist of the Beautiful" be called science fiction?

part 2

Alternate Futures:
The Present as Future

One of the characteristics of SF may be that it always involves some sort of warping of reality. If the future is happening now, and if we can observe it happening, there are doubtless many events that—were we to know about them—would cause enormous changes in our consciousness. SF is not realistic literature; the stories in this section are not "true"; the occurrences related here have not, as far as we know, actually happened. But the events spoken of in this section—unlike those of the next—are written in a perspective of the present; the probability of their happening does not necessarily depend upon the passing of chronological time.

Allen Ginsberg writes of the poet in the present, dreaming towards the future. His exploration is as much of mystical inner space as of outer space. Kenneth Koch's artist grows more and more ambitious with each completed project; the artist's creations, step by step, lead him into further explorations of the possible.

But suppose what we think of as reality is not the actual reality? Our understanding is limited; our conclusions and predictions are founded on a limited point of view. This world might actually be that hell in which Isaac Singer's characters love. Another view of reality might be the idea that either we are characters in someone's dream or we are dreaming up others, to the commands of such beings as those in Robert Heinlein's "They." We can ask who, in "The Country of the Blind," is really blind? How might humans of the past have acted when meeting members of other cultures? Are all utopias necessarily flawed? Change is upon us. How we will react, for instance, to the balloon that is about to settle over our city (or already has) tells us a great deal about how we shall meet the more distant tomorrow.

Allen Ginsberg is one of the culture heroes of the time, widely known for his peaceful involvement in demonstrations and riots. Ginsberg's books include Howl, Kaddish, Planet News, and Reality Sandwiches. H. G. Wells is (with Jules Verne) commonly regarded by many SF fans as the founder of modern science fiction. His novels include The Time Machine, The Shape of Things to Come, War of the Worlds, and The Invisible Man. Isaac Bashevis Singer, since his arrival in the United States in 1935, has become commonly regarded as one of America's leading writers. Singer's short stories, fables, and novels often combine *elements of fantasy and magic with harrowing portraits of strange townspeople and devils. His books include the novels* The Manor *and* Satan in Goray, *and the short story collections* Short Friday, Gimpel the Fool, *and* The Seance. *Robert Heinlein's* Stranger in a Strange Land *has achieved great popularity among college students—particularly for its treatment of religion and communal living. Heinlein has also written* Glory Road, The Puppet Masters, *and* The Moon Is a Harsh Mistress. *These, and his many other works, have earned him the title of the Dean of Modern Science Fiction. The New York poet Kenneth Koch's books include* Thank You and Other Poems; No, Or a Season on Earth; *and* Permanently. *Donald Barthelme is the author of* Come Back, Dr. Caligari; Snow White; Unspeakable Practices, Unnatural Acts; *and* City Life.

Poem Rocket

Allen Ginsberg

Be a Star-screwer!
Gregory Corso

Old moon my eyes are new moon with human footprint
no longer Romeo Sadface in drunken river Loony Pierre eyebrow,
    goof moon
O possible moon in Heaven we get to first of ageless constellations
    of names
as God is possible as All is possible so we'll reach another life.

Moon politicians earth weeping and warring in eternity

tho not one star disturbed by screaming madmen from Hollywood
oil tycoons from Romania making secret deals with flabby green
    Plutonians—
slave camps on Saturn Cuban revolutions on Mars?
Old life and new side by side, will Catholic church find Christ on
    Jupiter
Mohammed rave in Uranus will Buddha be acceptable on the
    stolid planets   10
or will we find Zoroastrian temples flowering on Neptune?
What monstrous new ecclesiastical designs on the entire universe
    unfold in the dying Pope's brain?
Scientist alone is true poet he gives us the moon
he promises the stars he'll make us a new universe if it comes to
    that
O Einstein I should have sent you my flaming mss.
O Einstein I should have pilgrimaged to your white hair!
O fellow travellers I write you a poem in Amsterdam in the Cosmos
where Spinoza ground his magic lenses long ago
I write you a poem long ago

already my feet are washed in death   20
Here I am naked without identity
with no more body than the fine black tracery of pen mark on soft
    paper
as star talks to star multiple beams of sunlight all the same myriad
    thought
in one fold of the universe where Whitman was
and Blake and Shelley saw Milton dwelling as in a starry temple
brooding in his blindness seeing all—
Now at last I can speak to you beloved brothers of an unknown
    moon
real Yous squatting in whatever form amidst Platonic Vapors of
    Eternity
I am another Star.
Will you eat my poems or read them   30
or gaze with aluminum blind plates on sunless pages?
do you dream or translate & accept data with indifferent droopings
    of antennae?
do I make sense to your flowery green receptor eyesockets? do you
    have visions of God?
Which way will the sunflower turn surrounded by millions of suns?

This is my rocket my personal rocket I send up my message Beyond
Someone to hear me there
My immortality
without steel or cobalt basalt or diamond gold or mercurial fire
without passports filing cabinets bits of paper warheads
without myself finally   40
pure thought
message all and everywhere the same
I send up my rocket to land on whatever planet awaits it
preferably religious sweet planets no money
fourth dimensional planets where Death shows movies
plants speak (courteously) of ancient physics and poetry itself is
    manufactured by the trees
the final Planet where the Great Brain of the Universe sits waiting
    for a poem to land in His golden pocket
joining the other notes mash-notes love-sighs complaints-musical
    shrieks of despair and the million unutterable thoughts of frogs
I send you my rocket of amazing chemical
more than my hair my sperm or the cells of my body   50

the speeding thought that flies upward with my desire as instanta-
neous as the universe and faster than light
and leave all other questions unfinished for the moment to turn
back to sleep in my dark bed on earth.

QUESTIONS

1. Explain how Ginsberg travels from God to All to "another
life" in line 4. How would you describe the logic of this progression?

2. What does Ginsberg mean in the line "Which way will the
sunflower turn surrounded by millions of suns"?

3. Compare the use of imagery in this poem with the imagery in
early Bob Dylan songs such as "Mr. Tambourine Man."

4. Is this primarily a "mystical" or "humorous" poem?

5. How do the form and style of "Poem Rocket" emphasize its
meanings? What, for instance, accounts for the tone of the final lines?

6. Discuss the scientist as poet.

The Country of the Blind

H. G. Wells

Three hundred miles and more from Chimborazo, one hundred from the snows of Cotopaxi, in the wildest wastes of Ecuador's Andes, there lies that mysterious mountain valley, cut off from the world of men, the Country of the Blind. Long years ago that valley lay so far open to the world that men might come at last through frightful gorges and over an icy pass into its equable meadows; and thither indeed men came, a family or so of Peruvian half-breeds fleeing from the lust and tyranny of an evil Spanish ruler. Then came the stupendous outbreak of Mindo-bamba, when it was night in Quito for seventeen days, and the water was boiling at Yaguachi and all the fish floating dying even as far as Guaya-quil; everywhere along the Pacific slopes there were landslips and swift thawings and sudden floods, and one whole side of the Arauca crest slipped and came down in thunder, and cut off the Country of the Blind for ever from the exploring feet of men. But one of these early settlers had chanced to be on the hither side of the gorges when the world had so terribly shaken itself, and he perforce had to forget his wife and his child and all the friends and possessions he had left up there, and start life over again in the lower world. He started it again but ill, blindness overtook him, and he died of punishment in the mines; but the story he told begot a legend that lingers along the length of the Cordilleras of the Andes to this day.

He told of his reason for venturing back from that fastness, into which he had first been carried lashed to a llama, beside a vast bale of gear, when he was a child. The valley, he said, had in it all that the heart of man could desire—sweet water, pasture, and even climate, slopes of rich brown soil with tangles of a shrub that bore an excellent fruit, and on one side great hanging forests of pine that held the avalanches high. Far overhead, on three sides, vast cliffs of grey-green rock were capped by cliffs of ice; but the glacier stream came not to them but flowed away by the farther slopes, and only now and then huge ice masses fell on the val-ley side. In this valley it neither rained nor snowed, but the abundant springs gave a rich green pasture, that irrigation would spread over all the valley space. The settlers did well indeed there. Their beasts did well and multiplied, and but one thing marred their happiness. Yet it was enough to mar it greatly. A strange disease had come upon them, and had made all the children born to them there—and indeed, several older children also—blind. It was to seek some charm or antidote against this plague of blindness that he had with fatigue and danger and difficulty returned down the gorge. In those days, in such cases, men did not think of germs and infections but of sins; and it seemed to him that the reason of this affliction must lie in the negligence of these priestless immigrants to set up a shrine so soon as they entered the valley. He wanted a shrine—a handsome, cheap, effectual shrine—to be erected in the valley; he wanted relics and such-like potent things of faith, blessed objects and mysterious medals and prayers. In his wallet he had a bar of native silver for which he would not account; he insisted there was none in the valley with something of the insistence of an inexpert liar. They had all clubbed their money and ornaments together, having little need for such treasure up there, he said, to buy them holy help against their ill. I figure this dim-eyed young mountaineer, sunburnt, gaunt, and anxious, hat-brim clutched feverishly, a man all unused to the ways of the lower world, telling this story to some keen-eyed, attentive priest before the great convulsion; I can picture him presently seeking to return with pious and infallible remedies against that trouble, and the infinite dismay with which he must have faced the tumbled vastness where the gorge had once come out. But the rest of his story of mischances is lost to me, save that I know of his evil death after several years. Poor stray from that remoteness! The stream that had once made the gorge now bursts from the mouth of a rocky cave, and the legend his poor, ill-told story set going developed into the legend of a race of blind men somewhere "over there" one may still hear to-day.

And amidst the little population of that now isolated and forgotten valley the disease ran its course. The old became groping and purblind, the young saw but dimly, and the children that were born to them saw never at all. But life was very easy in that snow-rimmed basin, lost to all the world, with neither thorns nor briars, with no evil insects nor any beasts save the gentle breed of llamas they had lugged and thrust and followed up the beds of the shrunken rivers in the gorges up which they had come. The seeing had become purblind so gradually that they scarcely noted their loss. They guided the sightless youngsters hither and thither until they knew the whole valley marvellously, and when at last sight died out among them the race lived on. They had even time to adapt themselves to the blind control of fire, which they made carefully in stoves of stone. They were a simple strain of people at the first, unlettered, only slightly touched with the Spanish civilisation, but with something of a tradition of the arts of old Peru and of its lost philosophy. Generation followed generation. They forgot many things; they devised many things. Their tradition of the greater world they came from became mythical in colour and uncertain. In all things save sight they were strong and able; and presently the chance of birth and heredity sent one who had an original mind and who could talk and persuade among them, and then afterwards another. These two passed, leaving their effects, and the little community grew in numbers and in understanding, and met and settled social and economic problems that arose. Generation followed generation. Generation followed generation. There came a time when a child was born who was fifteen generations from that ancestor who went out of the valley with a bar of silver to seek God's aid, and who never returned. Thereabouts it chanced that a man came into this community from the outer world. And this is the story of that man.

He was a mountaineer from the country near Quito, a man who had been down to the sea and had seen the world, a reader of books in an original way, an acute and enterprising man, and he was taken on by a party of Englishmen who had come out to Ecuador to climb mountains, to replace one of their three Swiss guides who had fallen ill. He climbed here and he climbed there, and then came the attempt on Parascotopetl, the Matterhorn of the Andes, in which he was lost to the outer world. The story of the accident has been written a dozen times. Pointer's narrative is the best. He tells how the party worked their difficult and almost vertical way up to the very foot of the last and greatest precipice, and how they built a night shelter amidst the snow upon a little shelf of rock, and, with a touch of real dramatic power, how presently they found Nunez had gone from them. They shouted, and there was no reply, shouted and whistled, and for the rest of that night they slept no more.

As the morning broke they saw the traces of his fall. It seems impossible he could have uttered a sound. He had slipped eastward towards the unknown side of the mountain; far below he had struck a steep slope of snow, and ploughed his way down it in the midst of a snow avalanche. His track went straight to the edge of a frightful precipice, and beyond that everything was hidden. Far, far below, and hazy with distance, they could see trees rising out of a narrow, shut-in valley—the lost Country of the Blind. But they did not know it was the lost Country of the Blind, nor distinguish it in any way from any other narrow streak of upland valley. Unnerved by this disaster, they abandoned their attempt in the afternoon, and Pointer was called away to the war before he could make another attack. To this day Parascotopetl lifts an unconquered crest, and Pointer's shelter crumbles unvisited amidst the snows.

And the man who fell survived.

At the end of the slope he fell a thousand feet, and came down in the midst of a cloud of snow upon a snow slope even steeper than the one above. Down this he was whirled, stunned and insensible, but without a bone broken in his body; and then at last came to gentler slopes, and at last rolled out and lay still, buried amidst a softening heap of the white masses that had accompanied and saved him. He came to himself with a dim fancy that he was ill in bed; then realised his position with a mountaineer's intelligence, and worked himself loose and, after a rest or so, out until he saw the stars. He rested flat upon his chest for a space, wondering where he was and what had happened to him. He explored his limbs, and discovered that several of his buttons were gone and his coat turned over his head. His knife had gone from his pocket and his hat was lost, though he had tied it under his chin. He recalled that he had been looking for loose stones to raise his piece of the shelter wall. His ice-axe had disappeared.

He decided he must have fallen, and looked up to see, exaggerated by the ghastly light of the rising moon, the tremendous flight he had taken. For a while he lay, gazing blankly at that vast pale cliff towering above, rising moment by moment out of a subsiding tide of darkness. Its phantasmal, mysterious beauty held him for a space, and then he was seized with a paroxysm of sobbing laughter. . . .

After a great interval of time he became aware that he was near the lower edge of the snow. Below, down what was now a moonlit and practicable slope, he saw the dark and broken appearance of rock-strewn turf. He struggled to his feet, aching in every joint and limb, got down painfully from the heaped loose snow about him, went downward until he was on the turf, and there dropped rather than lay beside a boulder, drank deep from the flask in his inner pocket, and instantly fell asleep.

He was awakened by the singing of birds in the trees far below.

He sat up and perceived he was on a little alp at the foot of a vast precipice, that was grooved by the gully down which he and his snow had come. Over against him another wall of rock reared itself against the sky. The gorge between these precipices ran east and west and was full of the morning sunlight, which lit to the westward the mass of fallen mountain that closed the descending gorge. Below him it seemed there was a precipice equally steep, but behind the snow in the gully he found a sort of chimney-cleft dripping with snow-water down which a desperate man might venture. He found it easier than it seemed, and came at last to another desolate alp, and then after a rock climb of no particular difficulty to a steep slope of trees. He took his bearings and turned his face up the gorge, for he saw it opened out above upon green meadows, among which he now glimpsed quite distinctly a cluster of stone huts of unfamiliar fashion. At times his progress was like clambering along the face of a wall, and after a time the rising sun ceased to strike along the gorge, the voices of the singing birds died away, and the air grew cold and dark about him. But the distant valley with its houses was all the brighter for that. He came presently to talus, and among the rocks he noted—for he was an observant man—an unfamiliar fern that seemed to clutch out of the crevices with intense green hands. He picked a frond or so and gnawed its stalk and found it helpful.

About midday he came at last out of the throat of the gorge into the plain and the sunlight. He was stiff and weary; he sat down in the shadow of a rock, filled up his flask with water from a spring and drank it down, and remained for a time resting before he went on to the houses.

They were very strange to his eyes, and indeed the whole aspect of that valley became, as he regarded it, queerer and more unfamiliar. The greater part of its surface was lush green meadow, starred with many beautiful flowers, irrigated with extraordinary care, and bearing evidence of systematic cropping piece by piece. High up and ringing the valley about was a wall, and what appeared to be a circumferential water-channel, from which the little trickles of water that fed the meadow plants came, and on the higher slopes above this flocks of llamas cropped the scanty herbage. Sheds, apparently shelters or feeding-places for the llamas, stood against the boundary wall here and there. The irrigation streams ran together into a main channel down the centre of the valley, and this was enclosed on either side by a wall breast high. This gave a singularly urban quality to this secluded place, a quality that was greatly enhanced by the fact that a number of paths paved with black and white stones, and each with a curious little kerb at the side, ran hither and thither in an orderly manner. The houses of the central village were quite unlike the casual and higgledy-piggledy agglomeration of the mountain villages he knew; they stood in a continuous row on either side of a central street of astonishing cleanness; here and there their parti-coloured façade was pierced by a door, and not a solitary window broke their even frontage. They were parti-coloured with extraordinary irregularity; smeared with a sort of plaster that was sometimes grey, sometimes drab, sometimes slate-coloured or dark brown; and it was the sight of this wild plastering first brought the word "blind" into the thoughts of the explorer. "The good man who did that," he thought, "must have been as blind as a bat."

He descended a steep place, and so came to the wall and channel that ran about the valley, near where the latter spouted out its surplus contents into the deeps of the gorge in a thin and wavering thread of cascade. He could now see a number of men and women resting on piled heaps of grass, as if taking a siesta, in the remoter part of the meadow, and nearer the village a number of recumbent children, and then nearer at hand three men carrying pails on yokes along a little path that ran from the encircling wall towards the houses. These latter were clad in garments of llama cloth and boots and belts of leather, and they wore caps of cloth with back and ear flaps. They followed one another in single file, walking slowly and yawning as they walked, like men who have been up all night. There was something so reassuringly prosperous and respectable in their bearing that after a moment's hesitation Nunez stood forward as conspicuously as possible upon his rock, and gave vent to a mighty shout that echoed round the valley.

The three men stopped, and moved their heads as though they were looking about them. They turned their faces this way and that, and Nunez gesticulated with freedom. But they did not appear to see him for all his gestures, and after a time, directing themselves towards the mountains far away to the right, they shouted as if in answer. Nunez bawled again, and then once more, and as he gestured ineffectually the word "blind" came up to the top of his thoughts. "The fools must be blind," he said.

When at last, after much shouting and wrath, Nunez crossed the stream by a little bridge, came through a gate in the wall, and approached them, he was sure that they were blind. He was sure that this was the Country of the Blind of which the legends told. Conviction had sprung upon him, and a sense of great and rather enviable adventure. The three stood side by side, not looking at him, but with their ears directed towards him, judging him by his unfamiliar steps. They stood close together like men a little afraid, and he could see their eyelids closed and sunken, as though the very balls beneath had shrunk away. There was an expression near awe on their faces.

"A man," one said, in hardly recognisable Spanish—"a man it is—a man or a spirit—coming down from the rocks."

But Nunez advanced with the confident steps of a youth who enters upon life. All the old stories of the lost valley and the Country of the Blind had come back to his mind, and through his thoughts ran this old proverb, as if it were a refrain—

"In the Country of the Blind the One-eyed Man is King."

"In the Country of the Blind the One-eyed Man is King."

And very civilly he gave them greeting. He talked to them and used his eyes.

"Where does he come from, brother Pedro?" asked one.

"Down out of the rocks."

"Over the mountains I come," said Nunez, "out of the country beyond there—where men can see. From near Bogota, where there are a hundred thousands of people, and where the city passes out of sight."

"Sight?" muttered Pedro. "Sight?"

"He comes," said the second blind man, "out of the rocks."

The cloth of their coats Nunez saw was curiously fashioned, each with a different sort of stitching.

They startled him by a simultaneous movement towards him, each with a hand outstretched. He stepped back from the advance of these spread fingers.

"Come hither," said the third blind man, following his motion and clutching him neatly.

And they held Nunez and felt him over, saying no word further until they had done so.

"Carefully," he cried, with a finger in his eye, and found they thought that organ, with its fluttering lids, a queer thing in him. They went over it again.

"A strange creature, Correa," said the one called Pedro. "Feel the coarseness of his hair. Like a llama's hair."

"Rough he is as the rocks that begot him," said Correa, investigating Nunez's unshaven chin with a soft and slightly moist hand. "Perhaps he will grow finer." Nunez struggled a little under their examination, but they gripped him firm.

"Carefully," he said again.

"He speaks," said the third man. "Certainly he is a man."

"Ugh!" said Pedro, at the roughness of his coat.

"And you have come into the world?" asked Pedro.

"Out of the world. Over mountains and glaciers; right over above there, half-way to the sun. Out of the great big world that goes down, twelve days' journey to the sea."

They scarcely seemed to heed him. "Our fathers have told us men may be made by the forces of Nature," said Correa. "It is the warmth of things and moisture, and rottenness—rottenness."

"Let us lead him to the elders," said Pedro.

"Shout first," said Correa, "lest the children be afraid. This is a marvellous occasion."

So they shouted, and Pedro went first and took Nunez by the hand to lead him to the houses.

He drew his hand away. "I can see," he said.

"See?" said Correa.

"Yes, see," said Nunez, turning towards him, and stumbled against Pedro's pail.

"His senses are still imperfect," said the third blind man. "He stumbles, and talks unmeaning words. Lead him by the hand."

"As you will," said Nunez, and was led along, laughing.

It seemed they knew nothing of sight.

Well, all in good time, he would teach them.

He heard people shouting, and saw a number of figures gathering together in the middle roadway of the village.

He found it taxed his nerve and patience more than he had anticipated, that first encounter with the population of the Country of the Blind. The place seemed larger as he drew near to it, and the smeared plasterings queerer, and a crowd of children and men and women (the women and girls, he was pleased to note, had some of them quite sweet faces, for all that their eyes were shut and sunken) came about him, holding on to him, touching him with soft, sensitive hands, smelling at him, and listening at every word he spoke. Some of the maidens and children, however, kept aloof as if afraid, and indeed his voice seemed coarse and rude beside their softer notes. They mobbed him. His three guides kept close to him with an effect of proprietorship, and said again and again, "A wild man out of the rocks."

"Bogota," he said. "Bogota. Over the mountain crests."

"A wild man—using wild words," said Pedro. "Did you hear that—*Bo-*

gota? His mind is hardly formed yet. He has only the beginnings of speech."

A little boy nipped his hand. "Bogota!" he said mockingly.

"Ay! A city to your village. I come from the great world—where men have eyes and see."

"His name's Bogota," they said.

"He stumbled," said Correa, "stumbled twice as we came hither."

"Bring him to the elders."

And they thrust him suddenly through a doorway into a room as black as pitch, save at the end there faintly glowed a fire. The crowd closed in behind him and shut out all but the faintest glimmer of day, and before he could arrest himself he had fallen headlong over the feet of a seated man. His arm, outflung, struck the face of someone else as he went down; he felt the soft impact of features and heard a cry of anger, and for a moment he struggled against a number of hands that clutched him. It was a one-sided fight. An inkling of the situation came to him, and he lay quiet.

"I fell down," he said; "I couldn't see in this pitchy darkness."

There was a pause as if the unseen persons about him tried to understand his words. Then the voice of Correa said: "He is but newly formed. He stumbles as he walks and mingles words that mean nothing with his speech."

Others also said things about him that he heard or understood imperfectly.

"May I sit up?" he asked, in a pause. "I will not struggle against you again."

They consulted and let him rise.

The voice of an older man began to question him, and Nunez found himself trying to explain the great world out of which he had fallen, and the sky and mountains and sight and such-like marvels, to these elders who sat in darkness in the Country of the Blind. And they would believe and understand nothing whatever he told them, a thing quite outside his expectation. They would not even understand many of his words. For fourteen generations these people had been blind and cut off from all the seeing world; the names for all the things of sight had faded and changed; the story of the outer world was faded and changed to a child's story; and they had ceased to concern themselves with anything beyond the rocky slopes above their circling wall. Blind men of genius had arisen among them and questioned the shreds of belief and tradition they had brought with them from their seeing days, and had dismissed all these things as idle fancies, and replaced them with new and saner explanations. Much of their imagination had shrivelled with their eyes, and they had made for themselves new imaginations with their ever more sensitive ears and finger-tips. Slowly Nunez realised this; that his expectation of wonder and reverence at his origin and his gifts was not to be borne out; and after his poor attempt to explain sight to them had been set aside as the confused version of a new-made being describing the marvels of his incoherent sensations, he subsided, a little dashed, into listening to their instruction. And the eldest of the blind men explained to him life and philosophy and religion, how that the world (meaning their valley) had been first an empty hollow in the rocks, and then had come, first, inanimate things without the gift of touch, and llamas and a few other creatures that had little sense, and then men, and at last angels, whom one could hear singing and making fluttering sounds, but whom no one could touch at all, which puzzled Nunez greatly until he thought of the birds.

He went on to tell Nunez how this time had been divided into the warm and the cold, which are the blind equivalents of day and night, and how it was good to sleep in the warm and work during the cold, so that now, but for his advent, the whole town of the blind would have been asleep. He said Nunez must have been specially created to learn and serve the wisdom they had acquired, and for that all his mental incoherency and stumbling behaviour he must have courage, and do his best to learn, and at that all the people in the doorway murmured encouragingly. He said the night—for the blind call their day night—was now far gone, and it behooved every one to go back to sleep. He asked Nunez if he knew how to sleep, and Nunez said he did, but that before sleep he wanted food.

They brought him food—llama's milk in a bowl, and rough salted bread—and led him into a lonely place to eat out of their hearing, and afterwards to slumber until the chill of the mountain evening roused them to begin their day again. But Nunez slumbered not at all.

Instead, he sat up in the place where they had left him, resting his limbs and turning the unanticipated circumstances of his arrival over and over in his mind.

Every now and then he laughed, sometimes with amusement, and sometimes with indignation.

"Unformed mind!" he said. "Got no senses yet! They little know they've been insulting their heaven-sent king and master. I see I must bring them to reason. Let me think—let me think."

He was still thinking when the sun set.

Nunez had an eye for all beautiful things, and it seemed to him that the glow upon the snowfields and glaciers that rose about the valley on every side was the most beautiful thing he had ever seen. His eyes went from that inaccessible glory to the village and irrigated fields, fast sinking into the twilight, and suddenly a wave of emotion took him, and he thanked God from the bottom of his heart that the power of sight had been given him.

He heard a voice calling to him from out of the village.

"Ya ho there, Bogota! Come hither!"

At that he stood up smiling. He would show these people once and for all what sight would do for a man. They would seek him, but not find him.

"You move not, Bogota," said the voice.

He laughed noiselessly, and made two stealthy steps aside from the path.

"Trample not on the grass, Bogota; that is not allowed."

Nunez had scarcely heard the sound he made himself. He stopped amazed.

The owner of the voice came running up the piebald path towards him.

He stepped back into the pathway. "Here I am," he said.

"Why did you not come when I called you?" said the blind man. "Must you be led like a child? Cannot you hear the path as you walk?"

Nunez laughed. "I can see it," he said.

"There is no such word as *see*," said the blind man, after a pause. "Cease this folly, and follow the sound of my feet."

Nunez followed, a little annoyed.

"My time will come," he said.

"You'll learn," the blind man answered. "There is much to learn in the world."

"Has no one told you, 'In the Country of the Blind the One-eyed Man is King'?"

"What is blind?" asked the blind man carelessly over his shoulder.

Four days passed, and the fifth found the King of the Blind still incognito, as a clumsy and useless stranger among his subjects.

It was, he found, much more difficult to proclaim himself than he had supposed, and in the meantime, while he meditated his *coup d'état*, he did what he was told and learned the manners and customs of the Country of the Blind. He found working and going about at night a particularly irksome thing, and he decided that that should be the first thing he would change.

They led a simple, laborious life, these people, with all the elements of virtue and happiness, as these things can be understood by men. They toiled, but not oppressively; they had food and clothing sufficient for their needs; they had days and seasons of rest; they made much of music and singing, and there was love among them, and little children.

It was marvellous with what confidence and precision they went about their ordered world. Everything, you see, had been made to fit their needs; each of the radiating paths of the valley area had a constant angle to the others, and was distinguished by a special notch upon its kerbing; all obstacles and irregularities of path or meadow had long since been cleared away; all their methods and procedure arose naturally from their special needs. Their senses had become marvellously acute; they could hear and judge the slightest gesture of a man a dozen paces away—could hear the very beating of his heart. Intonation had long replaced expres-

sion with them, and touches gesture, and their work with hoe and spade
and fork was as free and confident as garden work can be. Their sense of
smell was extraordinarily fine; they could distinguish individual differences as readily as a dog can, and they went about the tending of the llamas, who lived among the rocks above and came to the wall for food and
shelter, with ease and confidence. It was only when at last Nunez sought
to assert himself that he found how easy and confident their movements
could be.

He rebelled only after he had tried persuasion.

He tried at first on several occasions to tell them of sight. "Look you
here, you people," he said. "There are things you do not understand in
me."

Once or twice one or two of them attended to him; they sat with faces
downcast and ears turned intelligently towards him, and he did his best
to tell them what it was to see. Among his hearers was a girl, with eyelids
less red and sunken than the others, so that one could almost fancy she
was hiding eyes, whom especially he hoped to persuade. He spoke of the
beauties of sight, of watching the mountains, of the sky and the sunrise,
and they heard him with amused incredulity that presently became con-
demnatory. They told him there were indeed no mountains at all, but
that the end of the rocks where the llamas grazed was indeed the end of
the world; thence sprang a cavernous roof of the universe, from which
the dew and the avalanches fell; and when he maintained stoutly the
world had neither end nor roof such as they supposed, they said his
thoughts were wicked. So far as he could describe sky and clouds and
stars to them it seemed to them a hideous void, a terrible blankness in
the place of the smooth roof to things in which they believed—it was an
article of faith with them that the cavern roof was exquisitely smooth to
the touch. He saw that in some manner he shocked them, and gave up
that aspect of the matter altogether, and tried to show them the practical
value of sight. One morning he saw Pedro in the path called Seventeen
and coming towards the central houses, but still too far off for hearing or
scent, and he told them as much. "In a little while," he prophesied,
"Pedro will be here." An old man remarked that Pedro had no business
on Path Seventeen, and then, as if in confirmation, that individual as he
drew near turned and went transversely into Path Ten, and so back with
nimble paces towards the outer wall. They mocked Nunez when Pedro
did not arrive, and afterwards, when he asked Pedro questions to clear
his character, Pedro denied and outfaced him, and was afterwards hostile
to him.

Then he induced them to let him go a long way up the sloping meadows towards the wall with one complacent individual, and to him he
promised to describe all that happened among the houses. He noted certain goings and comings, but the things that really seemed to signify to
these people happened inside of or behind the windowless houses—the

only things they took note of to test him by—and of these he could see or tell nothing; and it was after the failure of this attempt, and the ridicule they could not repress, that he resorted to force. He thought of seizing a spade and suddenly smiting one or two of them to earth, and so in fair combat showing the advantage of eyes. He went so far with that resolution as to seize his spade, and then he discovered a new thing about himself, and that was that it was impossible for him to hit a blind man in cold blood.

He hesitated, and found them all aware that he snatched up the spade. They stood alert, with their heads on one side, and bent ears towards him for what he would do next.

"Put that spade down," said one, and he felt a sort of helpless horror. He came near obedience.

Then he thrust one backwards against a house wall, and fled past him and out of the village.

He went athwart one of their meadows, leaving a track of trampled grass behind his feet, and presently sat down by the side of one of their ways. He felt something of the buoyancy that comes to all men in the beginning of a fight, but more perplexity. He began to realise that you cannot even fight happily with creatures who stand upon a different mental basis to yourself. Far away he saw a number of men carrying spades and sticks come out of the street of houses, and advance in a spreading line along the several paths towards him. They advanced slowly, speaking frequently to one another, and ever and again the whole cordon would halt and sniff the air and listen.

The first time they did this Nunez laughed. But afterwards he did not laugh.

One struck his trail in the meadow grass, and came stooping and feeling his way along it.

For five minutes he watched the slow extension of the cordon, and then his vague disposition to do something forthwith became frantic. He stood up, went a pace or so towards the circumferential wall, turned, and went back a little way. There they all stood in a crescent, still and listening.

He also stood still, gripping his spade very tightly in both hands. Should he charge them?

The pulse in his ears ran into the rhythm of "In the Country of the Blind the One-eyed Man is King!"

Should he charge them?

He looked back at the high and unclimbable wall behind—unclimbable because of its smooth plastering, but withal pierced with many little doors, and at the approaching line of seekers. Behind these, others were now coming out of the street of houses.

Should he charge them?

"Bogota!" called one. "Bogota! where are you?"

He gripped his spade still tighter, and advanced down the meadows towards the place of habitations, and directly he moved they converged upon him. "I'll hit them if they touch me," he swore; "by Heaven, I will. I'll hit." He called aloud, "Look here, I'm going to do what I like in this valley. Do you hear? I'm going to do what I like and go where I like!"

They were moving in upon him quickly, groping, yet moving rapidly. It was like playing blind man's buff, with everyone blindfolded except one. "Get hold of him!" cried one. He found himself in the arc of a loose curve of pursuers. He felt suddenly he must be active and resolute.

"You don't understand," he cried in a voice that was meant to be great and resolute, and which broke. "You are blind, and I can see. Leave me alone!"

"Bogota! Put down that spade, and come off the grass!"

The last order, grotesque in its urban familiarity, produced a gust of anger.

"I'll hurt you," he said, sobbing with emotion. "By Heaven, I'll hurt you. Leave me alone!"

He began to run, not knowing clearly where to run. He ran from the nearest blind man, because it was a horror to hit him. He stopped, and then made a dash to escape from their closing ranks. He made for where a gap was wide, and the men on either side, with a quick perception of the approach of his paces, rushed in on one another. He sprang forward, and then saw he must be caught, and *swish!* the spade had struck. He felt the soft thud of hand and arm, and the man was down with a yell of pain, and he was through.

Through! And then he was close to the street of houses again, and blind men, whirling spades and stakes, were running with a sort of reasoned swiftness hither and thither.

He heard steps behind him just in time, and found a tall man rushing forward and swiping at the sound of him. He lost his nerve, hurled his spade a yard wide at his antagonist, and whirled about and fled, fairly yelling as he dodged another.

He was panic-stricken. He ran furiously to and fro, dodging when there was no need to dodge, and in his anxiety to see on every side of him at once, stumbling. For a moment he was down and they heard his fall. Far away in the circumferential wall a little doorway looked like heaven, and he set off in a wild rush for it. He did not even look round at his pursuers until it was gained, and he had stumbled across the bridge, clambered a little way among the rocks, to the surprise and dismay of a young llama, who went leaping out of sight, and lay down sobbing for breath.

And so his *coup d'état* came to an end.

He stayed outside the wall of the valley of the Blind for two nights and days without food or shelter, and meditated upon the unexpected. During these meditations he repeated very frequently and always with a profounder note of derision the exploded proverb: "In the Country of the

Blind the One-eyed Man is King." He thought chiefly of ways of fighting and conquering these people, and it grew clear that for him no practicable way was possible. He had no weapons, and now it would be hard to get one.

The canker of civilisation had got to him even in Bogota, and he could not find it in himself to go down and assassinate a blind man. Of course, if he did that, he might then dictate terms on the threat of assassinating them all. But—sooner or later he must sleep! . . .

He tried also to find food among the pine trees, to be comfortable under pine boughs while the frost fell at night, and—with less confidence—to catch a llama by artifice in order to try to kill it—perhaps by hammering it with a stone—and so finally, perhaps, to eat some of it. But the llamas had a doubt of him and regarded him with distrustful brown eyes, and spat when he drew near. Fear came on him the second day and fits of shivering. Finally he crawled down to the wall of the Country of the Blind and tried to make terms. He crawled along by the stream, shouting, until two blind men came out to the gate and talked to him.

"I was mad," he said. "But I was only newly made."

They said that was better.

He told them he was wiser now, and repented of all he had done.

Then he wept without intention, for he was very weak and ill now, and they took that as a favourable sign.

They asked him if he still thought he could "see."

"No," he said. "That was folly. The word means nothing—less than nothing!"

They asked him what was overhead.

"About ten times ten the height of a man there is a roof above the world of—of rock—and very, very smooth." . . . He burst again into hysterical tears. "Before you ask me any more, give me some food or I shall die."

He expected dire punishments, but these blind people were capable of toleration. They regarded his rebellion as but one more proof of his general idiocy and inferiority; and after they had whipped him they appointed him to do the simplest and heaviest work they had for anyone to do, and he, seeing no other way of living, did submissively what he was told.

He was ill for some days, and they nursed him kindly. That refined his submission. But they insisted on his lying in the dark, and that was a great misery. And blind philosophers came and talked to him of the wicked levity of his mind, and reproved him so impressively for his doubts about the lid of rock that covered their cosmic casserole that he almost doubted whether indeed he was not the victim of hallucination in not seeing it overhead.

So Nuncz became a citizen of the Country of the Blind, and these people ceased to be a generalised people and became individualities and familiar to him, while the world beyond the mountains became more and more remote and unreal. There was Yacob, his master, a kindly man when not annoyed; there was Pedro, Yacob's nephew; and there was Medina-saroté, who was the youngest daughter of Yacob. She was little esteemed in the world of the blind, because she had a clear-cut face, and lacked that satisfying, glossy smoothness that is the blind man's ideal of feminine beauty; but Nunez thought her beautiful at first, and presently the most beautiful thing in the whole creation. Her closed eyelids were not sunken and red after the common way of the valley, but lay as though they might open again at any moment; and she had long eyelashes, which were considered a grave disfigurement. And her voice was strong, and did not satisfy the acute hearing of the valley swains. So that she had no lover.

There came a time when Nunez thought that, could he win her, he would be resigned to live in the valley for all the rest of his days.

He watched her; he sought opportunities of doing her little services, and presently he found that she observed him. Once at a rest-day gathering they sat side by side in the dim starlight, and the music was sweet. His hand came upon hers and he dared to clasp it. Then very tenderly she returned his pressure. And one day, as they were at their meal in the darkness, he felt her hand very softly seeking him, and as it chanced the fire leaped then and he saw the tenderness of her face.

He sought to speak to her.

He went to her one day when she was sitting in the summer moonlight spinning. The light made her a thing of silver and mystery. He sat down at her feet and told her he loved her, and told her how beautiful she seemed to him. He had a lover's voice, he spoke with a tender reverence that came near to awe, and she had never before been touched by adoration. She made him no definite answer, but it was clear his words pleased her.

After that he talked to her whenever he could make an opportunity. The valley became the world for him, and the world beyond the mountains where men lived in sunlight seemed no more than a fairy tale he would some day pour into her ears. Very tentatively and timidly he spoke to her of sight.

Sight seemed to her the most poetical of fancies, and she listened to his description of the stars and the mountains and her own sweet white-lit beauty as though it was a guilty indulgence. She did not believe, she could only half understand, but she was mysteriously delighted, and it seemed to him that she completely understood.

His love lost its awe and took courage. Presently he was for demanding her of Yacob and the elders in marriage, but she became fearful and delayed. And it was one of her elder sisters who first told Yacob that Medina-saroté and Nunez were in love.

There was from the first very great opposition to the marriage of

Nunez and Medina-saroté; not so much because they valued her as because they held him as a being apart, an idiot, an incompetent thing below the permissible level of a man. Her sisters opposed it bitterly as bringing discredit on them all; and old Yacob, though he had formed a sort of liking for his clumsy, obedient serf, shook his head and said the thing could not be. The young men were all angry at the idea of corrupting the race, and one went so far as to revile and strike Nunez. He struck back. Then for the first time he found an advantage in seeing, even by twilight, and after that fight was over no one was disposed to raise a hand against him. But they still found his marriage impossible.

Old Yacob had a tenderness for his last little daughter, and was grieved to have her weep upon his shoulder.

"You see, my dear, he's an idiot. He has delusions; he can't do anything right."

"I know," wept Medina-saroté. "But he's better than he was. He's getting better. And he's strong, dear father, and kind—stronger and kinder than any other man in the world. And he loves me—and, father, I love him."

Old Yacob was greatly distressed to find her inconsolable, and, besides—what made it more distressing—he liked Nunez for many things. So he went and sat in the windowless council-chamber with the other elders and watched the trend of the talk, and said, at the proper time, "He's better than he was. Very likely, some day, we shall find him as sane as ourselves."

Then afterwards one of the elders, who thought deeply, had an idea. He was the great doctor among these people, their medicine-man, and he had a very philosophical and inventive mind, and the idea of curing Nunez of his peculiarities appealed to him. One day when Yacob was present he returned to the topic of Nunez.

"I have examined Bogota," he said, "and the case is clearer to me. I think very probably he might be cured."

"That is what I have always hoped," said old Yacob.

"His brain is affected," said the blind doctor.

The elders murmured assent.

"Now, *what* affects it?"

"Ah!" said old Yacob.

"*This*," said the doctor, answering his own question. "Those queer things that are called the eyes, and which exist to make an agreeable soft depression in the face, are diseased, in the case of Bogota, in such a way as to affect his brain. They are greatly distended, he has eyelashes, and his eyelids move, and consequently his brain is in a state of constant irritation and distraction."

"Yes?" said old Yacob. "Yes?"

"And I think I may say with reasonable certainty that, in order to cure him completely, all that we need do is a simple and easy surgical operation—namely, to remove these irritant bodies."

"And then he will be sane?"

"Then he will be perfectly sane, and a quite admirable citizen."

"Thank Heaven for science!" said old Yacob, and went forth at once to tell Nunez of his happy hopes.

But Nunez's manner of receiving the good news struck him as being cold and disappointing.

"One might think," he said, "from the tone you take, that you did not care for my daughter."

It was Medina-saroté who persuaded Nunez to face the blind surgeons.

"*You* do not want me," he said, "to lose my gift of sight?"

She shook her head.

"My world is sight."

Her head drooped lower.

"There are the beautiful things, the beautiful little things—the flowers, the lichens among the rocks, the lightness and softness on a piece of fur, the far sky with its drifting down of clouds, the sunsets and the stars. And there is *you*. For you alone it is good to have sight, to see your sweet, serene face, your kindly lips, your dear, beautiful hands folded together. . . . It is these eyes of mine you won, these eyes that hold me to you, that these idiots seek. Instead, I must touch you, hear you, and never see you again. I must come under that roof of rock and stone and darkness, that horrible roof under which your imagination stoops. . . . No; you would not have me do that?"

A disagreeable doubt had risen in him. He stopped, and left the thing a question.

"I wish," she said, "sometimes—" She paused.

"Yes?" said he, a little apprehensively.

"I wish sometimes—you would not talk like that."

"Like what?"

"I know it's pretty—it's your imagination. I love it, but now—"

He felt cold. "*Now?*" he said faintly.

She sat quite still.

"You mean—you think—I should be better, better perhaps—"

He was realising things very swiftly. He felt anger, indeed, anger at the dull course of fate, but also sympathy for her lack of understanding—a sympathy near akin to pity.

"Dear," he said, and he could see by her whiteness how intensely her spirit pressed against the things she could not say. He put his arms about her, he kissed her ear, and they sat for a time in silence.

"If I were to consent to this?" he said at last, in a voice that was very gentle.

She flung her arms about him, weeping wildly. "Oh, if you would," she sobbed, "if only you would!"

For a week before the operation that was to raise him from the servitude and inferiority to the level of a blind citizen, Nunez knew nothing of sleep, and all through the warm sunlit hours, while the others slumbered happily, he sat brooding or wandered aimlessly, trying to bring his mind to bear on his dilemma. He had given his answer, he had given his consent, and still he was not sure. And at last work-time was over, the sun rose in splendour over the golden crests, and his last day of vision began for him. He had a few minutes with Medina-saroté before she went apart to sleep.

"To-morrow," he said, "I shall see no more."

"Dear heart!" she answered, and pressed his hands with all her strength.

"They will hurt you but little," she said; "and you are going through this pain—you are going through it, dear lover, for *me*. . . . Dear, if a woman's heart and life can do it, I will repay you. My dearest one, my dearest with the tender voice, I will repay."

He was drenched in pity for himself and her.

He held her in his arms, and pressed his lips to hers, and looked on her sweet face for the last time. "Good-bye!" he whispered at that dear sight, "good-bye!"

And then in silence he turned away from her.

She could hear his slow retreating footsteps, and something in the rhythm of them threw her into a passion of weeping.

He had fully meant to go to a lonely place where the meadows were beautiful with white narcissus, and there remain until the hour of his sacrifice should come, but as he went he lifted up his eyes and saw the morning, the morning like an angel in golden armour, marching down the steeps. . . .

It seemed to him that before this splendour he, and this blind world in the valley, and his love, and all, were no more than a pit of sin.

He did not turn aside as he had meant to do, but went on, and passed through the wall of the circumference and out upon the rocks, and his eyes were always upon the sunlit ice and snow.

He saw their infinite beauty, and his imagination soared over them to the things beyond he was now to resign for ever.

He thought of that great free world he was parted from, the world that was his own, and he had a vision of those further slopes, distance beyond distance, with Bogota, a place of multitudinous stirring beauty, a glory by day, a luminous mystery by night, a place of palaces and fountains and statues and white houses, lying beautifully in the middle distance. He thought how for a day or so one might come down through passes, drawing ever nearer and nearer to its busy streets and ways. He thought of the river journey, day by day, from great Bogota to the still vaster world beyond, through towns and villages, forest and desert places, the rushing river day by day, until its banks receded and the big steamers came splashing by, and one had reached the sea—the limitless sea, with its thousand islands, its thousands of islands, and its ships seen dimly far away in their incessant journeyings round and about that greater world. And there, unpent by mountains, one saw the sky—the sky, not such a disc as one saw it here, but an arch of immeasurable blue, a deep of deeps in which the circling stars were floating. . . .

His eyes scrutinised the great curtain of the mountains with a keener inquiry.

For example, if one went so, up that gully and to that chimney there, then one might come out high among those stunted pines that ran round in a sort of shelf and rose still higher and higher as it passed above the gorge. And then? That talus might be managed. Thence perhaps a climb might be found to take him up to the precipice that came below the snow; and if that chimney failed, then another farther to the east might serve his purpose better. And then? Then one would be out upon the amber-lit snow there, and halfway up to the crest of those beautiful desolations.

He glanced back at the village, then turned right round and regarded it steadfastly.

He thought of Medina-saroté, and she had become small and remote.

He turned again towards the mountain wall, down which the day had come to him.

Then very circumspectly he began to climb.

When sunset came he was no longer climbing, but he was far and high. He had been higher, but he was still very high. His clothes were torn, his limbs were blood-stained, he was bruised in many places, but he lay as if he were at his ease, and there was a smile on his face.

From where he rested the valley seemed as if it were in a pit and nearly a mile below. Already it was dim with haze and shadow, though the mountain summits around him were things of light and fire. The little details of the rocks near at hand were drenched with subtle beauty—a vein of green mineral piercing the grey, the flash of crystal faces here and there, a minute, minutely beautiful orange lichen close beside his face. There were deep mysterious shadows in the gorge, blue deepening into purple, and purple into a luminous darkness, and overhead was the illimitable vastness of the sky. But he heeded these things no longer, but lay quite inactive there, smiling as if he were satisfied merely to have escaped from the valley of the Blind in which he had thought to be King.

The glow of the sunset passed, and the night came, and still he lay peacefully contented under the cold stars.

QUESTIONS

1. In what way can Nunez be called a prophet? How is this story similar to Richard Wilbur's poem "Advice to a Prophet"?

2. Discuss point of view in this story. If the story had a different setting, could it be considered an "alien encounter" story?

3. How perfect must a style of life be in order to have it called "utopian"?

4. Discuss the story's extended opening section in terms of the concept of "willing suspension of disbelief."

5. Explore the allegorical aspects of "The Country of the Blind."

6. What is the function of irony in this story?

7. Is it possible to make any final value judgment concerning the outcome of the story? That is, can we finally say that Nunez's decision was "right" or "wrong"?

Jachid and Jachidah

Isaac Bashevis Singer

In a prison where souls bound for Sheol—Earth they call it there—await destruction, there hovered the female soul Jachidah. Souls forgot their origin. Purah, the Angel of Forgetfulness, he who dissipates God's light and conceals His face, holds dominion everywhere beyond the Godhead. Jachidah, unmindful of her descent from the Throne of Glory, had sinned. Her jealousy had caused much trouble in the world where she dwelled. She had suspected all female angels of having affairs with her lover Jachid, had not only blasphemed God but even denied him. Souls, she said, were not created but had evolved out of nothing: they had neither mission nor purpose. Although the authorities were extremely patient and forgiving, Jachidah was finally sentenced to death. The judge fixed the moment of her descent to that cemetery called Earth.

The attorney for Jachidah appealed to the Superior Court of Heaven, even presented a petition to Metatron, the Lord of the Face. But Jachidah was so filled with sin and so impenitent that no power could save her. The attendants seized her, tore her from Jachid, clipped her wings, cut her hair, and clothed her in a long white shroud. She was no longer allowed to hear the music of the spheres, to smell the perfumes of Paradise and to meditate on the secrets of the Torah, which sustained the soul. She could no longer bathe in the wells of balsam oil. In the prison cell, the darkness of the nether world already surrounded her. But her greatest torment was her longing for Jachid. She could no longer reach him telepathically. Nor could she send a message to him, all of her servants having been taken away. Only the fear of death was left to Jachidah.

Death was no rare occurrence where Jachidah lived but it befell only vulgar, exhausted spirits. Exactly what happened to the dead, Jachidah did not know. She was convinced that when a soul descended to Earth it was to extinction, even though the pious maintained that a spark of life remained. A dead soul immediately began to rot and was soon covered with a slimy stuff called "semen." Then a grave digger put it into a womb where it turned into some sort of fungus and was henceforth known as a "child." Later on, began the tortures of Gehenna: birth, growth, toil. For according to the morality books, death was not the final stage. Purified, the soul returned to its source. But what evidence was there for such beliefs? So far as Jachidah knew, no one had ever returned from Earth. The enlightened Jachidah believed that the soul rots for a short time and then disintegrates into a darkness of no return.

Now the moment had come when Jachidah must die, must sink to Earth. Soon, the Angel of Death would appear with his fiery sword and thousand eyes.

At first Jachidah had wept incessantly, but then her tears had ceased. Awake or asleep she never stopped thinking of Jachid. Where was he? What was he doing? Whom was he with? Jachidah was well aware he would not mourn for her for ever. He was surrounded by beautiful females, sacred beasts, angels, seraphim, cherubs, ayralim, each one with powers of seduction. How long could someone like Jachid curb his desires? He, as she, was an unbeliever. It was he who had taught her that spirits were not created, but were products of evolution. Jachid did not acknowledge free will, nor believe in ultimate good and evil. What would restrain him? Most certainly he already lay in the lap of some other divinity, telling those stories about himself he had already told Jachidah.

But what could she do? In this dungeon all contact with the mansions ceased. All doors were closed: neither mercy, nor beauty entered here. The one way from this prison led down to Earth, and to the horrors called flesh, blood, marrow, nerves, and breath. The God-fearing angels promised resurrection. They preached that the soul did not linger forever on Earth, but that after it had endured its punishment, it returned to the Higher Sphere. But Jachidah, being a modernist, regarded all of this as superstition. How would a soul free itself from the corruption of the body? It was scientifically impossible. Resurrection was a dream, a silly comfort of primitive and frightened souls.

II

One night as Jachidah lay in a corner brooding about Jachid and the pleasures she had received from him, his kisses, his caresses, the secrets whispered in her ear, the many positions and games into which she had been initiated, Dumah, the thousand-eyed Angel of Death, looking just as the Sacred Books described him, entered bearing a fiery sword.

"Your time has come, little sister," he said.

"No further appeal is possible?"

"Those who are in this wing always go to Earth."

Jachidah shuddered. "Well, I am ready."

"Jachidah, repentance helps even now. Recite your confession."

"How can it help? My only regret is that I did not transgress more," said Jachidah rebelliously.

Both were silent. Finally Dumah said, "Jachidah, I know you are angry with me. But is it my fault, sister? Did I want to be the Angel of Death? I too am a sinner, exiled from a higher realm, my punishment to be the executioner of souls. Jachidah, I have not willed your death, but be comforted. Death is not as dreadful as you imagine. True, the first moments are not easy. But once you have been planted in the womb, the nine months that follow are not painful. You will forget all that you have learned here. Coming out of the womb will be a shock; but childhood is often pleasant. You will begin to study the lore of death, clothed in a fresh, pliant body, and soon will dread the end of your exile."

Jachidah interrupted him. "Kill me if you must, Dumah, but spare me your lies."

"I am telling you the truth, Jachidah. You will be absent no more than a hundred years, for even the wickedest do not suffer longer than that. Death is only the preparation for a new existence."

"Dumah, please. I don't want to listen."

"But it is important for you to know that good and evil exist there, too, and that the will remains free."

"What will? Why do you talk such nonsense?"

"Jachidah, listen carefully. Even among the dead there are laws and regulations. The way you act in death will determine what happens to you next. Death is a laboratory for the rehabilitation of souls."

"Make an end of me, I beseech you."

"Be patient, you still have a few more minutes to live and must receive your instructions. Know, then, that one may act well or evilly on Earth and that the most pernicious sin of all is to return a soul to life."

This idea was so ridiculous that Jachidah laughed despite her anguish. "How can one corpse give life to another?"

"It's not as difficult as you think. The body is composed of such weak material that a mere blow can make it disintegrate. Death is no stronger than a cobweb; a breeze blows and it disappears. But it is a great offense to destroy either another's death or one's own. Not only that, but you must not act or speak or even think in such a way as to threaten death. Here one's object is to preserve life, but there it is death that is succored."

"Nursery tales. The fantasies of an executioner."

"It is the truth, Jachidah. The Torah that applies to Earth is based on a single principle: Another man's death must be as dear to one as one's own. Remember my words. When you descend to Sheol, they will be of value to you."

"No, no, I won't listen to any more lies." And Jachidah covered her ears.

III

Years passed. Everyone in the higher realm had forgotten Jachidah except her mother, who still continued to light memorial candles for her daughter. On Earth Jachidah had a new mother as well as a father, several brothers and sisters, all dead. After attending a high school, she had begun to take courses at the university. She lived in a large necropolis where corpses are prepared for all kinds of mortuary functions.

It was spring, and Earth's corruption grew leprous with blossoms. From the graves with their memorial trees and cleansing waters arose a dreadful stench. Millions of creatures, forced to descend into the domains of death, were becoming flies, butterflies, worms, toads, frogs. They buzzed, croaked, screeched, rattled, already involved in the death struggle. But since Jachidah was totally inured to the habits of Earth, all this seemed to her part of life. She sat on a park bench staring up at the moon, which from the darkness of the nether world is sometimes recognized as a memorial candle set in a skull. Like all female corpses, Jachidah yearned to perpetuate death, to have her womb became a grave for the newly dead. But she couldn't do that without the help of a male with whom she would have to copulate in the hatred which corpses call "love."

As Jachidah sat staring into the sockets of the skull above her, a white-shrouded corpse came and sat beside her. For a while the two corpses gazed at each other, thinking they could see, although all corpses are actually blind. Finally the male corpse spoke:

"Pardon, Miss, could you tell me what time it is?"

Since deep within themselves all corpses long for the termination of their punishment, they are perpetually concerned with time.

"The time?" Jachidah answered. "Just a second." Strapped to her wrist was an instrument to measure time but the divisions were so minute and the symbols so tiny that she could not easily read the dial. The male corpse moved nearer to her.

"May I take a look? I have good eyes."

"If you wish."

Corpses never act straightforwardly but are always sly and devious. The male corpse took Jachidah's hand and bent his head toward the instrument. This was not the first time a male corpse had touched Jachidah but contact with this one made her limbs tremble. He stared intently but could not decide immediately. Then he said: "I think it's ten minutes after ten."

"Is it really so late?"

"Permit me to introduce myself. My name is Jachid."

"Jachid? Mine is Jachidah."

"What an odd coincidence."

Both hearing death race in their blood were silent for a long while. Then Jachid said: "How beautiful the night is!"

"Yes, beautiful!"

"There's something about spring that cannot be expressed in words."

"Words can express nothing," answered Jachidah.

As she made this remark, both knew they were destined to lie together and to prepare a grave for a new corpse. The fact is, no matter how dead the dead are, there remains some life in them, a trace of contact with that knowledge which fills the universe. Death only masks the truth. The sages speak of it as a soap bubble that bursts at the touch of a straw. The dead, ashamed of death, try to conceal their condition through cunning. The more moribund a corpse, the more voluble it is.

"May I ask where you live?" asked Jachid.

Where have I seen him before? How is it his voice sounds so familiar to me? Jachidah wondered. *And how does it happen that he's called Jachid? Such a rare name.*

"Not far from here," she answered.

"Would you object to my walking you home?"

"Thank you. You don't have to. But if you want . . . It is still too early to go to bed."

When Jachid rose, Jachidah did, too. Is this the one I have been searching for? Jachidah asked herself, the one destined for me? But what do I mean by "destiny"? According to my professor, only atoms and motion exist. A carriage approached them and Jachidah heard Jachid say:

"Would you like to take a ride?"

"Where to?"

"Oh, just around the park."

Instead of reproving him as she intended to, Jachidah said: "It would be nice. But I don't think you should spend the money."

"What's money? You only live once."

The carriage stopped and they both got in. Jachidah knew that no self-respecting girl would go riding with a strange young man. What did Jachid think of her? Did he believe she would go riding with anyone who asked her? She wanted to explain that she was shy by nature, but she knew she could not wipe out the impression she had already made. She sat in silence, astonished at her behavior. She felt nearer to this stranger than she ever had to anyone. She could almost read his mind. She wished the night would continue for ever. Was this love? Could one really fall in love so quickly? And am I happy? she asked herself. But no answer came from within her. For the dead are always melancholy, even in the midst of gaiety. After a while Jachidah said: "I have a strange feeling I have experienced all this before."

"*Déjà vu*—that's what psychology calls it."

"But maybe there's some truth to it. . . ."

"What do you mean?"

"Maybe we've known each other in some other world."

Jachid burst out laughing. "In what world? There is only one, ours, the earth."

"But maybe souls do exist."

"Impossible. What you call the 'soul' is nothing but vibrations of matter, the product of the nervous system. I should know, I'm a medical student." Suddenly he put his arm around her waist. And although Jachidah had never permitted any male to take such liberties before, she did not reprove him. She sat there perplexed by her acquiescence, fearful of the regrets that would be hers tomorrow. I'm completely without character, she chided herself. But he is right about one thing. If there is no soul and life is nothing but a short episode in an eternity of death, then why shouldn't one enjoy oneself without restraint? If there is no soul, there is no God, free will is meaningless. Morality, as my professor says, is nothing but a part of the ideological superstructure.

Jachidah closed her eyes and leaned back against the upholstery. The horse trotted slowly. In the dark all the corpses, men and beasts, lamented their death—howling, laughing, buzzing, chirping, sighing. Some of the corpses staggered, having drunk to forget for a while the tortures of hell. Jachidah had retreated into herself. She dozed off, then awoke again with a start. When the dead sleep, they once more connect themselves with the source of life. The illusion of time and space, cause and effect, number and relation ceases. In her dream Jachidah had ascended again into the world of her origin. There she saw her real mother, her friends, her teachers. Jachid was there, too. The two greeted each other, embraced, laughed and wept with joy. At that moment, they both recognized the truth, that death on Earth is temporary and illusory, a trial and a means of purification. They traveled together past heavenly mansions, gardens, oases for convalescent souls, forests for divine beasts, islands for heavenly birds. No, our meeting was not an accident, Jachidah murmured to herself. There is a God. There is a purpose in creation. Copulation, free will, fate—all are part of His plan. Jachid and Jachidah passed by a prison and gazed into its window. They saw a soul condemned to sink down to Earth. Jachidah knew that this soul would become her daughter. Just before she woke up, Jachidah heard a voice:

"The grave and the gravedigger have met. The burial will take place tonight."

QUESTIONS

1. Do you think that Singer's story provides, for you, an acceptable view of reality? Compare the view of reality shown here to that in the next story, Robert Heinlein's "They."

2. Does this strange story affirm or deny traditional religious beliefs?

3. What devices has Singer used to create the vaguely unpleasant feeling in part II?

4. Would you classify this story as allegory, satire, fantasy, or as something else?

They

Robert A. Heinlein

They would not let him alone.

They would never let him alone. He realized that that was part of the plot against him—never to leave him in peace, never to give him a chance to mull over the lies they had told him, time enough to pick out the flaws and to figure out the truth for himself.

That damned attendant this morning! He had come busting in with his breakfast tray, waking him, and causing him to forget his dream. If only he could remember that dream—

Someone was unlocking the door. He ignored it.

"Howdy, old boy. They tell me you refused your breakfast?" Dr. Hayward's professionally kindly mask hung over his bed.

"I wasn't hungry."

"But we can't have that. You'll get weak, and then I won't be able to get you well completely. Now, get up and get your clothes on and I'll order an eggnog for you. Come on, that's a good fellow!"

Unwilling, but still less willing at that moment to enter into any conflict of wills, he got out of bed and slipped on his bathrobe. "That's better," Hayward approved. "Have a cigarette?"

"No, thank you."

The doctor shook his head in a puzzled fashion. "Darned if I can figure you out. Loss of interest in physical pleasures does not fit your type of case."

"What is my type of case?" he inquired in flat tones.

"Tut! Tut!" Hayward tried to appear roguish. "If medicos told their professional secrets, they might have to work for a living."

"What is my type of case?"

"Well—the label doesn't matter, does it? Suppose you tell me. I really know nothing about your case as yet. Don't you think it is about time you talked?"

"I'll play chess with you."

"All right, all right." Hayward made a gesture of impatient concession. "We've played chess every day for a week. If you will talk, I'll play chess."

91

What could it matter? If he was right, they already understood perfectly that he had discovered their plot; there was nothing to be gained by concealing the obvious. Let them try to argue him out of it. Let the tail go with the hide! To hell with it!

He got out the chessmen and commenced setting them up. "What do you know of my case so far?"

"Very little. Physical examination, negative. Past history, negative. High intelligence, as shown by your record in school and your success in your profession. Occasional fits of moodiness but nothing exceptional. The only positive information was the incident that caused you to come here for treatment."

"To be brought here, you mean. Why should it cause comment?"

"Well, good gracious, man—if you barricade yourself in your room and insist that your wife is plotting against you, don't you expect people to notice?"

"But she was plotting against me—and so are you. White or black?"

"Black—it's your turn to attack. Why do you think we are plotting against you?"

"It's an involved story and goes way back into my early childhood. There was an immediate incident, however—" He opened by advancing the white king's knight to KB3. Hayward's eyebrows raised.

"You make a piano attack?"

"Why not? You know that it is not safe for me to risk a gambit with you."

The doctor shrugged his shoulders and answered the opening. "Suppose we start with your early childhood. It may shed more light than more recent incidents. Did you feel that you were being persecuted as a child?"

"No!" He half rose from his chair. "When I was a child, I was sure of myself. I knew then, I tell you; I knew! Life was worthwhile, and I knew it. I was at peace with myself and my surroundings. Life was good and I was good and I assumed that the creatures around me were like myself."

"And weren't they?"

"Not at all! Particularly the children. I didn't know what viciousness was until I was turned loose with other children. The little devils! And I was expected to be like them and play with them."

The doctor nodded. "I know. The herd compulsion. Children can be pretty savage at times."

"You've missed the point. This wasn't any healthy roughness; these creatures were different—not like myself at all. They looked like me, but they were not like me. If I tried to say anything to one of them about anything that mattered to me, all I could get was a stare and a scornful laugh. Then they would find some way to punish me for having said it."

Hayward nodded. "I see what you mean. How about grownups?"

"That is somewhat different. Adults don't matter to children at first—

or, rather, they did not matter to me. They were too big, and they did not bother me, and they were busy with things that did not enter into my considerations. It was only when I noticed that my presence affected them that I began to wonder about them."

"How do you mean?"

"Well, they never did the things when I was around that they did when I was not around."

Hayward looked at him carefully. "Won't that statement take quite a lot of justifying? How do you know what they did when you weren't around?"

He acknowledged the point. "But I used to catch them just stopping. If I came into a room, the conversation would stop suddenly, and then it would pick up about the weather or something equally inane. Then I took to hiding and listening and looking. Adults did not behave the same way in my presence as out of it."

"Your move, I believe. But see here, old man—that was when you were a child. Every child passes through that phase. Now that you are a man, you must see the adult point of view. Children are strange creatures and have to be protected—at least, we do protect them—from many adult interests. There is a whole code of conventions in the matter that—"

"Yes, yes," he interrupted impatiently, "I know all that. Nevertheless, I noticed enough and remembered enough that was never clear to me later. And it put me on my guard to notice the next thing."

"Which was?" He noticed that the doctor's eyes were averted as he adjusted a castle's position.

"The things I saw people doing and heard them talking about were never of any importance. They must be doing something else."

"I don't follow you."

"You don't choose to follow me. I'm telling this to you in exchange for a game of chess."

"Why do you like to play chess so well?"

"Because it is the only thing in the world where I can see all the factors and understand all the rules. Never mind—I saw all around me this enormous plant, cities, farms, factories, churches, schools, homes, railroads, luggage, roller coasters, trees, saxophones, libraries, people, and animals. People that looked like me and who should have felt very much like me, if what I was told was the truth. But what did they appear to be doing? 'They went to work to earn the money to buy the food to get the strength to go to work to earn the money to buy the food to get the strength to go to work to get the strength to buy the food to earn the money to go to—' until they fell over dead. Any slight variation in the basic pattern did not matter, for they always fell over dead. And everybody tried to tell me that I should be doing the same thing. I knew better!"

The doctor gave him a look apparently intended to denote helpless surrender and laughed. "I can't argue with you. Life does look like that and maybe it is just that futile. But it is the only life we have. Why not make up your mind to enjoy it as much as possible?"

"Oh, no!" He looked both sulky and stubborn. "You can't peddle nonsense to me by claiming to be fresh out of sense. How do I know? Because all this complex stage setting, all these swarms of actors, could not have been put here just to make idiot noises at each other. Some other explanation but not that one. An insanity as enormous, as complex, as the one around me had to be planned. I've found the plan!"

"Which is?"

He noticed that the doctor's eyes were again averted.

"It is a play intended to divert me, to occupy my mind and confuse me, to keep me so busy with details that I will not have time to think about the meaning. You are all in it, every one of you." He shook his finger in the doctor's face. "Most of them may be helpless automatons, but you're not. You are one of the conspirators. You've been sent in as a troubleshooter to try to force me to go back to playing the role assigned to me!"

He saw that the doctor was waiting for him to quiet down.

"Take it easy," Hayward finally managed to say. "Maybe it is all a conspiracy, but why do you think that you have been singled out for special attention? Maybe it is a joke on all of us. Why couldn't I be one of the victims as well as yourself?"

"Got you!" He pointed a long finger at Hayward. "That is the essence of the plot. All of these creatures have been set up to look like me in order to prevent me from realizing that I was the center of the arrangements. But I have noticed the key fact, the mathematically inescapable fact, that I am unique. Here am I, sitting on the inside. The world extends outward from me. I am the center—"

"Easy, man, easy! Don't you realize that the world looks that way to me, too. We are each the center of the universe—"

"Not so! That is what you have tried to make me believe, that I am just one of millions more just like me. Wrong! If they were like me, then I could get into communication with them. I can't. I have tried and tried and I can't. I've sent out my inner thoughts, seeking some one other being who has them, too. What have I gotten back? Wrong answers, jarring incongruities, meaningless obscenity. I've tried, I tell you. God!—how I've tried! But there is nothing out there to speak to me—nothing but emptiness and otherness!"

"Wait a minute. Do you mean to say that you think there is nobody home at my end of the line? Don't you believe that I am alive and conscious?"

He regarded the doctor soberly. "Yes, I think you are probably alive, but you are one of the others—my antagonists. But you have set thousands of others around me whose faces are blank, not lived in, and whose speech is a meaningless reflex of noise."

"Well, then, if you concede that I am an ego, why do you insist that I am so very different from yourself?"

"Why? Wait!" He pushed back from the chess table and strode over to the wardrobe, from which he took out a violin case.

While he was playing, the lines of suffering smoothed out of his face and his expression took a relaxed beatitude. For a while he recaptured the emotions, but not the knowledge, which he had possessed in dreams. The melody proceeded easily from proposition to proposition with inescapable, unforced logic. He finished with a triumphant statement of the essential thesis and turned to the doctor. "Well?"

"Hm-m-m." He seemed to detect an even greater degree of caution in the doctor's manner. "It's an odd bit but remarkable. 'S pity you didn't take up the violin seriously. You could have made quite a reputation. You could even now. Why don't you do it? You could afford to, I believe."

He stood and stared at the doctor for a long moment, then shook his head as if trying to clear it. "It's no use," he said slowly, "no use at all. There is no possibility of communication. I am alone." He replaced the instrument in its case and returned to the chess table. "My move, I believe?"

"Yes. Guard your queen."

He studied the board. "Not necessary. I no longer need my queen. Check."

The doctor interposed a pawn to parry the attack.

He nodded. "You use your pawns well, but I have learned to anticipate your play. Check again—and mate, I think."

The doctor examined the new situation. "No," he decided, "no—not quite." He retreated from the square under attack. "Not checkmate—stalemate at the worst. Yes, another stalemate."

He was upset by the doctor's visit. He couldn't be wrong, basically, yet the doctor had certainly pointed out logical holes in his position. From a logical standpoint the whole world might be a fraud perpetrated on everybody. But logic meant nothing—logic itself was a fraud, starting with unproved assumptions and capable of proving anything. The world is what it is!—and carries its own evidence of trickery.

But does it? What did he have to go on? Could he lay down a line between known facts and everything else and then make a reasonable interpretation of the world, based on facts alone—an interpretation free from complexities of logic and no hidden assumptions of points not certain? Very well—

First fact, himself. He knew himself directly. He existed.

Second fact, the evidence of his "five senses," everything that he himself saw and heard and smelled and tasted with his physical senses. Subject to their limitations, he must believe his senses. Without them he was entirely solitary, shut up in a locker of bone, blind, deaf, cut off, the only being in the world.

And that was not the case. He knew that he did not invent the information brought to him by his senses. There had to be something else out there, some otherness that produced the things his senses recorded. All philosophies that claimed that the physical world around him did not exist except in his imagination were sheer nonsense.

But beyond that, what? Were there any third facts on which he could rely? No, not at this point. He could not afford to believe anything that he was told, or that he read, or that was implicitly assumed to be true about the world around him. No, he could not believe any of it, for the sum total of what he had been told and read and been taught in school was so contradictory, so senseless, so wildly insane that none of it could be believed unless he personally confirmed it.

Wait a minute— The very telling of these lies, these senseless contradictions, was a fact in itself, known to him directly. To that extent they were data, probably very important data.

The world as it had been shown to him was a piece of unreason, an idiot's dream. Yet it was on too mammoth a scale to be without some reason. He came wearily back to his original point: Since the world could not be as crazy as it appeared to be, it must necessarily have been arranged to appear crazy in order to deceive him as to the truth.

Why had they done it to him? And what was the truth behind the sham? There must be some clue in the deception itself. What thread ran through it all? Well, in the first place he had been given a super-abundance of explanations of the world around him, philosophies, religions, "commonsense" explanations. Most of them were so clumsy, so obviously inadequate or meaningless, that they could hardly have expected him to take them seriously. They must have intended them simply as misdirection.

But there were certain basic assumptions running through all the hundreds of explanations of the craziness around him. It must be these basic assumptions that he was expected to believe. For example, there was the deep-seated assumption that he was a "human being," essentially like millions of others around him and billions more in the past and the future.

That was nonsense! He had never once managed to get into real communication with all those things that looked so much like him but were so different. In the agony of his loneliness he had deceived himself that Alice understood him and was a being like him. He knew now that he had suppressed and refused to examine thousands of little discrepancies because he could not bear the thought of returning to complete loneliness. He had needed to believe that his wife was a living, breathing being of his own kind who understood his inner thoughts. He had refused to consider the possibility that she was simply a mirror, an echo—or something unthinkably worse.

He had found a mate, and the world was tolerable, even though dull, stupid, and full of petty annoyance. He was moderately happy and had put away his suspicions. He had accepted, quite docilely, the treadmill he was expected to use, until a slight mischance had momentarily cut through the fraud—then his suspicions had returned with impounded force; the bitter knowledge of his childhood had been confirmed.

He supposed that he had been a fool to make a fuss about it. If he had kept his mouth shut, they would not have locked him up. He should have been as subtle and as shrewd as they, kept his eyes and ears open and learned the details of and the reasons for the plot against him. He might have learned how to circumvent it.

But what if they had locked him up—the whole world was an asylum and all of them his keepers.

A key scraped in the lock, and he looked up to see an attendant entering with a tray. "Here's your dinner, sir."

"Thanks, Joe," he said gently. "Just put it down."

"Movies tonight, sir," the attendant went on. "Wouldn't you like to go? Dr. Hayward said you could—"

"No, thank you. I prefer not to."

"I wish you would, sir." He noticed with amusement the persuasive intentness of the attendant's manner. "I think the doctor wants you to. It's a good movie. There's a Mickey Mouse cartoon—"

"You almost persuade me, Joe," he answered with passive agreeableness. "Mickey's trouble is the same as mine, essentially. However, I'm not going. They need not bother to hold movies tonight."

"Oh, there will be movies in any case, sir. Lots of our other guests will attend."

"Really? Is that an example of thoroughness, or are you simply keeping up the pretense in talking to me? It isn't necessary, Joe, if it's any strain on you. I know the game. If I don't attend, there is no point in holding movies."

He liked the grin with which the attendant answered this thrust. Was it possible that this being was created just as he appeared to be—big muscles, phlegmatic disposition, tolerant, doglike? Or was there nothing going on behind those kind eyes, nothing but robot reflex? No, it was more likely that he was one of them, since he was so closely in attendance on him.

The attendant left and he busied himself at his supper tray, scooping up the already-cut bites of meat with a spoon, the only implement provided. He smiled again at their caution and thoroughness. No danger of that—he would not destroy this body as long as it served him in investigating the truth of the matter. There were still many different avenues of research available before taking that possibly irrevocable step.

After supper he decided to put his thoughts in better order by writing them; he obtained paper. He should start with a general statement of some underlying postulate of the credos that had been drummed into him all his "life." Life? Yes, that was a good one. He wrote:

"I am told that I was born a certain number of years ago and that I will die a similar number of years hence. Various clumsy stories have been offered me to explain to me where I was before birth and what becomes of me after death, but they are rough lies, not intended to deceive, except as misdirection. In every other possible way the world around me assures me that I am mortal, here but a few years, and a few years hence gone completely—nonexistent.

"WRONG—I am immortal. I transcend this little time axis; a seventy-year span on it is but a casual phase in my experience. Second only to the prime datum of my own existence is the emotionally convincing certainty of my own continuity. I may be a closed curve, but, closed or open, I neither have a beginning nor an end. Self-awareness is not relational; it is absolute and cannot be reached to be destroyed or created. Memory, however, being a relational aspect of consciousness, may be tampered with and possibly destroyed.

"It is true that most religions which have been offered me teach immortality, but note the fashion in which they teach it. The surest way to lie convincingly is to tell the truth unconvincingly. They did not wish me to believe.

"Caution: Why have they tried so hard to convince me that I am going to die in a few years? There must be a very important reason. I infer that they are preparing me for some sort of a major change. It may be crucially important for me to figure out their intentions about this— probably I have several years in which to reach a decision. Note: Avoid using the types of reasoning they have taught me."

The attendant was back. "Your wife is here, sir."

"Tell her to go away."

"Please, sir— Dr. Hayward is most anxious that you should see her."

"Tell Dr. Hayward that I said that he is an excellent chess player."

"Yes, sir." The attendant waited for a moment. "Then, you won't see her, sir?"

"No, I won't see her."

He wandered around the room for some minutes after the attendant had left, too distrait to return to his recapitulation. By and large they had played very decently with him since they had brought him here. He was glad that they had allowed him to have a room alone and he certainly had more time free for contemplation than had ever been possible on the outside. To be sure, continuous effort to keep him busy and to distract him was made, but, by being stubborn, he was able to circumvent the rules and gain some hours each day for introspection.

But, damnation!—he did wish they would not persist in using Alice in their attempts to divert his thoughts. Although the intense terror and revulsion which she had inspired in him when he had first rediscovered the truth had now aged into a simple feeling of repugnance and distaste for her company, nevertheless it was emotionally upsetting to be reminded of her, to be forced into making decisions about her.

After all, she had been his wife for many years. Wife? What was a wife? Another soul like one's own, a complement, the other necessary pole to the couple, a sanctuary of understanding and sympathy in the boundless depths of aloneness. That was what he had thought, what he had needed to believe and had believed fiercely for years. The yearning need for companionship of his own kind had caused him to see himself reflected in those beautiful eyes and had made him quite uncritical of occasional incongruities in her responses.

He sighed. He felt that he had sloughed off most of the typed emotional reactions which they had taught him by precept and example, but Alice had gotten under his skin, 'way under, and it still hurt. He had been happy—what if it had been a dope dream? They had given him an excellent, a beautiful mirror to play with—the more fool he to have looked behind it!

Wearily he turned back to his summing up:

"The world is explained in either one of two ways; the commonsense way which says that the world is pretty much as it appears to be and that ordinary human conduct and motivations are reasonable, and the religiomystic solution which states that the world is dream stuff, unreal, insubstantial, with reality somewhere beyond.

"WRONG—both of them. The commonsense scheme has no sense to it of any sort. Life is short and full of trouble. Man born of woman is born to trouble as the sparks fly upward. His days are few and they are numbered. All is vanity and vexation. Those quotations may be jumbled and incorrect, but that is a fair statement of the commonsense world is-as-it-seems in its only possible evaluation. In such a world human striving is about as rational as the blind darting of a moth against a light bulb. The commonsense world is a blind insanity, out of nowhere, going nowhere, to no purpose.

"As for the other solution, it appears more rational on the surface, in that it rejects the utterly irrational world of commonsense. But it is not a rational solution, it is simply a flight from reality of any sort, for it refuses to believe the results of the only available direct communication between the ego and the Outside. Certainly the 'five senses' are poor enough channels of communication, but they are the only channels."

He crumpled up the paper and flung himself from the chair. Order and logic were no good—his answer was right because it smelled right. But he still did not know all the answers. Why the grand scale to the deception, countless creatures, whole continents, an enormously involved and minutely detailed matrix of insane history, insane tradition, insane culture? Why bother with more than a cell and a straitjacket?

It must be, it had to be, because it was supremely important to deceive him completely, because a lesser deception would not do. Could it be that they dare not let him suspect his real identity no matter how difficult and involved the fraud?

He had to know. In some fashion he must get behind the deception and see what went on when he was not looking. He had had one glimpse; this time he must see the actual workings, catch the puppet masters in their manipulations.

Obviously the first step must be to escape from this asylum, but to do it so craftily that they would never see him, never catch up with him, not have a chance to set the stage before him. That would be hard to do. He must excel them in shrewdness and subtlety.

Once decided, he spent the rest of the evening in considering the means by which he might accomplish his purpose. It seemed almost impossible—he must get away without once being seen and remain in strict hiding. They must lose track of him completely in order that they would not know where to center their deceptions. That would mean going without food for several days. Very well—he could do it. He must not give them any warning by unusual action or manner.

The lights blinked twice. Docilely he got up and commenced preparations for bed. When the attendant looked through the peephole, he was already in bed, with his face turned to the wall.

Gladness! Gladness everywhere! It was good to be with his own kind, to hear the music swelling out of every living thing, as it always had and always would—good to know that everything was living and aware of him, participating in him, as he participated in them. It was good to be, good to know the unity of many and the diversity of one. There had been one bad thought—the details escaped him—but it was gone—it had never been; there was no place for it.

The early-morning sounds from the adjacent ward penetrated the sleep-laden body which served him here and gradually recalled him to awareness of the hospital room. The transition was so gentle that he carried over full recollection of what he had been doing and why. He lay still, a gentle smile on his face, and savored the uncouth, but not unpleasant, languor of the body he wore. Strange that he had ever forgotten despite their tricks and stratagems. Well, now that he had recalled the key, he would quickly set things right in this odd place. He would call them in at once and announce the new order. It would be amusing to see old Glaroon's expression when he realized that the cycle had ended—

The click of the peephole and the rasp of the door being unlocked guillotined his line of thought. The morning attendant pushed briskly in with the breakfast tray and placed it on the tip table. "Morning, sir. Nice, bright day—want it in bed, or will you get up?"

Don't answer! Don't listen! Suppress this distraction! This is part of their plan— But it was too late, too late. He felt himself slipping, falling, wrenched from reality back into the fraud world in which they had kept him. It was gone, gone completely, with no single association around him to which to anchor memory. There was nothing left but the sense of heartbreaking loss and the acute ache of unsatisfied catharsis.

"Leave it where it is. I'll take care of it."

"Okey-doke." The attendant bustled out, slamming the door, and noisily locked it.

He lay quite still for a long time, every nerve end in his body screaming for relief.

At last he got out of bed, still miserably unhappy, and attempted to concentrate on his plans for escape. But the psychic wrench he had received in being recalled so suddenly from his plane of reality had left him bruised and emotionally disturbed. His mind insisted on rechewing its doubts, rather than engage in constructive thought. Was it possible that the doctor was right, that he was not alone in his miserable dilemma? Was he really simply suffering from paronoia, delusions of self-importance?

Could it be that each unit in this yeasty swarm around him was the prison of another lonely ego—helpless, blind, and speechless, condemned to an eternity of miserable loneliness? Was the look of suffering which he had brought to Alice's face a true reflection of inner torment and not simply a piece of playacting intended to maneuver him into compliance with their plans?

A knock sounded at the door. He said "Come in," without looking up. Their comings and goings did not matter to him.

"Dearest—" A well-known voice spoke slowly and hesitantly.

"Alice!" He was on his feet at once and facing her. "Who let you in here?"

"Please, dear, please—I had to see you."

"It isn't fair. It isn't fair." He spoke more to himself than to her. Then: "Why did you come?"

She stood up to him with a dignity he had hardly expected. The beauty of her childlike face had been marred by line and shadow, but it shone with an unexpected courage. "I love you," she answered quietly. "You can tell me to go away, but you can't make me stop loving you and trying to help you."

He turned away from her in an agony of indecision. Could it be possible that he had misjudged her? Was there, behind that barrier of flesh and sound symbols, a spirit that truly yearned toward his? Lovers whispering in the dark— *"You do understand, don't you?"*

"Yes, dear heart, I understand."

"Then nothing that happens to us can matter, as long as we are together and understand—" Words, words, rebounding hollowly from an unbroken wall—

No, he couldn't be wrong! Test her again— "Why did you keep me on that job in Omaha?"

"But I didn't make you keep that job. I simply pointed out that we should think twice before—"

"Never mind. Never mind." Soft hands and a sweet face preventing him with mild stubbornness from ever doing the thing that his heart told him to do. Always with the best of intentions, the best of intentions, but always so that he had never quite managed to do the silly, unreasonable things that he knew were worthwhile. Hurry, hurry, hurry, and strive, with an angel-faced jockey to see that you don't stop long enough to think for yourself—

"Why did you try to stop me from going back upstairs that day?"

She managed to smile, although her eyes were already spilling over with tears. "I didn't know it really mattered to you. I didn't want us to miss the train."

It had been a small thing, an unimportant thing. For some reason not clear even to him he had insisted on going back upstairs to his study when they were about to leave the house for a short vacation. It was raining, and she had pointed out that there was barely enough time to get to the station. He had surprised himself and her, too, by insisting on his own way in circumstances in which he had never been known to be stubborn.

He had actually pushed her to one side and forced his way up the stairs. Even then nothing might have come of it had he not—quite unnecessarily—raised the shade of the window that faced toward the rear of the house.

It was a very small matter. It had been raining, hard, out in front. From this window the weather was clear and sunny, with no sign of rain.

He had stood there quite a long while, gazing out at the impossible sunshine and rearranging his cosmos in his mind. He reexamined long-suppressed doubts in the light of this one small but totally unexplainable discrepancy. Then he had turned and had found that she was standing behind him.

He had been trying ever since to forget the expression that he had surprised on her face.

"What about the rain?"

"The rain?" she repeated in a small, puzzled voice. "Why, it was raining, of course. What about it?"

"But it was not raining out my study window."

"What? But of course it was. I did notice the sun break through the clouds for a moment, but that was all."

"Nonsense!"

"But darling, what has the weather to do with you and me? What difference does it make whether it rains or not—to us?" She approached him timidly and slid a small hand between his arm and side. "Am I responsible for the weather?"

"I think you are. Now please go."

She withdrew from him, brushed blindly at her eyes, gulped once, then said in a voice held steady: "All right. I'll go. But remember—you can come home if you want to. And I'll be there, if you want me." She waited a moment, then added hesitantly: "Would you . . . would you kiss me good-bye?"

He made no answer of any sort, neither with voice nor eyes. She looked at him, then turned, fumbled blindly for the door, and rushed through it.

The creature he knew as Alice went to the place of assembly without stopping to change form. "It is necessary to adjourn this sequence. I am no longer able to influence his decisions."

They had expected it; nevertheless they stirred with dismay.

The Glaroon addressed the First for Manipulation. "Prepare to graft the selected memory track at once."

Then, turning to the First for Operations, the Glaroon said: "The extrapolation shows that he will tend to escape within two of his days. This sequence degenerated primarily through your failure to extend that rainfall all around him. Be advised."

"It would be simpler if we understood his motives."

"In my capacity as Dr. Hayward, I have often thought so," commented the Glaroon acidly, "but if we understood his motives, we would be part of him. Bear in mind the Treaty! He almost remembered."

The creature known as Alice spoke up. "Could he not have the Taj Mahal next sequence? For some reason he values it."

"You are becoming assimilated!"

"Perhaps. I am not in fear. Will he receive it?"

"It will be considered."

The Glaroon continued with orders: "Leave structures standing until adjournment. New York City and Harvard University are now dismantled. Divert him from those sectors.

"Move!"

QUESTIONS

1. Is the fantasy of Heinlein's main character a common one?

2. Discuss this story in terms of childhood and adolescence as times of slavery.

3. Paraphrase the ending of "They." Do you feel that the device of the surprise ending adds or detracts from the story?

4. In the future, do you think the government's control of the mind will be more acceptable than its present control of the body?

The Artist

Kenneth Koch

Ah, well, I abandon you, cherrywood smokestack,
Near the entrance to this old green park! . . .

* * *

Cherrywood avalanche, my statue of you
Is still standing in Toledo, Ohio.
O places, summer, boredom, the static of an acrobatic blue!

And I made an amazing zinc airliner
It is standing to this day in the Minneapolis zoo . . .

Old times are not so long ago, plaster-of-paris haircut!

* * *

I often think *Play* was my best work.
It is an open field with a few boards in it.   10

Children are allowed to come and play in *Play*
By permission of the Cleveland Museum.
I look up at the white clouds, I wonder what I shall do, and smile.

Perhaps somebody will grow up having been influenced by *Play*,
I think—but what good will that do?
Meanwhile I am interested in steel cigarettes . . .

* * *

The orders are coming in thick and fast for steel cigarettes, steel ci-
  gars.
The Indianapolis Museum has requested six dozen packages.
I wonder if I'd still have the courage to do a thing like *Play*?   20
I think I may go to Cleveland . . .

*   *   *

Well, here I am! Pardon me, can you tell me how to get to the
    Cleveland Museum's monumental area, *Play*?

"Mother, that was torn down a long time ago. You ought to go and
    see the new thing they have now—*Gun.*"
What? *Play* torn down?
"Yes, Mister, and I loved to climb in it too, when I was a kid!" And
    he shakes his head
Sadly . . . But I am thrilled beyond expectation!
He liked my work!   30
And I guess there must be others like that man in Cleveland
    too . . .

So you see, *Play* has really had its effect!
Now I am on the outskirts of town
And . . . here it is! But it has changed! There are some blue merds
    lying in the field
And it's not marked *Play* anymore—and here's a calf!
I'm so happy, I can't tell why!
Was this how I originally imagined *Play*, but lacked the courage?

It would be hard now, though, to sell it to another museum.   40
I wonder if the man I met's children will come and play in it?
How does one's audience survive?

*   *   *

Pittsburgh, May 16th. I have abandoned the steel cigarettes. I am
    working on *Bee*.
Bee will be a sixty-yards-long covering for the elevator shaft open-
    ing in the foundry sub-basement
Near my home. So far it's white sailcloth with streams of golden
    paint evenly spaced out
With a small blue pond at one end, and around it orange and
    green flowers. My experience in Cleveland affected me so   50
That my throat aches whenever I am not working at full speed. I
    have never been so happy and inspired and
Play seems to me now like a juvenile experience!

*   *   *

June 8th. *Bee* is still not finished. I have introduced a huge number
    of red balloons into it. How will it work?

Yesterday X. said, "Are you still working on *Bee*? What's happened
to your interest in steel cigarettes?"
Y. said, "He hasn't been doing any work at all on them since he
went to Cleveland." A shrewd guess! But how much can they
possibly know?   60

*   *   *

November 19th. Disaster! *Bee* was almost completed, and now the
immense central piece of sailcloth has torn. Impossible to repair
it!

December 4th. I've gone back to work on *Bee*! I suddenly thought
(after weeks of despair), "I can place the balloons over the tear in
the canvas!" So that is what I am doing. All promises to be well!

December 6th. The foreman of the foundry wants to look at my
work. It seems that he too is an "artist"—does sketches and wa-
tercolors and such . . . What will he think of *Bee*?

*   *   *

Cherrywood! I had left you far from my home   70
And the foreman came to look at *Bee*
And the zinc airliner flew into *Play*!

The pink balloons aren't heavy, but the yellow ones break.
The foreman says, "It's the greatest thing I ever saw!"
Cleveland heard too and wants me to come back and reinaugurate
    Play.

I dream of going to Cleveland but never will.
Bee has obsessed my mind.

*   *   *

March 14th. A cold spring day. It is snowing. *Bee* is completed.

*   *   *

O *Bee* I think you are my best work   80
In the blue snow-filled air
I feel my heart break
I lie down in the snow
They come from the foundry and take *Bee* away
Oh what can I create now, Earth,

Green Earth on which everything blossoms anew?
"A bathroom floor cardboard trolley line
The shape and size of a lemon seed with on the inside
A passenger the size of a pomegranate seed
Who is an invalid and has to lean on the cardboard side   90
Of the lemon-seed-sized trolley line so that he won't fall off the
    train."

*   *   *
*   *   *

I just found these notes written many years ago.
How seriously I always take myself! Let it be a lesson to me.
To bring things up to date: I have just finished *Campaign*, which is
    a tremendous piece of charcoal.
Its shape is difficult to describe; but it is extremely large and would
    reach to the sixth floor of the Empire State Building. I have been
    very successful in the past fourteen or fifteen years.

*   *   *

Summer Night, shall I never succeed in finishing you? Oh you are   100
    the absolute end of all my creation! The ethereal beauty of that
    practically infinite number of white stone slabs stretching into
    the blue secrecy of ink! O stabs in my heart!

. . . Why not a work *Stabs in My Heart?* But *Summer Night?*

January . . . A troubled sleep. Can I make two things at once?
    What way is there to be sure that the impulse to work on *Stabs
    in My Heart* is serious? It seems occasioned only by my problem
    about finishing *Summer Night* . . . ?

*   *   *

The *Magician of Cincinnati* is now ready for human use. They
    are twenty-five tremendous stone staircases, each over six hun-   110
    dred feet high, which will be placed in the Ohio River between
    Cincinnati and Louisville, Kentucky. All the boats coming down
    the Ohio River will presumably be smashed up against the im-
    mense statues, which are the most recent work of the creator of
    Flowers, Bee, Play, Again, and *Human Use.* Five thousand cit-
    izens are thronged on the banks of the Ohio waiting to see the
    installation of the work, and the crowd is expected to be more

than fifteen times its present number before morning. There will
be a game of water baseball in the early afternoon, before the beginning of the ceremonies, between the Cincinnati Redlegs and   120
the Pittsburgh Pirates. The *Magician of Cincinnati*, incidentally,
is said to be absolutely impregnable to destruction of any kind,
and will therefore presumably always be a feature of this part of
the Ohio . . .

✳   ✳   ✳

May 16th. With what an intense joy I watched the installation of
the *Magician of Cincinnati* today, in the Ohio River, where it
belongs, and which is so much a part of my original scheme . . .

May 17th. I feel suddenly freed from life—not so much as if my
work were going to change, but as though I had at last seen what
I had so long been prevented (perhaps I prevented myself!) from   130
seeing: that there is too much for me to do. Somehow this en-
ables me to relax, to breathe easily . . .

✳   ✳   ✳

There's the *Magician of Cincinnati*
In the distance.
Here I am in the green trees of Pennsylvania.
How strange I felt when they had installed
The *Magician*! . . . Now a bluebird trills, I am busy making my
    polished stones
For *Dresser*.

The stream the stone the birds the reddish-pink Pennsylvania hills   140
All go to make up *Dresser*.
Why am I camping out?
I am waiting for the thousands of tons of embalming fluid
That have to come and with which I can make these hills.

✳   ✳   ✳

GREATEST ARTISTIC EVENT HINTED BY GOVERNOR
Reading, June 4. Greatest artistic event was hinted today by gover-
    nor. Animals converge on meadow where artist working.

CONVERGE ON MEADOW WHERE WORKING

ARTIST HINTED, SAME MAN

. . . the *Magician of Cincinnati*   150

THREE YEARS

October 14th. I want these hills to be striated! How naive the *Magician of Cincinnati* was! Though it makes me happy to think of
it . . . Here, I am plunged into such real earth! Striate, hills!
What is this deer's head of green stone? I can't fabricate anything less than what I think should girdle the earth . . .

PHOTOGRAPH

PHOTOGRAPH

PHOTOGRAPH

Artist who created the *Magician of Cincinnati*; Now at work in   160
Pennsylvania; The Project—*Dresser*—So Far.

*   *   *

Ah! . . .

*   *   *

TONS

SILICON, GRASS AND DEER-HEAD RANGE
Philadelphia. Your voice as well as mine will be appreciated to express the appreciation of *Dresser*, which makes of Pennsylvania the
silicon, grass and stone deer-head center of the world . . . Artist
says he may change his mind about the central bridges. Fountains
to give forth real tar-water. Mountain lake in center. Real chalk
cliffs. Also cliffs of clay. Deep declivities nearby. "Wanted forest at-   170
mosphere, yet to be open." Gas . . .

*   *   *

PHOTOGRAPH

SKETCH

DEDICATION CEREMONY

GOES SWIMMING IN OWN STREAM

SHAKING HANDS WITH GOVERNOR

COLOR PICTURE

THE HEAD OF THE ARTIST

THE ARTIST'S HAND

STACK OF ACTUAL BILLS NEEDED TO PAY FOR PROJ-   180
ECT

Story of *Dresser*

PENNSYLVANIA'S PRIDE: *DRESSER*

Creator of *Dresser*

                    ✻   ✻   ✻

STILL SMILING AT FORGE
Beverly, South Dakota, April 18. Still smiling at forge, artist of
Dresser says, "No, of course I haven't forgotten *Dresser*. Though
how quickly the years have gone by since I have been doing *Too!*"
We glanced up at the sky and saw a large white bird, somewhat
similar to an immense seagull, which was as if fixed above our   190
heads. Its eyes were blue sapphires, and its wings were formed by an
ingenious arrangement of whitened daffodil-blossom parts. Its body
seemed mainly charcoal, on the whole, with a good deal of sand
mixed in. As we watched it, the creature actually seemed to
move . . .

August 4th . . . Three four five, and it's finished! I can see it in
    Beverly . . .

                    ✻   ✻   ✻

BEVERLY   HONORS   ARTIST.   CALLED   "FOUNDING
FATHER"

Beverly, South Dakota, August 14 . . .   200

MISSISSIPPI CLAIMS BIRTHPLACE

HONORS BIRTHPLACE

BIRTHPLACE HONORS HELD

* * *

INDIANS AND SAVANTS MEET TO PRAISE *WEST WIND*

PAT HONORED

PAT AND *WEST WIND* HONORED

* * *

June 3rd. It doesn't seem possible—the Pacific Ocean! I have ordered sixteen million tons of blue paint. Waiting anxiously for it
to arrive. How would grass be as a substitute? cement?

* * *

QUESTIONS

1. Would it be actually possible to build a project in the Ohio
River such as the poem describes?
2. What does this poem say about the nature of ambition?
3. Why does "The Artist" receive so much adulation?
4. In what way is the adulation related to the sheer size of his
projects?
5. How do you think Koch, in this poem, conceives of the nature of time?
6. Is it ridiculous to compare "The Artist" to God?

The Balloon

Donald Barthelme

The balloon, beginning at a point on Fourteenth Street, the exact location of which I cannot reveal, expanded northward all one night, while people were sleeping, until it reached the Park. There, I stopped it; at dawn the northernmost edges lay over the Plaza; the free-hanging motion was frivolous and gentle. But experiencing a faint irritation at stopping, even to protect the trees, and seeing no reason the balloon should not be allowed to expand upward, over the parts of the city it was already covering, into the "air space" to be found there, I asked the engineers to see to it. This expansion took place throughout the morning, soft imperceptible sighing of gas through the valves. The balloon then covered forty-five blocks north-south and an irregular area east-west, as many as six crosstown blocks on either side of the Avenue in some places. That was the situation, then.

But it is wrong to speak of "situations," implying sets of circumstances leading to some resolution, some escape of tension; there were no situations, simply the balloon hanging there—muted heavy grays and browns for the most part, contrasting with walnut and soft yellows. A deliberate lack of finish, enhanced by skillful installation, gave the surface a rough, forgotten equality; sliding weights on the inside, carefully adjusted, anchored the great, vari-shaped mass at a number of points. Now, we have had a flood of original ideas in all media, works of singular beauty as well as significant milestones in the history of inflation, but at that moment there was only *this balloon*, concrete particular, hanging there.

There were reactions. Some people found the balloon "interesting." As a response this seemed inadequate to the immensity of the balloon, the suddenness of its appearance over the city; on the other hand, in the absence of hysteria or other societally-induced anxiety, it must be judged a calm, "mature" one. There was a certain amount of initial argumentation about the "meaning" of the balloon; this subsided, because we have learned not to insist on meanings, and they are rarely even looked for now, except in cases involving the simplest, safest phenomena. It was agreed that since the meaning of the balloon could never be known absolutely, extended discussion was pointless, or at least less meaningful than the activities of those who, for example, hung green and blue paper lanterns from the warm gray underside, in certain streets, or seized the occasion to write messages on the surface, announcing their availability for the performance of unnatural acts, or the availability of acquaintances.

Daring children jumped, especially at those points where the balloon hovered close to a building, so that the gap between balloon and building was a matter of a few inches, or points where the balloon actually made contact, exerting an ever-so-slight pressure against the side of a building, so that balloon and building seemed a unity. The upper surface was so structured that a "landscape" was presented, small valleys as well as slight knolls, or mounds; once atop the balloon, a stroll was possible, or even a trip, from one place to another. There was pleasure in being able to run down an incline, then up the opposing slope, both gently graded, or in making a leap from one side to the other. Bouncing was possible, because of the pneumaticity of the surface, and even falling, if that was your wish. That all these varied motions, as well as others, were within one's possibilities, in experiencing the "up" side of the balloon, was extremely exciting for children, accustomed to the city's flat, hard skin. But the purpose of the balloon was not to amuse children.

Too, the number of people, children and adults, who took advantage of the opportunities described was not so large as it might have been: a certain timidity, lack of trust in the balloon, was seen. There was, furthermore, some hostility. Because we had hidden the pumps, which fed helium to the interior, and because the surface was so vast that the authorities could not determine the point of entry—that is, the point at which the gas was injected—a degree of frustration was evidenced by those city officers into whose province such manifestations normally fell. The apparent purposelessness of the balloon was vexing (as was the fact that it was "there" at all). Had we painted, in great letters, "LABORATORY TESTS PROVE" or "18% MORE EFFECTIVE" on the sides of the balloon, this difficulty would have been circumvented, but I could not bear to do so. On the whole, these officers were remarkably tolerant, considering the dimensions of the anomaly, this tolerance being the result of, first, secret tests conducted by night that convinced them that little or nothing could be done in the way of removing or destroying the balloon, and, secondly, a public warmth that arose (not uncolored by touches of the aforementioned hostility) toward the balloon, from ordinary citizens.

As a single balloon must stand for a lifetime of thinking about balloons, so each citizen expressed, in the attitude he chose, a complex of attitudes. One man might consider that the balloon had to do with the notion *sullied*, as in the sentence *The big balloon sullied the otherwise clear and radiant Manhattan sky.* That is, the balloon was, in this man's view, an imposture, something inferior to the sky that had formerly been there, something interposed between the people and their "sky." But in fact it was January, the sky was dark and ugly; it was not a sky you could look up into, lying on your back in the street, with pleasure, unless pleasure, for you, proceeded from having been threatened, from having been misused. And the underside of the balloon, by contrast, was a pleasure to look up into—we had seen to that. Muted grays and browns for the most part, contrasted with walnut and soft, forgotten yellows. And so, while this man was thinking *sullied*, still there was an admixture of pleasurable cognition in his thinking, struggling with the original perception.

Another man, on the other hand, might view the balloon as if it were part of a system of unanticipated rewards, as when one's employer walks in and says, "Here, Henry, take this package of money I have wrapped for you, because we have been doing so well in the business here, and I admire the way you bruise the tulips, without which bruising your department would not be a success, or at least not the success that it is." For this man the balloon might be a brilliantly heroic "muscle and pluck" experience, even if an experience poorly understood.

Another man might say, "Without the example of ——— it is doubtful that ——— would exist today in its present form," and find many to agree with him, or to argue with him. Ideas of "bloat" and "float" were introduced, as well as concepts of dream and responsibility. Others engaged in remarkably detailed fantasies having to do with a wish either to lose themselves in the balloon, or to engorge it. The private character of these wishes, of their origins, deeply buried and unknown, was such that they were not much spoken of; yet there is evidence that they were widespread. It was also argued that what was important was what you felt when you stood under the balloon; some people claimed that they felt sheltered, warmed, as never before, while enemies of the balloon felt, or reported feeling, constrained, a "heavy" feeling.

Critical opinion was divided:

"monstrous pourings"

"harp"

XXXXXXX "certain contrasts with darker portions"

"inner joy"

"large, square corners"

"conservative eclecticism that has so far governed modern balloon design"

::::::: "abnormal vigor"

"warm, soft, lazy passages"

"Has unity been sacrificed for a sprawling quality?"

"Quelle catastrophe!"

"munching"

People began, in a curious way, to locate themselves in relation to aspects of the balloon: "I'll be at that place where it dips down into Forty-seventh Street almost to the sidewalk, near the Alamo Chile House," or "Why don't we go stand on top, and take the air, and maybe walk about a bit, where it forms a tight, curving line with the façade of the Gallery of Modern Art—" Marginal intersections offered entrances within a given time duration, as well as "warm, soft, lazy passages" in which . . . But it is wrong to speak of "marginal intersections." Each intersection was crucial, none could be ignored (as if, walking there, you might not find someone capable of turning your attention, in a flash, from old exercises to new exercises). Each intersection was crucial, meeting of balloon and building, meeting of balloon and man, meeting of balloon and balloon.

It was suggested that what was admired about the balloon was finally this: that it was not limited, or defined. Sometimes a bulge, blister, or sub-section would carry all the way east to the river on its own initiative, in the manner of an army's movements on a map, as seen in a headquarters remote from the fighting. Then that part would be, as it were, thrown back again, or would withdraw into new dispositions; the next morning, that part would have made another sortie, or disappeared altogether. This ability on the part of the balloon to shift its shape, to change, was very pleasing, especially to people whose lives were rather rigidly patterned, persons to whom change, although desired, was not available. The balloon, for the twenty-two days of its existence, offered the possibility, in its randomness, of getting lost, of losing oneself, in contradistinction to the grid of precise, rectangular pathways under our feet. The amount of specialized training currently needed, and the consequent desirability of long-term commitments, has been occasioned by the steadily growing importance of complex machinery, in virtually all kinds of operations; as this tendency increases, more and more people will turn, in bewildered inadequacy, to solutions for which the balloon may stand as a prototype, or "rough draft."

I met you under the balloon, on the occasion of your return from Norway. You asked if it was mine; I said it was. The balloon, I said, is a spontaneous autobiographical disclosure, having to do with the unease I felt at your absence, and with sexual deprivation, but now that your visit to Bergen has been terminated, it is no longer necessary or appropriate. Removal of the balloon was easy; trailer trucks carried away the depleted fabric, which is now stored in West Virginia, awaiting some other time of unhappiness, sometime, perhaps, when we are angry with one another.

QUESTIONS

1. Compare the ease with which people adjusted to the balloon to the ease with which they adjust to any major change in their lives—a new season, airport, or President.

2. The balloon is obviously symbolic. Is it important to decide upon an ultimate meaning or set of meanings for the balloon?

3. In what way is the desire for simplicity a natural outgrowth of a society overwhelmed by complexity? Is this a dangerous desire?

4. Explain the possible meanings of the story's final paragraph.

5. Is this story actually a satire of symbolic stories?

6. Has contemporary lack of imagination reached such an extent that we need physical objects and gigantic events in order to set our imaginations to work once more?

The Future

"Future shock," wrote Alvin Toffler in 1970,

> *is the head-on collision between an accelerative push forever pressing us to live faster, to adapt more quickly, to make or break our environmental ties more frequently, to make speedier decisions, and the equally powerful counter-pressures of novelty and diversity which demand that we process more data, that we break out of our old, carefully honed routines, that we examine each situation anew before we make a decision.**

Science fiction may be one of the most useful devices modern man is learning to employ as he anticipates such collisions and prepares for the inevitable clashes.

All of the selections in this part of the book take place in the future, but all of them postulate alternative futures, depending on the particular author's point of view. Although the emphasis in most of these selections is less on science than on speculation—reflecting this book's concentration on "social science fiction" —all of the stories do depend on technological changes having taken place. The stories are much less fantasies than those in the previous part.

The first selection, Ray Bradbury's "To the Chicago Abyss," forecasts the individual human's adjustments to a post Third World War future. But if the war does not come tomorrow, there are other alternatives with which mankind might have to cope. In contrast to preceding selections in which adjustment to change was explored through psychologically oriented allegory, Bob Shaw's "Light of Other Days" is a more science-oriented "new invention" type of SF story. In fact, "slow glass" is noted among SF writers and fans as one of the first truly new and usable "inventions" of contemporary science fiction.

The satirist Kurt Vonnegut, Jr. uses the typical "what if" SF device in "Harrison Bergeron." What if a day comes when there is perfect equality? In that time, what will happen to the human spirit? The prospects seem gloomy. Perhaps, though, the future will bring us such individual personalities as Robert Hein-

---

* "New York Faces Future Shock," *New York* Magazine, Vol. 3, No. 30 (July 27, 1970), p. 26.

lein's poet Rhysling, and Roger Zelazny's poet who offers hope and beauty to a doomed race. Love, SF writers seem to assure their readers, will forever be one of the verities, even the fantastic kind of love taken up in Frederik Pohl's "Day Million"—a story which asks us to reexamine our own limited points of view—and in D. M. Thomas "Tithonus." The latter poem may also serve as a warning of the wretched things we may become capable of doing in the name of science.

Even more frightening are the consequences of worshiping the machine and the future—a problem that E. M. Forster's long short story touches upon. "The Machine Stops" concerns a city where everyone is in communication, yet physically isolated, and secure, yet frightened, dependent, and doomed by an increasingly self-imposed slavery. We may ask if the future holds either this city or the time-obsessed city of Harlan Ellison's harlequin.

Yet even the possibilities of these alternative futures will some day pass. Arthur Clarke posits the end of the human race and shows what record of ourselves we may inadvertently leave to the universe. H. G. Wells's The Time Machine *takes us to the end of Earth's time, as the sun burns out and monsters rise from the sea.*

Ray Bradbury, the author of "To the Chicago Abyss," is one of the best known of modern science fiction writers. His novels Fahrenheit 451 *and* The Illustrated Man *have both appeared in film versions. He has published many short story collections, in addition to his widely known books* The Martian Chronicles *and* Dandelion Wine. *Irish writer Bob Shaw's "Light of Other Days" tied for a 1966 Nebula Award. Kurt Vonnegut, Jr.'s books* Player Piano; Mother Night; Sirens of Titan; Cat's Cradle; God Bless You, Mr. Rosewater; Welcome to the Monkey House; *and* Slaughterhouse-Five *bridge whatever gap there might be between science fiction and "mainstream" literature, and have won Vonnegut wide popularity.*

Robert Heinlein's "The Green Hills of Earth" is one of Heinlein's series of stories dealing with man's future, recorded from the present until the year 2600 when, Heinlein predicts, there will come "the end of human adolescence and the beginning of the first mature culture." More science fiction poetry by D. M. Thomas appears in Penguin Modern Poets, *No. 11. Of E. M. Forster's "The Machine Stops" critic Mark R. Hillegas writes "unquestionably 'The Machine Stops' attacks the Wellsian vision"—most probably that given in Wells's* A Modern Utopia—*while "ironically, it is science fiction as developed by Wells that Forster uses as the vehicle for his polemic against the machine." † E. M. Forster's most famous works include* Passage to India *and* Howard's End. *In Wells's* The Time Machine, *from which a selection is reprinted here, the time traveler reaches a postwar future world where he is able to help a small group of humans free itself from slavery; yet he is unable to change the whole course of time.*

The Hugo and Nebula Awards are given each year to the year's most out-

---

† *The Future as Nightmare: H. G. Wells and the Anti-Utopians* (New York: Oxford University Press, 1967), pp. 85, 91.

standing SF works as judged by SF fans, critics, and writers. "A Rose for Ecclesiastes" won Roger Zelazny a Hugo Award nomination; his other stories and novels have won him Hugo and Nebula awards. Zelazny's books include Land of Light, Damnation Alley, Four for Tomorrow, *and* This Immortal. *Hugo and Nebula awards have also been won by Harlan Ellison, who is commonly regarded as science fiction's most iconoclastic writer. Ellison has been a television writer (whose credits include* The Man from U.N.C.L.E., *and* Star Trek), *newspaper columnist, editor of the anthology* Dangerous Visions, *and author of such works as* I Have No Mouth and I Must Scream *and* From the Land of Fear. *"Day Million" is one of the many stories that have made Frederik Pohl a leading SF writer. His novel* The Space Merchants, *written with C. M. Kornbluth, is regarded as a modern SF classic. Arthur Clarke, in collaboration with Stanley Kubrick, wrote the screenplay for* 2001: A Space Odyssey, *a film based on one of Clarke's early short stories. Clarke's other fiction includes* Childhood's End, The City and the Stars, *and* The Nine Billion Names of God. *His nonfiction includes* Profiles of the Future, Voices from the Sky, *and* The Promise of Space.

To the Chicago Abyss

Ray Bradbury

Under a pale April sky in a faint wind that blew out of a memory of winter, the old man shuffled into the almost empty park at noon. His slow feet were bandaged with nicotine-stained swathes, his hair was wild, long and gray as was his beard which enclosed a mouth which seemed always atremble with revelation.

Now he gazed back as if he had lost so many things he could not begin to guess there in the tumbled ruin, the toothless skyline of the city. Finding nothing, he shuffled on until he found a bench where sat a woman alone. Examining her, he nodded and sat to the far end of the bench and did not look at her again.

He remained, eyes shut, mouth working, for three minutes, head moving as if his nose were printing a single word on the air. Once it was written, he opened his mouth to pronounce it in a clear, fine voice:

"Coffee."

The woman gasped and stiffened.

The old man's gnarled fingers tumbled in pantomime on his unseen lap.

"Twist the key! Bright-red, yellow-letter can! Compressed air. Hisss! Vacuum pack. Ssst! Like a snake!"

The woman snapped her head about as if slapped, to stare in dreadful fascination at the old man's moving tongue.

"The scent, the odor, the smell. Rich, dark, wondrous Brazilian beans, fresh-ground!"

Leaping up, reeling as if gun-shot, the woman tottered.

The old man flicked his eyes wide. "No! I—"

But she was running, gone.

The old man sighed and walked on through the park until he reached a bench where sat a young man completely involved with wrapping dried grass in a small square of thin tissue paper. His thin fingers shaped the grass tenderly, in an almost holy ritual, trembling as he rolled the tube, put it to his mouth and, hypnotically, lit it. He leaned back, squinting deliciously, communing with the strange rank air in his mouth and lungs.

The old man watched the smoke blow away on the noon wind and said, "Chesterfields."

The young man gripped his knees tight.

"Raleighs," said the old man. "Lucky Strikes."

The young man stared at him.

"Kent. Kool. Marlboro," said the old man, not looking at him. "Those were the names. White, red, amber packs, grass green, sky blue, pure gold, with the red slick small ribbon that ran around the top that you pulled to zip away the crinkly cellophane, and the blue government tax stamp—"

"Shut up," said the young man.

"Buy them in drugstores, fountains, subways—"

"Shut up!"

"Gently," said the old man. "It's just, that smoke of yours made me think—"

"Don't think!" The young man jerked so violently his homemade cigarette fell in chaff to his lap. "Now look what you made me do!"

"I'm sorry. It was such a nice friendly day."

"I'm no friend!"

"We're all friends now, or why live?"

"Friends!" the young man snorted, aimlessly plucking at the shredded grass and paper. "Maybe there were 'friends' back in 1970, but now . . ."

"1970. You must have been a baby then. They still had Butterfingers then in bright-yellow wrappers. Baby Ruths. Clark Bars in orange paper. Milky Ways—swallow a universe of stars, comets, meteors. Nice."

"It was never nice." The young man stood suddenly. "What's wrong with you?"

"I remember limes, and lemons, that's what's wrong with me. Do you remember oranges?"

"Damn right. Oranges, hell. You calling me a liar? You want me to feel bad? You nuts? Don't you know the law? You know I could turn you in, you?"

"I know, I know," said the old man, shrugging. "The weather fooled me. It made me want to compare—"

"Compare rumors, that's what they'd say, the police, the special cops, they'd say it, rumors, you trouble making bastard, you."

He seized the old man's lapels, which ripped so he had to grab another handful, yelling down into his face. "Why don't I just blast the living Jesus out of you? I ain't hurt no one in so long, I . . ."

He shoved the old man. Which gave him the idea to pummel, and when he pummeled he began to punch, and punching made it easy to strike, and soon he rained blows upon the old man, who stood like one caught in thunder and down-poured storm, using only his fingers to ward off blows that fleshed his cheeks, shoulders, his brow, his chin, as the young man shrieked cigarettes, moaned candies, yelled smokes, cried sweets until the old man fell to be kick-rolled and shivering. The young man stopped and began to cry. At the sound, the old man, cuddled, clenched into his pain, took his fingers away from his broken mouth and opened his eyes to gaze with astonishment at his assailant. The young man wept.

"Please . . ." begged the old man.

The young man wept louder, tears falling from his eyes.

"Don't cry," said the old man. "We won't be hungry forever. We'll rebuild the cities. Listen, I didn't mean for you to cry, only to think, Where are we going, what are we doing, what've we done? You weren't hitting me. You meant to hit something else, but I was handy. Look, I'm sitting up. I'm okay."

The young man stopped crying and blinked down at the old man, who forced a bloody smile.

"You . . . you can't go around," said the young man, "making people unhappy. I'll find someone to fix you!"

"Wait!" The old man struggled to his knees. "No!"

But the young man ran wildly off out of the park, yelling.

Crouched alone, the old man felt his bones, found one of his teeth lying red amongst the strewn gravel, handled it sadly.

"Fool," said a voice.

The old man glanced over and up.

A lean man of some forty years stood leaning against a tree nearby, a look of pale weariness and curiosity on his long face.

"Fool," he said again.

The old man gasped. "You were there, all the time, and did *nothing?*"

"What, fight one fool to save another? No." The stranger helped him up and brushed him off. "I do my fighting where it pays. Come on. You're going home with me."

The old man gasped again. "Why?"

"That boy'll be back with the police any second. I don't want you stolen away, you're a very precious commodity. I've heard of you, looked for you for days now. Good grief, and when I find you you're up to your famous tricks. What did you say to the boy made him mad?"

"I said about oranges and lemons, candy, cigarettes. I was just getting ready to recollect in detail wind-up toys, briar pipes and back scratchers, when he dropped the sky on me."

"I almost don't blame him. Half of me wants to hit you itself. Come on, double time. There's a siren, quick!"

And they went swiftly, another way, out of the park.

He drank the homemade wine because it was easiest. The food must wait until his hunger overcame the pain in his broken mouth. He sipped, nodding.

"Good, many thanks, good."

The stranger who had walked him swiftly out of the park sat across from him at the flimsy dining-room table as the stranger's wife placed broken and mended plates on the worn cloth.

"The beating," said the husband at last. "How did it happen!"
At this the wife almost dropped a plate.
"Relax," said the husband. "No one followed us. Go ahead, old man, tell us, why do you behave like a saint panting after martyrdom? You're famous, you know. Everyone's heard about you. Many would like to meet you. Myself, first, I want to know what makes you tick. Well?"
But the old man was only entranced with the vegetables on the chipped plate before him. Twenty-six, no, twenty-eight peas! He counted the impossible sum! He bent to the incredible vegetables like a man praying over his quietest beads. Twenty-eight glorious green peas, plus a few graphs of half-raw spaghetti announcing that today business was fair. But under the line of *pasta*, the cracked line of the plate showed where business for years now was more than terrible. The old man hovered counting above the food like a great and inexplicable buzzard crazily fallen and roosting in this cold apartment, watched by his Samaritan hosts until at last he said, "These twenty-eight peas remind me of a film I saw as a child. A comedian—do you know the word?—a funny man met a lunatic in a midnight house in this film and . . ."
The husband and wife laughed quietly.
"No, that's not the joke yet, sorry," the old man apologized. "The lunatic sat the comedian down to an empty table, no knives, no forks, no food. 'Dinner is served!' he cried. Afraid of murder, the comedian fell in with the make-believe. 'Great!' he cried, pretending to chew steak, vegetables, dessert. He bit nothings. 'Fine!' he swallowed air. 'Wonderful!' Eh . . . you may laugh now."
But the husband and wife, grown still, only looked at their sparsely strewn plates.
The old man shook his head and went on. "The comedian, thinking to impress the madman, exclaimed, 'And these spiced brandy peaches! Superb!' 'Peaches?' screamed the madman, drawing a gun. 'I served no peaches! You must be insane!' And shot the comedian in the behind!"
The old man, in the silence which ensued, picked up the first pea and weighed its lovely bulk upon his bent tin fork. He was about to put it in his mouth when—
There was a sharp rap on the door.
"Special police!" a voice cried.
Silent but trembling, the wife hid the extra plate.
The husband rose calmly to lead the old man to a wall where a panel hissed open, and he stepped in and the panel hissed shut and he stood in darkness hidden away as, beyond, unseen, the apartment door opened. Voices murmured excitedly. The old man could imagine the special policeman in his midnight-blue uniform, with drawn gun, entering to see only the flimsy furniture, the bare walls, the echoing linoleum floor, the glassless, cardboarded-over windows, this thin and oily film of civilization left on an empty shore when the storm tide of war went away.

"I'm looking for an old man," said the tired voice of authority beyond the wall. Strange, thought the old man, even the law sounds tired now. "Patched clothes . . ." But, thought the old man, I thought everyone's clothes were patched! "Dirty. About eighty years old . . ." But isn't everyone dirty, everyone old? the old man cried out to himself. "If you turn him in, there's a week's rations as reward," said the police voice. "Plus ten cans of vegetables, five cans of soup, bonus."

Real tin cans with bright printed labels, thought the old man. The cans flashed like meteors rushing by in the dark over his eyelids. What a fine reward! Not ten thousand dollars, not twenty thousand dollars, no no, but five incredible cans of real, not imitation soup, and ten, count them, ten brilliant circus-colored cans of exotic vegetables like string beans and sun-yellow corn! Think of it. Think!

There was a long silence in which the old man almost thought he heard faint murmurs of stomachs turning uneasily, slumbering but dreaming of dinners much finer than the hairballs of old illusion gone nightmare and politics gone sour in the long twilight since A. D., Annihilation Day.

"Soup. Vegetables," said the police voice, a final time. "Fifteen solid-pack cans!"

The door slammed.

The boots stomped away through the ramshackle tenement, pounding coffin-lid doors to stir other Lazarus souls alive to cry aloud of bright tins and real soups. The poundings faded. There was a last banging slam.

And at last the hidden panel whispered up. The husband and wife did not look at him as he stepped out. He knew why and wanted to touch their elbows.

"Even I," he said gently, "even I was tempted to turn myself in, to claim the reward, to eat the soup."

Still they would not look at him.

"Why?" he asked. "Why didn't you hand me over? Why?"

The husband, as if suddenly remembering, nodded to his wife. She went to the door, hesitated, her husband nodded again impatiently, and she went out, noiseless as a puff of cobweb. They heard her rustling along the hall, scratching softly at doors, which opened to gasps and murmurs.

"What's she up to? What are *you* up to?" asked the old man.

"You'll find out. Sit. Finish your dinner," said the husband. "Tell me why you're such a fool you make us fools who seek you out and bring you here."

"Why am I such a fool?" The old man sat. The old man munched slowly, taking peas one at a time from the plate which had been returned to him. "Yes, I am a fool. How did I start my foolishness? Years ago I looked at the ruined world, the dictatorships, the desiccated states and nations, and said, 'What can I do? Me, a weak old man, what? Rebuild a devastation? Ha!' But as I lay half asleep one night an old phonograph record played in my head. Two sisters named Duncan sang out of my childhood a song called 'Remembering.' 'Remembering is all I do, dear, so try and remember, too.' I sang the song, and it wasn't a song but a way of life. What did I have to offer a world that was forgetting? My memory! How could this help? By offering a standard of comparison. By telling the young *what once was*, by considering our losses. I found the more I remembered, the more I *could* remember! Depending on who I sat down with I remembered imitation flowers, dial telephones, refrigerators, kazoos (you ever play a kazoo?!), thimbles, bicycle clips, not bicycles, no, but bicycle *clips!* isn't that wild and strange? Antimacassars. Do you know them? Never mind. Once a man asked me to remember just the dashboard dials on a Cadillac. I remembered. I told him in detail. He listened. He cried great tears down his face. Happy tears or sad? I can't say. I only remember. Not literature, no, I never had a head for plays or poems, they slip away, they die. All I am, really, is a trash heap of the mediocre, the third-best-hand-me-down useless and chromed-over slush and junk of a race-track civilization that ran last over a precipice. So all I offer really is scintillant junk, the clamored-after chronometers and absurd machineries of a never-ending river of robots and robot-mad owners. Yet, one way or another, civilization must get back on the road. Those who can offer fine butterfly poetry, let them remember, let them offer. Those who can weave and build butterfly nets, let them weave, let them build. My gift is smaller than both, and perhaps contemptible in the long hoist, climb, jump toward the old and amiably silly peak. But I *must* dream myself worthy. For the things, silly or not, that people remember are the things they will search for again. I will, then, ulcerate their half-dead desires with vinegar-gnat memory. Then perhaps they'll rattle-bang the Big Clock together again, which is the city, the state and then the world. Let one man want wine, another lounge chairs, a third a batwing glider to soar the March winds on and build bigger electropterodactyls to scour even greater winds, with even greater peoples. Someone wants moron Christmas trees and some wise man goes to cut them. Pack this all together, wheel in want, want in wheel, and I'm just there to oil them, but oil them I do. Ho, once I would have raved, 'Only the best is best, only quality is true!' But roses grow from blood manure. Mediocre must be, so most-excellent can bloom. So I shall be the *best* mediocre there is and fight all who say, Slide under, sink back, dust-wallow, let brambles scurry over your living grave. I shall protest the roving apeman tribes, the sheep-people munching the far fields prayed on by the feudal land-baron wolves who rarefy themselves in the few skyscraper summits and horde unremembered foods. And these villains I will kill with can opener and corkscrew. I shall run them down with ghosts of Buick, Kissel-Kar and Moon, thrash them with licorice whips until they cry for some sort of unqualified mercy. Can I *do* all this? One can only try."

The old man rummaged the last pea, with the last words, in his mouth, while his Samaritan host simply looked at him with gently amazed eyes, and far off up through the house people moved, doors tapped open and shut, and there was a gathering outside the door of this apartment where now the husband said, "And *you* asked why we didn't turn you in? Do you hear that out there?"

"It sounds like everyone in the apartment house."

"Everyone. Old man, old fool, do you remember . . . motion picture houses, or, better, drive-in movies?"

The old man smiled. "Do *you?*"

"Almost. Look, listen, today, now, if you're going to be a fool, if you want to run risks, do it in the aggregate, in one fell blow. Why waste your breath on one, or two, or even three, if . . ."

The husband opened the door and nodded outside. Silently, one at a time and in couples, the people of the house entered. Entered this room as if entering a synagogue or church or the kind of church known as a movie or the kind of movie known as a drive-in and the hour was growing late in the day, with the sun going down the sky, and soon in the early evening hours, in the dark, the room would be dim and in the one light the voice of the old man would speak and these would listen and hold hands and it would be like the old days with the balconies and the dark, or the cars and the dark, and just the memory, the words, of popcorn, and the words for the gum and the sweet drinks and candy, but the words, anyway, the words . . .

And while the people were coming in and settling on the floor, and the old man watched them, incredulous that he had summoned them here without knowing, the husband said, "Isn't this better than taking a chance in the open?"

"Yes. Strange. I hate pain. I hate being hit and chased. But my tongue moves. I must hear what it has to say. Still this is better."

"Good." The husband pressed a red ticket into his palm. "When this is all over, an hour from now, here is a ticket from a friend of mine in Transportation. One train crosses the country each week. Each week I get a ticket for some idiot I want to help. This week it's you."

The old man read the destination on the folded red paper: " 'Chicago Abyss,' " and added, "Is the Abyss still there?"

"This time next year Lake Michigan may break through the last crust and make a new lake in the pit where the city once was. There's life of sorts around the crater rim, and a branch train goes west once a month. Once you leave here, keep moving, forget you met or know us. I'll give you a small list of people like ourselves. A long time from now, look them up, out in the wilderness. But, for God's sake, in the open, alone for a year, declare a moratorium. Keep your wonderful mouth shut. And here—" The husband gave him a yellow card. "A dentist I know. Tell him to make you a new set of teeth that will only open at mealtimes."

A few people, hearing, laughed, and the old man laughed quietly and the people were in now, dozens of them, and the day was late, and the husband and wife shut the door and stood by it and turned and waited for this last special time when the old man might open his mouth.

The old man stood up.

His audience grew very still.

The train came, rusty and loud at midnight, into a suddenly snow-filled station. Under a cruel dusting of white, the ill-washed people crowded into and through the ancient chair cars, mashing the old man along the corridor and into an empty compartment that had once been a lavatory. Soon the floor was a solid mass of bed roll on which sixteen people twisted and turned in darkness, fighting their way into sleep.

The train rushed forth to white emptiness.

The old man, thinking, Quiet, shut up, no, don't speak, nothing, no, stay still, think, careful, cease! found himself now swayed, joggled, hurled this way and that as he half crouched against a wall. He and just one other were upright in this monster room of dreadful sleep. A few feet away, similarly shoved against the wall, sat an eight-year-old boy with a drawn sick paleness escaping from his cheeks. Full awake, eyes bright, he seemed to watch, he *did* watch, the old man's mouth. The boy gazed because he must. The train hooted, roared, swayed, yelled and ran.

Half an hour passed in a thunderous grinding passage by night under the snow-hidden moon, and the old man's mouth was tight-nailed shut. Another hour, and still boned shut. Another hour, and the muscles around his cheeks began to slacken. Another, and his lips parted to wet themselves. The boy stayed awake. The boy saw. The boy waited. Immense sifts of silence came down the night air outside, tunneled by avalanche train. The travelers, very deep in invoiced terror, numbed by flight, slept each separate, but the boy did not take his eyes away and at last the old man leaned forward, softly.

"Sh. Boy. Your name?"

"Joseph."

The train swayed and groaned in its sleep, a monster floundering through timeless dark toward a morn that could not be imagined.

"Joseph . . ." The old man savored the word, bent forward, his eyes gentle and shining. His face filled with pale beauty. His eyes widened until they seemed blind. He gazed at a distant and hidden thing. He cleared his throat ever so softly. "Ah . . ."

The train roared round a curve. The people rocked in their snowing sleep.

"Well, Joseph," whispered the old man. He lifted his fingers softly in the air. "Once upon a time . . ."

QUESTIONS

1. Why do you think the old man cannot seem to stop talking?
2. Why does Bradbury's hero recite so many brand names?
3. What assumptions does the story make about man's motivations for building the future? Are the types of self-help motivations given here not the very ones likely to bring on conditions that may lead to the Third World War?
4. Discuss the social and intellectual role of the storyteller, particularly in the days before radio, movies, and television.

Light of Other Days

Bob Shaw

Leaving the village behind, we followed the heady sweeps of the road up into a land of slow glass.

I had never seen one of the farms before and at first found them slightly eerie—an effect heightened by imagination and circumstance. The car's turbine was pulling smoothly and quietly in the damp air so that we seemed to be carried over the convolutions of the road in a kind of supernatural silence. On our right the mountain sifted down into an incredibly perfect valley of timeless pine, and everywhere stood the great frames of slow glass, drinking light. An occasional flash of afternoon sunlight on their wind bracing created an illusion of movement, but in fact the frames were deserted. The rows of windows had been standing on the hillside for years, staring into the valley, and men only cleaned them in the middle of the night when their human presence would not matter to the thirsty glass.

They were fascinating, but Selina and I didn't mention the windows. I think we hated each other so much we both were reluctant to sully anything new by drawing it into the nexus of our emotions. The holiday, I had begun to realize, was a stupid idea in the first place. I had thought it would cure everything, but, of course, it didn't stop Selina being pregnant and, worse still, it didn't even stop her being angry about being pregnant.

Rationalizing our dismay over her condition, we had circulated the usual statements to the effect that we would have *liked* having children—but later on, at the proper time. Selina's pregnancy had cost us her well-paid job and with it the new house we had been negotiating and which was far beyond the reach of my income from poetry. But the real source of our annoyance was that we were face to face with the realization that people who say they want children later always mean they want children never. Our nerves were thrumming with the knowledge that we, who had thought ourselves so unique, had fallen into the same biological trap as every mindless rutting creature which ever existed.

The road took us along the southern slopes of Ben Cruachan until we began to catch glimpses of the gray Atlantic far ahead. I had just cut our speed to absorb the view better when I noticed the sign spiked to a gatepost. It said: "SLOW GLASS—Quality High, Prices Low—J. R. Hagan." On an impulse I stopped the car on the verge, wincing slightly as tough grasses whipped noisily at the bodywork.

"Why have we stopped?" Selina's neat, smoke-silver head turned in surprise.

"Look at that sign. Let's go up and see what there is. The stuff might be reasonably priced out here."

Selina's voice was pitched high with scorn as she refused, but I was too taken with my idea to listen. I had an illogical conviction that doing something extravagant and crazy would set us right again.

"Come on," I said, "the exercise might do us some good. We've been driving too long anyway."

She shrugged in a way that hurt me and got out of the car. We walked up a path made of irregular, packed clay steps nosed with short lengths of sapling. The path curved through trees which clothed the edge of the hill and at its end we found a low farmhouse. Beyond the little stone building tall frames of slow glass gazed out towards the voice-stilling sight of Cruachan's ponderous descent towards the waters of Loch Linnhe. Most of the panes were perfectly transparent but a few were dark, like panels of polished ebony.

As we approached the house through a neat cobbled yard a tall middle-aged man in ash-colored tweeds arose and waved to us. He had been sitting on the low rubble wall which bounded the yard, smoking a pipe and staring towards the house. At the front window of the cottage a young woman in a tangerine dress stood with a small boy in her arms, but she turned disinterestedly and moved out of sight as we drew near.

"Mr. Hagan?" I guessed.

"Correct. Come to see some glass, have you? Well, you've come to the right place." Hagan spoke crisply, with traces of the pure highland which sounds so much like Irish to the unaccustomed ear. He had one of those calmly dismayed faces one finds on elderly roadmenders and philosophers.

"Yes," I said. "We're on holiday. We saw your sign."

Selina, who usually has a natural fluency with strangers, said nothing. She was looking towards the now empty window with what I thought was a slightly puzzled expression.

"Up from London, are you? Well, as I said, you've come to the right place—and at the right time, too. My wife and I don't see many people this early in the season."

I laughed. "Does that mean we might be able to buy a little glass without mortgaging our home?"

"Look at that now," Hagan said, smiling helplessly. "I've thrown away any advantage I might have had in the transaction. Rose, that's my wife, says I never learn. Still, let's sit down and talk it over." He pointed at the rubble wall then glanced doubtfully at Selina's immaculate blue skirt.

"Wait till I fetch a rug from the house." Hagan limped quickly into the cottage, closing the door behind him.

"Perhaps it wasn't such a marvelous idea to come up here," I whispered to Selina, "but you might at least be pleasant to the man. I think I can smell a bargain."

"Some hope," she said with deliberate coarseness. "Surely even you must have noticed that ancient dress his wife is wearing? He won't give much away to strangers."

"Was that his wife?"

"Of course that was his wife."

"Well, well," I said, surprised. "Anyway, try to be civil with him. I don't want to be embarrassed."

Selina snorted, but she smiled whitely when Hagan reappeared and I relaxed a little. Strange how a man can love a woman and yet at the same time pray for her to fall under a train.

Hagan spread a tartan blanket on the wall and we sat down, feeling slightly self-conscious at having been translated from our city-oriented lives into a rural tableau. On the distant slate of the Loch, beyond the watchful frames of slow glass, a slow-moving steamer drew a white line towards the south. The boisterous mountain air seemed almost to invade our lungs, giving us more oxygen than we required.

"Some of the glass farmers around here," Hagan began, "give strangers, such as yourselves, a sales talk about how beautiful the autumn is in this part of Argyll. Or it might be the spring, or the winter. I don't do that—any fool knows that a place which doesn't look right in summer never looks right. What do you say?"

I nodded compliantly.

"I want you just to take a good look out towards Mull, Mr. . . . ."

"Garland."

". . . Garland. That's what you're buying if you buy my glass, and it never looks better than it does at this minute. The glass is in perfect phase, none of it is less than ten years thick—and a four-foot window will cost you two hundred pounds."

"*Two hundred!*" Selina was shocked. "That's as much as they charge at the Scenedow shop in Bond Street."

Hagan smiled patiently, then looked closely at me to see if I knew enough about slow glass to appreciate what he had been saying. His price had been much higher than I had hoped—but *ten years thick!* The cheap glass one found in places like the Vistaplex and Pane-o-rama stores usually consisted of a quarter of an inch of ordinary glass faced with a veneer of slow glass perhaps only ten or twelve months thick.

"You don't understand, darling," I said, already determined to buy. "This glass will last ten years and it's in phase."

"Doesn't that only mean it keeps time?"

Hagan smiled at her again, realizing he had no further necessity to bother with me. "Only, you say! Pardon me, Mrs. Garland, but you don't seem to appreciate the miracle, the genuine honest-to-goodness miracle, of engineering precision needed to produce a piece of glass in phase. When I say the glass is ten years thick it means it takes light ten years to pass through it. In effect, each one of those panes is ten light-years thick —more than twice the distance to the nearest star—so a variation in actual thickness of only a millionth of an inch would . . ."

He stopped talking for a moment and sat quietly looking towards the house. I turned my head from the view of the Loch and saw the young woman standing at the window again. Hagan's eyes were filled with a kind of greedy reverence which made me feel uncomfortable and at the same time convinced me Selina had been wrong. In my experience husbands never looked at wives that way, at least, not at their own.

The girl remained in view for a few seconds, dress glowing warmly, then moved back into the room. Suddenly I received a distinct, though inexplicable, impression she was blind. My feeling was that Selina and I were perhaps blundering through an emotional interplay as violent as our own.

"I'm sorry," Hagan continued, "I thought Rose was going to call me for something. Now, where was I, Mrs. Garland? Ten light-years compressed into a quarter of an inch means . . ."

I ceased to listen, partly because I was already sold, partly because I had heard the story of slow glass many times before and had never yet understood the principles involved. An acquaintance with scientific training had once tried to be helpful by telling me to visualize a pane of slow glass as a hologram which did not need coherent light from a laser for the reconstitution of its visual information, and in which every photon of ordinary light passed through a spiral tunnel coiled outside the radius of capture of each atom in the glass. This gem of, to me, incomprehensibility not only told me nothing, it convinced me once again that a mind as nontechnical as mine should concern itself less with causes than effects.

The most important effect, in the eyes of the average individual, was that light took a long time to pass through a sheet of slow glass. A new piece was always jet black because nothing had yet come through, but one could stand the glass beside, say, a woodland lake until the scene emerged, perhaps a year later. If the glass was then removed and installed in a dismal city flat, the flat would—for that year—appear to overlook the woodland lake. During the year it wouldn't be merely a very realistic but still picture—the water would ripple in sunlight, silent animals would come to drink, birds would cross the sky, night would follow day, season would follow season. Until one day, a year later, the beauty held in the subatomic pipelines would be exhausted and the familiar gray cityscape would reappear.

Apart from its stupendous novelty value, the commercial success of slow glass was founded on the fact that having a scenedow was the exact emotional equivalent of owning land. The meanest cave dweller could look out on misty parks—and who was to say they weren't his? A man who really owns tailored gardens and estates doesn't spend his time proving his ownership by crawling on his ground, feeling, smelling, tasting it. All he receives from the land are light patterns, and with scenedows those patterns could be taken into coal mines, submarines, prison cells.

On several occasions I have tried to write short pieces about the enchanted crystal but, to me, the theme is so ineffably poetic as to be, paradoxically, beyond the reach of poetry—mine at any rate. Besides, the best songs and verse had already been written, with prescient inspiration, by men who had died long before slow glass was discovered. I had no hope of equaling, for example, Moore with his:

> Oft in the stilly night,
> Ere slumber's chain has bound me,
> Fond Memory brings the light,
> Of other days around me . . .

It took only a few years for slow glass to develop from a scientific curiosity to a sizable industry. And much to the astonishment of we poets—those of us who remain convinced that beauty lives though lilies die—the trappings of that industry were no different from those of any other. There were good scenedows which cost a lot of money, and there were inferior scenedows which cost rather less. The thickness, measured in years, was an important factor in the cost but there was also the question of *actual* thickness, or phase.

Even with the most sophisticated engineering techniques available thickness control was something of a hit-and-miss affair. A coarse discrepancy could mean that a pane intended to be five years thick might be five and a half, so that light which entered in summer emerged in winter; a fine discrepancy could mean that noon sunshine emerged at midnight. These incompatibilities had their peculiar charm—many night workers, for example, liked having their own private time zones—but, in general, it cost more to buy scenedows which kept closely in step with real time.

Selina still looked unconvinced when Hagan had finished speaking. She shook her head almost imperceptibly and I knew he had been using the wrong approach. Quite suddenly the pewter helmet of her hair was disturbed by a cool gust of wind, and huge clean tumbling drops of rain began to spang round us from an almost cloudless sky.

"I'll give you a check now," I said abruptly, and saw Selina's green eyes triangulate angrily on my face. "You can arrange delivery?"

"Aye, delivery's no problem," Hagan said, getting to his feet. "But wouldn't you rather take the glass with you?"

"Well, yes—if you don't mind." I was shamed by his readiness to trust my scrip.

"I'll unclip a pane for you. Wait here. It won't take long to slip it into a carrying frame." Hagan limped down the slope towards the seriate windows, through some of which the view towards Linnhe was sunny, while others were cloudy and a few pure black.

Selina drew the collar of her blouse closed at her throat. "The least he could have done was invite us inside. There can't be so many fools passing through that he can afford to neglect them."

I tried to ignore the insult and concentrated on writing the check. One of the outsize drops broke across my knuckles, splattering the pink paper.

"All right," I said, "let's move in under the eaves till he gets back." You worm, I thought as I felt the whole thing go completely wrong. I just had to be a fool to marry you. A prize fool, a fool's fool—and now that you've trapped part of me inside you I'll never ever, never ever, *never ever* get away.

Feeling my stomach clench itself painfully, I ran behind Selina to the side of the cottage. Beyond the window the neat living room, with its coal fire, was empty but the child's toys were scattered on the floor. Alphabet blocks and a wheelbarrow the exact color of freshly pared carrots. As I stared in, the boy came running from the other room and began kicking the blocks. He didn't notice me. A few moments later the young woman entered the room and lifted him, laughing easily and wholeheartedly as she swung the boy under her arm. She came to the window as she had done earlier. I smiled self-consciously, but neither she nor the child responded.

My forehead prickled icily. *Could they both be blind?* I sidled away.

Selina gave a little scream and I spun towards her.

"The rug!" she said. "It's getting soaked."

She ran across the yard in the rain, snatched the reddish square from the dappling wall and ran back, towards the cottage door. Something heaved convulsively in my subconscious.

"Selina," I shouted. "Don't open it!"

But I was too late. She had pushed open the latched wooden door and was standing, hand over mouth, looking into the cottage. I moved close to her and took the rug from her unresisting fingers.

As I was closing the door I let my eyes traverse the cottage's interior. The neat living room in which I had just seen the woman and child was, in reality, a sickening clutter of shabby furniture, old newspapers, cast-off clothing and smeared dishes. It was damp, stinking and utterly deserted. The only object I recognized from my view through the window was the little wheelbarrow, paintless and broken.

I latched the door firmly and ordered myself to forget what I had seen. Some men who live alone are good housekeepers; others just don't know how.

Selina's face was white. "I don't understand. I don't understand it."

"Slow glass works both ways," I said gently. "Light passes out of a house, as well as in."

"You mean . . . ?"

"I don't know. It isn't our business. Now steady up—Hagan's coming back with our glass." The churning in my stomach was beginning to subside.

Hagan came into the yard carrying an oblong, plastic-covered frame. I held the check out to him, but he was staring at Selina's face. He seemed to know immediately that our uncomprehending fingers had rummaged through his soul. Selina avoided his gaze. She was old and ill-looking, and her eyes stared determinedly towards the nearing horizon.

"I'll take the rug from you, Mr. Garland," Hagan finally said. "You shouldn't have troubled yourself over it."

"No trouble. Here's the check."

"Thank you." He was still looking at Selina with a strange kind of supplication. "It's been a pleasure to do business with you."

"The pleasure was mine," I said with equal, senseless formality. I picked up the heavy frame and guided Selina towards the path which led to the road. Just as we reached the head of the now slippery steps Hagan spoke again.

"Mr. Garland!"

I turned unwillingly.

"It wasn't my fault," he said steadily. "A hit-and-run driver got them both, down on the Oban road six years ago. My boy was only seven when it happened. I'm entitled to keep something."

I nodded wordlessly and moved down the path, holding my wife close to me, treasuring the feel of her arms locked around me. At the bend I looked back through the rain and saw Hagan sitting with squared shoulders on the wall where we had first seen him.

He was looking at the house, but I was unable to tell if there was anyone at the window.

QUESTIONS

1. Explain why Shaw starts the story with the characters arguing. What have they learned by the end of the story?

2. Is it necessary to the story that the main character is a poet?

3. How plausible is the invention of "slow glass"? Is an understanding of the "science" in this story necessary for a complete enjoyment of the story?

4. Compare the use of "slow glass" to the use of home movies.

Harrison Bergeron

Kurt Vonnegut, Jr.

The year was 2081, and everybody was finally equal. They weren't only equal before God and the law. They were equal every which way. Nobody was smarter than anybody else. Nobody was better looking than anybody else. Nobody was stronger or quicker than anybody else. All this equality was due to the 211th, 212th, and 213th Amendments to the Constitution, and to the unceasing vigilance of agents of the United States Handicapper General.

Some things about living still weren't quite right, though. April, for instance, still drove people crazy by not being springtime. And it was in that clammy month that the H-G men took George and Hazel Bergeron's fourteen-year-old son, Harrison, away.

It was tragic, all right, but George and Hazel couldn't think about it very hard. Hazel had a perfectly average intelligence, which meant she couldn't think about anything except in short bursts. And George, while his intelligence was way above normal, had a little mental handicap radio in his ear. He was required by law to wear it at all times. It was tuned to a government transmitter. Every twenty seconds or so, the transmitter would send out some sharp noise to keep people like George from taking unfair advantage of their brains.

George and Hazel were watching television. There were tears on Hazel's cheeks, but she'd forgotten for the moment what they were about.

On the television screen were ballerinas.

A buzzer sounded in George's head. His thoughts fled in panic, like bandits from a burglar alarm.

"That was a real pretty dance, that dance they just did," said Hazel.

"Huh?" said George.

"That dance—it was nice," said Hazel.

"Yup," said George. He tried to think a little about the ballerinas. They weren't really very good—no better than anybody else would have been, anyway. They were burdened with sash-weights and bags of birdshot, and their faces were masked, so that no one, seeing a free and graceful gesture or a pretty face, would feel like something the cat drug in. George was toying with the vague notion that maybe dancers shouldn't be handicapped. But he didn't get very far with it before another noise in his ear radio scattered his thoughts.

George winced. So did two out of the eight ballerinas.

Hazel saw him wince. Having no mental handicap herself, she had to ask George what the latest sound had been.

"Sounded like somebody hitting a milk bottle with a ball peen hammer," said George.

"I'd think it would be real interesting, hearing all the different sounds," said Hazel, a little envious. "All the things they think up."

"Um," said George.

"Only, if I was Handicapper General, you know what I would do?" said Hazel. Hazel, as a matter of fact, bore a strong resemblance to the Handicapper General, a woman named Diana Moon Glampers. "If I was Diana Moon Glampers," said Hazel, "I'd have chimes on Sunday—just chimes. Kind of in honor of religion."

"I could think, if it was just chimes," said George.

"Well—maybe make 'em real loud," said Hazel. "I think I'd make a good Handicapper General."

"Good as anybody else," said George.

"Who knows better'n I do what normal is?" said Hazel.

"Right," said George. He began to think glimmeringly about his abnormal son who was now in jail, about Harrison, but a twenty-one-gun salute in his head stopped that.

"Boy!" said Hazel, "that was a doozy, wasn't it?"

It was such a doozy that George was white and trembling, and tears stood on the rims of his red eyes. Two of the eight ballerinas had collapsed to the studio floor, were holding their temples.

"All of a sudden you look so tired," said Hazel. "Why don't you stretch out on the sofa, so's you can rest your handicap bag on the pillows, honeybunch." She was referring to the forty-seven pounds of birdshot in a canvas bag, which was padlocked around George's neck. "Go on and rest the bag for a little while," she said. "I don't care if you're not equal to me for a while."

George weighed the bag with his hands. "I don't mind it," he said. "I don't notice it any more. It's just a part of me."

"You been so tired lately—kind of wore out," said Hazel. "If there was just some way we could make a little hole in the bottom of the bag, and just take out a few of them lead balls. Just a few."

"Two years in prison and two thousand dollars fine for every ball I took out," said George. "I don't call that a bargain."

"If you could just take a few out when you came home from work," said Hazel. "I mean—you don't compete with anybody around here. You just set around."

"If I tried to get away with it," said George, "then other people'd get away with it—and pretty soon we'd be right back to the dark ages again, with everybody competing against everybody else. You wouldn't like that, would you?"

"I'd hate it," said Hazel.

"There you are," said George. "The minute people start cheating on laws, what do you think happens to society?"

If Hazel hadn't been able to come up with an answer to this question, George couldn't have supplied one. A siren was going off in his head.

"Reckon it'd fall all apart," said Hazel.

"What would?" said George blankly.

"Society," said Hazel uncertainly. "Wasn't that what you just said?"

"Who knows?" said George.

The television program was suddenly interrupted for a news bulletin. It wasn't clear at first as to what the bulletin was about, since the announcer, like all announcers, had a serious speech impediment. For about half a minute, and in a state of high excitement, the announcer tried to say, "Ladies and gentlemen—"

He finally gave up, handed the bulletin to a ballerina to read.

"That's all right—" Hazel said of the announcer, "he tried. That's the big thing. He tried to do the best he could with what God gave him. He should get a nice raise for trying so hard."

"Ladies and gentlemen—" said the ballerina, reading the bulletin. She must have been extraordinarily beautiful, because the mask she wore was hideous. And it was easy to see that she was the strongest and most graceful of all the dancers, for her handicap bags were as big as those worn by two-hundred-pound men.

And she had to apologize at once for her voice, which was a very unfair voice for a woman to use. Her voice was a warm, luminous, timeless melody. "Excuse me—" she said, and she began again, making her voice absolutely uncompetitive.

"Harrison Bergeron, age fourteen," she said in a grackle squawk, "has just escaped from jail, where he was held on suspicion of plotting to overthrow the government. He is a genius and an athlete, is under-handicapped, and should be regarded as extremely dangerous."

A police photograph of Harrison Bergeron was flashed on the screen— upside down, then sideways, upside down again, then right side up. The picture showed the full length of Harrison against a background calibrated in feet and inches. He was exactly seven feet tall.

The rest of Harrison's appearance was Halloween and hardware. Nobody had ever borne heavier handicaps. He had outgrown hindrances faster than the H-G men could think them up. Instead of a little ear radio for a mental handicap, he wore a tremendous pair of earphones, and spectacles with thick wavy lenses. The spectacles were intended to make him not only half blind, but to give him whanging headaches besides.

Scrap metal was hung all over him. Ordinarily, there was a certain symmetry, a military neatness to the handicaps issued to strong people, but Harrison looked like a walking junkyard. In the race of life, Harrison carried three hundred pounds.

And to offset his good looks, the H-G men required that he wear at all times a red rubber ball for a nose, keep his eyebrows shaved off, and cover his even white teeth with black caps at snaggle-tooth random.

"If you see this boy," said the ballerina, "do not—I repeat, do not— try to reason with him."

There was the shriek of a door being torn from its hinges.

Screams and barking cries of consternation came from the television set. The photograph of Harrison Bergeron on the screen jumped again and again, as though dancing to the tune of an earthquake.

George Bergeron correctly identified the earthquake, and well he might have—for many was the time his own home had danced to the same crashing tune. "My God—" said George, "that must be Harrison!"

The realization was blasted from his mind instantly by the sound of an automobile collision in his head.

When George could open his eyes again, the photograph of Harrison was gone. A living, breathing Harrison filled the screen.

Clanking, clownish, and huge, Harrison stood in the center of the studio. The knob of the uprooted studio door was still in his hand. Ballerinas, technicians, musicians, and announcers cowered on their knees before him, expecting to die.

"I am the Emperor!" cried Harrison. "Do you hear? I am the Emperor! Everybody must do what I say at once!" He stamped his foot and the studio shook.

"Even as I stand here—" he bellowed, "crippled, hobbled, sickened—I am a greater ruler than any man who ever lived! Now watch me become what I *can* become!"

Harrison tore the straps of his handicap harness like wet tissue paper, tore straps guaranteed to support five thousand pounds.

Harrison's scrap-iron handicaps crashed to the floor.

Harrison thrust his thumbs under the bar of the padlock that secured his head harness. The bar snapped like celery. Harrison smashed his headphones and spectacles against the wall.

He flung away his rubber-ball nose, revealed a man that would have awed Thor, the god of thunder.

"I shall now select my Empress!" he said, looking down on the cowering people. "Let the first woman who dares rise to her feet claim her mate and her throne!"

A moment passed, and then a ballerina arose, swaying like a willow.

Harrison plucked the mental handicap from her ear, snapped off her physical handicaps with marvellous delicacy. Last of all, he removed her mask.

She was blindingly beautiful.

"Now—" said Harrison, taking her hand, "shall we show the people the meaning of the word dance? Music!" he commanded.

The musicians scrambled back into their chairs, and Harrison stripped them of their handicaps, too. "Play your best," he told them, "and I'll make you barons and dukes and earls."

The music began. It was normal at first—cheap, silly, false. But Harrison snatched two musicians from their chairs, waved them like batons as he sang the music as he wanted it played. He slammed them back into their chairs.

The music began again and was much improved.

Harrison and his Empress merely listened to the music for a while—listened gravely, as though synchronizing their heartbeats with it.

They shifted their weights to their toes.

Harrison placed his big hands on the girl's tiny waist, letting her sense the weightlessness that would soon be hers.

And then, in an explosion of joy and grace, into the air they sprang!

Not only were the laws of the land abandoned, but the law of gravity and the laws of motion as well.

They reeled, whirled, swiveled, flounced, capered, gamboled, and spun.

They leaped like deer on the moon.

The studio ceiling was thirty feet high, but each leap brought the dancers nearer to it.

It became their obvious intention to kiss the ceiling.

They kissed it.

And then, neutralizing gravity with love and pure will, they remained suspended in air inches below the ceiling, and they kissed each other for a long, long time.

It was then that Diana Moon Glampers, the Handicapper General, came into the studio with a double-barreled ten-gauge shotgun. She fired twice, and the Emperor and the Empress were dead before they hit the floor.

Diana Moon Glampers loaded the gun again. She aimed it at the musicians and told them they had ten seconds to get their handicaps back on.

It was then that the Bergerons' television tube burned out.

Hazel turned to comment about the blackout to George. But George had gone out into the kitchen for a can of beer.

George came back in with the beer, paused while a handicap signal shook him up. And then he sat down again. "You been crying?" he said to Hazel.

"Yup," she said.

"What about?" he said.

"I forget," she said. "Something real sad on television."

"What was it?" he said.

"It's all kind of mixed up in my mind," said Hazel.

"Forget sad things," said George.

"I always do," said Hazel.

"That's my girl," said George. He winced. There was the sound of a rivetting gun in his head.

"Gee—I could tell that one was a doozy," said Hazel.

"You can say that again," said George.

"Gee—" said Hazel, "I could tell that one was a doozy."

QUESTIONS

1. This story might seem rather believable until Vonnegut writes, "Not only were the laws of the land abandoned, but the law of gravity and the laws of motion as well." Why do you feel Vonnegut chose to so completely abandon reality at this point?

2. In what ways does the "Handicapper General" already function in our lives?

3. Discuss the difference between everyone being "average" and everyone being "equal."

4. Could this story be considered as a parable concerning both man's unconquerable will and the persistence of beauty? Or do we harm the story's humor when we take it too seriously?

The Green Hills of Earth

Robert A. Heinlein

This is the story of Rhysling, the Blind Singer of the Spaceways
—but not the official version. You sang his words in school:

> "I pray for one last landing
> On the globe that gave me birth;
> Let me rest my eyes on the fleecy skies
> And the cool, green hills of Earth."

Or perhaps you sang in French, or German. Or it might have been Es-
peranto, while Terra's rainbow banner rippled over your head.

The language does not matter—it was certainly an *Earth* tongue. No
one has ever translated *"Green Hills"* into the lisping Venerian speech;
no Martian ever croaked and whispered it in the dry corridors. This is
ours. We of Earth have exported everything from Hollywood crawlies to
synthetic radioactives, but this belongs solely to Terra, and to her sons
and daughters wherever they may be.

We have all heard many stories of Rhysling. You may even be one of
the many who have sought degrees, or acclaim, by scholarly evaluations
of his published works—*Songs of the Spaceways, The Grand Canal, and
other Poems, High and Far,* and *"UP SHIP!"*

Nevertheless, although you have sung his songs and read his verses, in
school and out your whole life, it is at least an even money bet—unless
you are a spaceman yourself—that you have never even heard of most of
Rhysling's unpublished songs, such items as *Since the Pusher Met My
Cousin, That Red-Headed Venusburg Gal, Keep Your Pants On, Skipper,* or *A Space Suit Built for Two.*

Nor can we quote them in a family magazine.

Rhysling's reputation was protected by a careful literary executor and
by the happy chance that he was never interviewed. *Songs of the Spaceways* appeared the week he died; when it became a best seller, the publicity stories about him were pieced together from what people remembered about him plus the highly colored handouts from his publishers.

The resulting traditional picture of Rhysling is about as authentic as
George Washington's hatchet or King Alfred's cakes.

In truth you would not have wanted him in your parlor; he was not socially acceptable. He had a permanent case of sun itch, which he scratched continually, adding nothing to his negligible beauty.

Van der Voort's portrait of him for the Harriman Centennial edition of his works shows a figure of high tragedy, a solemn mouth, sightless eyes concealed by black silk bandage. He was never solemn! His mouth was always open, singing, grinning, drinking, or eating. The bandage was any rag, usually dirty. After he lost his sight he became less and less neat about his person.

"Noisy" Rhysling was a jetman, second class, with eyes as good as yours, when he signed on for a loop trip to the Jovian asteroids in the R.S. *Goshawk*. The crew signed releases for everything in those days; a Lloyd's associate would have laughed in your face at the notion of insuring a spaceman. The Space Precautionary Act had never been heard of, and the Company was responsible only for wages, if and when. Half the ships that went further than Luna City never came back. Spacemen did not care; by preference they signed for shares, and any one of them would have bet you that he could jump from the 200th floor of Harriman Tower and ground safely, if you offered him three to two and allowed him rubber heels for the landing.

Jetmen were the most carefree of the lot and the meanest. Compared with them the masters, the radarmen, and the astrogators (there were no supers or stewards in those days) were gentle vegetarians. Jetmen knew too much. The others trusted the skill of the captain to get them down safely; jetmen knew that skill was useless against the blind and fitful devils chained inside their rocket motors.

The *Goshawk* was the first of Harriman's ships to be converted from chemical fuel to atomic power-piles—or rather the first that did not blow up. Rhysling knew her well; she was an old tub that had plied the Luna City run, Supra-New York space station to Leyport and back, before she was converted for deep space. He had worked the Luna run in her and had been along on the first deep space trip, Drywater on Mars—and back, to everyone's surprise.

He should have made chief engineer by the time he signed for the Jovian loop trip, but, after the Drywater pioneer trip, he had been fired, blacklisted, and grounded at Luna City for having spent his time writing a chorus and several verses at a time when he should have been watching his gauges. The song was the infamous *The Skipper is a Father to his Crew*, with the uproariously unprintable final couplet.

The blacklist did not bother him. He won an accordion from a Chinese barkeep in Luna City by cheating at one-thumb and thereafter kept going by singing to the miners for drinks and tips until the rapid attrition in spacemen caused the Company agent there to give him another chance. He kept his nose clean on the Luna run for a year or two, got back into deep space, helped give Venusburg its original ripe reputation, strolled the banks of the Grand Canal when a second colony was established at the ancient Martian capital, and froze his toes and ears on the second trip to Titan.

Things moved fast in those days. Once the power-pile drive was accepted the number of ships that put out from the Luna-Terra system was limited only by the availability of crews. Jetmen were scarce; the shielding was cut to a minimum to save weight and few married men cared to risk possible exposure to radioactivity. Rhysling did not want to be a father, so jobs were always open to him during the golden days of the claiming boom. He crossed and recrossed the system, singing the doggerel that boiled up in his head and chording it out on his accordion.

The master of the *Goshawk* knew him; Captain Hicks had been astrogator on Rhysling's first trip in her. "Welcome home, Noisy," Hicks had greeted him. "Are you sober, or shall I sign the book for you?"

"You can't get drunk on the bug juice they sell here, Skipper." He signed and went below, lugging his accordion.

Ten minutes later he was back. "Captain," he stated darkly, "that number two jet ain't fit. The cadmium dampers are warped."

"Why tell me? Tell the Chief."

"I did, but he says they will do. He's wrong."

The captain gestured at the book. "Scratch out your name and scram. We raise ship in thirty minutes."

Rhysling looked at him, shrugged, and went below again.

It is a long climb to the Jovian planetoids; a Hawk-class clunker had to blast for three watches before going into free flight. Rhysling had the second watch. Damping was done by hand then, with a multiplying vernier and a danger gauge. When the gauge showed red, he tried to correct it— no luck.

Jetmen don't wait; that's why they are jetmen. He slapped the emergency discover and fished at the hot stuff with the tongs. The lights went out, he went right ahead. A jetman has to know his power room the way your tongue knows the inside of your mouth.

He sneaked a quick look over the top of the lead baffle when the lights went out. The blue radioactive glow did not help him any; he jerked his head back and went on fishing by touch.

When he was done he called over the tube, "Number two jet out. And for crissake get me some light down here!"

There was light—the emergency circuit—but not for him. The blue radioactive glow was the last thing his optic nerve ever responded to.

II

"As Time and Space come bending back to shape this star-specked
scene,
The tranquil tears of tragic joy still spread their silver sheen;
Along the Grand Canal still soar the fragile Towers of Truth;
Their fairy grace defends this place of Beauty, calm and couth.

Bone-tired the race that raised the Towers, forgotten are their lores;
Long gone the gods who shed the tears that lap these crystal shores.
Slow beats the time-worn heart of Mars beneath this icy sky;
The thin air whispers voicelessly that all who live must die—

"Yet still the lacy Spires of Truth sing Beauty's madrigal
And she herself will ever dwell along the Grand Canal!"

from THE GRAND CANAL, by permission of
Lux Transcriptions, Ltd., London and Luna City

On the swing back they set Rhysling down on Mars at Drywater; the
boys passed the hat and the skipper kicked in a half month's pay. That
was all—*finish*—just another space bum who had not had the good fortune to finish it off when his luck ran out. He holed up with the prospec-
tors and archeologists at How-Far? for a month or so, and could probably have stayed forever in exchange for his songs and his accordion
playing. But spacemen die if they stay in one place; he hooked a crawler
over to Drywater again and thence to Marsopolis.

The capital was well into its boom; the processing plants lined the
Grand Canal on both sides and roiled the ancient waters with the filth of
the run-off. This was before the Tri-Planet Treaty forbade disturbing cultural relics for commerce; half the slender, fairylike towers had been torn
down, and others were disfigured to adapt them as pressurized buildings
for Earthmen.

Now Rhysling had never seen any of these changes and no one described them to him; when he "saw" Marsopolis again, he visualized it as
it had been, before it was rationalized for trade. His memory was good.
He stood on the riparian esplanade where the ancient great of Mars had
taken their ease and saw its beauty spreading out before his blinded eyes
—ice blue plain of water unmoved by tide, untouched by breeze, and
reflecting serenely the sharp, bright stars of the Martian sky, and beyond
the water the lacy buttresses and flying towers of an architecture too delicate for our rumbling, heavy planet.

The result was *Grand Canal.*

The subtle change in his orientation which enabled him to see beauty at Marsopolis where beauty was not now began to affect his whole life. All women became beautiful to him. He knew them by their voices and fitted their appearances to the sounds. It is a mean spirit indeed who will speak to a blind man other than in gentle friendliness; scolds who had given their husbands no peace sweetened their voices to Rhysling.

It populated his world with beautiful women and gracious men. *Dark Star Passing, Berenice's Hair, Death Song of a Wood's Colt,* and his other love songs of the wanderers, the womenless men of space, where the direct result of the fact that his conceptions were unsullied by tawdry truths. It mellowed his approach, changed his doggerel to verse, and sometimes even to poetry.

He had plenty of time to think now, time to get all the lovely words just so, and to worry a verse until it sang true in his head. The monotonous beat of *Jet Song*–

> When the field is clear, the reports all seen,
> When the lock sighs shut, when the lights wink green,
> When the check-off's done, when it's time to pray,
> When the Captain nods, when she blasts away—

> Hear the jets!
> Hear them snarl at your back
> When you're stretched on the rack;
> Feel your ribs clamp your chest,
> Feel your neck grind its rest.
> Feel the pain in your ship,
> Feel her strain in their grip.
> Feel her rise! Feel her drive!
> Straining steel, come alive,
> On her jets!

—came to him not while he himself was a jetman but later while he was hitchhiking from Mars to Venus and sitting out a watch with an old shipmate.

At Venusburg he sang his new songs and some of the old, in the bars. Someone would start a hat around for him; it would come back with a minstrel's usual take doubled or tripled in recognition of the gallant spirit behind the bandaged eyes.

It was an easy life. Any space port was his home and any ship his private carriage. No skipper cared to refuse to lift the extra mass of blind Rhysling and his squeeze box; he shuttled from Venusburg to Leyport to Drywater to New Shanghai, or back again, as the whim took him.

He never went closer to Earth than Supra-New York Space Station. Even when signing the contract for *Songs of the Spaceways* he made his mark in a cabin-class liner somewhere between Luna City and Ganymede. Horowitz, the original publisher, was aboard for a second honeymoon and heard Rhysling sing at a ship's party. Horowitz knew a good thing for the publishing trade when he heard it; the entire contents of *Songs* were sung directly into the tape in the communications room of the ship before he let Rhysling out of his sight. The next three volumes were squeezed out of Rhysling at Venusburg, where Horowitz had sent an agent to keep him liquored up until he had sung all he could remember.

UP SHIP! is not certainly authentic Rhysling throughout. Much of it is Rhysling's, no doubt, and *Jet Song* is unquestionably his, but most of the verses were collected after his death from people who had known him during his wanderings.

The Green Hills of Earth grew through twenty years. The earliest form we know about was composed before Rhysling was blinded, during a drinking bout with some of the indentured men on Venus. The verses were concerned mostly with the things the labor clients intended to do back on Earth if and when they ever managed to pay their bounties and thereby be allowed to go home. Some of the stanzas were vulgar, some were not, but the chorus was recognizably that of *Green Hills.*

We know exactly where the final form of *Green Hills* came from, and when.

There was a ship in at Venus Ellis Isle which was scheduled for the direct jump from there to Great Lakes, Illinois. She was the old *Falcon,* youngest of the Hawk class and the first ship to apply the Harriman Trust's new policy of extrafare express service between Earth cities and any colony with scheduled stops.

Rhysling decided to ride her back to Earth. Perhaps his own song had gotten under his skin—or perhaps he just hankered to see his native Ozarks one more time.

The Company no longer permitted deadheads; Rhysling knew this but it never occurred to him that the ruling might apply to him. He was getting old, for a spaceman, and just a little matter of fact about his privileges. Not senile—he simply knew that he was one of the landmarks in space, along with Halley's Comet, the Rings, and Brewster's Ridge. He walked in the crew's port, went below, and made himself at home in the first empty acceleration couch.

The Captain found him there while making a last minute tour of his ship. "What are you doing here?" he demanded.

"Dragging it back to Earth, Captain," Rhysling needed no eyes to see a skipper's four stripes.

"You can't drag in this ship; you know the rules. Shake a leg and get out of here. We raise ship at once." The Captain was young; he had come up after Rhysling's active time, but Rhysling knew the type—five years at Harriman Hall with only cadet practice trips instead of solid, deep space experience. The two men did not touch in background nor spirit; space was changing.

"Now, Captain, you wouldn't begrudge an old man a trip home."

The officer hesitated—several of the crew had stopped to listen. "I can't do it. 'Space Precautionary Act, Clause Six: No one shall enter space save as a licensed member of a crew of a chartered vessel, or as a paying passenger of such a vessel under such regulations as may be issued pursuant to this act.' Up you get and out you go."

Rhysling lolled back, his hands under his head. "If I've goot to go, I'm damned if I'll walk. Carry me."

The Captain bit his lip and said, "Master-at-Arms! Have this man removed."

The ship's policeman fixed his eyes on the overhead struts. "Can't rightly do it, Captain. I've sprained my shoulder." The other crew members, present a moment before, had faded into the bulkhead paint.

"Well, get a working party!"

"Aye, aye, sir." He, too, went away.

Rhysling spoke again. "Now look, Skipper—let's not have any hard feelings about this. You've got an out to carry me if you want to—the 'Distressed Spaceman' clause."

" 'Distressed Spaceman,' my eye! You're no distressed spaceman; you're a space-lawyer. I know who you are; you've been bumming around the system for years. Well, you won't do it in my ship. That clause was intended to succor men who had missed their ships, not to let a man drag free all over space."

"Well, now, Captain, can you properly say I haven't missed my ship? I've never been back home since my last trip as a signed-on crew member. The law says I can have a trip back."

"But that was years ago. You've used up your chance."

"Have I now? The clause doesn't say a word about how soon a man has to take his trip back; it just says he's got it coming to him. Go look it up, Skipper. If I'm wrong, I'll not only walk out on my two legs, I'll beg your humble pardon in front of your crew. Go on—look it up. Be a sport."

Rhysling could feel the man's glare, but he turned and stomped out of the compartment. Rhysling knew that he had used his blindness to place the Captain in an impossible position, but this did not embarrass Rhysling—he rather enjoyed it.

Ten minutes later the siren sounded, he heard the orders on the bull horn for Up-Stations. When the soft sighing of the locks and the slight pressure change in his ears let him know that take-off was imminent he got up and shuffled down to the power room, as he wanted to be near the jets when they blasted off. He needed no one to guide him in any ship of the Hawk class.

Trouble started during the first watch. Rhysling had been lounging in the inspector's chair, fiddling with the keys of his accordion and trying out a new version of *Green Hills.*

> "Let me breathe unrationed air again
> Where there's no lack nor dearth

And something, something, something 'Earth' "—it would not come out right. He tried again.

> "Let the sweet fresh breezes heal me
> As they rove around the girth
> Of our lovely mother planet,
> Of the cool green hills of Earth."

That was better, he thought. "How do you like that, Archie?" he asked over the muted roar.

"Pretty good. Give out with the whole thing." Archie Macdougal, Chief Jetman, was an old friend, both spaceside and in bars; he had been an apprentice under Rhysling many years and millions of miles back.

Rhysling obliged, then said, "You youngsters have got it soft. Everything automatic. When I was twisting her tail you had to stay awake."

"You still have to stay awake." They fell to talking shop and Macdougal showed him the direct response damping rig which had replaced the manual vernier control which Rhysling had used. Rhysling felt out the controls and asked questions until he was familiar with the new installation. It was his conceit that he was still a jetman and that his present occupation as a troubadour was simply an expedient during one of the fusses with the company that any man could get into.

"I see you still have the old hand damping plates installed," he remarked, his agile fingers flitting over the equipment.

"All except the links. I unshipped them because they obscure the dials."

"You ought to have them shipped. You might need them."

"Oh, I don't know. I think—" Rhysling never did find out what Macdougal thought for it was at that moment the trouble tore loose. Macdougal caught it square, a blast of radioactivity that burned him down where he stood.

Rhysling sensed what had happened. Automatic reflexes of old habit came out. He slapped the discover and rang the alarm to the control room simultaneously. Then he remembered the unshipped links. He had to grope until he found them, while trying to keep as low as he could to get maximum benefit from the baffles. Nothing but the links bothered him as to location. The place was as light to him as any place could be;

he knew every spot, every control, the way he knew the keys of his accordion.

"Power room! Power room! What's the alarm?"

"Stay out!" Rhysling shouted. "The place is 'hot.' " He could feel it on his face and in his bones, like desert sunshine.

The links he got into place, after cursing someone, anyone, for having failed to rack the wrench he needed. Then he commenced trying to reduce the trouble by hand. It was a long job and ticklish. Presently he decided that the jet would have to be spilled, pile and all.

First he reported. "Control!"

"Control aye aye!"

"Spilling jet three—emergency."

"Is this Macdougal?"

"Macdougal is dead. This is Rhysling, on watch. Stand by to record."

There was no answer; dumbfounded the Skipper may have been, but he could not interfere in a power room emergency. He had the ship to consider, and the passengers and crew. The doors had to stay closed.

The Captain must have been still more surprised at what Rhysling sent for record. It was:

> "We rot in the molds of Venus,
> We retch at her tainted breath.
> Foul are her flooded jungles,
> Crawling with unclean death."

Rhysling went on cataloguing the Solar System as he worked, "—harsh bright soil of Luna—," "—Saturn's rainbow rings—," "—the frozen night of Titan—," all the while opening and spilling the jet and fishing it clean. He finished with an alternate chorus—

> "We've tried each spinning space mote
> And reckoned its true worth:
> Take us back again to the homes of men
> On the cool, green hills of Earth."

—then, almost absentmindedly remembered to tack on his revised first verse:

> "The arching sky is calling
> Spacemen back to their trade.
> *All hands! Stand by! Free falling!*
> And the lights below us fade.
> Out ride the sons of Terra,
> Far drives the thundering jet,
> Up leaps the race of Earthmen,
> Out, far, and onward yet—"

The ship was safe now and ready to limp home shy one jet. As for himself, Rhysling was not so sure. That "sunburn" seemed sharp, he thought. He was unable to see the bright, rosy fog in which he worked but he knew it was there. He went on with the business of flushing the air out through the outer valve, repeating it several times to permit the level of radioaction to drop to something a man might stand under suitable armor. While he did this he sent one more chorus, the last bit of authentic Rhysling that ever could be:

> "We pray for one last landing
> On the globe that gave us birth;
> Let us rest our eyes on fleecy skies
> And the cool, green hills of Earth."

QUESTIONS

1. What are the qualities that go toward the creation of a hero?
2. Why does Heinlein write of a *blind* poet?
3. Discuss Rhysling's songs as they compare with others that use references to space subjects.
4. Is this story typical of the way the SF writer humanizes space?
5. Discuss the romance of space-traveling. What kinds of new art forms are space voyages likely to motivate? Do new experiences necessarily demand new art forms?

Tithonus

D. M. Thomas

And finally, ladies and gentlemen, perhaps in his quiet way
As exciting as many of our other exhibits,
Just group around and let me introduce you to
Our very first immortal *homo sapiens.*
Yes, here we have—but a word of caution, sir,
These tubes are delicate—the first *immortal.*
Let that word chime. Forget Jesus, forget
—Well, all the other man-gods of pre-history,
And fix your eyes instead on Edgar L. Cummings
As he floats here, bottled greyly in solution.   10
Death, Thou art Dead!
And isn't that typical scientific hooh-hah for something
So unimpressive—a mere pulsing sponge!
I don't blame you— But believe me when I say
That all Man's dreams of immortality,
—Penny for old Charon, them pearly gates,
Or some lotus-isle where falls not rain or hail—
Are here made coldly but thrillingly *fact.*
He just can't die! . . . —oh, barring some cosmic disaster.
Our Institute, you've seen, 's impregnable—   20
Fire-proof, bomb-proof, radiation-proof,
Sterilized; and when in a few billion billion years
Our sun threatens to blow up, he'll be whipped off
Like all the rest, to some more genial star.

Professor Wiggins will perhaps fill you in on
His case-history later—
She's rather busy fussing over his welfare as usual!
Miss Wiggins, my colleague in the Department of Tithonics,
Was actually present twenty years ago,

In student capacity, when Professor Joseph performed ⁣ ⁣ ⁣ 30
The historic excision. Briefly though: Edgar L. Cummings,
Born 1961, transfigured, so to speak, 2025
While dying, in coma, of arterio-sclerosis;
No relative surviving to worry about names,
Re-christened Tithonus, after an old Greek story
Which you will find briefly summarized on this plaque.
Unfortunately we can't provide an Eos,
Unless indeed Miss Wiggins—good EVENING, professor!—
Could be said to fill that category . . . She certainly clucks
Tenderly over him all hours of the day and night, ⁣ ⁣ ⁣ 40
Spends less and less time at her East Side apartment,
Burns midnight fluorescence rivalling the splendour
Of her own auburn—*Why Dawn, I believe you're BLUSHING!*
Well, well—! many a true word in jest, folks!
You'll bear me out, we've *proved* a real Heart beats
Under that tall and intellectual white,
That those spiky heels take the strain of Feminine passions! . . .
What's that? you'll get me later? . . . I'll look forward . . . !
Seriously, ladies and gentlemen, I know the question
You all must be dying to pose: in what queer sense ⁣ ⁣ ⁣ 50
Can this blob of matter be called a human being,
Whether Tithonus or Edgar L. Cummings.
In answer: in the *only* sense: he thinks,
He feels himself to be; a continent,
Lapped everywhere by our amniotic flood,
He contains the mystery of his mystery,
Is infinitely more important to himself
Than all the infinitely more important cosmos
He only senses over a few square inches.
All that he's lost was excrescence—desirable, ⁣ ⁣ ⁣ 60
To see, hear, move, speak—but not essential;
You lose a nail—not YOU; your legs—a pity;
But YOU remain, clenched in the brittle skull.
Here fed with tubers, that's the only difference.

Take a crane-fly wandering in from the river,
Settling on a door you've sprayed with paint.
One leg goes, in the frenzy to escape
—Two more—a wing—thick pencil scrawls

Grotesque millimetres away; now it knows
Not even God could separate paint from crane-fly   70
And leave enough of the latter. So it subsides,
Despairing. When you come along—my God, the paint!—
You expect it to welcome the tenderly offered rag,
The quick-crunch-and-it's-over. But no, it fights!
It tries to cringe. Not that it has any illusions
About ever getting away from this obscenity, it knows
The kindness of your gesture, but it just CAN'T
But try to protect its tiny brain from your pity.
Its little ego shrieks silently, LEAVE ME INTACT!
YOU DON'T KNOW HOW VITAL I AM.   80
Here, in this case, we've kept that ego intact.
I think I used the word excision,
As though what we cut *out* was expendable;
Call it rather a vast *amputation*
Of the body hacked clear away from the brain.
The *man* remains: meditates, desires, remembers.

Just to prove our point, watch now while Miss Wiggins
Stimulates a memory-cell. (Don't worry, he likes it;
Even when we happen to hit on a *bad* memory
He still enjoys the emotive exercise.)   90
Now . . . Watch . . . Keep one eye on the electro-
Encephalograph—WOOSH! See how the pencil goes
—Boy!—shooting up and up in fantastic hieroglyphics;
We've obviously hit on something pretty big.
That cell-twitch we gave him means that he's now re-living
—Down to the very colours, textures of garments—
A moment in his past: living it more *intensely*
Almost, in that memory-cell, than he did at the time.
A green coat *feels* itself slipping to the floor!
Maybe he's walking down a lane with his first girl,   100
Stepping carefully over a puddle, the scent of rain
Mixing with hers, while a blackberry branch whips
Across his leg, or maybe bending over a cot,
Yellow, with elephants pasted on it,
Where his son's fighting for breath against pneumonia.
Here's where the absence of speech, etcetera,
Proves a barrier. We never get through to him, or vice versa.

This memory is obviously emotional, but whether
Lust, anger, fear—your guess is as good as ours.
Our stubborn de-cipherers will wrestle with it   110
Seeking as always some clue to find the verbal
Equivalent, break the code. It's a helluva problem, *but*—
Sooner or later they'll do it.
The last twenty years, of course, haven't been exactly rich
In memories, except of his own thought-processes.
(These violent scribbles certainly relate back to
An earlier period.)
                                How far, you ask, is he
Aware of his situation? Well, obviously
He *can't* be aware of it at all, lacking
The normal apparati of discovery.   120
He only knows the contiguous bloodwarm
Solution, and our various probes—but this
Again is relative; aren't we, too, blissfully
Ignorant of our environment, outside
The (compared with infinity) contiguous
Galaxies a billion light-years away?
I admit the idea seems rather gruesome at first,
But he's happy because he *himself* exists.
"Ay, but to die, and go we know not where!"
—That's something he'll NEVER have to experience.   130
I hope and believe he'd thank us—no, that's an under-
Statement—if he could,
And say moreover how proud he is being
Our proto-immortal, paving the way for ALL
To escape even three days' extinction. What a niche
In history! Why, may I end by making the outrageous
Suggestion that already our grateful Tithonus
Is gropingly beginning to sense
The presence somewhere *"out there"* of a Miss Wiggins,
As she bends over: *senses* the auburn angel   140
Who watched Prof. Joseph roll back the stone
Before the stone was needed? That may sound a crazy
Hypothesis; Dr Reiner, our E.S.P. expert,
Reckons ten thousand years at least before
Our guest starts to develop his "sixth sense,"
But I've an idea this may be under-estimating
The powers of human adaptability.

QUESTIONS

1. What accounts for the horror of this poem?
2. What devices does Thomas use to create sympathy for Tithonus?
3. How does this poem parody the concept of immortality?
4. Is there any "evil" in those who watch Tithonus?
5. Use this poem as a basis for discussing the responsibility of the scientist for his inventions and that of the doctor for his patients.

The Machine Stops

E. M. Forster

I

The Air-ship

Imagine, if you can, a small room, hexagonal in shape, like the cell of a bee. It is lighted neither by window nor by lamp, yet it is filled with a soft radiance. There are no apertures for ventilation, yet the air is fresh. There are no musical instruments, and yet, at the moment that my meditation opens, this room is throbbing with melodious sounds. An armchair is in the centre, by its side a reading-desk—that is all the furniture. And in the arm-chair there sits a swaddled lump of flesh—a woman, about five feet high, with a face as white as a fungus. It is to her that the little room belongs.

An electric bell rang.

The woman touched a switch and the music was silent.

"I suppose I must see who it is," she thought, and set her chair in motion. The chair, like the music, was worked by machinery, and it rolled her to the other side of the room, where the bell still rang importunately.

"Who is it?" she called. Her voice was irritable, for she had been interrupted often since the music began. She knew several thousand people; in certain directions human intercourse had advanced enormously.

But when she listened into the receiver, her white face wrinkled into smiles, and she said:

"Very well. Let us talk, I will isolate myself. I do not expect anything important will happen for the next five minutes—for I can give you fully five minutes, Kuno. Then I must deliver my lecture on 'Music during the Australian Period.'"

She touched the isolation knob, so that no one else could speak to her. Then she touched the lighting apparatus, and the little room was plunged into darkness.

"Be quick!" she called, her irritation returning. "Be quick, Kuno; here I am in the dark wasting my time."

But it was fully fifteen seconds before the round plate that she held in her hands began to glow. A faint blue light shot across it, darkening to purple, and presently she could see the image of her son, who lived on the other side of the earth, and he could see her.

"Kuno, how slow you are."

He smiled gravely.

"I really believe you enjoy dawdling."

"I have called you before, mother, but you were always busy or isolated. I have something particular to say."

"What is it, dearest boy? Be quick. Why could you not send it by pneumatic post?"

"Because I prefer saying such a thing. I want—"

"Well?"

"I want you to come and see me."

Vashti watched his face in the blue plate.

"But I can see you!" she exclaimed. "What more do you want?"

"I want to see you not through the Machine," said Kuno. "I want to speak to you not through the wearisome Machine."

"Oh, hush!" said his mother, vaguely shocked. "You mustn't say anything against the Machine."

"Why not?"

"One mustn't."

"You talk as if a god had made the Machine," cried the other. "I believe that you pray to it when you are unhappy. Men made it, do not forget that. Great men, but men. The Machine is much, but it is not everything. I see something like you in this plate, but I do not see you. I hear something like you through this telephone, but I do not hear you. That is why I want you to come. Come and stop with me. Pay me a visit, so that we can meet face to face, and talk about the hopes that are in my mind."

She replied that she could scarcely spare the time for a visit.

"The air-ship barely takes two days to fly between me and you."

"I dislike air-ships."

"Why?"

"I dislike seeing the horrible brown earth, and the sea, and the stars when it is dark. I get no ideas in an air-ship."

"I do not get them anywhere else."

"What kind of ideas can the air give you?"

He paused for an instant.

"Do you not know four big stars that form an oblong, and three stars close together in the middle of the oblong, and hanging from these stars, three other stars?"

"No, I do not. I dislike the stars. But did they give you an idea? How interesting; tell me."

"I had an idea that they were like a man."

"I do not understand."

"The four big stars are the man's shoulders and his knees. The three stars in the middle are like the belts that men wore once, and the three stars hanging are like a sword."

"A sword?"

"Men carried swords about with them, to kill animals and other men."

"It does not strike me as a very good idea, but it is certainly original. When did it come to you first?"

"In the air-ship—" He broke off, and she fancied that he looked sad. She could not be sure, for the Machine did not transmit *nuances* of expression. It only gave a general idea of people—an idea that was good enough for all practical purposes, Vashti thought. The imponderable bloom, declared by a discredited philosophy to be the actual essence of intercourse, was rightly ignored by the Machine, just as the imponderable bloom of the grape was ignored by the manufacturers of artificial fruit. Something "good enough" had long since been accepted by our race.

"The truth is," he continued, "that I want to see these stars again. They are curious stars. I want to see them not from the air-ship, but from the surface of the earth, as our ancestors did, thousands of years ago. I want to visit the surface of the earth."

She was shocked again.

"Mother, you must come, if only to explain to me what is the harm of visiting the surface of the earth."

"No harm," she replied, controlling herself. "But no advantage. The surface of the earth is only dust and mud, no life remains on it, and you would need a respirator, or the cold of the outer air would kill you. One dies immediately in the outer air."

"I know; of course I shall take all precautions."

"And besides—"

"Well?"

She considered, and chose her words with care. Her son had a queer temper, and she wished to dissuade him from the expedition.

"It is contrary to the spirit of the age," she asserted.

"Do you mean by that, contrary to the Machine?"

"In a sense, but—"

His image in the blue plate faded.

"Kuno!"

He had isolated himself.

For a moment Vashti felt lonely.

Then she generated the light, and the sight of her room, flooded with radiance and studded with electric buttons, revived her. There were buttons and switches everywhere—buttons to call for food, for music, for clothing. There was the hot-bath button, by pressure of which a basin of (imitation) marble rose out of the floor, filled to the brim with a warm deodorised liquid. There was the cold-bath button. There was the button that produced literature. And there were of course the buttons by which she communicated with her friends. The room, though it contained nothing, was in touch with all that she cared for in the world.

Vashti's next move was to turn off the isolation-switch, and all the accumulations of the last three minutes burst upon her. The room was filled with the noise of bells, and speaking-tubes. What was the new food like? Could she recommend it? Had she had any ideas lately? Might one tell her one's own ideas? Would she make an engagement to visit the public nurseries at an early date?—say this day month.

To most of these questions she replied with irritation—a growing quality in that accelerated age. She said that the new food was horrible. That she could not visit the public nurseries through press of engagements. That she had no ideas of her own but had just been told one—that four stars and three in the middle were like a man: she doubted there was much in it. Then she switched off her correspondents, for it was time to deliver her lecture on Australian music.

The clumsy system of public gatherings had been long since abandoned; neither Vashti nor her audience stirred from their rooms. Seated in her arm-chair she spoke, while they in their arm-chairs heard her, fairly well, and saw her, fairly well. She opened with a humorous account of music in the pre-Mongolian epoch, and went on to describe the great outburst of song that followed the Chinese conquest. Remote and primæval as were the methods of I-San-So and the Brisbane school, she yet felt (she said) that study of them might repay the musician of today: they had freshness; they had, above all, ideas.

Her lecture, which lasted ten minutes, was well received, and at its conclusion she and many of her audience listened to a lecture on the sea; there were ideas to be got from the sea; the speaker had donned a respirator and visited it lately. Then she fed, talked to many friends, had a bath, talked again, and summoned her bed.

The bed was not to her liking. It was too large, and she had a feeling for a small bed. Complaint was useless, for beds were of the same dimension all over the world, and to have had an alternative size would have involved vast alterations in the Machine. Vashti isolated herself—it was necessary, for neither day nor night existed under the ground—and reviewed all that had happened since she had summoned the bed last. Ideas? Scarcely any. Events—was Kuno's invitation an event?

By her side, on the little reading-desk, was a survival from the ages of litter—one book. This was the Book of the Machine. In it were instructions against every possible contingency. If she was hot or cold or dyspeptic or at loss for a word, she went to the book, and it told her which button to press. The Central Committee published it. In accordance with a growing habit, it was richly bound.

Sitting up in the bed, she took it reverently in her hands. She glanced round the glowing room as if some one might be watching her. Then, half ashamed, half joyful, she murmured "O Machine! O Machine!" and raised the volume to her lips. Thrice she kissed it, thrice inclined her head, thrice she felt the delirium of acquiescence. Her ritual performed, she turned to page 1367, which gave the times of the departure of the air-ships from the island in the southern hemisphere, under whose soil she lived, to the island in the northern hemisphere, wherunder lived her son.

She thought, "I have not the time."

She made the room dark and slept; she awoke and made the room light; she ate and exchanged ideas with her friends, and listened to music and attended lectures; she made the room dark and slept. Above her, beneath her, and around her, the Machine hummed eternally; she did not notice the noise, for she had been born with it in her ears. The earth, carrying her, hummed as it sped through silence, turning her now to the invisible sun, now to the invisible stars. She awoke and made the room light.

"Kuno!"

"I will not talk to you," he answered, "until you come."

"Have you been on the surface of the earth since we spoke last?"

His image faded.

Again she consulted the book. She became very nervous and lay back in her chair palpitating. Think of her as without teeth or hair. Presently she directed the chair to the wall, and pressed an unfamiliar button. The wall swung apart slowly. Through the opening she saw a tunnel that curved slightly, so that its goal was not visible. Should she go to see her son, here was the beginning of the journey.

Of course she knew all about the communication-system. There was nothing mysterious in it. She would summon a car and it would fly with her down the tunnel until it reached the lift that communicated with the air-ship station: the system had been in use for many, many years, long before the universal establishment of the Machine. And of course she had studied the civilisation that had immediately preceded her own—the civilisation that had mistaken the functions of the system, and had used it for bringing people to things, instead of for bringing things to people. Those funny old days, when men went for change of air instead of changing the air in their rooms! And yet—she was frightened of the tunnel: she had not seen it since her last child was born. It curved—but not quite as she remembered; it was brilliant—but not quite as brilliant as a lecturer had suggested. Vashti was seized with the terrors of direct experience. She shrank back into the room, and the wall closed up again.

"Kuno," she said, "I cannot come to see you. I am not well."

Immediately an enormous apparatus fell on to her out of the ceiling, a thermometer was automatically inserted between her lips, a stethoscope was automatically laid upon her heart. She lay powerless. Cool pads soothed her forehead. Kuno had telegraphed to her doctor.

So the human passions still blundered up and down in the Machine. Vashti drank the medicine that the doctor projected into her mouth, and the machinery retired into the ceiling. The voice of Kuno was heard asking how she felt.

"Better." Then with irritation: "But why do you not come to me instead?"

"Because I cannot leave this place."

"Why?"

"Because, any moment, something tremendous may happen."

"Have you been on the surface of the earth yet?"

"Not yet."

"Then what is it?"

"I will not tell you through the Machine."

She resumed her life.

But she thought of Kuno as a baby, his birth, his removal to the public nurseries, her one visit to him there, his visits to her—visits which stopped when the Machine had assigned him a room on the other side of the earth. "Parents, duties of," said the book of the Machine, "cease at the moment of birth. P. 422327483." True, but there was something special about Kuno—indeed there had been something special about all her children—and, after all, she must brave the journey if he desired it. And "something tremendous might happen." What did that mean? The nonsense of a youthful man, no doubt, but she must go. Again she pressed the unfamiliar button, again the wall swung back, and she saw the tunnel that curved out of sight. Clasping the Book, she rose, tottered on to the platform, and summoned the car. Her room closed behind her: the journey to the northern hemisphere had begun.

Of course it was perfectly easy. The car approached and in it she found arm-chairs exactly like her own. When she signalled, it stopped, and she tottered into the lift. One other passenger was in the lift, the first fellow creature she had seen face to face for months. Few travelled in these days, for, thanks to the advance of science, the earth was exactly alike all over. Rapid intercourse, from which the previous civilisation had hoped so much, had ended by defeating itself. What was the good of going to Pekin when it was just like Shrewsbury? Why return to Shrewsbury when it would be just like Pekin? Men seldom moved their bodies; all unrest was concentrated in the soul.

The air-ship service was a relic from the former age. It was kept up, because it was easier to keep it up than to stop it or to diminish it, but it now far exceeded the wants of the population. Vessel after vessel would rise from the vomitories of Rye or of Christchurch (I use the antique names), would sail into the crowded sky, and would draw up at the wharves of the south—empty. So nicely adjusted was the system, so independent of meteorology, that the sky, whether calm or cloudy, resembled a vast kaleidoscope whereon the same patterns periodically recurred. The ship on which Vashti sailed started now at sunset, now at dawn. But always, as it passed above Rheims, it would neighbour the ship that served between Helsingfors and the Brazils, and, every third time it surmounted the Alps, the fleet of Palermo would cross its track behind. Night and day, wind and storm, tide and earthquake, impeded man no longer. He had harnessed Leviathan. All the old literature, with its praise of Nature, and its fear of Nature, rang false as the prattle of a child.

Yet as Vashti saw the vast flank of the ship, stained with exposure to the outer air, her horror of direct experience returned. It was not quite like the air-ship in the cinematophote. For one thing it smelt—not strongly or unpleasantly, but it did smell, and with her eyes shut she should have known that a new thing was close to her. Then she had to walk to it from the lift, had to submit to glances from the other passengers. The man in front dropped his Book—no great matter, but it disquieted them all. In the rooms, if the Book was dropped, the floor raised it mechanically, but the gangway to the air-ship was not so prepared, and the sacred volume lay motionless. They stopped—the thing was unforeseen—and the man, instead of picking up his property, felt the muscles of his arm to see how they had failed him. Then some one actually said with direct utterance: "We shall be late"—and they trooped on board, Vashti treading on the pages as she did so.

Inside, her anxiety increased. The arrangements were old-fashioned and rough. There was even a female attendant, to whom she would have to announce her wants during the voyage. Of course a revolving platform ran the length of the boat, but she was expected to walk from it to her cabin. Some cabins were better than others, and she did not get the best. She thought the attendant had been unfair, and spasms of rage shook her. The glass valves had closed, she could not go back. She saw, at the end of the vestibule, the lift in which she had ascended going quietly up and down, empty. Beneath those corridors of shining tiles were rooms, tier below tier, reaching far into the earth, and in each room there sat a human being, eating, or sleeping, or producing ideas. And buried deep in the hive was her own room. Vashti was afraid.

"O Machine! O Machine!" she murmured, and caressed her Book, and was comforted.

Then the sides of the vestibule seemed to melt together, as do the passages that we see in dreams, the lift vanished, the Book that had been dropped slid to the left and vanished, polished tiles rushed by like a stream of water, there was a slight jar, and the air-ship, issuing from its tunnel, soared above the waters of a tropical ocean.

It was night. For a moment she saw the coast of Sumatra edged by the phosphorescence of waves, and crowned by lighthouses, still sending forth their disregarded beams. These also vanished, and only the stars distracted her. They were not motionless, but swayed to and fro above her head, thronging out of one skylight into another, as if the universe and not the air-ship was careening. And, as often happens on clear nights, they seemed now to be in perspective, now on a plane; now piled tier beyond tier into the infinite heavens, now concealing infinity, a roof limiting for ever the visions of men. In either case they seemed intolerable. "Are we to travel in the dark?" called the passengers angrily, and the attendant, who had been careless, generated the light, and pulled down the blinds of pliable metal. When the air-ships had been built, the desire to look direct at things still lingered in the world. Hence the extraordinary number of skylights and windows, and the proportionate discomfort to those who were civilised and refined. Even in Vashti's cabin one star peeped through a flaw in the blind, and after a few hours' uneasy slumber, she was disturbed by an unfamiliar glow, which was the dawn.

Quick as the ship had sped westwards, the earth had rolled eastwards quicker still, and had dragged back Vashti and her companions towards the sun. Science could prolong the night, but only for a little, and those high hopes of neutralising the earth's diurnal revolution had passed, together with hopes that were possibly higher. To "keep pace with the sun," or even to outstrip it, had been the aim of the civilisation preceding this. Racing aeroplanes had been built for the purpose, capable of enormous speed, and steered by the greatest intellects of the epoch. Round the globe they went, round and round, westward, westward, round and round, amidst humanity's applause. In vain. The globe went eastward quicker still, horrible accidents occurred, and the Committee of the Machine, at the time rising into prominence, declared the pursuit illegal, unmechanical, and punishable by Homelessness.

Of Homelessness more will be said later.

Doubtless the Committee was right. Yet the attempt to "defeat the sun" aroused the last common interest that our race experienced about the heavenly bodies, or indeed about anything. It was the last time that men were compacted by thinking of a power outside the world. The sun had conquered, yet it was the end of his spiritual dominion. Dawn, midday, twilight, the zodiacal path, touched neither men's lives nor their hearts, and science retreated into the ground, to concentrate herself upon problems that she was certain of solving.

So when Vashti found her cabin invaded by a rosy finger of light, she was annoyed, and tried to adjust the blind. But the blind flew up altogether, and she saw through the skylight small pink clouds, swaying against a background of blue, and as the sun crept higher, its radiance entered direct, brimming down the wall, like a golden sea. It rose and fell with the air-ship's motion, just as waves rise and fall, but it advanced steadily, as a tide advances. Unless she was careful, it would strike her face. A spasm of horror shook her and she rang for the attendant. The attendant too was horrified, but she could do nothing; it was not her place to mend the blind. She could only suggest that the lady should change her cabin, which she accordingly prepared to do.

People were almost exactly alike all over the world, but the attendant of the air-ship, perhaps owing to her exceptional duties, had grown a little out of the common. She had often to address passengers with direct speech, and this had given her a certain roughness and originality of manner. When Vashti swerved away from the sunbeams with a cry, she behaved barbarically—she put out her hand to steady her.

"How dare you!" exclaimed the passenger. "You forget yourself!"

The woman was confused, and apologised for not having let her fall. People never touched one another. The custom had become obsolete, owing to the Machine.

"Where are we now?" asked Vashti haughtily.

"We are over Asia," said the attendant, anxious to be polite.

"Asia?"

"You must excuse my common way of speaking. I have got into the habit of calling places over which I pass by their unmechanical names."

"Oh, I remember Asia. The Mongols came from it."

"Beneath us, in the open air, stood a city that was once called Simla."

"Have you ever heard of the Mongols and of the Brisbane school?"

"No."

"Brisbane also stood in the open air."

"Those mountains to the right—let me show you them." She pushed back a metal blind. The main chain of the Himalayas was revealed. "They were once called the Roof of the World, those mountains."

"What a foolish name!"

"You must remember that, before the dawn of civilisation, they seemed to be an impenetrable wall that touched the stars. It was supposed that no one but the gods could exist above their summits. How we have advanced, thanks to the Machine!"

"How we have advanced, thanks to the Machine!" said Vashti.

"How we have advanced, thanks to the Machine!" echoed the passenger who had dropped his Book the night before, and who was standing in the passage.

"And that white stuff in the cracks?—what is it?"

"I have forgotten its name."

"Cover the window, please. These mountains give me no ideas."

The northern aspect of the Himalayas was in deep shadow: on the Indian slope the sun had just prevailed. The forests had been destroyed during the literature epoch for the purpose of making newspaper-pulp, but the snows were awakening to their morning glory, and clouds still hung on the breasts of Kinchinjunga. In the plain were seen the ruins of cities, with diminished rivers creeping by their walls, and by the sides of these were sometimes the signs of vomitories, marking the cities of today. Over the whole prospect air-ships rushed, crossing and intercrossing with incredible *aplomb*, and rising nonchalantly when they desired to escape the perturbations of the lower atmosphere and to traverse the Roof of the World.

"We have indeed advanced, thanks to the Machine," repeated the attendant, and hid the Himalayas behind a metal blind.

The day dragged wearily forward. The passengers sat each in his cabin, avoiding one another with an almost physical repulsion and longing to be once more under the surface of the earth. There were eight or ten of them, mostly young males, sent out from the public nurseries to inhabit the rooms of those who had died in various parts of the earth. The man who had dropped his Book was on the homeward journey. He had been sent to Sumatra for the purpose of propagating the race. Vashti alone was travelling by her private will.

At midday she took a second glance at the earth. The air-ship was crossing another range of mountains, but she could see little, owing to clouds. Masses of black rock hovered below her, and merged indistinctly into grey. Their shapes were fantastic; one of them resembled a prostrate man.

"No ideas here," murmured Vashti, and hid the Caucasus behind a metal blind.

In the evening she looked again. They were crossing a golden sea, in which lay many small islands and one peninsula.

She repeated, "No ideas here," and hid Greece behind a metal blind.

II

The Mending Apparatus

By a vestibule, by a lift, by a tubular railway, by a platform, by a sliding door—by reversing all the steps of her departure did Vashti arrive at her son's room, which exactly resembled her own. She might well declare that the visit was superfluous. The buttons, the knobs, the reading-desk with the Book, the temperature, the atmosphere, the illumination—all were exactly the same. And if Kuno himself, flesh of her flesh, stood close beside her at last, what profit was there in that? She was too well-bred to shake him by the hand.

Averting her eyes, she spoke as follows:

"Here I am. I have had the most terrible journey and greatly retarded the development of my soul. It is not worth it, Kuno, it is not worth it. My time is too precious. The sunlight almost touched me, and I have met with the rudest people. I can only stop a few minutes. Say what you want to say, and then I must return."

"I have been threatened with Homelessness," said Kuno.

She looked at him now.

"I have been threatened with Homelessness, and I could not tell you such a thing through the Machine."

Homelessness means death. The victim is exposed to the air, which kills him.

"I have been outside since I spoke to you last. The tremendous thing has happened, and they have discovered me."

"But why shouldn't you go outside!" she exclaimed. "It is perfectly legal, perfectly mechanical, to visit the surface of the earth. I have lately been to a lecture on the sea; there is no objection to that; one simply summons a respirator and gets an Egression-permit. It is not the kind of thing that spiritually-minded people do, and I begged you not to do it, but there is no legal objection to it."

"I did not get an Egression-permit."

"Then how did you get out?"

"I found out a way of my own."

The phrase conveyed no meaning to her, and he had to repeat it.

"A way of your own?" she whispered. "But that would be wrong."

"Why?"

The question shocked her beyond measure.

"You are beginning to worship the Machine," he said coldly. "You think it irreligious of me to have found out a way of my own. It was just what the Committee thought, when they threatened me with Homelessness."

At this she grew angry. "I worship nothing!" she cried. "I am most advanced. I don't think you irreligious, for there is no such thing as religion left. All the fear and the superstition that existed once have been destroyed by the Machine. I only meant that to find out a way of your own was—Besides, there is no new way out."

"So it is always supposed."

"Except through the vomitories, for which one must have an Egression-permit, it is impossible to get out. The Book says so."

"Well, the Book's wrong, for I have been out on my feet."

For Kuno was possessed of a certain physical strength.

By these days it was a demerit to be muscular. Each infant was examined at birth, and all who promised undue strength were destroyed. Humanitarians may protest, but it would have been no true kindness to let an athlete live; he would never have been happy in that state of life to which the Machine had called him; he would have yearned for trees to climb, rivers to bathe in, meadows and hills against which he might measure his body. Man must be adapted to his surroundings, must he not? In the dawn of the world our weakly must be exposed on Mount Taygetus, in its twilight our strong will suffer euthanasia, that the Machine may progress, that the Machine may progress, that the Machine may progress eternally.

"You know that we have lost the sense of space. We say 'space is annihilated,' but we have annihilated not space, but the sense thereof. We have lost a part of ourselves. I determined to recover it, and I began by walking up and down the platform of the railway outside my room. Up and down, until I was tired, and so did recapture the meaning of 'Near' and 'Far.' 'Near' is a place to which I can get quickly *on my feet*, not a place to which the train or the air-ship will take me quickly. 'Far' is a place to which I cannot get quickly on my feet; the vomitory is 'far,' though I could be there in thirty-eight seconds by summoning the train. Man is the measure. That was my first lesson. Man's feet are the measure for distance, his hands are the measure for ownership, his body is the measure for all that is lovable and desirable and strong. Then I went further: it was then that I called to you for the first time, and you would not come.

"This city, as you know, is built deep beneath the surface of the earth, with only the vomitories protruding. Having paced the platform outside my own room, I took the lift to the next platform and paced that also, and so with each in turn, until I came to the topmost, above which begins the earth. All the platforms were exactly alike, and all that I gained by visiting them was to develop my sense of space and my muscles. I think I should have been content with this—it is not a little thing—but as I walked and brooded, it occurred to me that our cities had been built in the days when men still breathed the outer air, and that there had been ventilation shafts for the workmen. I could think of nothing but these ventilation shafts. Had they been destroyed by all the food-tubes and medicine-tubes and music-tubes that the Machine has evolved lately? Or did traces of them remain? One thing was certain. If I came upon them anywhere, it would be in the railway-tunnels of the topmost story. Everywhere else, all space was accounted for.

"I am telling my story quickly, but don't think that I was not a coward or that your answers never depressed me. It is not the proper thing, it is not mechanical, it is not decent to walk along a railway-tunnel. I did not fear that I might tread upon a live rail and be killed. I feared something far more intangible—doing what was not contemplated by the Machine. Then I said to myself, 'Man is the measure,' and I went, and after many visits I found an opening.

"The tunnels, of course, were lighted. Everything is light, artificial light; darkness is the exception. So when I saw a black gap in the tiles, I knew that it was an exception, and rejoiced. I put in my arm—I could put in no more at first—and waved it round and round in ecstasy. I loosened another tile, and put in my head, and shouted into the darkness: 'I am coming, I shall do it yet,' and my voice reverberated down endless passages. I seemed to hear the spirits of those dead workmen who had returned each evening to the starlight and to their wives, and all the generations who had lived in the open air called back to me, 'You will do it yet, you are coming.' "

He paused, and, absurd as he was, his last words moved her. For Kuno had lately asked to be a father, and his request had been refused by the Committee. His was not a type that the Machine desired to hand on.

"Then a train passed. It brushed by me, but I thrust my head and arms into the hole. I had done enough for one day, so I crawled back to the platform, went down in the lift, and summoned my bed. Ah, what dreams! And again I called you, and again you refused."

She shook her head and said:

"Don't. Don't talk of these terrible things. You make me miserable. You are throwing civilisation away."

"But I had got back the sense of space and a man cannot rest then. I determined to get in at the hole and climb the shaft. And so I exercised my arms. Day after day I went through ridiculous movements, until my flesh ached, and I could hang by my hands and hold the pillow of my bed outstretched for many minutes. Then I summoned a respirator, and started.

"It was easy at first. The mortar had somehow rotted, and I soon pushed some more tiles in, and clambered after them into the darkness, and the spirits of the dead comforted me. I don't know what I mean by that. I just say what I felt. I felt, for the first time, that a protest had been lodged against corruption, and that even as the dead were comforting me, so I was comforting the unborn. I felt that humanity existed, and that it existed without clothes. How can I possibly explain this? It was naked, humanity seemed naked, and all these tubes and buttons and machineries neither came into the world with us, nor will they follow us out, nor do they matter supremely while we are here. Had I been strong, I would have torn off every garment I had, and gone out into the outer air unswaddled. But this is not for me, nor perhaps for my generation. I climbed with my respirator and my hygienic clothes and my dietetic tabloids! Better thus than not at all.

"There was a ladder, made of some primæval metal. The light from the railway fell upon its lowest rungs, and I saw that it led straight upwards out of the rubble at the bottom of the shaft. Perhaps our ancestors ran up and down it a dozen times daily, in their building. As I climbed, the rough edges cut through my gloves so that my hands bled. The light helped me for a little, and then came darkness and, worse still, silence which pierced my ears like a sword. The Machine hums! Did you know that? Its hum penetrates our blood, and may even guide our thoughts. Who knows! I was getting beyond its power. Then I thought: 'This silence means that I am doing wrong.' But I heard voices in the silence, and again they strengthened me." He laughed. "I had need of them. The next moment I cracked my head against something."

She sighed.

"I had reached one of those pneumatic stoppers that defend us from the outer air. You may have noticed them on the air-ship. Pitch dark, my feet on the rungs of an invisible ladder, my hands cut; I cannot explain how I lived through this part, but the voices still comforted me, and I felt for fastenings. The stopper, I suppose, was about eight feet across. I passed my hand over it as far as I could reach. It was perfectly smooth. I felt it almost to the centre. Not quite to the centre, for my arm was too short. Then the voice said: 'Jump. It is worth it. There may be a handle in the centre, and you may catch hold of it and so come to us your own way. And if there is no handle, so that you may fall and are dashed to pieces—it is still worth it: you will still come to us your own way.' So I jumped. There was a handle, and—"

He paused. Tears gathered in his mother's eyes. She knew that he was fated. If he did not die today he would die tomorrow. There was not room for such a person in the world. And with her pity disgust mingled. She was ashamed at having borne such a son, she who had always been so respectable and so full of ideas. Was he really the little boy to whom she had taught the use of his stops and buttons, and to whom she had given his first lessons in the Book? The very hair that disfigured his lip showed that he was reverting to some savage type. On atavism the Machine can have no mercy.

"There was a handle, and I did catch it. I hung tranced over the darkness and heard the hum of these workings as the last whisper in a dying dream. All the things I had cared about and all the people I had spoken to through tubes appeared infinitely little. Meanwhile the handle revolved. My weight had set something in motion and I span slowly, and then—

"I cannot describe it. I was lying with my face to the sunshine. Blood poured from my nose and ears and I heard a tremendous roaring. The stopper, with me clinging to it, had simply been blown out of the earth, and the air that we make down here was escaping through the vent into the air above. It burst up like a fountain. I crawled back to it—for the upper air hurts—and, as it were, I took great sips from the edge. My respirator had flown goodness knows where, my clothes were torn. I just lay with my lips close to the hole, and I sipped until the bleeding stopped. You can imagine nothing so curious. This hollow in the grass—I will speak of it in a minute,—the sun shining into it, not brilliantly but through marbled clouds,—the peace, the nonchalance, the sense of space, and, brushing my cheek, the roaring fountain of our artificial air! Soon I spied my respirator, bobbing up and down in the current high above my head, and higher still were many air-ships. But no one ever looks out of air-ships, and in my case they could not have picked me up. There I was, stranded. The sun shone a little way down the shaft, and revealed the topmost rung of the ladder, but it was hopeless trying to reach it. I should either have been tossed up again by the escape, or else have fallen in, and died. I could only lie on the grass, sipping and sipping, and from time to time glancing around me.

"I knew that I was in Wessex, for I had taken care to go to a lecture on the subject before starting. Wessex lies above the room in which we are talking now. It was once an important state. Its kings held all the southern coast from the Andredswald to Cornwall, while the Wansdyke protected them on the north, running over the high ground. The lecturer was only concerned with the rise of Wessex, so I do not know how long it remained an international power, nor would the knowledge have assisted me. To tell the truth I could do nothing but laugh, during this part. There was I, with a pneumatic stopper by my side and a respirator bobbing over my head, imprisoned, all three of us, in a grass-grown hollow that was edged with fern."

Then he grew grave again.

"Lucky for me that it was a hollow. For the air began to fall back into it and to fill it as water fills a bowl. I could crawl about. Presently I stood. I breathed a mixture, in which the air that hurts predominated whenever I tried to climb the sides. This was not so bad. I had not lost my tabloids and remained ridiculously cheerful, and as for the Machine, I forgot about it altogether. My one aim now was to get to the top, where the ferns were, and to view whatever objects lay beyond.

"I rushed the slope. The new air was still too bitter for me and I came rolling back, after a momentary vision of something grey. The sun grew very feeble, and I remembered that he was in Scorpio—I had been to a lecture on that too. If the sun is in Scorpio and you are in Wessex, it means that you must be as quick as you can, or it will get too dark. (This is the first bit of useful information I have ever got from a lecture, and I expect it will be the last.) It made me try frantically to breath the new air, and to advance as far as I dared out of my pond. The hollow filled so slowly. At times I thought that the fountain played with less vigour. My respirator seemed to dance nearer the earth; the roar was decreasing."

He broke off.

"I don't think this is interesting you. The rest will interest you even less. There are no ideas in it, and I wish that I had not troubled you to come. We are too different, mother."

She told him to continue.

"It was evening before I climbed the bank. The sun had very nearly slipped out of the sky by this time, and I could not get a good view. You, who have just crossed the Roof of the World, will not want to hear an account of the little hills that I saw—low colourless hills. But to me they were living and the turf that covered them was a skin, under which their muscles rippled, and I felt that those hills had called with incalculable force to men in the past, and that men had loved them. Now they sleep —perhaps for ever. They commune with humanity in dreams. Happy the man, happy the woman, who awakes the hills of Wessex. For though they sleep, they will never die."

His voice rose passionately.

"Cannot you see, cannot all your lecturers see, that it is we who are dying, and that down here the only thing that really lives is the Machine? We created the Machine, to do our will, but we cannot make it do our will now. It has robbed us of the sense of space and of the sense of touch, it has blurred every human relation and narrowed down love to a carnal act, it has paralysed our bodies and our wills, and now it compels us to worship it. The Machine develops—but not on our lines. The Machine proceeds—but not to our goal. We only exist as the blood corpuscles that course through its arteries, and if it could work without us, it would let us die. Oh, I have no remedy—or, at least, only one—to tell men again and again that I have seen the hills of Wessex as Ælfrid saw them when he overthrew the Danes.

"So the sun set. I forgot to mention that a belt of mist lay between my hill and other hills, and that it was the colour of pearl."

He broke off for the second time.

"Go on," said his mother wearily.

He shook his head.

"Go on. Nothing that you say can distress me now. I am hardened."

"I had meant to tell you the rest, but I cannot: I know that I cannot: good-bye."

Vashti stood irresolute. All her nerves were tingling with his blasphemies. But she was also inquisitive.

"This is unfair," she complained. "You have called me across the world to hear your story, and hear it I will. Tell me—as briefly as possible, for this is a disastrous waste of time—tell me how you returned to civilisation."

"Oh—that!" he said, starting. "You would like to hear about civilisation. Certainly. Had I got to where my respirator fell down?"

"No—but I understand everything now. You put on your respirator, and managed to walk along the surface of the earth to a vomitory, and there your conduct was reported to the Central Committee."

"By no means."

He passed his hand over his forehead, as if dispelling some strong impression. Then, resuming his narrative, he warmed to it again.

"My respirator fell about sunset. I had mentioned that the fountain seemed feebler, had I not."

"Yes."

"About sunset, it let the respirator fall. As I said, I had entirely forgotten about the Machine, and I paid no great attention at the time, being occupied with other things. I had my pool of air, into which I could dip when the outer keenness became intolerable, and which would possibly remain for days, provided that no wind sprang up to disperse it. Not until it was too late, did I realize what the stoppage of the escape implied. You see—the gap in the tunnel had been mended; the Mending Apparatus; the Mending Apparatus, was after me.

"One other warning I had, but I neglected it. The sky at night was clearer than it had been in the day, and the moon, which was about half the sky behind the sun, shone into the dell at moments quite brightly. I was in my usual place—on the boundary between the two atmospheres—when I thought I saw something dark move across the bottom of the dell, and vanish into the shaft. In my folly, I ran down. I bent over and listened, and I thought I heard a faint scraping noise in the depths.

"At this—but it was too late—I took alarm. I determined to put on my respirator and to walk right out of the dell. But my respirator had gone. I knew exactly where it had fallen—between the stopper and the aperture—and I could even feel the mark that it had made in the turf. It had gone, and I realized that something evil was at work, and I had better escape to the other air, and, if I must die, die running towards the cloud that had been the colour of a pearl. I never started. Out of the shaft—it is too horrible. A worm, a long white worm, had crawled out of the shaft and was gliding over the moonlit grass.

"I screamed. I did everything that I should not have done, I stamped upon the creature instead of flying from it, and it at once curled round the ankle. Then we fought. The worm let me run all over the dell, but edged up my leg as I ran. 'Help!' I cried. (That part is too awful. It belongs to the part that you will never know.) 'Help!' I cried. (Why cannot we suffer in silence?) 'Help!' I cried. Then my feet were wound together, I fell, I was dragged away from the dear ferns and the living hills, and past the great metal stopper (I can tell you this part), and I thought it might save me again if I caught hold of the handle. It also was enwrapped, it also. Oh, the whole dell was full of the things. They were searching it in all directions, they were denuding it, and the white snouts of others peeped out of the hole, ready if needed. Everything that could be moved they brought—brushwood, bundles of fern, everything, and down we all went intertwined into hell. The last things that I saw, ere the stopper closed after us, were certain stars, and I felt that a man of my sort lived in the sky. For I did fight, I fought till the very end, and it was only my head hitting against the ladder that quieted me. I woke up in this room. The worms had vanished. I was surrounded by artificial air, artificial light, artificial peace, and my friends were calling to me down speaking-tubes to know whether I had come across any new ideas lately."

Here his story ended. Discussion of it was impossible, and Vashti turned to go.

"It will end in Homelessness," she said quietly.

"I wish it would," retorted Kuno.

"The Machine has been most merciful."

"I prefer the mercy of God."

"By that superstitious phrase, do you mean that you could live in the outer air?"

"Yes."

"Have you ever seen, round the vomitories, the bones of those who were extruded after the Great Rebellion?"

"Yes."

"They were left where they perished for our edification. A few crawled away, but they perished, too—who can doubt it? And so with the Homeless of our own day. The surface of the earth supports life no longer."

"Indeed."

"Ferns and a little grass may survive, but all higher forms have perished. Has any air-ship detected them?"

"No."

"Has any lecturer dealt with them?"

"No."

"Then why this obstinacy?"

"Because I have seen them," he exploded.

"Seen *what?*"

"Because I have seen her in the twilight—because she came to my help when I called—because she, too, was entangled by the worms, and, luckier than I, was killed by one of them piercing her throat."

He was mad. Vashti departed, nor, in the troubles that followed, did she ever see his face again.

III

The Homeless

During the years that followed Kuno's escapade, two important developments took place in the Machine. On the surface they were revolutionary, but in either case men's minds had been prepared beforehand, and they did but express tendencies that were latent already.

The first of these was the abolition of respirators.

Advanced thinkers, like Vashti, had always held it foolish to visit the surface of the earth. Air-ships might be necessary, but what was the good of going out for mere curiosity and crawling along for a mile or two in a terrestrial motor? The habit was vulgar and perhaps faintly improper: it was unproductive of ideas, and had no connection with the habits that really mattered. So respirators were abolished, and with them, of course, the terrestrial motors, and except for a few lecturers, who complained that they were debarred access to their subject-matter, the development was accepted quietly. Those who still wanted to know what the earth was like had after all only to listen to some gramophone, or to look into some cinematophote. And even the lecturers acquiesced when they found that a lecture on the sea was none the less stimulating when compiled out of other lectures that had already been delivered on the same subject. "Beware of first-hand ideas!" exclaimed one of the most advanced of them. "First-hand ideas do not really exist. They are but the physical impressions produced by love and fear, and on this gross foundation who could erect a philosophy? Let your ideas be second-hand, and if possible tenth-hand, for then they will be far removed from that disturbing element—direct observation. Do not learn anything about this subject of mine—the French Revolution. Learn instead what I think that Enicharmon thought Urizen thought Gutch thought Ho-Yung thought Chi-Bo-Sing thought Lafcadio Hearn thought Carlyle thought Mirabeau said about the French Revolution. Through the medium of these eight great minds, the blood that was shed at Paris and the windows that were broken at Versailles will be clarified to an idea which you may employ most profitably in your daily lives. But be sure that the intermediates are many and varied, for in history one authority exists to counteract another. Urizen must counteract the scepticism of Ho-Yung and Enicharmon, I must myself counteract the impetuosity of Gutch. You who listen to me are in a better position to judge about the French Revolution than I am. Your descendants will be even in a better position than you, for they will learn what you think I think, and yet another intermediate will be added to the chain. And in time"—his voice rose— "there will come a generation that has got beyond facts, beyond impressions, a generation absolutely colourless, a generation

'seraphically free
From taint of personality,'

which will see the French Revolution not as it happened, nor as they would like it to have happened, but as it would have happened, had it taken place in the days of the Machine."

Tremendous applause greeted this lecture, which did but voice a feeling already latent in the minds of men—a feeling that terrestrial facts must be ignored, and that the abolition of respirators was a positive gain. It was even suggested that air-ships should be abolished too. This was not done, because air-ships had somehow worked themselves into the Machine's system. But year by year they were used less, and mentioned less by thoughtful men.

The second great development was the reestablishment of religion.

This, too, had been voiced in the celebrated lecture. No one could mistake the reverent tone in which the peroration had concluded, and it awakened a responsive echo in the heart of each. Those who had long worshipped silently, now began to talk. They described the strange feeling of peace that came over them when they handled the Book of the Machine, the pleasure that it was to repeat certain numerals out of it, however little meaning those numerals conveyed to the outward ear, the ecstasy of touching a button, however unimportant, or of ringing an electric bell, however superfluously.

"The Machine," they exclaimed, "feeds us and clothes us and houses us; through it we speak to one another, through it we see one another, in it we have our being. The Machine is the friend of ideas and the enemy of superstition: the Machine is omnipotent, eternal; blessed is the Machine." And before long this allocution was printed on the first page of the Book, and in subsequent editions the ritual swelled into a complicated system of praise and prayer. The word "religion" was sedulously avoided, and in theory the Machine was still the creation and the implement of man. But in practice all, save a few retrogrades, worshipped it as divine. Nor was it worshipped in unity. One believer would be chiefly impressed by the blue optic plates, through which he saw other believers; another by the mending apparatus, which sinful Kuno had compared to worms; another by the lifts, another by the Book. And each would pray to this or to that, and ask it to intercede for him with the Machine as a whole. Persecution—that also was present. It did not break out, for reasons that will be set forward shortly. But it was latent, and all who did not accept the minimum known as "undenominational Mechanism" lived in danger of Homelessness, which means death, as we know.

To attribute these two great developments to the Central Committee, is to take a very narrow view of civilisation. The Central Committee announced the developments, it is true, but they were no more the cause of them than were the kings of the imperialistic period the cause of war. Rather did they yield to some invincible pressure, which came no one knew whither, and which, when gratified, was succeeded by some new pressure equally invincible. To such a state of affairs it is convenient to give the name of progress. No one confessed the Machine was out of hand. Year by year it was served with increased efficiency and decreased intelligence. The better a man knew his own duties upon it, the less he understood the duties of his neighbour, and in all the world there was not one who understood the monster as a whole. Those master brains had perished. They had left full directions, it is true, and their successors had each of them mastered a portion of those directions. But Humanity, in its desire for comfort, had over-reached itself. It had exploited the riches of nature too far. Quietly and complacently, it was sinking into decadence, and progress had come to mean the progress of the Machine.

As for Vashti, her life went peacefully forward until the final disaster. She made her room dark and slept; she awoke and made the room light. She lectured and attended lectures. She exchanged ideas with her innumerable friends and believed she was growing more spiritual. At times a friend was granted Euthanasia, and left his or her room for the homelessness that is beyond all human conception. Vashti did not much mind. After an unsuccessful lecture, she would sometimes ask for Euthanasia herself. But the death-rate was not permitted to exceed the birth-rate, and the Machine had hitherto refused it to her.

The troubles began quietly, long before she was conscious of them.

One day she was astonished at receiving a message from her son. They never communicated, having nothing in common, and she had only heard indirectly that he was still alive, and had been transferred from the northern hemisphere, where he had behaved so mischievously, to the southern—indeed, to a room not far from her own.

"Does he want me to visit him?" she thought. "Never again, never. And I have not the time."

No, it was madness of another kind.

He refused to visualize his face upon the blue plate, and speaking out of the darkness with solemnity said:

"The Machine stops."

"What do you say?"

"The Machine is stopping, I know it, I know the signs."

She burst into a peal of laughter. He heard her and was angry, and they spoke no more.

"Can you imagine anything more absurd?" she cried to a friend. "A man who was my son believes that the Machine is stopping. It would be impious if it was not mad."

"The Machine is stopping?" her friend replied. "What does that mean? The phrase conveys nothing to me."

"Nor to me."

"He does not refer, I suppose, to the trouble there has been lately with the music?"

"Oh no, of course not. Let us talk about music."

"Have you complained to the authorities?"

"Yes, and they say it wants mending, and referred me to the Committee of the Mending Apparatus. I complained of those curious gasping sighs that disfigure the symphonies of the Brisbane school. They sound like some one in pain. The Committee of the Mending Apparatus say that it shall be remedied shortly."

Obscurely worried, she resumed her life. For one thing, the defect in the music irritated her. For another thing, she could not forget Kuno's speech. If he had known that the music was out of repair—he could not know it, for he detested music—if he had known that it was wrong, "the Machine stops" was exactly the venomous sort of remark he would have made. Of course he had made it at a venture, but the coincidence annoyed her, and she spoke with some petulance to the Committee of the Mending Apparatus.

They replied, as before, that the defect would be set right shortly.

"Shortly! At once!" she retorted. "Why should I be worried by imperfect music? Things are always put right at once. If you do not mend it at once, I shall complain to the Central Committee."

"No personal complaints are received by the Central Committee," the Committee of the Mending Apparatus replied.

"Through whom am I to make my complaint, then?"

"Through us."

"I complain then."

"Your complaint shall be forwarded in its turn."

"Have others complained?"

This question was unmechanical, and the Committee of the Mending Apparatus refused to answer it.

"It is too bad!" she exclaimed to another of her friends. "There never was such an unfortunate woman as myself. I can never be sure of my music now. It gets worse and worse each time I summon it."

"I too have my troubles," the friend replied. "Sometimes my ideas are interrupted by a slight jarring noise."

"What is it?"

"I do not know whether it is inside my head, or inside the wall."

"Complain, in either case."

"I have complained, and my complaint will be forwarded in its turn to the Central Committee."

Time passed, and they resented the defects no longer. The defects had not been remedied, but the human tissues in that latter day had become so subservient, that they readily adapted themselves to every caprice of the Machine. The sigh at the crisis of the Brisbane symphony no longer irritated Vashti; she accepted it as part of the melody. The jarring noise, whether in the head or in the wall, was no longer resented by her friend. And so with the mouldy artificial fruit, so with the bath water that began to stink, so with the defective rhymes that the poetry machine had taken to emit. All were bitterly complained of at first, and then acquiesced in and forgotten. Things went from bad to worse unchallenged.

It was otherwise with the failure of the sleeping apparatus. That was a more serious stoppage. There came a day when over the whole world—in Sumatra, in Wessex, in the innumerable cities of Courland and Brazil—the beds, when summoned by their tired owners, failed to appear. It may seem a ludicrous matter, but from it we may date the collapse of humanity. The Committee responsible for the failure was assailed by complainants, whom it referred, as usual, to the Committee of the Mending Apparatus, who in its turn assured them that their complaints would be forwarded to the Central Committee. But the discontent grew, for mankind was not yet sufficiently adaptable to do without sleeping.

"Some one is meddling with the Machine—" they began.

"Some one is trying to make himself king, to reintroduce the personal element."

"Punish that man with Homelessness."

"To the rescue! Avenge the Machine! Avenge the Machine!"

"War! Kill the man!"

But the Committee of the Mending Apparatus now came forward, and allayed the panic with well-chosen words. It confessed that the Mending Apparatus was itself in need of repair.

The effect of this frank confession was admirable.

"Of course," said a famous lecturer—he of the French Revolution, who gilded each new decay with splendour—"of course we shall not press our complaints now. The Mending Apparatus has treated us so well in the past that we all sympathize with it, and will wait patiently for its recovery. In its own good time it will resume its duties. Meanwhile let us do without our beds, our tabloids, our other little wants. Such, I feel sure, would be the wish of the Machine."

Thousands of miles away his audience applauded. The Machine still linked them. Under the seas, beneath the roots of the mountains, ran the wires through which they saw and heard, the enormous eyes and ears that were their heritage, and the hum of many workings clothed their thoughts in one garment of subserviency. Only the old and the sick remained ungrateful, for it was rumoured that Euthanasia, too, was out of order, and that pain had reappeared among men.

It became difficult to read. A blight entered the atmosphere and dulled its luminosity. At times Vashti could scarcely see across her room. The air, too, was foul. Loud were the complaints, impotent the remedies, heroic the tone of the lecturer as he cried: "Courage, courage! What matter so long as the Machine goes on? To it the darkness and the light are one." And though things improved again after a time, the old brilliancy was never recaptured, and humanity never recovered from its entrance into twilight. There was an hysterical talk of "measures," of "provisional dictatorship," and the inhabitants of Sumatra were asked to familiarize themselves with the workings of the central power station, the said power station being situated in France. But for the most part panic reigned, and men spent their strength praying to their Books, tangible proofs of the Machine's omnipotence. There were gradations of terror—at times came rumours of hope—the Mending Apparatus was almost mended—the enemies of the Machine had been got under—new "nerve-centres" were evolving which would do the work even more magnificently than before. But there came a day when, without the slightest warning, without any previous hint of feebleness, the entire communication-system broke down, all over the world, and the world, as they understood it, ended.

Vashti was lecturing at the time and her earlier remarks had been punctuated with applause. As she proceeded the audience became silent, and at the conclusion there was no sound. Somewhat displeased, she called to a friend who was a specialist in sympathy. No sound: doubtless the friend was sleeping. And so with the next friend whom she tried to summon, and so with the next, until she remembered Kuno's cryptic remark, "The Machine stops."

The phrase still conveyed nothing. If Eternity was stopping it would of course be set going shortly.

For example, there was still a little light and air—the atmosphere had improved a few hours previously. There was still the Book, and while there was the Book there was security.

Then she broke down, for with the cessation of activity came an unexpected terror—silence.

She had never known silence, and the coming of it nearly killed her—it did kill many thousands of people outright. Ever since her birth she had been surrounded by the steady hum. It was to the ear what artificial air was to the lungs, and agonizing pains shot across her head. And scarcely knowing what she did, she stumbled forward and pressed the unfamiliar button, the one that opened the door of her cell.

Now the door of the cell worked on a simple hinge of its own. It was not connected with the central power station, dying far away in France. It opened, rousing immoderate hopes in Vashti, for she thought that the Machine had been mended. It opened, and she saw the dim tunnel that curved far away towards freedom. One look, and then she shrank back. For the tunnel was full of people—she was almost the last in that city to have taken alarm.

People at any time repelled her, and these were nightmares from her worst dreams. People were crawling about, people were screaming, whimpering, gasping for breath, touching each other, vanishing in the dark, and ever and anon being pushed off the platform on to the live rail. Some were fighting round the electric bells, trying to summon trains which could not be summoned. Others were yelling for Euthanasia or for respirators, or blaspheming the Machine. Others stood at the doors of their cells fearing, like herself, either to stop in them or to leave them. And behind all the uproar was silence—the silence which is the voice of the earth and of the generations who have gone.

No—it was worse than solitude. She closed the door again and sat down to wait for the end. The disintegration went on, accompanied by horrible cracks and rumbling. The valves that restrained the Medical Apparatus must have been weakened, for it ruptured and hung hideously from the ceiling. The floor heaved and fell and flung her from her chair. A tube oozed towards her serpent fashion. And at last the final horror approached—light began to ebb, and she knew that civilisation's long day was closing.

She whirled round, praying to be saved from this, at any rate, kissing the Book, pressing button after button. The uproar outside was increasing, and even penetrated the wall. Slowly the brilliancy of her cell was dimmed, the reflections faded from her metal switches. Now she could not see the reading-stand, now not the Book, though she held it in her hand. Light followed the flight of sound, air was following light, and the original void returned to the cavern from which it had been so long excluded. Vashti continued to whirl, like the devotees of an earlier religion, screaming, praying, striking at the buttons with bleeding hands.

It was thus that she opened her prison and escaped—escaped in the

spirit: at least so it seems to me, ere my meditation closes. That she es-
capes in the body—I cannot perceive that. She struck, by chance, the
switch that released the door, and the rush of foul air on her skin, the
loud throbbing whispers in her ears, told her that she was facing the tunnel again, and that tremendous platform on which she had seen men
fighting. They were not fighting now. Only the whispers remained, and
the little whimpering groans. They were dying by hundreds out in the
dark.

She burst into tears.

Tears answered her.

They wept for humanity, those two, not for themselves. They could
not bear that this should be the end. Ere silence was completed their
hearts were opened, and they knew what had been important on the
earth. Man, the flower of all flesh, the noblest of all creatures visible,
man who had once made god in his image, and had mirrored his strength
on the constellations, beautiful naked man was dying, strangled in the
garments that he had woven. Century after century had he toiled, and
here was his reward. Truly the garment had seemed heavenly at first, shot
with the colours of culture, sewn with the threads of self-denial. And
heavenly it had been so long as it was a garment and no more, so long as
man could shed it at will and live by the essence that is his soul, and the
essence, equally divine, that is his body. The sin against the body—it was
for that they wept in chief; the centuries of wrong against the muscles
and the nerves, and those five portals by which we can alone apprehend
—glozing it over with talk of evolution, until the body was white pap,
the home of ideas as colourless, last sloshy stirrings of a spirit that had
grasped the stars.

"Where are you?" she sobbed.

His voice in the darkness said, "Here."

"Is there any hope, Kuno?"

"None for us."

"Where are you?"

She crawled towards him over the bodies of the dead. His blood
spurted over her hands.

"Quicker," he gasped, "I am dying—but we touch, we talk, not
through the Machine."

He kissed her.

"We have come back to our own. We die, but we have recaptured life,
as it was in Wessex, when Ælfrid overthrew the Danes. We know what
they know outside, they who dwelt in the cloud that is the colour of a
pearl."

"But, Kuno, is it true? Are there still men on the surface of the earth?
Is this—this tunnel, this poisoned darkness—really not the end?"

He replied:

"I have seen them, spoken to them, loved them. They are hiding in the mist and the ferns until our civilisation stops. Today they are the Home-less—tomorrow—"

"Oh, tomorrow—some fool will start the Machine again, tomorrow."

"Never," said Kuno, "never. Humanity has learnt its lesson."

As he spoke, the whole city was broken like a honeycomb. An air-ship had sailed in through the vomitory into a ruined wharf. It crashed downwards, exploding as it went, rending gallery after gallery with its wings of steel. For a moment they saw the nations of the dead, and, before they joined them, scraps of the untainted sky.

QUESTIONS

1. Could the world described in this story be considered utopian or the opposite of utopian?

2. Why have family relationships become so muted in "The Machine Stops"?

3. Compare the regulation of lives in "The Machine Stops" to that written of in "Harrison Bergeron" and " 'Repent Harlequin!' Said the Ticktockman" (page 215).

4. Why does the Book of the Machine take on religious significance?

5. In "Day Million" human contact also seems at a minimum. What accounts for the authors' different attitudes toward this lack of physical closeness?

6. Does "The Machine Stops" say that man's need for security or his need for adventure is stronger?

7. Discuss the story in the context of the use of leisure time. What is its judgment on "intellectuals"?

8. Do we, in any real sense, already inhabit cities like the one Forster writes about?

A Rose for Ecclesiastes

Roger Zelazny

I

I was busy translating one of my *Madrigals Macabre* into Martian on the morning I was found acceptable. The intercom had buzzed briefly, and I dropped my pencil and flipped on the toggle in a single motion.

"Mister G," piped Morton's youthful contralto, "the old man says I should 'get hold of that damned conceited rhymer' right away, and send him to his cabin.—Since there's only one damned conceited rhymer . . ."

"Let not ambition mock thy useful toil." I cut him off.

So, the Martians had finally made up their minds! I knocked an inch and a half of ash from a smouldering butt, and took my first drag since I had lit it. The entire month's anticipation tried hard to crowd itself into the moment, but could not quite make it. I was frightened to walk those forty feet and hear Emory say the words I already knew he would say; and that feeling elbowed the other one into the background.

So I finished the stanza I was translating before I got up.

It took only a moment to reach Emory's door. I knocked twice and opened it, just as he growled, "Come in."

"You wanted to see me?" I sat down quickly to save him the trouble of offering me a seat.

"That was fast. What did you do, run?"

I regarded his paternal discontent:

Little fatty flecks beneath pale eyes, thinning hair, and an Irish nose; a voice a decibel louder than anyone else's . . .

Hamlet to Claudius: "I was working."

"Hah! he snorted. "Come off it. No one's ever seen you do any of that stuff."

I shrugged my shoulders and started to rise.

"If that's what you called me down here—"

"Sit down!"

He stood up. He walked around his desk. He hovered above me and glared down. (A hard trick, even when I'm in a low chair.)

"You are undoubtedly the most antagonistic bastard I've ever had to work with!" he bellowed, like a belly-stung buffalo. "Why the hell don't you act like a human being sometime and surprise everybody? I'm willing to admit you're smart, maybe even a genius, but—oh, Hell!" He made a heaving gesture with both hands and walked back to his chair.

"Betty has finally talked them into letting you go in." His voice was normal again. "They'll receive you this afternoon. Draw one of the jeepsters after lunch, and get down there."

"Okay," I said.

"That's all, then."

I nodded, got to my feet. My hand was on the doorknob when he said:

"I don't have to tell you how important this is. Don't treat them the way you treat us."

I closed the door behind me.

I don't remember what I had for lunch. I was nervous, but I knew instinctively that I wouldn't muff it. My Boston publishers expected a Martian Idyll, or at least a Saint-Exupéry job on space flight. The National Science Association wanted a complete report on the Rise and Fall of the Martian Empire.

They would both be pleased. I knew.

That's the reason everyone is jealous—why they hate me. I always come through, and I can come through better than anyone else.

I shoveled in a final anthill of slop, and made my way to our car barn. I drew one jeepster and headed it toward Tirellian.

Flames of sand, lousy with iron oxide, set fire to the buggy. They swarmed over the open top and bit through my scarf; they set to work pitting my goggles.

The jeepster, swaying and panting like a little donkey I once rode through the Himalayas, kept kicking me in the seat of the pants. The Mountains of Tirellian shuffled their feet and moved toward me at a cockeyed angle.

Suddenly I was heading uphill, and I shifted gears to accommodate the engine's braying. Not like Gobi, not like the Great Southwestern Desert, I mused. Just red, just dead . . . without even a cactus.

I reached the crest of the hill, but I had raised too much dust to see what was ahead. It didn't matter, though, I have a head full of maps. I bore to the left and downhill, adjusting the throttle. A cross-wind and solid ground beat down the fires. I felt like Ulysses in Malebolge—with a terza-rima speech in one hand and an eye out for Dante.

I sounded a rock pagoda and arrived.

Betty waved as I crunched to a halt, then jumped down.

"Hi," I choked, unwinding my scarf and shaking out a pound and a half of grit. "Like, where do I go and who do I see?"

She permitted herself a brief Germanic giggle—more at my starting a sentence with "like" than at my discomfort—then she started talking. (She is a top linguist, so a word from the Village Idiom still tickles her!)

I appreciated her precise, furry talk; informational, and all that. I had enough in the way of social pleasantries before me to last at least the rest of my life. I looked at her chocolate-bar eyes and perfect teeth, at her sun-bleached hair, close-cropped to the head (I hate blondes!), and decided that she was in love with me.

"Mr. Gallinger, the Matriarch is waiting inside to be introduced. She has consented to open the Temple records for your study." She paused here to pat her hair and squirm a little. Did my gaze make her nervous?

"They are religious documents, as well as their only history," she continued, "sort of like the Mahabharata. She expects you to observe certain rituals in handling them, like repeating the sacred words when you turn pages—she will teach you the system."

I nodded quickly, several times.

"Fine, let's go in."

"Uh—" she paused. "Do not forget their Eleven Forms of Politeness and Degree. They take matters of form quite seriously—and do not get into any discussions over the equality of the sexes—"

"I know all about their taboos," I broke in. "Don't worry. I've lived in the Orient, remember?"

She dropped her eyes and seized my hand. I almost jerked it away.

"It will look better if I enter leading you."

I swallowed my comments and followed her, like Samson in Gaza.

Inside, my last thought met with a strange correspondence. The Matriarch's quarters were a rather abstract version of what I imagine the tents of the tribes of Israel to have been like. Abstract, I say, because it was all frescoed brick, peaked like a huge tent, with animal-skin representations, like gray-blue scars, that looked as if they had been laid on the walls with a palette knife.

The Matriarch, M'Cwyie, was short, white-haired, fiftyish, and dressed like a Gypsy queen. With her rainbow of voluminous skirts she looked like an inverted punch bowl set atop a cushion.

Accepting my obeisances, she regarded me as an owl might a rabbit. The lids of those black, black eyes jumped upwards as she discovered my perfect accent.—The tape recorder Betty had carried on her interviews had done its part, and I knew the language reports from the first two expeditions, verbatim. I'm all hell when it comes to picking up accents.

"You are the poet?"

"Yes," I replied.

"Recite one of your poems, please."

"I'm sorry, but nothing short of a thorough translating job would do justice to your language and my poetry, and I don't know enough of your language yet."

"Oh?"

"But I've been making such translations for my own amusement, as an exercise in grammar," I continued. "I'd be honored to bring a few of them along one of the times that I come here."

"Yes. Do so."

Score one for me!

She turned to Betty.

"You may go now."

Betty muttered the parting formalities, gave me a strange sidewise look, and was gone. She apparently had expected to stay and "assist" me. She wanted a piece of the glory, like everyone else. But I was the Schliemann at this Troy, and there would be only one name on the Association report!

M'Cwyie rose, and I noticed that she gained very little height by standing. But then I'm six-six and look like a poplar in October: thin, bright red on top, and towering above everyone else.

"Our records are very, very old," she began. "Betty says that your word for their age is 'millennia'."

I nodded appreciatively.

"I'm very eager to see them."

"They are not here. We will have to go into the Temple—they may not be removed."

I was suddenly wary.

"You have no objections to my copying them, do you?"

"No. I see that you respect them, or your desire would not be so great."

"Excellent."

She seemed amused. I asked her what was funny.

"The High Tongue may not be so easy for a foreigner to learn."

It came through fast.

No one on the first expedition had gotten this close. I had no way of knowing that this was a double-language deal—a classical as well as a vulgar. I knew some of their Prakrit, now I had to learn all their Sanskrit.

"Ouch! and damn!"

"Pardon, please?"

"It's nontranslatable, M'Cwyie. But imagine yourself having to learn the High Tongue in a hurry, and you can guess at the sentiment."

She seemed amused again, and told me to remove my shoes.

She guided me through an alcove . . .

. . . and into a burst of Byzantine brilliance!

No Earthman had ever been in this room before, or I would have heard about it. Carter, the first expedition's linguist, with the help of one Mary Allen, M.D., had learned all the grammar and vocabulary that I knew while sitting cross-legged in the antechamber.

We had had no idea this existed. Greedily, I cast my eyes about. A highly sophisticated system of esthetics lay behind the décor. We would have to revise our entire estimation of Martian culture.

For one thing, the ceiling was vaulted and corbeled; for another, there were side columns with reverse flutings; for another—oh hell! The place was big. Posh. You could never have guessed it from the shaggy outsides.

I bent forward to study the gilt filigree on a ceremonial table. M'Cwyie seemed a bit smug at my intentness, but I'd still have hated to play poker with her.

The table was loaded with books.

With my toe, I traced a mosaic on the floor.

"Is your entire city within this one building?"

"Yes, it goes far back into the mountain."

"I see," I said, seeing nothing.

I couldn't ask her for a conducted tour, yet.

She moved to a small stool by the table.

"Shall we begin your friendship with the High Tongue?"

I was trying to photograph the hall with my eyes, knowing I would have to get a camera in here, somehow, sooner or later. I tore my gaze from a statuette and nodded, hard.

"Yes, introduce me."

I sat down.

For the next three weeks alphabet-bugs chased each other behind my eyelids whenever I tried to sleep. The sky was an unclouded pool of turquoise that rippled calligraphies whenever I swept my eyes across it. I drank quarts of coffee while I worked and mixed cocktails of Benzedrine and champagne for my coffee breaks.

M'Cwyie tutored me two hours every morning, and occasionally for another two in the evening. I spent an additional fourteen hours a day on my own, once I had gotten up sufficient momentum to go ahead alone.

And at night the elevator of time dropped me to its bottom floors . . .

I was six again, learning my Hebrew, Greek, Latin, and Aramaic. I was ten, sneaking peeks at the *Iliad*. When Daddy wasn't spreading hellfire, brimstone, and brotherly love, he was teaching me to dig the Word, like in the original.

Lord! There are so many originals and so *many* words! When I was twelve I started pointing out the little differences between what he was preaching and what I was reading.

The fundamentalist vigor of his reply brooked no debate. It was worse than any beating. I kept my mouth shut after that and learned to appreciate Old Testament poetry.

—Lord, I am sorry! Daddy—Sir—I am sorry!—It couldn't be! It couldn't be . . .

On the day the boy graduated from high school, with the French, German, Spanish, and Latin awards, Dad Gallinger had told his fourteen-year-old, six-foot scarecrow of a son that he wanted him to enter the ministry. I remember how his son was evasive:

"Sir," he had said, "I'd sort of like to study on my own for a year or so, and then take pre-theology courses at some liberal-arts university. I feel I'm still sort of young to try a seminary, straight off."

The Voice of God: "But you have the gift of tongues, my son. You can preach the Gospel in all the lands of Babel. You were born to be a missionary. You say you are young, but time is rushing by you like a whirlwind. Start early, and you will enjoy added years of service."

The added years of service were so many added tails to the cat repeatedly laid on my back. I can't see his face now, I never can. Maybe it is because I was always afraid to look at it then.

And years later, when he was dead, and laid out, in black, amidst bouquets, amidst weeping congregationalists, amidst prayers, red faces, handkerchiefs, hands patting your shoulders, solemn-faced comforters . . . I looked at him and did not recognize him.

We had met nine months before my birth, this stranger and I. He had never been cruel—stern, demanding, with contempt for everyone's shortcomings—but never cruel. He was also all that I had had of a mother. And brothers. And sisters. He had tolerated my three years at St. John's, possibly because of its name, never knowing how liberal and delightful a place it really was.

But I never knew him, and the man atop the catafalque demanded nothing now; I was free not to preach the Word.

But now I wanted to, in a different way. I wanted to preach a word that I could never have voiced while he lived.

I did not return for my Senior year in the fall. I had a small inheritance coming, and a bit of trouble getting control of it since I was still under eighteen. But I managed.

It was Greenwich Village I finally settled upon.

Not telling any well-meaning parishioners my new address, I entered into a daily routine of writing poetry and teaching myself Japanese and Hindustani. I grew a fiery beard, drank espresso, and learned to play chess. I wanted to try a couple of the other paths to salvation.

After that, it was two years in India with the Old Peace Corps—which broke me of my Buddhism, and gave me my *Pipes of Krishna* lyrics and the Pulitzer they deserved.

Then back to the States for my degree, grad work in linguistics, and more prizes.

Then one day a ship went to Mars. The vessel settling in its New Mexico nest of fires contained a new language.—It was fantastic, exotic, and esthetically overpowering. After I had learned all there was to know about it, and written my book, I was famous in new circles:

"Go, Gallinger. Dip your bucket in the well, and bring us a drink of

Mars. Go, learn another world—but remain aloof, rail at it gently like Auden—and hand us its soul in iambics."

And I came to the land where the sun is a tarnished penny, where the wind is a whip, where two moons play at hot-rod games, and a hell of sand gives you the incendiary itches whenever you look at it.

I rose from my twistings on the bunk and crossed the darkened cabin to a port. The desert was a carpet of endless orange, bulging from the sweepings of centuries beneath it.

"I a stranger, unafraid—This is the land—I've got it made!"

I laughed.

I had the High Tongue by the tail already—or the roots, if you want your puns anatomical, as well as correct.

The High and Low Tongues were not so dissimilar as they had first seemed. I had enough of the one to get me through the murkier parts of the other. I had the grammar and all the commoner irregular verbs down cold; the dictionary I was constructing grew by the day, like a tulip, and would bloom shortly. Every time I played the tapes, the stem lengthened.

Now was the time to tax my ingenuity, to really drive the lessons home. I had purposely refrained from plunging into the major texts until I could do justice to them. I had been reading minor commentaries, bits of verse, fragments of history. And one thing had impressed me strongly in all that I read.

They wrote about concrete things: rocks, sand, water, winds; and the tenor couched within these elemental symbols was fiercely pessimistic. It reminded me of some Buddhist texts, but even more so, I realized from my recent *recherches*, it was like parts of the Old Testament. Specifically it reminded me of the Book of Ecclesiastes.

That, then, would be it. The sentiment, as well as the vocabulary, was so similar that it would be a perfect exercise. Like putting Poe into French. I would never be a convert to the Way of Malann, but I would show them that an Earthman had once thought the same thoughts, felt similarly.

I switched on my desk lamp and sought King James amidst my books.

Vanity of vanities, saith the Preacher, vanity of vanities; all is vanity. What profit hath a man . . .

My progress seemed to startle M'Cwyie. She peered at me, like Sartre's Other, across the tabletop. I ran through a chapter in the Book of Locar. I didn't look up, but I could feel the tight net her eyes were working about my head, shoulders, and rapid hands. I turned another page.

Was she weighing the net, judging the size of the catch? And what for? The books said nothing of fishers on Mars. Especially of men. They said that some god named Malann had spat, or had done something disgust-

ing (depending on the version you read), and that life had gotten underway as a disease in inorganic matter. They said that movement was its
first law, its first law, and that the dance was the only legitimate reply to
the inorganic . . . the dance's quality its justification,—fication . . . and
love is a disease in organic matter—Inorganic matter?

I shook my head. I had almost been asleep.

"M'narra."

I stood and stretched. Her eyes outlined me greedily now. So I met
them, and they dropped.

"I grow tired. I want to rest awhile. I didn't sleep much last night."

She nodded, Earth's shorthand for "yes," as she had learned from me.

"You wish to relax, and see the explicitness of the doctrine of Locar in
its fullness?"

"Pardon me?"

"You wish to see a Dance of Locar?"

"Oh." Their damned circuits of form and periphrasis here ran worse
than the Koreans! "Yes. Surely. Any time it's going to be done, I'd be
happy to watch."

I continued, "In the meantime, I've been meaning to ask you whether
I might take some pictures—"

"Now is the time. Sit down. Rest. I will call the musicians."

She bustled out through a door I had never been past.

Well now, the dance was the highest art, according to Locar, not to
mention Havelock Ellis, and I was about to see how their centuries-dead
philosopher felt it should be conducted. I rubbed my eyes and snapped
over, touching my toes a few times.

The blood began pounding in my head, and I sucked in a couple deep
breaths. I bent again and there was a flurry of motion at the door.

To the trio who entered with M'Cwyie I must have looked as if I were
searching for the marbles I had just lost, bent over like that.

I grinned weakly and straightened up, my face red from more than
exertion. I hadn't expected them *that* quickly.

Suddenly I thought of Havelock Ellis again in his area of greatest popularity.

The little redheaded doll, wearing, sari-like, a diaphanous piece of the
Martian sky, looked up in wonder—as a child at some colorful flag on a
high pole.

"Hello," I said, or its equivalent.

She bowed before replying. Evidently I had been promoted in status.

"I shall dance," said the red wound in that pale, pale cameo, her face.
Eyes, the color of dream and her dress, pulled away from mine.

She drifted to the center of the room.

Standing there, like a figure in an Etruscan frieze, she was either medi-
tating or regarding the design on the floor.

Was the mosaic symbolic of something? I studied it. If it was, it eluded me; it would make an attractive bathroom floor or patio, but I couldn't see much in it beyond that.

The other two were paint-spattered sparrows like M'Cwyie, in their middle years. One settled to the floor with a triple-stringed instrument fantly resembling a *samisen*. The other held a simple woodblock and two drumsticks.

M'Cwyie disdained her stool and was seated upon the floor before I realized it. I followed suit.

The *samisen* player was still tuning up, so I leaned toward M'Cwyie. "What is the dancer's name?"

"Braxa," she replied, without looking at me, and raised her left hand, slowly, which meant yes, and go ahead, and let it begin.

The stringed thing throbbed like a toothache, and a tick-tocking, like ghosts of all the clocks they had never invented, sprang from the block.

Braxa was a statue, both hands raised to her face, elbows high and out-spread.

The music became a metaphor for fire.

Crackle, purr, snap . . .

She did not move.

The hissing altered to splashes. The cadence slowed. It was water now, the most precious thing in the world, gurgling clear then green over mossy rocks.

Still she did not move.

Glissandos. A pause.

Then, so faint I could hardly be sure at first, the tremble of the winds began. Softly, gently, sighing and halting, uncertain. A pause, a sob, then a repetition of the first statement, only louder.

Were my eyes completely bugged from my reading, or was Braxa actually trembling, all over, head to foot.

She was.

She began a microscopic swaying. A fraction of an inch right, then left. Her fingers opened like the petals of a flower, and I could see that her eyes were closed.

Her eyes opened. They were distant, glassy, looking through me and the walls. Her swaying became more pronounced, merged with the beat.

The wind was sweeping in from the desert now, falling against Tirellian like waves on a dike. Her fingers moved, they were the gusts. Her arms, slow pendulums, descended, began a countermovement.

The gale was coming now. She began an axial movement and her hands caught up with the rest of her body, only now her shoulders commenced to writhe out a figure eight.

The wind! The wind, I say. O wild, enigmatic! O muse of St.-John Perse!

The cyclone was twisting round those eyes, its still center. Her head was thrown back, but I knew there was no ceiling between her gaze, pas-

sive as Buddha's, and the unchanging skies. Only the two moons, perhaps, interrupted their slumber in that elemental Nirvana of uninhabited
turquoise.

Years ago, I had seen the Devadasis in India, the street dancers, spinning their colorful webs, drawing in the male insect. But Braxa was more
than this: she was a Ramadjany, like those votaries of Rama, incarnation
of Vishnu, who had given the dance to man: the sacred dancers.

The clicking was monotonously steady now; the whine of the strings
made me think of the stinging rays of the sun, their heat stolen by the
wind's halations; the blue was Sarasvati and Mary, and a girl named
Laura. I heard a sitar from somewhere, watched this statue come to life,
and inhaled a divine afflatus.

I was again Rimbaud with his hashish, Baudelaire with his laudanum,
Poe, De Quincy, Wilde, Mallarmé, and Aleister Crowley. I was, for a
fleeting second, my father in his dark pulpit and darker suit, the hymns
and the organ's wheeze transmuted to bright wind.

She was a spun weather vane, a feathered crucifix hovering in the air, a
clothesline holding one bright garment lashed parallel to the ground.
Her shoulder was bare now, and her right breast moved up and down like
a moon in the sky, its red nipple appearing momently above a fold and
vanishing again. The music was as formal as Job's argument with God.
Her dance was God's reply.

The music slowed, settled; it had been met, matched, answered. Her
garment, as if alive, crept back into the more sedate folds it originally
held.

She dropped low, lower, to the floor. Her head fell upon her raised
knees. She did not move.

There was silence.

I realized, from the ache across my shoulders, how tensely I had been
sitting. My armpits were wet. Rivulets had been running down my sides.
What did one do now? Applaud?

I sought M'Cwyie from the corner of my eye. She raised her right
hand.

As if by telepathy the girl shuddered all over and stood. The musicians
also rose. So did M'Cwyie.

I got to my feet, with a charley horse in my left leg, and said, "It was
beautiful," inane as that sounds.

I received three different High Forms of "thank you."

There was a flurry of color and I was alone again with M'Cwyie.

"That is the one hundred seventeenth of the two thousand two hundred twenty-four dances of Locar."

I looked down at her.

"Whether Locar was right or wrong, he worked out a fine reply to the
inorganic."

She smiled.

"Are the dances of your world like this?"

"Some of them are similar. I was reminded of them as I watched Braxa—but I've never seen anything exactly like hers."

"She is good," M'Cwyie said. "She knows all the dances."

A hint of her earlier expression which had troubled me . . .

It was gone in an instant.

"I must tend to my duties now." She moved to the table and closed the books. "M'narra."

"Good-bye." I slipped into my boots.

"Good-bye, Gallinger."

I walked out the door, mounted the jeepster, and roared across the evening into night, my wings of risen desert flapping slowly behind me.

II

I had just closed the door behind Betty, after a brief grammar session, when I heard the voices in the hall. My vent was opened a fraction, so I stood there and eavesdropped:

Morton's fruity treble: "Guess what? He said 'hello' to me a while ago."

"Hmmph!" Emory's elephant lungs exploded. "Either he's slipping, or you were standing in his way and he wanted you to move."

"Probably didn't recognize me. I don't think he sleeps any more, now he has that language to play with. I had night watch last week, and every night I passed his door at 0300—I always heard that recorder going. At 0500, when I got off, he was still at it."

"The guy *is* working hard," Emory admitted, grudgingly. "In fact, I think he's taking some kind of dope to keep awake. He looks sort of glassy-eyed these days. Maybe that's natural for a poet, though."

Betty had been standing there, because she broke in then:

"Regardless of what you think of him, it's going to take me at least a year to learn what he's picked up in three weeks. And I'm just a linguist, not a poet."

Morton must have been nursing a crush on her bovine charms. It's the only reason I can think of for his dropping his guns to say what he did.

"I took a course in modern poetry when I was back at the university," he began. "We read six authors—Yeats, Pound, Eliot, Crane, Stevens, and Gallinger—and on the last day of the semester, when the prof was feeling a little rhetorical, he said, 'These six names are written on the century, and all the gates of criticism and Hell shall not prevail against them.'"

"Myself," he continued. "I thought his *Pipes of Krishna* and his *Madrigals* were great. I was honored to be chosen for an expedition he was going on.

"I think he's spoken two dozen words to me since I met him," he finished.

The Defence: "Did it ever occur to you," Betty said, "that he might be tremendously self-conscious about his appearance? He was also a precocious child, and probably never even had school friends. He's sensitive and very introverted."

"Sensitive? Self-conscious?" Emory choked and gagged. "The man is as proud as Lucifer, and he's a walking insult machine. You press a button like 'Hello' or 'Nice day' and he thumbs his nose at you. He's got it down to a reflex."

They muttered a few other pleasantries and drifted away.

Well, bless you, Morton boy. You little pimple-faced, Ivy-bred connoisseur! I've never taken a course in my poetry, but I'm glad someone said that. The Gates of Hell. Well, now! Maybe Daddy's prayers got heard somewhere, and I am a missionary, after all!

Only . . .

. . . Only a missionary needs something to convert people to. I have my private system of esthetics, and I suppose it oozes an ethical by-product somewhere. But if I ever had anything to preach, really, even in my poems, I wouldn't care to preach it to such lowlifes as you. If you think I'm a slob, I'm also a snob, and there's no room for you in Heaven—it's a private place, where Swift, Shaw, and Petronius Arbiter come to dinner.

And oh, the feasts we have! The Trimalchio's, the Emory's we dissect! We finish you with the soup, Morton!

I turned and settled at my desk. I wanted to write something. Ecclesiastes could take a night off. I wanted to write a poem, a poem about the one hundred seventeenth dance of Locar; about a rose following the light, traced by the wind, sick, like Blake's rose, dying . . .

I found a pencil and began.

When I had finished I was pleased. It wasn't great—at least, it was no greater than it needed to be—High Martian not being my strongest tongue. I groped, and put it into English, with partial rhymes. Maybe I'd stick it in my next book. I called it *Braxa*:

> In a land of wind and red,
> where the icy evening of Time
> freezes milk in the breasts of Life,
> as two moons overhead—
> cat and dog in alleyways of dream—
> scratch and scramble agelessly my
>   flight . . .
> This final flower turns a burning
>   head.

I put it away and found some phenobarbitol. I was suddenly tired.

When I showed my poem to M'Cwyie the next day, she read it through several times, very slowly.

"It is lovely," she said. "But you used three words from your own language. 'Cat' and 'dog,' I assume, are two small animals with a hereditary hatred for one another. But what is 'flower'?"

"Oh," I said. "I've never come across your word for 'flower,' but I was actually thinking of an Earth flower, the rose."

"What is it like?"

"Well, its petals are generally bright red. That's what I meant, on one level, by 'burning head.' I also wanted it to imply fever, though, and red hair, and the fire of life. The rose, itself, has a thorny stem, green leaves, and a distinct, pleasant aroma."

"I wish I could see one."

"I suppose it could be arranged. I'll check."

"Do it, please. You are a—" She used the word for "prophet," or religious poet, like Isaiah or Locar. "—and your poem is inspired. I shall tell Braxa of it."

I declined the nomination, but felt flattered.

This, then, I decided, was the strategic day, the day on which to ask whether I might bring in the microfilm machine and the camera. I wanted to copy all their texts, I explained, and I couldn't write fast enough to do it.

She surprised me by agreeing immediately. But she bowled me over with her invitation.

"Would you like to come and stay here while you do this thing? Then you can work night and day, any time you want—except when the Temple is being used, of course."

I bowed.

"I should be honored."

"Good. Bring your machines when you want, and I will show you a room."

"Will this afternoon be all right?"

"Certainly."

"Then I will go now and get things ready. Until this afternoon . . ."

"Good-bye."

I anticipated a little trouble from Emory, but not much. Everyone back at the ship was anxious to see the Martians, talk with the Martians, poke needles in the Martians, ask them about Martian climate, diseases, soil chemistry, politics, and mushrooms (our botanist was a fungus nut, but a reasonably good guy)—and only four or five had actually gotten to see them. The crew had been spending most of its time excavating dead cities and their acropolises. We played the game by strict rules, and the natives were as fiercely insular as the nineteenth-century Japanese. I figured I would meet with little resistance, and I figured right.

In fact, I got the distinct impression that everyone was happy to see me move out.

I stopped in the hydroponics room to speak with our mushroom master.

"Hi, Kane. Grow any toadstools in the sand yet?"

He sniffed. He always sniffs. Maybe he's allergic to plants.

"Hello, Gallinger. No, I haven't had any success with toadstools, but look behind the car barn next time you're out there. I've got a few cacti going."

"Great," I observed. Doc Kane was about my only friend aboard, not counting Betty.

"Say, I came down to ask you a favor."

"Name it."

"I want a rose."

"A what?"

"A rose. You know, a nice red American Beauty job—thorns, pretty smelling—"

"I don't think it will take in this soil. *Sniff, sniff.*"

"No, you don't understand. I don't want to plant it, I just want the flowers."

"I'd have to use the tanks." He scratched his hairless dome. "It would take at least three months to get you flowers, even under forced growth."

"Will you do it?"

"Sure, if you don't mind the wait."

"Not at all. In fact, three months will just make it before we leave." I looked about at the pools of crawling slime, at the trays of shoots. "—I'm moving up to Tirellian today, but I'll be in and out all the time. I'll be here when it blooms."

"Moving up there, eh? Moore said they're an in-group."

"I guess I'm 'in' then."

"Looks that way—I still don't see how you learned their language, though. Of course, I had trouble with French and German for my PhD., but last week I heard Betty demonstrate it at lunch. It just sounds like a lot of weird noises. She says speaking it is like working a *Times* crossword and trying to imitate birdcalls at the same time."

I laughed, and took the cigarette he offered me.

"It's complicated," I acknowledged. "But, well, it's as if you suddenly came across a whole new class of mycetae here—you'd dream about it at night."

His eyes were gleaming.

"Wouldn't that be something! I might, yet, you know."

"Maybe you will."

He chuckled as we walked to the door.

"I'll start your roses tonight. Take it easy down there."

"You bet. Thanks."

Like I said, a fungus nut, but a fairly good guy.

My quarters in the Citadel of Tirellian were directly adjacent to the Temple, on the inward side and slightly to the left. They were a considerable improvement over my cramped cabin, and I was pleased that Martian culture had progressed sufficiently to discover the desirability of the mattress over the pallet. Also, the bed was long enough to accommodate me, which *was* surprising.

So I unpacked and took 16 35 mm. shots of the Temple, before starting on the books.

I took 'stats until I was sick of turning pages without knowing what they said. So I started translating a work of history.

"Lo. In the thirty-seventh year of the Process of Cillen the rains came, which gave rise to rejoicing, for it was a rare and untoward occurrence, and commonly construed a blessing.

"But it was not the life-giving semen of Malann which fell from the heavens. It was the blood of the universe, spurting from an artery. And the last days were upon us. The final dance was to begin.

"The rains brought the plague that does not kill, and the last passes of Locar began with their drumming . . ."

I asked myself what the hell Tamur meant, for he was an historian and supposedly committed to fact. This was not their Apocalypse.

Unless they could be one and the same . . . ?

Why not? I mused. Tirellian's handful of people were the remnant of what had obviously once been a highly developed culture. They had had wars, but no holocausts; science, but little technology. A plague, a plague that did not kill . . . ? Could that have done it? How, if it wasn't fatal?

I read on, but the nature of the plague was not discussed. I turned pages, skipped ahead, and drew a blank.

M'Cwyie! M'Cwyie! When I want to question you most, you are not around!

Would it be a *faux pas* to go looking for her? Yes, I decided. I was restricted to the rooms I had been shown, that had been an implicit understanding. I would have to wait to find out.

So I cursed long and loud, in many languages, doubtless burning Malann's sacred ears, there in his Temple.

He did not see fit to strike me dead, so I decided to call it a day and hit the sack.

I must have been asleep for several hours when Braxa entered my room with a tiny lamp. She dragged me awake by tugging at my pajama sleeve.

I said hello. Thinking back, there is not much else I could have said. "Hello."

"I have come," she said, "to hear the poem."

"What poem?"

"Yours."

"Oh."

I yawned, sat up, and did things people usually do when awakened in the middle of the night to read poetry.

"That is very kind of you, but isn't the hour a trifle awkward?"

"I don't mind," she said.

Someday I am going to write an article for the *Journal of Semantics*, called "Tone of Voice: An Insufficient Vehicle for Irony."

However, I was awake, so I grabbed my robe.

"What sort of animal is that?" she asked, pointing at the silk dragon on my lapel.

"Mythical," I replied. "Now look, it's late. I am tired. I have much to do in the morning. And M'Cwyie just might get the wrong idea if she learns you were here."

"Wrong idea?"

"You know damned well what I mean!" It was the first time I had had an opportunity to use Martian profanity, and it failed.

"No," she said, "I do not know."

She seemed frightened, like a puppy being scolded without knowing what it has done wrong.

I softened. Her red cloak matched her hair and lips so perfectly, and those lips were trembling.

"Here now, I didn't mean to upset you. On my world there are certain, uh, mores, concerning people of different sex alone together in bedrooms, and not allied by marriage . . . Um, I mean, you see what I mean?"

"No."

They were jade, her eyes.

"Well, it's sort of . . . Well, it's sex, that's what it is."

A light was switched on in those jade lamps.

"Oh, you mean having children!"

"Yes. That's it! Exactly."

She laughed. It was the first time I had heard laughter in Tirellian. It sounded like a violinist striking his high strings with the bow, in short little chops. It was not an altogether pleasant thing to hear, especially because she laughed too long.

When she had finished she moved closer.

"I remember, now," she said. "We used to have such rules. Half a Process ago, when I was a child, we had such rules. But," she looked as if she were ready to laugh again, "there is no need for them now."

My mind moved like a tape recorder played at triple speed.

Half a Process! HalfaProcessaProcessaProcess! No! Yes!

Half a Process was two hundred forty-three years, roughly speaking!

—Time enough to learn the 2,224 dances of Locar.

—Time enough to grow old, if you were human.

—Earth-style human, I mean.

I looked at her again, pale as the white queen in an ivory chess set.

She was human, I'd stake my soul—alive, normal, healthy, I'd stake my life—woman, my body . . .

But she was two and a half centuries old, which made M'Cwyie Methuselah's grandma. It flattered me to think of their repeated complimenting of my skills, as linguist, as poet. These superior beings!

But what did she mean 'there is no such need for them now'? Why the near-hysteria? Why all those funny looks I'd been getting from M'Cwyie?

I suddenly knew I was close to something important, besides a beautiful girl.

"Tell me," I said, in my Casual Voice, "did it have anything to do with 'the plague that does not kill,' of which Tamur wrote?"

"Yes," she replied, "the children born after the Rains could have no children of their own, and—"

"And what?" I was leaning forward, memory set at "record."

"—and the men had no desire to get any."

I sagged backward against the bedpost. Racial sterility, masculine impotence, following phenomenal weather. Had some vagabond cloud of radioactive junk from God knows where penetrated their weak atmosphere one day? One day long before Schiaparelli saw the canals, mythical as my dragon, before those "canals" had given rise to some correct guesses for all the wrong reasons, had Braxa been alive, dancing, here— damned in the womb since blind Milton had written of another paradise, equally lost?

I found a cigarette. Good thing I had thought to bring ashtrays. Mars had never had a tobacco industry either. Or booze. The ascetics I had met in India had been Dionysiac compared to this.

"What is that tube of fire?"

"A cigarette. Want one?"

"Yes, please."

She sat beside me, and I lighted it for her.

"It irritates the nose."

"Yes. Draw some into your lungs, hold it there, and exhale."

A moment passed.

"Ooh," she said.

A pause, then, "Is it sacred?"

"No, it's nicotine," I answered, "a very *ersatz* form of divinity."

Another pause.

"Please don't ask me to translate 'ersatz'."

"I won't. I get this feeling sometimes when I dance."

"It will pass in a moment."

"Tell me your poem now."

An idea hit me.

"Wait a minute," I said, "I may have something better."

I got up and rummaged through my notebooks, then I returned and sat beside her.

"These are the first three chapters of the Book of Ecclesiastes," I explained. "It is very similiar to your own sacred books."

I started reading.

I got through eleven verses before she cried out, "Please don't read that! Tell me one of yours!"

I stopped and tossed the notebook onto a nearby table. She was shaking, not as she had quivered that day she danced as the wind, but with the jitter of unshed tears. She held her cigarette awkwardly, like a pencil. Clumsily, I put my arm about her shoulders.

"He is so sad," she said, "like all the others."

So I twisted my mind like a bright ribbon, folded it, and tied the crazy Christmas knots I love so well. From German to Martian, with love, I did an impromptu paraphrasal of a poem about a Spanish dancer. I thought it would please her. I was right.

"Ooh," she said again. "Did you write that?"

"No, it's by a better man than I."

"I don't believe you. You wrote it."

"No, a man named Rilke did."

"But you brought it across to my language.—Light another match, so I can see how she danced."

I did.

" 'The fires of forever,' " she mused, "and she stamped them out, 'with small, firm feet.' I wish I could dance like that."

"You're better than any Gipsy," I laughed, blowing it out.

"No, I'm not. I couldn't do that."

Her cigarette was burning down, so I removed it from her fingers and put it out, along with my own.

"Do you want me to dance for you?"

"No," I said. "Go to bed."

She smiled, and before I realized it, had unclasped the fold of red at her shoulder.

And everything fell away.

And I swallowed, with some difficulty.

"All right," she said.

So I kissed her, as the breath of fallen cloth extinguished the lamp.

III

The days were like Shelley's leaves: yellow, red, brown, whipped in bright gusts by the west wind. They swirled past me with the rattle of microfilm. Almost all the books were recorded now. It would take scholars years to get through them, to properly assess their value. Mars was locked in my desk.

Ecclesiastes, abandoned and returned to a dozen times, was almost ready to speak in the High Tongue.

I whistled when I wasn't in the Temple. I wrote reams of poetry I would have been ashamed of before. Evenings I would walk with Braxa, across the dunes or up into the mountains. Sometimes she would dance for me; and I would read something long, and in dactylic hexameter. She still thought I was Rilke, and I almost kidded myself into believing it. Here I was, staying at the Castle Duino, writing his *Elegies*.

> . . . It is strange to inhabit the Earth no more,
> to use no longer customs scarce acquired,
> nor interpret roses . . .

No! Never interpret roses! Don't. Smell them (sniff, Kane!), pick them, enjoy them. Live in the moment. Hold to it tightly. But charge not the gods to explain. So fast the leaves go by, are blown . . .

And no one ever noticed us. Or cared.

Laura. Laura and Braxa. They rhyme, you know, with a bit of a clash. Tall, cool, and blonde was she (I hate blondes!), and Daddy had turned me inside out, like a pocket, and I thought she could fill me again. But the big, beat word-slinger, with Judas-beard and dog-trust in his eyes, oh, he had been a fine decoration at her parties. And that was all.

How the machine cursed me in the Temple! It blasphemed Malann and Gallinger. And the wild west wind went by and something was not far behind.

The last days were upon us.

A day went by and I did not see Braxa, and a night.

And a second. A third.

I was half-mad. I hadn't realized how close we had become, how important she had been. With the dumb assurance of presence, I had fought against questioning roses.

I had to ask. I didn't want to, but I had no choice.

"Where is she, M'Cwyie? Where is Braxa?"

"She is gone," she said.

"Where?"

"I do not know."

I looked at those devil-bird eyes. Anathema maranatha rose to my lips.

"I must know."

She looked through me.

"She has left us. She is gone. Up into the hills, I suppose. Or the desert. It does not matter. What does anything matter? The dance draws to a close. The Temple will soon be empty."

"Why? Why did she leave?"

"I do not know."

"I must see her again. We lift off in a matter of days."

"I am sorry, Gallinger."

"So am I," I said, and slammed shut a book without saying "m'narra." I stood up.

"I will find her."

I left the Temple. M'Cwyie was a seated statue. My boots were still where I had left them.

All day I roared up and down the dunes, going nowhere. To the crew of the *Aspic* I must have looked like a sandstorm, all by myself. Finally, I had to return for more fuel.

Emory came stalking out.

"Okay, make it good. You look like the abominable dust man. Why the rodeo?"

"Why, I, uh, lost something."

"In the middle of the desert? Was it one of your sonnets? They're the only thing I can think of that you'd make such a fuss over."

"No, dammit! It was something personal."

George had finished filling the tank. I started to mount the jeepster again.

"Hold on there!" He grabbed my arm.

"You're not going back until you tell me what this is all about."

I could have broken his grip, but then he could order me dragged back by the heels, and quite a few people would enjoy doing the dragging. So I forced myself to speak slowly, softly:

"It's simply that I lost my watch. My mother gave it to me and it's a family heirloom. I want to find it before we leave."

"You sure it's not in your cabin, or down in Tirellian?"

"I've already checked."

"Maybe somebody hid it to irritate you. You know you're not the most popular guy around."

I shook my head.

"I thought of that. But I always carry it in my right pocket. I think it might have bounced out going over the dunes."

He narrowed his eyes.

"I remember reading on a book jacket that your mother died when you were born."

"That's right," I said, biting my tongue. "The watch belonged to her father and she wanted me to have it. My father kept it for me."

"Hmph!" he snorted. "That's a pretty strange way to look for a watch, riding up and down in a jeepster."

"I could see the light shining off it that way," I offered, lamely.

"Well, it's starting to get dark," he observed. "No sense looking any more today.

"Throw a dust sheet over the jeepster," he directed a mechanic.

He patted my arm.

"Come on in and get a shower, and something to eat. You look as if you could use both."

Little fatty flecks beneath pale eyes, thinning hair, and an Irish nose; a voice a decibel louder than anyone else's . . .

His only qualifications for leadership!

I stood there, hating him. Claudius! If only this were the fifth act!

But suddenly the idea of a shower, and food, came through to me. I could use both badly. If I insisted on hurrying back immediately, I might arouse more suspicion.

So I brushed some sand from my sleeve.

"You're right. That sounds like a good idea."

"Come on, we'll eat in my cabin."

The shower was a blessing, clean khakis were the grace of God, and the food smelled like Heaven.

"Smells pretty good," I said.

We hacked up our steaks in silence. When we got to the dessert and coffee, he suggested:

"Why don't you take the night off? Stay here and get some sleep."

I shook my head.

"I'm pretty busy. Finishing up. There's not much time left."

"A couple days ago you said you were almost finished."

"Almost, but not quite."

"You also said they'll be holding a service in the Temple tonight."

"That's right. I'm going to work in my room."

He shrugged his shoulders.

Finally, he said, "Gallinger," and I looked up because my name means trouble.

"It shouldn't be any of my business," he said, "but it is. Betty says you have a girl down there."

There was no question mark. It was a statement hanging in the air. Waiting.

—Betty, you're a bitch. You're a cow and a bitch. And a jealous one, at that. Why didn't you keep your nose where it belonged, shut your eyes? Your mouth?

"So?" I said, a statement with a question mark.

"So," he answered it, "it is my duty, as head of this expedition, to see that relations with the natives are carried on in a friendly, and diplomatic, manner."

"You speak of them," I said, "as though they are aborigines. Nothing could be further from the truth."

I rose.

"When my papers are published, everyone on Earth will know that truth. I'll tell them things Doctor Moore never even guessed at. I'll tell the tragedy of a doomed race, waiting for death, resigned and disinterested. I'll tell why, and it will break hard, scholarly hearts. I'll write about it, and they will give me more prizes, and this time I won't want them.

"My God!" I exclaimed. "They had a culture when our ancestors were clubbing the sabre-tooth and finding out how fire works!"

"Do you have a girl down there?"

"Yes!" I said. *Yes, Claudius! Yes, Daddy! Yes, Emory!* "I do. But I'm going to let you in on a scholarly scoop now. They're already dead. They're sterile. In one more generation there won't be any Martians."

I paused, then added, "Except in my papers, except on a few pieces of microfilm and tape. And in some poems, about a girl who did give a damn and could only bitch about the unfairness of it all by dancing."

"Oh," he said.

After awhile:

"You *have* been behaving differently these past couple months. You've even been downright civil on occasion, you know. I couldn't help wondering what was happening. I didn't know anything mattered that strongly to you."

I bowed my head.

"Is she the reason you were racing around the desert?"

I nodded.

"Why?"

I looked up.

"Because she's out there, somewhere. I don't know where, or why. And I've got to find her before we go."

"Oh," he said again.

Then he leaned back, opened a drawer, and took out something wrapped in a towel. He unwound it. A framed photo of a woman lay on the table.

"My wife," he said.

It was an attractive face, with big, almond eyes.

"I'm a Navy man, you know," he began. "Young officer once. Met her in Japan.

"Where I come from it wasn't considered right to marry into another race, so we never did. But she was my wife. When she died I was on the other side of the world. They took my children, and I've never seen them since. I couldn't learn what orphanage, what home, they were put into. That was long ago. Very few people know about it."

"I'm sorry," I said.

"Don't be. Forget it. But," he shifted in his chair and looked at me, "if you do want to take her back with you—do it. It'll mean my neck, but I'm too old to ever head another expedition like this one. So go ahead."

He gulped his cold coffee.

"Get your jeepster."

He swiveled the chair around.

I tried to say "thank you" twice, but I couldn't. So I got up and walked out.

"Sayonara, and all that," he muttered behind me.

"Here it is, Gallinger!" I heard a shout.

I turned on my heel and looked back up the ramp.

"Kane!"

He was limned in the port, shadow against light, but I had heard him sniff.

I returned the few steps.

"Here what is?"

"Your rose."

He produced a plastic container, divided internally. The lower half was filled with liquid. The stem ran down into it. The other half, a glass of claret in this horrible night, was a large, newly opened rose.

"Thank you," I said, tucking it into my jacket.

"Going back to Tirellian, eh?"

"Yes."

"I saw you come aboard, so I got it ready. Just missed you at the Captain's cabin. He was busy. Hollered out that I could catch you at the barns."

"Thanks again."

"It's chemically treated. It will stay in bloom for weeks."

I nodded. I was gone.

Up into the mountains now. Far. Far. The sky was a bucket of ice in which no moons floated. The going became steeper, and the little donkey protested. I whipped him with the throttle and went on. Up. Up. I spotted a green, unwinking star, and felt a lump in my throat. The uncased rose beat against my chest like an extra heart. The donkey brayed, long and loudly, then began to cough. I lashed him some more and he died.

I threw the emergency brake on and got out. I began to walk.

So cold, so cold it grows. Up here. At night? Why? Why did she do it? Why flee the campfire when night comes on?

And I was up, down around, and through every chasm, gorge, and pass, with my long-legged strides and an ease of movement never known on Earth.

Barely two days remain, my love, and thou hast forsaken me. Why?

I crawled under overhangs. I leapt over ridges. I scraped my knees, an elbow. I heard my jacket tear.

No answer, Malann? Do you really hate your people this much? Then I'll try someone else. Vishnu, you're the Preserver. Preserve her, please! Let me find her.

Jehovah?

Adonis? Osiris? Thammuz? Manitou? Legba? Where is she?

I ranged far and high, and I slipped.

Stones ground underfoot and I dangled over an edge. My fingers so cold. It was hard to grip the rock.

I looked down.

Twelve feet or so. I let go and dropped, landed rolling.

Then I heard her scream.

I lay there, not moving, looking up. Against the night, above, she called.

"Gallinger!"

I lay still.

"Gallinger!"

And she was gone.

I heard stones rattle and knew she was coming down some path to the right of me.

I jumped up and ducked into the shadow of a boulder.

She rounded a cut-off, and picked her way, uncertainly, through the stones.

"Gallinger?"

I stepped out and seized her shoulders.

"Braxa."

She screamed again, then began to cry, crowding against me. It was the first time I had ever heard her cry.

"Why?" I asked. "Why?"

But she only clung to me and sobbed.

Finally, "I thought you had killed yourself."

"Maybe I would have," I said. "Why did you leave Tirellian? And me?"

"Didn't M'Cwyie tell you? Didn't you guess?"

"I didn't guess, and M'Cwyie said she didn't know."

"Then she lied. She knows."

"What? What is it she knows?"

She shook all over, then was silent for a long time. I realized suddenly that she was wearing only her flimsy dancer's costume. I pushed her from me, took off my jacket, and put it about her shoulders.

"Great Malann!" I cried. "You'll freeze to death!"

"No," she said, "I won't."

I was transferring the rose case to my pocket.

"What is that?" she asked.

"A rose," I answered. "You can't make it out much in the dark. I once compared you to one. Remember?"

"Yu-Yes. May I carry it?"

"Sure." I stuck it in the jacket pocket.

"Well? I'm still waiting for an explanation."

"You really do not know?" she asked.

"No!"

"When the Rains came," she said, "apparently only our men were affected, which was enough. . . . Because I—wasn't—affected—apparently—"

"Oh," I said. "Oh."

We stood there, and I thought.

"Well, why did you run? What's wrong with being pregnant on Mars? Tamur was mistaken. Your people can live again."

She laughed, again that wild violin played by a Paganini gone mad. I stopped her before it went too far.

"How?" she finally asked, rubbing her cheek.

"Your people live longer than ours. If our child is normal it will mean our races can intermarry. There must still be other fertile women of your race. Why not?"

"You have read the Book of Locar," she said, "and yet you ask me that? Death was decided, voted upon, and passed, shortly after it appeared in this form. But long before, the followers of Locar knew. They decided it long ago. 'We have done all things,' they said, 'we have seen all things, we have heard and felt all things. The dance was good. Now let it end.' "

"You can't believe that."

"What I believe does not matter," she replied. "M'Cwyie and the Mothers have decided we must die. Their very title is now a mockery, but their decisions will be upheld. There is only one prophecy left, and it is mistaken. We will die."

"No," I said.

"What, then?"

"Come back with me, to Earth."

"No."

"All right, then. Come with me now."

"Where?"

"Back to Tirellian. I'm going to talk to the Mothers."

"You can't! There is a Ceremony tonight!"

I laughed.

"A ceremony for a god who knocks you down, and then kicks you in the teeth?"

"He is still Malann," she answered. "We are still his people."

"You and my father would have gotten along fine," I snarled. "But I am going, and you are coming with me, even if I have to carry you—and I'm bigger than you are."

"But you are not bigger than Ontro."

"Who the hell is Ontro?"

"He will stop you, Gallinger. He is the Fist of Malann."

IV

I scudded the jeepster to a halt in front of the only entrance I knew, M'Cwyie's. Braxa, who had seen the rose in a headlamp, now cradled it in her lap, like our child, and said nothing. There was a passive, lovely look on her face.

"Are they in the Temple now?" I wanted to know.

The Madonna expression did not change. I repeated the question. She stirred.

"Yes," she said, from a distance, "but you cannot go in."

"We'll see."

I circled and helped her down.

I led her by the hand, and she moved as if in a trance. In the light of the new-risen moon, her eyes looked as they had the day I met her, when she had danced. I snapped my fingers. Nothing happened.

So I pushed the door open and led her in. The room was half-lighted.

And she screamed for the third time that evening:

"Do not harm him, Ontro! It is Gallinger!"

I had never seen a Martian man before, only women. So I had no way of knowing whether he was a freak, though I suspected it strongly.

I looked up at him.

His half-naked body was covered with moles and swellings. Gland trouble, I guessed.

I had thought I was the tallest man on the planet, but he was seven feet tall and overweight. Now I knew where my giant bed had come from!

"Go back," he said. "She may enter. You may not."

"I must get my books and things."

He raised a huge left arm. I followed it. All my belongings lay neatly stacked in the corner.

"I must go in. I must talk with M'Cwyie and the Mothers."

"You may not."

"The lives of your people depend on it."

"Go back," he boomed. "Go home to *your* people, Gallinger. Leave *us!*"

My name sounded so different on his lips, like someone else's. How old was he? I wondered. Three hundred? Four? Had he been a Temple guardian all his life? Why? Who was there to guard against? I didn't like the way he moved. I had seen men who moved like that before.

"Go back," he repeated.

If they had refined their martial arts as far as they had their dances, or, worse yet, if their fighting arts were a part of the dance, I was in for trouble.

"Go on in," I said to Braxa. "Give the rose to M'Cwyie. Tell her that I sent it. Tell her I'll be there shortly."

"I will do as you ask. Remember me on Earth, Gallinger. Good-bye."

I did not answer her, and she walked past Ontro and into the next room, bearing her rose.

"Now will you leave?" he asked. "If you like, I will tell her that we fought and you almost beat me, but I knocked you unconscious and carried you back to your ship."

"No," I said, "either I go around you or go over you, but I am going through."

He dropped into a crouch, arms extended.

"It is a sin to lay hands on a holy man," he rumbled, "but I will stop you, Gallinger."

My memory was a fogged window, suddenly exposed to fresh air. Things cleared. I looked back six years.

I was a student of Oriental Languages at the University of Tokyo. It was my twice-weekly night of recreation. I stood in a 30-foot circle in the Kodokan, the *judogi* lashed about my high hips by a brown belt. I was *Ikkyu*, one notch below the lowest degree of expert. A brown diamond above my right breast said "Jiu-Jitsu" in Japanese, and it meant *atemi-waza*, really, because of the one striking technique I had worked out, found unbelievably suitable to my size, and won matches with.

But I had never used it on a man, and it was five years since I had practiced. I was out of shape, I knew, but I tried hard to force my mind *tsuki no kokoro*, like the moon, reflecting the all of Ontro.

Somewhere, out of the past, a voice said, "*Hajime*, let it begin."

I snapped into my *neko-ashi-dachi* cat stance, and his eyes burned strangely. He hurried to correct his own position—and I threw it at him!

My one trick!

My long left leg lashed up like a broken spring. Seven feet off the ground my foot connected with his jaw as he tried to leap backward.

His head snapped back and he fell. A soft moan escaped his lips. *That's all there is to it,* I thought. *Sorry, old fellow.*

And as I stepped over him, somehow, groggily, he tripped me, and I fell across his body. I couldn't believe he had strength enough to remain conscious after that blow, let alone move. I hated to punish him any more.

But he found my throat and slipped a forearm across it before I realized there was a purpose to his action.

No! Don't let it end like this!

It was a bar of steel across my windpipe, my carotids. Then I realized that he was still unconscious, and that this was a reflex instilled by countless years of training. I had seen it happen once, in *shiai*. The man had died because he had been choked unconscious and still fought on, and his opponent thought he had not been applying the choke properly. He tried harder.

But it was rare, so very rare!

I jammed my elbows into his ribs and threw my head back in his face. The grip eased, but not enough. I hated to do it, but I reached up and broke his little finger.

The arm went loose and I twisted free.

He lay there panting, face contorted. My heart went out to the fallen giant, defending his people, his religion, following his orders. I cursed myself as I had never cursed before, for walking over him, instead of around.

I staggered across the room to my little heap of possessions. I sat on the projector case and lit a cigarette.

I couldn't go into the Temple until I got my breath back, until I thought of something to say?

How do you talk a race out of killing itself?

Suddenly—

—Could it happen? Would it work that way? If I read them the Book of Ecclesiastes—if I read them a greater piece of literature than any Locar ever wrote—and as somber—and as pessimistic—and showed them that our race had gone on despite one man's condemning all of life in the highest poetry—showed them that the vanity he had mocked had borne us to the Heavens—would they believe it?—would they change their minds?

I ground out my cigarette on the beautiful floor, and found my notebook. A strange fury rose within me as I stood.

And I walked into the Temple to preach the Black Gospel according to Gallinger, from the Book of Life.

There was silence all about me.

M'Cwyie had been reading Locar, the rose set at her right hand, target of all eyes.

Until I entered.

Hundreds of people were seated on the floor, barefoot. The few men were as small as the women, I noted.

I had my boots on.

Go all the way, I figured. *You either lose or you win—everything!*

A dozen crones sat in a semicircle behind M'Cwyie. The Mothers.

The barren earth, the dry wombs, the fire-touched.

I moved to the table.

"Dying yourselves, you would condemn your people," I addressed them, "that they may not know the life you have known—the joys, the sorrows, the fullness.—But it is not true that you all must die." I addressed the multitude now. "Those who say this lie. Braxa knows, for she will bear a child—"

They sat there, like rows of Buddhas. M'Cwyie drew back into the semicircle.

"—my child!" I continued, wondering what my father would have thought of this sermon.

". . . And all the women young enough may bear children. It is only your men who are sterile.—And if you permit the doctors of the next expedition to examine you, perhaps even the men may be helped. But if they cannot, you can mate with the men of Earth.

"And ours is not an insignificant people, an insignificant place," I went on. "Thousands of years ago, the Locar of our world wrote a book saying that it was. He spoke as Locar did, but we did not lie down, despite plagues, wars, and famines. We did not die. One by one we beat down the diseases, we fed the hungry, we fought the wars, and, recently, have gone a long time without them. We may finally have conquered them. I do not know.

"But we have crossed millions of miles of nothingness. We have visited another world. And our Locar had said, 'Why bother? What is the worth of it? It is all vanity, anyhow.'

"And the secret is," I lowered my voice, as at a poetry reading, "he was right! It *is* vanity, it *is* pride! It is the *hybris* of rationalism to always attack the prophet, the mystic, the god. It is our blasphemy which has made us great, and will sustain us, and which the gods secretly admire in us.—All the truly sacred names of God are blasphemous things to speak!"

I was working up a sweat. I paused dizzily.

"Here is the Book of Ecclesiastes," I announced, and began:

" 'Vanity of vanities, saith the Preacher, vanity of vanities; all is vanity. What profit hath a man . . .' "

I spotted Braxa in the back, mute, rapt.

I wondered what she was thinking.

And I wound the hours of night about me, like black thread on a spool.

Oh, it was late! I had spoken till day came, and still I spoke. I finished Ecclesiastes and continued Gallinger.

And when I finished, there was still only a silence.

The Buddhas, all in a row, had not stirred through the night. And after a long while M'Cwyie raised her right hand. One by one the Mothers did the same.

And I knew what that meant.

It meant no, do not, cease, and stop.

It meant that I had failed.

I walked slowly from the room and slumped beside my baggage.

Ontro was gone. Good that I had not killed him . . .

After a thousand years M'Cwyie entered.

She said, "Your job is finished."

I did not move.

"The prophecy is fulfilled," she said. "My people are rejoicing. You have won, holy man. Now leave us quickly."

My mind was a deflated balloon. I pumped a little air back into it.

"I'm not a holy man," I said, "just a second-rate poet with a bad case of *hybris*."

I lit my last cigarette.

Finally, "All right, what prophecy?"

"The Promise of Locar," she replied, as though the explaining were unnecessary, "that a holy man would come from the heavens to save us in our last hours, if all the dances of Locar were completed. He would defeat the Fist of Malann and bring us life."

"How?"

"As with Braxa, and as the example in the Temple."

"Example?"

"You read us his words, as great as Locar's. You read to us how there is 'nothing new under the sun.' And you mocked his words as you read them—showing us a new thing.

"There has never been a flower on Mars," she said, "but we will learn to grow them.

"You are the Sacred Scoffer," she finished. "He-Who-Must-Mock-in-the-Temple—you go shod on holy ground."

"But you voted 'no'," I said.

"I voted not to carry out our original plan, and to let Braxa's child live instead."

"Oh." The cigarette fell from my fingers. How close it had been! How little I had known!

"And Braxa?"

"She was chosen half a Process ago to do the dances—to wait for you."

"But she said that Ontro would stop me."

M'Cwyie stood there for a long time.

"She had never believed the prophecy herself. Things are not well with her now. She ran away, fearing it was true. When you completed it and we voted, she knew."

"Then she does not love me? Never did?"

"I am sorry, Gallinger. It was the one part of her duty she never managed."

"Duty," I said flatly. . . . Dutydutyduty! Tra-la!

"She has said good-bye, she does not wish to see you again.

". . . and we will never forget your teachings," she added.

"Don't," I said, automatically, suddenly knowing the great paradox which lies at the heart of all miracles. I did not believe a word of my own gospel, never had.

I stood, like a drunken man, and muttered "M'narra."

I went outside, into my last day on Mars.

I have conquered thee, Malann—and the victory is thine! Rest easy on thy starry bed. God damned!

I left the jeepster there and walked back to the *Aspic*, leaving the burden of life so many footsteps behind me. I went to my cabin, locked the door, and took forty-four sleeping pills.

But when I awakened, I was in the dispensary, and alive.
I felt the throb of engines as I slowly stood up and somehow made it to the port.
Blurred Mars hung like a swollen belly above me, until it dissolved, brimmed over, and streamed down my face.

QUESTIONS

1. What kind of person is Gallinger? Is he at all like the character Rhysling in "The Green Hills of Earth"?
2. Discuss the function of the numerous literary allusions made in this story.
3. How does the end of the story relate to the meaning of *The Book of Ecclesiastes*?
4. Does the unlikelihood of any life ever having existed on Mars seriously flaw this story?
5. Does Zelazny intend you to feel sympathy for Gallinger, especially at the end of the story?
6. Is Zelazny's prose style effective? Would the story gain or lose in effect if he had used, for example, longer paragraphs?

"Repent, Harlequin!" Said the Ticktockman

Harlan Ellison

There are always those who ask, what is it all about? For those who need to ask, for those who need points sharply made, who need to know "where it's at," this:

> The mass of men serve the state thus, not as men mainly, but as machines, with their bodies. They are the standing army, and the militia, jailors, constables, posse comitatus, etc. In most cases there is no free exercise whatever of the judgment or of the moral sense; but they put themselves on a level with wood and earth and stones; and wooden men can perhaps be manufactured that will serve the purposes as well. Such command no more respect than men of straw or a lump of dirt. They have the same sort of worth only as horses and dogs. Yet such as these even are commonly esteemed good citizens. Others—as most legislators, politicians, lawyers, ministers, and office-holders—serve the state chiefly with their heads; and, as they rarely make any moral distinctions, they are as likely to serve the Devil, without intending it, as God. A very few, as heroes, patriots, martyrs, reformers in the great sense, and *men*, serve the state with their consciences also, and so necessarily resist it for the most part; and they are commonly treated as enemies by it.*

That is the heart of it. Now begin in the middle, and later learn the beginning; the end will take care of itself.

But because it was the very world it was, the very world they had allowed it to *become*, for months his activities did not come to the alarmed attention of The Ones Who Kept The Machine Functioning Smoothly, the ones who poured the very best butter over the cams and mainsprings of the culture. Not until it had become obvious that somehow, someway, he had become a notoriety, a celebrity, perhaps even a hero for (what Officialdom inescapably tagged) "an emotionally disturbed segment of the populace," did they turn it over to the Ticktockman and his legal machinery. But by then, because it was the very world

---

* Henry David Thoreau, "Civil Disobedience."

it was, and they had no way to predict he would happen—possibly a strain of disease long-defunct, now, suddenly, reborn in a system where immunity had been forgotten, had lapsed—he had been allowed to become too real. Now he had form and substance.

He had become a *personality*, something they had filtered out of the system many decades ago. But there it was, and there *he* was, a very definitely imposing personality. In certain circles—middle-class circles— it was thought disgusting. Vulgar ostentation. Anarchistic. Shameful. In others, there was only sniggering, those strata where thought is subjugated to form and ritual, niceties, proprieties. But down below, ah, down below, where the people always needed their saints and sinners, their bread and circuses, their heroes and villains, he was considered a Bolivar; a Napoleon; a Robin Hood; a Dick Bong (Ace of Aces); a Jesus; a Jomo Kenyatta.

And at the top—where, like socially-attuned Shipwreck Kellys, even tremor and vibration threatens to dislodge the wealthy, powerful and titled from their flagpoles—he was considered a menace; a heretic; a rebel; a disgrace; a peril. He was known down the line, to the very heartmeat core, but the important reactions were high above and far below. At the very top, at the very bottom.

So his file was turned over, along with his time-card and his cardioplate, to the office of the Ticktockman.

The Ticktockman: very much over six feet tall, often silent, a soft purring man when things went timewise. The Ticktockman.

Even in the cubicles of the hierarchy, where fear was generated, seldom suffered, he was called the Ticktockman. But no one called him that to his mask.

You don't call a man a hated name, not when that man, behind his mask, is capable of revoking the minutes, the hours, the days and nights, the years of your life. He was called the Master Timekeeper to his mask. It was safer that way.

"This is *what* he is," said the Ticktockman with genuine softness, "but not *who* he is? This time-card I'm holding in my left hand has a name on it, but it is the name of *what* he is, not *who* he is. This cardioplate here in my right hand is also named, but not whom named, merely what named. Before I can exercise proper revocation, I have to know who this what is."

To his staff, all the ferrets, all the loggers, all the finks, all the commex, even the mineez, he said, "Who is this Harlequin?"

He was not purring smoothly. Timewise, it was jangle.

However, it *was* the longest single speech they had ever heard him utter at one time, the staff, the ferrets, the loggers, the finks, the commex, but not the mineez, who usually weren't around to know, in any case. But even they scurried to find out.

Who is the Harlequin?

High above the third level of the city, he crouched on the humming aluminum-frame platform of the air-boat (foof! air-boat, indeed! swizzleskid is what it was, with a tow-rack jerry-rigged) and stared down at the neat Mondrian arrangement of the buildings.

Somewhere nearby, he could hear the metronomic left-right-left of the 2:47 P.M. shift, entering the Timkin roller-bearing plant in their sneakers. A minute later, precisely, he heard the softer right-left-right of the 5:00 A.M. formation, going home.

An elfish grin spread across his tanned features, and his dimples appeared for a moment. Then, scratching at his thatch of auburn hair, he shrugged within his motley, as though girding himself for what came next, and threw the joystick forward, and bent into the wind as the air-boat dropped. He skimmed over a slidewalk, purposely dropping a few feet to crease the tassels of the ladies of fashion, and—inserting thumbs in large ears—he stuck out his tongue, rolled his eyes and went wugga-wugga-wugga. It was a minor diversion. One pedestrian skittered and tumbled, sending parcels everywhichway, another wet herself, a third keeled slantwise and the walk was stopped automatically by the servitors till she could be resuscitated. It was a minor diversion.

Then he swirled away on a vagrant breeze, and was gone. Hi-ho.

As he rounded the cornice of the Time-Motion Study Building, he saw the shift, just boarding the slidewalk. With practiced motion and an absolute conservation of movement, they sidestepped up onto the slowstrip and (in a chorus line reminiscent of a Busby Berkeley film of the antediluvian 1930's) advanced across the strips ostrich-walking till they were lined up on the expresstrip.

Once more, in anticipation, the elfin grin spread, and there was a tooth missing back there on the left side. He dipped, skimmed, and swooped over them; and then, scrunching about on the air-boat, he released the holding pins that fastened shut the ends of the home-made pouring troughs that kept his cargo from dumping prematurely. And as he pulled the trough-pins, the air-boat slid over the factory workers and one hundred and fifty thousand dollars worth of jelly beans cascaded down on the expresstrip.

Jelly beans! Millions and billions of purples and yellows and greens and licorice and grape and raspberry and mint and round and smooth and crunchy outside and soft-mealy inside and sugary and bouncing jouncing tumbling clittering clattering skittering fell on the heads and shoulders and hardhats and carapaces of the Timkin workers, tinkling on the slidewalk and bouncing away and rolling about underfoot and filling the sky on their way down with all the colors of joy and childhood and holidays, coming down in a steady rain, a solid wash, a torrent of color and sweetness out of the sky from above, and entering a universe of sanity and metronomic order with quite-mad coocoo newness. Jelly beans!

The shift workers howled and laughed and were pelted, and broke ranks, and the jelly beans managed to work their way into the mechanism of the slidewalks after which there was a hideous scraping as the sound of a million fingernails rasped down a quarter of a million blackboards, followed by a coughing and a sputtering, and then the slidewalks all stopped and everyone was dumped thisawayandthataway in a jackstraw tumble, and still laughing and popping little jelly bean eggs of childish color into their mouths. It was a holiday, and a jollity, an absolute insanity, a giggle. But . . .

The shift was delayed seven minutes.

They did not get home for seven minutes.

The master schedule was thrown off by seven minutes.

Quotas were delayed by inoperative slidewalks for seven minutes.

He had tapped the first domino in the line, and one after another, like chik chik chik, the others had fallen.

The System had been seven minutes worth of disrupted. It was a tiny matter, one hardly worthy of note, but in a society where the single driving force was order and unity and promptness and clocklike precision and attention to the clock, reverence of the gods of the passage of time, it was a disaster of major importance.

So he was ordered to appear before the Ticktockman. It was broadcast across every channel of the communications web. He was ordered to be *there* at 7:00 dammit on time. And they waited, and they waited, but he didn't show up till almost ten-thirty, at which time he merely sang a little song about moonlight in a place no one had ever heard of, called Vermont, and vanished again. But they had all been waiting since seven, and it wrecked *hell* with their schedules. So the question remained: Who is the Harlequin?

But the *unasked* question (more important of the two) was: how did we get *into* this position, where a laughing, irresponsible japer of jabberwocky and jive could disrupt our entire economic and cultural life with a hundred and fifty thousand dollars worth of jelly beans . . .

Jelly for God's sake beans! This is madness! Where did he get the money to buy a hundred and fifty thousand dollars worth of jelly beans? (They knew it would have cost that much, because they had a team of Situation Analysts pulled off another assignment, and rushed to the slidewalk scene to sweep up and count the candies, and produce findings, which disrupted *their* schedules and threw their entire branch at least a day behind.) Jelly beans! Jelly . . . *beans?* Now wait a second—a second accounted for—no one has manufactured jelly beans for over a hundred years. Where did he get jelly beans?

That's another good question. More than likely it will never be answered to your complete satisfaction. But then, how many questions ever are?

The middle you know. Here is the beginning. How it starts:

A desk pad. Day for day, and turn each day. 9:00—open the mail. 9:45—appointment with planning commission board. 10:30—discuss installation progress charts with J.L. 11:45—pray for rain. 12:00—lunch. *And so it goes.*

"I'm sorry, Miss Grant, but the time for interviews was set at 2:30, and it's almost five now. I'm sorry you're late, but those are the rules. You'll have to wait till next year to submit application for this college again." *And so it goes.*

The 10:10 local stops at Cresthaven, Galesville, Tonawanda Junction, Selby and Farnhurst, but not at Indiana City, Lucasville and Colton, except on Sunday. The 10:35 express stops at Galesville, Selby and Indiana City, except on Sundays & Holidays, at which time it stops at . . . *and so it goes.*

"I couldn't wait, Fred. I had to be at Pierre Cartain's by 3:00, and you said you'd meet me under the clock in the terminal at 2:45, and you weren't there, so I had to go on. You're always late, Fred. If you'd been there, we could have sewed it up together, but as it was, well, I took the order alone . . ." *And so it goes.*

Dear Mr. and Mrs. Atterley: in reference to your son Gerold's constant tardiness, I am afraid we will have to suspend him from school unless some more reliable method can be instituted guaranteeing he will arrive at his classes on time. Granted he is an exemplary student, and his marks are high, his constant flouting of the schedules of this school makes it impractical to maintain him in a system where the other children seem capable of getting where they are supposed to be on time *and so it goes.*

YOU CANNOT VOTE UNLESS YOU APPEAR AT 8:45 A.M.

"I don't care if the script is *good*, I need it Thursday!"

CHECK-OUT TIME IS 2:00 P.M.

"You got here late. The job's taken. Sorry."

YOUR SALARY HAS BEEN DOCKED FOR TWENTY MINUTES TIME LOST.

"God, what time is it, I've gotta run!"

And so it goes. And so it goes. And so it goes. And so it goes goes goes goes goes tick tock tick tock tick tock and one day we no longer let time serve us, we serve time and we are slaves of the schedule, worshippers of the sun's passing, bound into a life predicated on restrictions because the system will not function if we don't keep the schedule tight.

Until it becomes more than a minor inconvenience to be late. It becomes a sin. Then a crime. Then a crime punishable by this:

EFFECTIVE 15 JULY 2389, 12:00 midnight, the office of the Master Timekeeper will require all citizens to submit their time-cards and cardioplates for processing. In accordance with Statute 555-7-SGH-999 governing the revocation of time per capita, all cardioplates will be keyed to the individual holder and—

What they had done, was devise a method of curtailing the amount of life a person could have. If he was ten minutes late, he lost ten minutes of his life. An hour was proportionately worth more revocation. If someone was consistently tardy, he might find himself, on a Sunday night, receiving a communique from the Master Timekeeper that his time had run out, and he would be "turned off" at high noon on Monday, please straighten your affairs, sir.

And so, by this simple scientific expedient (utilizing a scientific process held dearly secret by the Ticktockman's office) the System was maintained. It was the only expedient thing to do. It was, after all, patriotic. The schedules had to be met. After all, there *was* a war on!

But, wasn't there always?

"Now that is really disgusting," the Harlequin said, when pretty Alice showed him the wanted poster. "Disgusting and *highly* improbable. After all, this isn't the days of desperadoes. A *wanted* poster!"

"You know," Alice noted, "you speak with a great deal of inflection."

"I'm sorry," said the Harlequin, humbly.

"No need to be sorry. You're always saying 'I'm sorry.' You have such massive guilt, Everett, it's really very sad."

"I'm sorry," he repeated, then pursed his lips so the dimples appeared momentarily. He hadn't wanted to say that at all. "I have to go out again. I have to *do* something."

Alice slammed her coffee-bulb down on the counter. "Oh for God's *sake*, Everett, can't you stay home just *one* night! Must you always be out in that ghastly clown suit, running around annoying people?"

"I'm—" he stopped, and clapped the jester's hat onto his auburn thatch with a tiny tingling of bells. He rose, rinsed out his coffee-bulb at the tap, and put it into the drier for a moment. "I have to go."

She didn't answer. The faxbox was purring, and she pulled a sheet out, read it, threw it toward him on the counter. "It's about you. Of course. You're ridiculous."

He read it quickly. It said the Ticktockman was trying to locate him. He didn't care, he was going out to be late again. At the door, dredging for an exit line, he hurled back petulantly, "Well, *you* speak with inflection, *too!*"

Alice rolled her pretty eyes heavenward. "You're ridiculous." The Harlequin stalked out, slamming the door, which sighed shut softly, and locked itself.

There was a gentle knock, and Alice got up with an exhalation of exasperated breath, and opened the door. He stood there. "I'll be back about ten-thirty, okay?"

She pulled a rueful face. "Why do you tell me that? Why? You *know* you'll be late! You *know it!* You're *always* late, so why do you tell me these dumb things?" She closed the door.

On the other side, the Harlequin nodded to himself. *She's right. She's always right. I'll be late. I'm always late. Why do I tell her these dumb things?*

He shrugged again, and went off to be late once more.

He had fired off the firecracker rockets that said: I will attend the 115th annual International Medical Association Invocation at 8:00 P.M. precisely. I do hope you will all be able to join me.

The words had burned in the sky, and of course the authorities were there, lying in wait for him. They assumed, naturally, that he would be late. He arrived twenty minutes early, while they were setting up the spiderwebs to trap and hold him, and blowing a large bullhorn, he frightened and unnerved them so, their own moisturized encirclement webs sucked closed, and they were hauled up, kicking and shrieking, high above the amphitheater's floor. The Harlequin laughed and laughed, and apologized profusely. The physicians, gathered in solemn conclave, roared with laughter, and accepted the Harlequin's apologies with exaggerated bowing and posturing, and a merry time was had by all, who thought the Harlequin was a regular foofaraw in fancy pants; all, that is, but the authorities, who had been sent out by the office of the Ticktockman, who hung there like so much dockside cargo, hauled up above the floor of the amphitheater in a most unseemly fashion.

(In another part of the same city where the Harlequin carried on his "activities," totally unrelated in every way to what concerns here, save that it illustrates the Ticktockman's power and import, a man named Marshall Delahanty received his turn-off notice from the Ticktockman's office. His wife received the notification from the grey-suited minee who delivered it, with the traditional "look of sorrow" plastered hideously across his face. She knew what it was, even without unsealing it. It was a billet-doux of immediate recognition to everyone these days. She gasped, and held it as though it were a glass slide tinged with botulism, and prayed it was not for her. Let it be for Marsh, she thought, brutally, realistically, or one of the kids, but not for me, please dear God, not for me. And then she opened it, and it *was* for Marsh, and she was at one and the same time horrified and relieved. The next trooper in the line had caught the bullet. "Marshall," she screamed, "Marshall! Termination, Marshall! OhmiGod, Marshall, whattl we do, whattl we do, Marshall omigodmarshall . . ." and in their home that night was the sound of tearing paper and fear, and the stink of madness went up the flue and there was nothing, absolutely nothing they could do about it.

(But Marshall Delahanty tried to run. And early the next day, when turn-off time came, he was deep in the forest two hundred miles away, and the office of the Ticktockman blanked his cardioplate, and Marshall Delahanty keeled over, running, and his heart stopped, and the blood dried up on its way to his brain, and he was dead that's all. One light went out on his sector map in the office of the Master Timekeeper, while notification was entered for fax reproduction, and Georgette Delahanty's name was entered on the dole roles till she could re-marry. Which is the end of the footnote, and all the point that need be made, except don't laugh, because that is what would happen to the Harlequin if ever the Ticktockman found out his real name. It isn't funny.)

The shopping level of the city was thronged with the Thursday-colors of the buyers. Women in canary yellow chitons and men in pseudo-Tyrolean outfits that were jade and leather and fit very tightly, save for the balloon pants.

When the Harlequin appeared on the still-being-constructed shell of the new Efficiency Shopping Center, his bullhorn to his elfishly-laughing lips, everyone pointed and stared, and he berated them:

"Why let them order you about? Why let them tell you to hurry and scurry like ants or maggots? Take your time! Saunter a while! Enjoy the sunshine, enjoy the breeze, let life carry you at your own pace! Don't be slaves of time, it's a helluva way to die, slowly, by degrees . . . down with the Ticktockman!"

Who's the nut? most of the shoppers wanted to know. Who's the nut oh wow I'm gonna be late I gotta run . . .

And the construction gang on the Shopping Center received an urgent order from the office of the Master Timekeeper that the dangerous criminal known as the Harlequin was atop their spire, and their aid was urgently needed in apprehending him. The work crew said no, they would lose time on their construction schedule, but the Ticktockman managed to pull the proper threads of governmental webbing, and they were told to cease work and catch that nitwit up there on the spire with the bullhorn. So a dozen and more burly workers began climbing into their construction platforms, releasing the a-grav plates, and rising toward the Harlequin.

After the debacle (in which, through the Harlequin's attention to personal safety, no one was seriously injured), the workers tried to reassemble, and assault him again, but it was too late. He had vanished. It had attracted quite a crowd, however, and the shopping cycle was thrown off by hours, simply hours. The purchasing needs of the system were therefore falling behind, and so measures were taken to accelerate the cycle for the rest of the day, but it got bogged down and speeded up and they sold too many float-valves and not nearly enough wegglers, which meant that the popli ratio was off, which made it necessary to rush cases and cases of spoiling Smash-O to stores that usually needed a case only every three or four hours. The shipments were bollixed, the trans-shipments were misrouted, and in the end, even the swizzleskid industries felt it.

"Don't come back till you have him!" the Ticktockman said, very quietly, very sincerely, extremely dangerously.

They used dogs. They used probes. They used cardioplate crossoffs.

They used teepers. They used bribery. They used stiktytes. They used intimidation. They used torment. They used torture. They used finks. They used cops. They used search&seizure. They used fallaron. They used betterment incentive. They used fingerprints. They used Bertillon. They used cunning. They used guile. They used treachery. They used Raoul Mitgong, but he didn't help much. They used applied physics. They used techniques of criminology.

And what the hell: they caught him.

After all, his name was Everett C. Marm, and he wasn't much to begin with, except a man who had no sense of time.

"Repent, Harlequin!" said the Ticktockman.

"Get stuffed!" the Harlequin replied, sneering.

"You've been late a total of sixty-three years, five months, three weeks, two days, twelve hours, forty-one minutes, fifty-nine seconds, point oh three six one one one microseconds. You've used up everything you can, and more. I'm going to turn you off."

"Scare someone else. I'd rather be dead than live in a dumb world with a bogeyman like you."

"It's my job."

"You're full of it. You're a tyrant. You have no right to order people around and kill them if they show up late."

"You can't adjust. You can't fit in."

"Unstrap me, and I'll fit my fist into your mouth."

"You're a non-conformist."

"That didn't used to be a felony."

"It is now. Live in the world around you."

"I hate it. It's a terrible world."

"Not everyone thinks so. Most people enjoy order."

"I don't, and most of the people I know don't."

"That's not true. How do you think we caught you?"

"I'm not interested."

"A girl named pretty Alice told us who you were."

"That's a lie."

"It's true. You unnerve her. She wants to belong, she wants to conform, I'm going to turn you off."

"Then do it already, and stop arguing with me."

"I'm not going to turn you off."

"You're an idiot!"

"Repent, Harlequin!" said the Ticktockman.

"Get stuffed."

So they sent him to Coventry. And in Coventry they worked him over. It was just like what they did to Winston Smith in "1984," which was a book none of them knew about, but the techniques are really quite ancient, and so they did it to Everett C. Marm, and one day quite a long time later, the Harlequin appeared on the communications web, appearing elfish and dimpled and bright-eyed, and not at all brainwashed, and he said he had been wrong, that it was a good, a very good thing indeed, to belong, and be right on time hip-ho and away we go, and everyone stared up at him on the public screens that covered an entire city block, and they said to themselves, well, you see, he was just a nut after all, and if that's the way the system is run, then let's do it that way, because it doesn't pay to fight city hall, or in this case, the Ticktockman. So Everett C. Marm was destroyed, which was a loss, because of what Thoreau said earlier, but you can't make an omelet without breaking a few eggs, and in every revolution, a few die who shouldn't, but they have to, because that's the way it happens, and if you make only a little change, then it seems to be worthwhile. Or, to make the point lucidly:

"Uh, excuse me, sir, I, uh, don't know how to uh, to uh, tell you this, but you were three minutes late. The schedule is a little, uh, bit off."

He grinned sheepishly.

"That's ridiculous!" murmured the Ticktockman behind his mask. "Check your watch." And then he went into his office, going mrmee, mrmee, mrmee, mrmee.

QUESTIONS

1. Explain what happens to the Ticktockman at the story's ending.

2. How does this story demonstrate an awareness of ecological concepts?

3. Compare this story to "Harrison Bergeron."

4. Discuss the contribution of Ellison's style to the story.

5. Would the story have significantly lost in effectiveness had it been written without the focus on Thoreau?

6. Use this story as a basis for discussing the American obsession with time.

Day Million

Frederik Pohl

On this day I want to tell you about, which will be about ten thousand years from now, there were a boy, a girl and a love story. Now, although I haven't said much so far, none of it is true. The boy was not what you and I would normally think of as a boy, because he was a hundred and eighty-seven years old. Nor was the girl a girl, for other reasons. And the love story did not entail that sublimation of the urge to rape, and concurrent postponement of the instinct to submit, which we at present understand in such matters. You won't care much for this story if you don't grasp these facts at once. If, however, you will make the effort you'll likely enough find it jampacked, chockful and tip-top-crammed with laughter, tears and poignant sentiment which may, or may not, be worthwhile. The reason the girl was not a girl was that she was a boy.

How angrily you recoil from the page! You say, who the hell wants to read about a pair of queers? Calm yourself. Here are no hot-breathing secrets of perversion for the coterie trade. In fact, if you were to see this girl you would not guess that she was in any sense a boy. Breasts, two; reproductive organs, female. Hips, callipygean; face hairless, supra-orbital lobes non-existent. You would term her female on sight, although it is true that you might wonder just what species she was a female of, being confused by the tail, the silky pelt and the gill slits behind each ear.

Now you recoil again. Cripes, man, take my word for it. This is a sweet kid, and if you, as a normal male, spent as much as an hour in a room with her you would bend heaven and Earth to get her in the sack. Dora — We will call her that; her "name" was omicron-Dibase seven-group-totter-oot S Doradus 5314, the last part of which is a colour specification corresponding to a shade of green—Dora, I say, was feminine, charming and cute. I admit she doesn't sound that way. She was, as you might put it, a dancer. Her art involved qualities of intellection and expertise of a very high order, requiring both tremendous natural capacities and endless practice; it was performed in null-gravity and I can best describe it by saying that it was something like the performance of a contortionist and something like classical ballet, maybe resembling Danilova's dying swan.

225

It was also pretty damned sexy. In a symbolic way, to be sure; but face it, most of the things we call "sexy" are symbolic, you know, except perhaps an exhibitionist's open clothing. On Day Million when Dora danced, the people who saw her panted, and you would too.

About this business of her being a boy. It didn't matter to her audiences that genetically she was male. It wouldn't matter to you, if you were among them, because you wouldn't know it—not unless you took a biopsy cutting of her flesh and put it under an electron-microscope to find the XY chromosome—and it didn't matter to them because they didn't care. Through techniques which are not only complex but haven't yet been discovered, these people were able to determine a great deal about the aptitudes and easements of babies quite a long time before they were born—at about the second horizon of cell-division, to be exact, when the segmenting egg is becoming a free blastocyst—and then they naturally helped those aptitudes along. Wouldn't we? If we find a child with an aptitude for music we give him a scholarship to Juilliard. If they found a child whose aptitudes were for being a woman, they made him one. As sex had long been dissociated from reproduction this was relatively easy to do and caused no trouble and no, or at least very little, comment.

How much is "very little"? Oh, about as much as would be caused by our own tampering with Divine Will by filling a tooth. Less than would be caused by wearing a hearing aid. Does it still sound awful? Then look closely at the next busty babe you meet and reflect that she may be a Dora, for adults who are genetically male but somatically female are far from unknown even in our own time. An accident of environment in the womb overwhelms the blueprints of heredity. The difference is that with us it happens only by accident and we don't know about it except rarely, after close study; whereas the people of Day Million did it often, on purpose, because they wanted to.

Well, that's enough to tell you about Dora. It would only confuse you to add that she was seven feet tall and smelled of peanut butter. Let us begin our story.

On Day Million, Dora swam out of her house, entered a transportation tube, was sucked briskly to the surface in its flow of water and ejected in its plume of spray to an elastic platform in front of her—ah—call it her rehearsal hall.

"Oh, hell!" she cried in pretty confusion, reaching out to catch her balance and finding herself tumbled against a total stranger, whom we will call Don.

They met cute. Don was on his way to have his legs renewed. Love was the farthest thing from his mind. But when, absentmindedly taking a shortcut across the landing platform for submarinites and finding himself drenched, he discovered his arms full of the loveliest girl he had ever seen, he knew at once they were meant for each other. "Will you marry me?" he asked. She said softly, "Wednesday," and the promise was like a caress.

Don was tall, muscular, bronze and exciting. His name was no more Don than Dora's was Dora, but the personal part of it was Adonis in tribute to his vibrant maleness, and so we will call him Don for short. His personality colour-code, in Angstrom units, was 5,290, or only a few degrees bluer than Dora's 5,314—a measure of what they had intuitively discovered at first sight; that they possessed many affinities of taste and interest.

I despair of telling you exactly what it was that Don did for a living—I don't mean for the sake of making money, I mean for the sake of giving purpose and meaning to his life, to keep him from going off his nut with boredom—except to say that it involved a lot of travelling. He travelled in interstellar spaceships. In order to make a spaceship go really fast, about thirty-one male and seven genetically female human beings had to do certain things, and Don was one of the thirty-one. Actually, he contemplated options. This involved a lot of exposure to radiation flux—not so much from his own station in the propulsive system as in the spillover from the next stage, where a genetic female preferred selections, and the sub-nuclear particles making the selections she preferred demolished themselves in a shower of quanta. Well, you don't give a rat's ass for that, but it meant that Don had to be clad at all times in a skin of light, resilient, extremely strong copper-coloured metal. I have already mentioned this, but you probably thought I meant he was sunburned.

More than that, he was a cybernetic man. Most of his ruder parts had been long since replaced with mechanisms of vastly more permanence and use. A cadmium centrifuge, not a heart, pumped his blood. His lungs moved only when he wanted to speak out loud, for a cascade of osmotic filters rebreathed oxygen out of his own wastes. In a way, he probably would have looked peculiar to a man from the 20th century, with his glowing eyes and seven-fingered hands. But to himself, and of course to Dora, he looked mighty manly and grand. In the course of his voyages Don had circled Proxima Centauri, Procyon and the puzzling worlds of Mira Ceti; he had carried agricultural templates to the planets of Canopus and brought back warm, witty pets from the pale companion of Aldebaran. Blue-hot or red-cool, he had seen a thousand stars and their ten thousand planets. He had, in fact, been travelling the starlanes, with only brief leaves on Earth, for pushing two centuries. But you don't care about that, either. It is people who make stories, not the circumstances they find themselves in, and you want to hear about these two people. Well, they made it. The great thing they had for each other grew and flowered and burst into fruition on Wednesday, just as Dora had promised. They met at the encoding room, with a couple of well-wishing friends apiece to cheer them on, and while their identities were being taped and stored they smiled and whispered to each other and bore the jokes of their friends with blushing repartee. Then they exchanged their mathematical analogues and went away, Dora to her dwelling beneath the surface of the sea and Don to his ship.

It was an idyll, really. They lived happily ever after—or anyway, until they decided not to bother any more and died.

Of course, they never set eyes on each other again.

Oh, I can see you now, you eaters of charcoal-broiled steak, scratching an incipient bunion with one hand and holding this story with the other, while the stereo plays d'Indy or Monk. You don't believe a word of it, do you? Not for one minute. People wouldn't live like that, you say with a grunt as you get up to put fresh ice in a drink.

And yet there's Dora, hurrying back through the flushing commuter pipes toward her underwater home (she prefers it there; has had herself somatically altered to breathe the stuff). If I tell you with what sweet fulfilment she fits the recorded analogue of Don into the symbol manipulator, hooks herself in and turns herself on . . . if I try to tell you any of that you will simply stare. Or glare; and grumble, what the hell kind of love-making is this? And yet I assure you, friend, I really do assure you that Dora's ecstasies are as creamy and passionate as any of James Bond's lady spies', and one hell of a lot more so than anything you are going to find in "real life." Go ahead, glare and grumble. Dora doesn't care. If she thinks of you at all, her thirty-times-great-great-grandfather, she thinks you're a pretty primordial sort of brute. You are. Why, Dora is farther removed from you than you are from the australopithecines of five thousand centuries ago. You could not swim a second in the strong currents of her life. You don't think progress goes in a straight line, do you? Do you recognize that it is an ascending, accelerating, maybe even exponential curve? It takes hell's own time to get started, but when it goes it goes like a bomb. And you, you Scotch-drinking steak-eater in your relaxacizing chair, you've just barely lighted the primacord of the fuse. What is it now, the six or seven hundred thousandth day after Christ? Dora lives in Day Million, the millionth day of the Christian Era. Ten thousand years from now. Her body fats are polyunsaturated, like Crisco. Her wastes are haemodialysed out of her bloodstream while she sleeps—that means she doesn't have to go to the bathroom. On whim, to pass a slow half-hour, she can command more energy than the entire nation of Portugal can spend today, and use it to launch a weekend satellite or remould a crater on the Moon. She loves Don very much. She keeps his every gesture, mannerism, nuance, touch of hand, thrill of intercourse, passion of kiss stored in symbolic-mathematical form. And when she wants him, all she has to do is turn the machine on and she has him.

And Don, of course, has Dora. Adrift on a sponson city a few hundred yards over her head, or orbiting Arcturus fifty light-years away, Don has only to command his own symbol-manipulator to rescue Dora from the ferrite files and bring her to life for him, and there she is; and rapturously, tirelessly they love all night. Not in the flesh, of course; but then his flesh has been extensively altered and it wouldn't really be much fun. He doesn't need the flesh for pleasure. Genital organs feel nothing. Neither do hands, nor breasts, nor lips; they are only receptors, accepting and transmitting impulses. It is the brain that feels; it is the interpretation of those impulses that makes agony or orgasm, and Don's symbol manipulator gives him the analogue of cuddling, the analogue of kissing, the analogue of wild, ardent hours with the eternal, exquisite and incorruptible analogue of Dora. Or Diane. Or sweet Rose, or laughing Alicia; for to be sure, they have each of them exchanged analogues before, and will again.

Rats, you say, it looks crazy to me. And you—with your aftershave lotion and your little red car, pushing papers across a desk all day and chasing tail all night—tell me, just how the hell do you think you would look to Tiglath-Pileser, say, or Attila the Hun?

QUESTIONS

1. How does the tone of this story affect its contents? Why do you think Pohl chose to address his readers so directly?

2. Is this story offensive, or does Pohl seem to misread the audience's response?

3. Compare "Day Million" to D. M. Thomas' "Tithonus" as you discuss the future of biological engineering and its consequences.

4. Why is there so little mention of children in "Day Million"?

History Lesson

Arthur C. Clarke

No one could remember when the tribe had begun its long journey. The land of great rolling plains that had been its first home was now no more than a half-forgotten dream.

For many years Shann and his people had been fleeing through a country of low hills and sparkling lakes, and now the mountains lay ahead. This summer they must cross them to the southern lands. There was little time to lose. The white terror that had come down from the Poles, grinding continents to dust and freezing the very air before it, was less than a day's march behind.

Shann wondered if the glaciers could climb the mountains ahead, and within his heart he dared to kindle a little flame of hope. This might prove a barrier against which even the remorseless ice would batter in vain. In the southern lands of which the legends spoke, his people might find refuge at last.

It took weeks to discover a pass through which the tribe and the animals could travel. When midsummer came, they had camped in a lonely valley where the air was thin and the stars shone with a brilliance no one had ever seen before.

The summer was waning when Shann took his two sons and went ahead to explore the way. For three days they climbed, and for three nights slept as best they could on the freezing rocks. And on the fourth morning there was nothing ahead but a gentle rise to a cairn of gray stones built by other travelers, centuries ago.

Shann felt himself trembling, and not with cold, as they walked toward the little pyramid of stones. His sons had fallen behind. No one spoke, for too much was at stake. In a little while they would know if all their hopes had been betrayed.

To east and west, the wall of mountains curved away as if embracing the land beneath. Below lay endless miles of undulating plain, with a great river swinging across it in tremendous loops. It was a fertile land; one in which the tribe could raise crops knowing that there would be no need to flee before the harvest came.

Then Shann lifted his eyes to the south, and saw the doom of all his hopes. For there at the edge of the world glimmered that deadly light he had seen so often to the north—the glint of ice below the horizon.

There was no way forward. Through all the years of flight, the glaciers from the south had been advancing to meet them. Soon they would be crushed beneath the moving walls of ice. . . .

Southern glaciers did not reach the mountains until a generation later. In that last summer the sons of Shann carried the sacred treasures of the tribe to the lonely cairn overlooking the plain. The ice that had once gleamed below the horizon was now almost at their feet. By spring it would be splintering against the mountain walls.

No one understood the treasures now. They were from a past too distant for the understanding of any man alive. Their origins were lost in the mists that surrounded the Golden Age, and how they had come at last into the possession of this wandering tribe was a story that now would never be told. For it was the story of a civilization that had passed beyond recall.

Once, all these pitiful relics had been treasured for some good reason and now they had become sacred though their meaning had long been lost. The print in the old books had faded centuries ago though much of the lettering was still visible—if there had been any to read it. But many generations had passed since anyone had had a use for a set of seven figure logarithms, an atlas of the world, and the score of Sibelius' Seventh Symphony, printed, according to the flyleaf, by H. K. Chu and Sons, at the City of Pekin in the year 2371 A.D.

The old books were placed reverently in the little crypt that had been made to receive them. There followed a motley collection of fragments —gold and platinum coins, a broken telephoto lens, a watch, a cold-light lamp, a microphone, the cutter from an electric shaver, some midget radio tubes, the flotsam that had been left behind when the great tide of civilization had ebbed forever.

All these treasures were carefully stowed away in their resting place. Then came three more relics, the most sacred of all because the least understood.

The first was a strangely shaped piece of metal, showing the coloration of intense heat. It was, in its way, the most pathetic of all these symbols from the past, for it told of man's greatest achievement and of the future he might have known. The mahogany stand on which it was mounted bore a silver plate with the inscription.

Auxiliary Igniter from Starboard Jet
Spaceship "Morning Star"
Earth-Moon, A.D. 1985

Next followed another miracle of the ancient science—a sphere of transparent plastic with strangely shaped pieces of metal embedded in it. At its centre was a tiny capsule of synthetic radio-element, surrounded by the converting screens that shifted its radiation far down the spectrum. As long as the material remained active, the sphere would be a tiny radio transmitter, broadcasting power in all directions. Only a few of these spheres had ever been made. They had been designed as perpetual beacons to mark the orbits of the asteroids. But man had never reached the asteroids and the beacons had never been used.

Last of all was a flat, circular tin, wide in comparison with its depth. It was heavily sealed, and rattled when shaken. The tribal lore predicted that disaster would follow if it were ever opened, and no one knew that it held one of the great works of art of nearly a thousand years before.

The work was finished. The two men rolled the stones back into place and slowly began to descend the mountainside. Even to the last, man had given some thought to the future and had tried to preserve something for posterity.

That winter the great waves of ice began their first assault on the mountains, attacking from north and south. The foothills were overwhelmed in the first onslaught, and the glaciers ground them into dust. But the mountains stood firm, and when the summer came the ice retreated for a while.

So, winter after winter, the battle continued, and the roar of the avalanches, the grinding of rock and the explosions of splintering ice filled the air with tumult. No war of man's had been fiercer than this, and even man's battles had not quite engulfed the globe as this had done.

At last the tidal waves of ice began to subside and to creep slowly down the flanks of the mountains they had never quite subdued. The valleys and passes were still firmly in their grip. It was stalemate. The glaciers had met their match, but their defeat was too late to be of any use to Man.

So the centuries passed, and presently there happened something that must occur once at least in the history of every world in the universe, no matter how remote and lonely it may be.

The ship from Venus came five thousand years too late, but its crew knew nothing of this. While still many millions of miles away, the telescopes had seen the great shroud of ice that made Earth the most brilliant object in the sky next to the sun itself.

Here and there the dazzling sheet was marred by black specks that revealed the presence of almost buried mountains. That was all. The rolling oceans, the plains and forests, the deserts and lakes—all that had been the world of man was sealed beneath the ice, perhaps forever.

The ship closed in to Earth and established an orbit less than a thousand miles away. For five days it circled the planet, while cameras recorded all that was left to see and a hundred instruments gathered information that would give the Venusian scientists many years of work.

An actual landing was not intended. There seemed little purpose in it.

But on the sixth day the picture changed. A panoramic monitor, driven to the limit of its amplification, detected the dying radiation of the five-thousand-year-old-beacon. Through all the centuries, it had been sending out its signals with ever-failing strength as its radioactive heart steadily weakened.

The monitor locked on the beacon frequency. In the control room, a bell clamored for attention. A little later, the Venusian ship broke free from its orbit and slanted down toward Earth, toward a range of mountains that still towered proudly above the ice, and to a cairn of gray stones that the years had scarcely touched. . . .

The great disc of the sun blazed fiercely in a sky no longer veiled with mist, for the clouds that had once hidden Venus had now completely gone. Whatever force had caused the change in the sun's radiation had doomed one civilization, but had given birth to another. Less than five thousand years before, the half-savage people of Venus had seen Sun and stars for the first time. Just as the science of Earth had begun with astronomy, so had that of Venus, and on the warm, rich world that man had never seen progress had been incredibly rapid.

Perhaps the Venusians had been lucky. They never knew the Dark Age that held Man enchained for a thousand years. They missed the long detour into chemistry and mechanics but came at once to the more fundamental laws of radiation physics. In the time that man had taken to progress from the Pyramids to the rocket-propelled spaceship, the Venusians had passed from the discovery of agriculture to anti-gravity itself—the ultimate secret that Man had never learned.

The warm ocean that still bore most of the young planet's life rolled its breakers languidly against the sandy shore. So new was this continent that the very sands were coarse and gritty. There had not yet been time enough for the sea to wear them smooth.

The scientists lay half in the water, their beautiful reptilian bodies gleaming in the sunlight. The greatest minds of Venus had gathered on this shore from all the islands of the planet. What they were going to hear they did not yet know, except that it concerned the Third World and the mysterious race that had peopled it before the coming of the ice.

The Historian was standing on the land, for the instruments he wished to use had no love of water. By his side was a large machine which attracted many curious glances from his colleagues. It was clearly concerned with optics, for a lens system projected from it toward a screen of white material a dozen yards away.

The Historian began to speak. Briefly he recapitulated what little had been discovered concerning the third planet and its people.

He mentioned the centuries of fruitless research that had failed to interpret a single word of the writings of Earth. The planet had been inhabited by a race of great technical ability. That, at least, was proved by the few pieces of machinery that had been found in the cairn upon the mountain.

"We do not know why so advanced a civilization came to an end," he observed. "Almost certainly, it had sufficient knowledge to survive an Ice Age. There must have been some factor of which we know nothing. Possibly disease or racial degeneration may have been responsible. It has even been suggested that the tribal conflicts endemic to our own species in prehistoric times may have continued on the third planet after the coming of technology.

"Some philosophers maintain that knowledge of machinery does not necessarily imply a high degree of civilization, and it is theoretically possible to have wars in a society possessing mechanical power, flight, and even radio. Such a conception is alien to our thoughts, but we must admit its possibility. It would certainly account for the downfall of the lost race.

"It has always been assumed that we should never know anything of the physical form of the creatures who lived in Planet Three. For centuries our artists have been depicting scenes from the history of the dead world, peopling it with all manner of fantastic beings. Most of these creations have resembled us more or less closely, though it has often been pointed out that because *we* are reptiles it does not follow that all intelligent life must necessarily be reptilian.

"We now know the answer to one of the most baffling problems of history. At last, after a hundred years of research, we have discovered the exact form and nature of the ruling life on the Third Planet."

There was a murmur of astonishment from the assembled scientists. Some were so taken aback that they disappeared for a while into the comfort of the ocean, as all Venusians were apt to do in moments of stress. The Historian waited until his colleagues reemerged into the element they so disliked. He himself was quite comfortable, thanks to the tiny sprays that were continually playing over his body. With their help he could live on land for many hours before having to return to the ocean.

The excitement slowly subsided and the lecturer continued:

"One of the most puzzling of the objects found on Planet Three was a flat metal container holding a great length of transparent plastic material, perforated at the edges and wound tightly into a spool. This transparent tape at first seemed quite featureless, but an examination with the new subelectronic microscope has shown that this is not the case. Along the surface of the material, invisible to our eyes but perfectly clear under the correct radiation, are literally thousands of tiny pictures. It is believed that they were imprinted on the material by some chemical means, and have faded with the passage of time.

"These pictures apparently form a record of life as it was on the Third Planet at the height of its civilization. They are not independent. Consecutive pictures are almost identical, differing only in the detail of movement. The purpose of such a record is obvious. It is only necessary to project the scenes in rapid succession to give an illusion of continuous movement. We have made a machine to do this, and I have here an exact reproduction of the picture sequence.

"The scenes you are now going to witness take us back many thousands of years, to the great days of our sister planet. They show a complex civilization, many of whose activities we can only dimly understand. Life seems to have been very violent and energetic, and much that you will see is quite baffling.

"It is clear that the Third Planet was inhabited by a number of different species, none of them reptilian. That is a blow to our pride, but the conclusion is inescapable. The dominant type of life appears to have been a two-armed biped. It walked upright and covered its body with some flexible material, possibly for protection against the cold, since even before the Ice Age the planet was at a much lower temperature than our own world. But I will not try your patience any further. You will now see the record of which I have been speaking."

A brilliant light flashed from the projector. There was a gentle whirring, and on the screen appeared hundreds of strange beings moving rather jerkily to and fro. The picture expanded to embrace one of the creatures, and the scientists could see that the Historian's description had been correct.

The creature possessed two eyes, set rather close together, but the other facial adornments were a little obscure. There was a large orifice in the lower portion of the head that was continually opening and closing. Possibly it had something to do with the creature's breathing.

The scientists watched spellbound as the strange being became involved in a series of fantastic adventures. There was an incredibly violent conflict with another, slightly different creature. It seemed certain that they must both be killed, but when it was all over neither seemed any the worse.

Then came a furious drive over miles of country in a four-wheeled mechanical device which was capable of extraordinary feats of locomotion. The ride ended in a city packed with other vehicles moving in all directions at breath-taking speeds. No one was surprised to see two of the machines meet headon with devastating results.

After that, events became even more complicated. It was now quite obvious that it would take many years of research to analyze and understand all that was happening. It was also clear that the record was a work of art, somewhat stylized, rather than an exact reproduction of life as it actually had been on the Third Planet.

Most of the scientists felt themselves completely dazed when the sequence of pictures came to an end. There was a final flurry of motion, in which the creature that had been the center of interest became involved in some tremendous but incomprehensible catastrophe. The picture contracted to a circle, centered on the creature's head.

The last scene of all was an expanded view of its face, obviously expressing some powerful emotion. But whether it was rage, grief, defiance, resignation or some other feeling could not be guessed. The picture vanished. For a moment some lettering appeared on the screen, then it was all over.

For several minutes there was complete silence, save the lapping of the waves upon the sand. The scientists were too stunned to speak. The fleeting glimpse of Earth's civilization had had a shattering effect on their minds. Then little groups began to start talking together, first in whispers and then more and more loudly as the implications of what they had seen became clearer. Presently the Historian called for attention and addressed the meeting again.

"We are now planning," he said, "a vast program of research to extract all available knowledge from this record. Thousands of copies are being made for distribution to all workers. You will appreciate the problems involved. The psychologists in particular have an immense task confronting them.

"But I do not doubt that we shall succeed. In another generation, who can say what we may not have learned of this wonderful race? Before we leave, let us look again at our remote cousins, whose wisdom may have surpassed our own but of whom so little has survived."

Once more the final picture flashed on the screen, motionless this time, for the projector had been stopped. With something like awe, the scientists gazed at the still figure from the past, while in turn the little biped stared back at them with its characteristic expression of arrogant bad temper.

For the rest of time it would symbolize the human race. The psychologists of Venus would analyze its actions and watch its every movement until they could reconstruct its mind. Thousands of books would be written about it. Intricate philosophies would be contrived to account for its behavior.

But all this labor, all this research, would be utterly in vain. Perhaps the proud and lonely figure on the screen was smiling sardonically at the scientists who were starting on their age-long fruitless quest.

Its secret would be safe as long as the universe endured, for no one now would ever read the lost language of Earth. Millions of times in the ages to come those last few words would flash across the screen, and none could ever guess their meaning:

A Walt Disney Production.

QUESTIONS

1. Why is there so little use of characterization in this story?
2. Compare "History Lesson" with the selection from H. G. Wells's *The Time Machine* that follows.

3. Did you guess the ending of the story before you reached it?

4. Why do you think Clarke chose "A Walt Disney Production"?

5. Is this story the serious equivalent of a "sick joke"? Why is the ending so satisfactory, so final?

from The Time Machine

H. G. Wells

XI

"I have already told you of the sickness and confusion that comes with time travelling. And this time I was not seated properly in the saddle, but sideways and in an unstable fashion. For an indefinite time I clung to the machine as it swayed and vibrated, quite unheeding how I went, and when I brought myself to look at the dials again I was amazed to find where I had arrived. One dial records days, another thousands of days, another millions of days, and another thousands of millions. Now, instead of reversing the levers I had pulled them over so as to go forward with them, and when I came to look at these indicators I found that the thousands hand was sweeping round as fast as the seconds hand of a watch—into futurity.

"As I drove on, a peculiar change crept over the appearance of things. The palpitating greyness grew darker; then—though I was still travelling with prodigious velocity—the blinking succession of day and night, which was usually indicative of a slower pace, returned, and grew more and more marked. This puzzled me very much at first. The alternations of night and day grew slower and slower, and so did the passage of the sun across the sky, until they seemed to stretch through centuries. At last a steady twilight brooded over the earth, a twilight only broken now and then when a comet glared across the darkling sky. The band of light that had indicated the sun had long since disappeared; for the sun had ceased to set—it simply rose and fell in the west, and grew ever broader and more red. All trace of the moon had vanished. The circling of the stars, growing slower and slower, had given place to creeping points of light. At last, some time before I stopped, the sun, red and very large, halted motionless upon the horizon, a vast dome glowing with a dull heat, and now and then suffering a momentary extinction. At one time it had for a little while glowed more brilliantly again, but it speedily reverted to its sullen red-heat. I perceived by this slowing down of its rising and setting that the work of the tidal drag was done. The earth had come to rest with one face to the sun, even as in our own time the moon faces the earth. Very cautiously, for I remembered my former headlong fall, I began to reverse my motion. Slower and slower went the circling hands until the thousands one seemed motionless, and the daily one was no longer a mere mist upon its scale. Still slower, until the dim outlines of a desolate beach grew visible.

"I stopped very gently and sat upon the Time Machine, looking round. The sky was no longer blue. North-eastward it was inky black, and out of the blackness shone brightly and steadily the pale white stars. Overhead it was a deep Indian red and starless, and south-eastward it grew brighter to a glowing scarlet where, cut by the horizon, lay the huge hull of the sun, red and motionless. The rocks about me were of a harsh reddish colour, and all the trace of life that I could see at first was the intensely green vegetation that covered every projecting point on their south-eastern face. It was the same rich green that one sees on forest moss or on the lichen in caves: plants which like these grow in a perpetual twilight.

"The machine was standing on a sloping beach. The sea stretched away to the south-west, to rise into a sharp bright horizon against the wan sky. There were no breakers and no waves, for not a breath of wind was stirring. Only a slight oily swell rose and fell like a gentle breathing, and showed that the eternal sea was still moving and living. And along the margin where the water sometimes broke was a thick incrustation of salt—pink under the lurid sky. There was a sense of oppression in my head, and I noticed that I was breathing very fast. The sensation reminded me of my only experience of mountaineering, and from that I judged the air to be more rarefied than it is now.

"Far away up the desolate slope I heard a harsh scream, and saw a thing like a huge white butterfly go slanting and fluttering up into the sky and, circling, disappear over some low hillocks beyond. The sound of its voice was so dismal that I shivered and seated myself more firmly upon the machine. Looking round me again, I saw that, quite near, what I had taken to be a reddish mass of rock was moving slowly towards me. Then I saw the thing was really a monstrous crab-like creature. Can you imagine a crab as large as yonder table, with its many legs moving slowly and uncertainly, its big claws swaying, its long antennæ, like carters' whips, waving and feeling, and its stalked eyes gleaming at you on either side of its metallic front? Its back was corrugated and ornamented with ungainly bosses, and a greenish incrustation blotched it here and there. I could see the many palps of its complicated mouth flickering and feeling as it moved.

"As I stared at this sinister apparition crawling towards me, I felt a tickling on my cheek as though a fly had lighted there. I tried to brush it away with my hand, but in a moment it returned, and almost immediately came another by my ear. I struck at this, and caught something threadlike. It was drawn swiftly out of my hand. With a frightful qualm, I turned, and saw that I had grasped the antenna of another monster crab that stood just behind me. Its evil eyes were wriggling on their stalks, its mouth was all alive with appetite, and its vast ungainly claws, smeared with an algal slime, were descending upon me. In a moment my hand was on the lever, and I had placed a month between myself and these monsters. But I was still on the same beach, and I saw them distinctly now as soon as I stopped. Dozens of them seemed to be crawling here and there, in the sombre light, among the foliated sheets of intense green.

"I cannot convey the sense of abominable desolation that hung over the world. The red eastern sky, the northward blackness, the salt Dead Sea, the stony beach crawling with these foul, slow-stirring monsters, the uniform poisonous-looking green of the lichenous plants, the thin air that hurt one's lungs; all contributed to an appalling effect. I moved on a hundred years, and there was the same red sun—a little larger, a little duller—the same dying sea, the same chill air, and the same crowd of earthly crustacea creeping in and out among the green weed and the red rocks. And in the westward sky I saw a curved pale line like a vast new moon.

"So I travelled, stopping ever and again, in great strides of a thousand years or more, drawn on by the mystery of the earth's fate, watching with a strange fascination the sun grow larger and duller in the westward sky, and the life of the old earth ebb away. At last, more than thirty million years hence, the huge red-hot dome of the sun had come to obscure nearly a tenth part of the darkling heavens. Then I stopped once more, for the crawling multitude of crabs had disappeared, and the red beach, save for its livid green liverworts and lichens, seemed lifeless. And now it was flecked with white. A bitter cold assailed me. Rare white flakes ever and again came eddying down. To the north-eastward, the glare of snow lay under the starlight of the sable sky, and I could see an undulating crest of hillocks pinkish-white. There were fringes of ice along the sea margin, with drifting masses further out; but the main expanse of that salt ocean, all bloody under the eternal sunset, was still unfrozen.

"I looked about me to see if any traces of animal-life remained. A certain indefinable apprehension still kept me in the saddle of the machine. But I saw nothing moving, in earth or sky or sea. The green slime on the rocks alone testified that life was not extinct. A shallow sandbank had appeared in the sea and the water had receded from the beach. I fancied I saw some black object flopping about upon this bank, but it became motionless as I looked at it, and I judged that my eye had been deceived, and that the black object was merely a rock. The stars in the sky were intensely bright and seemed to me to twinkle very little.

"Suddenly I noticed that the circular westward outline of the sun had changed; that a concavity, a bay, had appeared in the curve. I saw this grow larger. For a minute perhaps I stared aghast at this blackness that was creeping over the day, and then I realized that an eclipse was beginning. Either the moon or the planet Mercury was passing across the sun's disk. Naturally, at first I took it to be the moon, but there is much to incline me to believe that what I really saw was the transit of an inner planet passing very near to the earth.

"The darkness grew apace; a cold wind began to blow in freshening gusts from the east, and the showering white flakes in the air increased in number. From the edge of the sea came a ripple and whisper. Beyond these lifeless sounds the world was silent. Silent? It would be hard to convey the stillness of it. All the sounds of man, the bleating of sheep, the cries of birds, the hum of insects, the stir that makes the background of our lives—all that was over. As the darkness thickened, the eddying flakes grew more abundant, dancing before my eyes; and the cold of the air more intense. At last, one by one, swiftly, one after the other, the white peaks of the distant hills vanished into blackness. The breeze rose to a moaning wind. I saw the black central shadow of the eclipse sweeping towards me. In another moment the pale stars alone were visible. All else was rayless obscurity. The sky was absolutely black.

"A horror of this great darkness came on me. The cold, that smote to my marrow, and the pain I felt in breathing overcame me. I shivered, and a deadly nausea seized me. Then like a red-hot bow in the sky appeared the edge of the sun. I got off the machine to recover myself. I felt giddy and incapable of facing the return journey. As I stood sick and confused I saw again the moving thing upon the shoal—there was no mistake now that it was a moving thing—against the red water of the sea. It was a round thing, the size of a football perhaps, or, it may be, bigger, and tentacles trailed down from it; it seemed black against the weltering blood-red water, and it was hopping fitfully about. Then I felt I was fainting. But a terrible dread of lying helpless in that remote and awful twilight sustained me while I clambered upon the saddle."

QUESTIONS

1. Do you believe this vision of the end of the world? Or does your belief in it not really matter?

2. What is the effect created by the colors Wells chooses in his descriptions?

3. Why do not descriptions of space flight—where similar sensations could conceivably be felt—produce the same feeling of terror of absolute blackness and silence that Wells's description of the end of the world does?

4. If there is no way for man to prevent this sort of future, what implication does this have for the individual human life of this time and this place?

part 3

Theories

Science fiction is a genre of literature that has received relatively little serious critical attention from those who do not make their living as SF writers. It has commonly been regarded as lacking the "art" of mainstream literature; the exceptions to this judgment are generally George Orwell's 1984 and Aldous Huxley's Brave New World, which Arthur Koestler maintains have qualities of outstanding literature mainly because of their non-SF elements. However, as more and more mainstream writers have begun working with futurist themes—a number of them represented in this book—the criticism and critical attention paid to science fiction is increasing. The selections that follow indicate some of the concerns that merit further study.

A brief look at the history of science fiction and some suggestions as to how it might be best defined are provided by Kingsley Amis' "Starting Points." Further suggestions as to definitions are given by Isaac Asimov, whose conceptions of "social science fiction" and adjustment to change have provided a rationale for the kind of science fiction most heavily represented in this book. Both Asimov and Gerald Heard write about the role of science fiction in preparing its readers for the future, and both indicate possibilities not only of what that future will be, but also of how we shall adapt individuals and institutions to it.*

Arthur Koestler and Susan Sontag's essays relate more to the "popular" and "escapist" science fiction than do the first three essays. Koestler presents a strong argument as to why science fiction will not provide the most significant and necessary literature of the future. Miss Sontag examines, in "The Imagination of Disaster," what science fiction reveals about contemporary hopes and fears. The final article, by John Sisk, is an intensive examination of the "futurists," and asks the reader to consider whether the future predicted in the present is necessarily bound to the limited perspective of the present, and is therefore at once revealing and dangerous.

---

* In reading Asimov's "Social Science Fiction," remember that it was first published in 1953. It is reprinted in this book essentially as it appeared then; no attempt at updating has been made.

"*Starting Points*" *is the first chapter of Kingsley Amis'* New Maps of Hell: A Survey of Science Fiction. *Published in* 1960, *this study was one of the first widely read critical examinations of the form. Amis is also the author of* Lucky Jim, That Uncertain Feeling, *and* The Anti-Death League. *With Robert Conquest, he is the editor of the* Spectrum *series of science fiction anthologies. Isaac Asimov is one of the most prolific authors of the twentieth century, with more than one hundred books to his credit, ranging from SF novels and short stories to studies of science and history. Gerald Heard has written such mysteries as* A Taste for Honey *and* Reply Paid. *His science fiction and fantasy includes* The Doppelgangers *and* The Lost Cavern.

Arthur Koestler is the author of Darkness at Noon, Arrival and Departure, The Lotus and the Robot, *and* The Sleepwalkers. "*The Imagination of Disaster*" *is included in* Against Interpretation, *a collection of Susan Sontag's critical essays, some of which appeared in such journals as* The Partisan Review, The New York Review of Books, Evergreen Review, *and* Commenntary. *She is also the author of* The Benefactor *and* Death Kit. *John Sisk is a member of the English Department at Gonzaga University.*

Starting Points

Kingsley Amis

Those who have never seen a living Martian can scarcely imagine the strange horror of its appearance. The peculiar V-shaped mouth with its pointed upper lip, the absence of brow ridges, the absence of a chin beneath the wedge-like lower lip, the incessant quivering of this mouth, the Gorgon groups of tentacles, the tumultuous breathing of the lungs in a strange atmosphere, the evident heaviness and painfulness of movement due to the greater gravitational energy of the earth—above all, the extraordinary intensity of the immense eyes—were at once vital, intense, inhuman, crippled and monstrous. There was something fungoid in the oily brown skin, something in the clumsy deliberation of the tedious movements unspeakably nasty. Even at this first encounter, this first glimpse, I was overcome with disgust and dread.

If that produces no special reaction—it comes, of course, from an early chapter of *The War of the Worlds*—perhaps this passage will:

"I don't have to tell you men that Point-of-Sale has its special problems," Harvey said, puffing his thin cheeks. "I swear, the whole damned Government must be infiltrated with [Conservationists]! You know what they've done. They outlawed compulsive subsonics in our aural advertising—but we've bounced back with a list of semantic cue words that tie in with every basic trauma and neurosis in American life today. They listened to the safety cranks and stopped us from projecting our messages on aircar windows—but we bounced back. Lab tells me," he nodded to our Director of Research across the table, "that soon we'll be testing a system that projects direct on the retina of the eye. . . ." He broke off, "Excuse me, Mr. Schocken," he whispered. "Has Security checked this room?"

Fowler Schocken nodded. "Absolutely clean. Nothing but the usual State Department and House of Representatives spy-mikes. And of course we're feeding a canned playback into them."

I quote that extract from *The Space Merchants* (a novel published in 1953) and the H. G. Wells piece in order to make possible a tiny experiment in self-analysis: anybody encountering such passages who fails to experience a peculiar interest, related to, but distinct from, ordinary literary interest, will never be an addict of science fiction. Now I acknowledge that people can live out happy and useful lives in complete indifference to this form of writing, but the point about addiction is the one where investigation should start. Those who decide that they ought to "find out about" science fiction, suspecting that it furnishes a new vantage point from which to survey "our culture," will find much to confirm that suspicion and also, I hope, much incidental entertainment, but they are unlikely to be able to share, nor even perhaps to comprehend, the experience of the addicts, who form the overwhelming majority of science-fiction readers, and to whom, naturally, entertainment is not incidental but essential. As is the way with addictions, this one is mostly contracted in adolescence or not at all, like addiction to jazz. The two have much in common, and their actual coexistence in the same person is not unusual.

The two modes themselves, indeed, show marked similarities. Both emerged as self-contained entities some time in the second or third decade of the century, and both, far more precisely, underwent rapid internal change around 1940. Both have strong connections with what I might call mass culture without being, as I hope to show in the case of science fiction, mass media in themselves. Both are characteristically American* products with a large audience and a growing band of practitioners in Western Europe, excluding the Iberian peninsula and, probably, Ireland. Both in their different ways have a noticeably radical tinge, showing itself again and again in the content of science fiction, while as regards jazz, whose material is perforce non-political, radicalism of some sort often appears in the attitudes of those connected with it; a recent article in the *Spectator* claimed that one might as well give up hope of meeting a British intellectual committed to jazz who was not firmly over to the left in politics. Both of these fields, again, have thrown up a large number of interesting and competent figures without producing anybody of first-rate importance; both have arrived at a state of anxious and largely naïve self-consciousness; both, having decisively and for something like half a century separated themselves from the main streams of serious music and serious literature, show signs of bending back towards those streams. One shouldn't go on like this all night; the two forms have no helpful resemblance, for example, in origin or in role, but I should like to round off this catalogue of supposed parallels by observing that both jazz and

---

* The prehistory of science fiction, up until 1914 or later, is admittedly as much British as American, and until quite recently the phenomenon of the serious author who takes an occasional trip into science fiction (Huxley, Orwell, William Golding—in a rather different sense) has been British rather than American. But the general run is so firmly American that British science-fiction writers will often fabricate American backgrounds and fill their dialogue with what they believe to be American idioms. (Compare the British "tough" thriller, at any rate on its lower levels.)

science fiction have in the last dozen years begun to attract the attention of the cultural diagnostician, or trend-hound, who becomes interested in them not for or as themselves, but for the light they can be made to throw on some other thing. By saying this I mean only to distinguish this interest, not to denigrate it; it seems worthy enough, even praiseworthy.

A definition of science fiction, though attempted with enormous and significant frequency by commentators inside the field, is bound to be cumbersome rather than memorable. With the "fiction" part we are on reasonably secure ground; the "science" part raises several kinds of difficulty, one of which is that science fiction is not necessarily fiction about science or scientists, nor is science necessarily important in it. Prolonged cogitation, however, would lead one to something like this: Science fiction is that class of prose narrative treating of a situation that could not arise in the world we know, but which is hypothesised on the basis of some innovation in science or technology, or pseudo-science or pseudo-technology, whether human or extra-terrestrial in origin. This is the kind of definition that demands footnotes. "Prose narrative," then, because the appearance of science-fiction interests in verse form have so far been of minor extent. An occasional dreadful poem about the majesty of the stars and so on struggles into one or another of the magazines as a page-filler, and there is in England a poet of some standing, Robert Conquest, whose works include an ode to the first explorers of Mars and a report on Terran culture imagined as the work of a survey team constituted by the headquarters of the Galactic Federation (plus a whole science-fiction novel, *A World of Difference*). But Conquest is at the moment a rather lonely figure, or perhaps a pioneer. I draw attention also to the existence of a volume called *The Space Child's Mother Goose*, which contains ingenious, but not always striking, variations on nursery rhymes—"This is the theory that Jack built," and so on—with contemporary *art-nouveau* illustrations. The work falls into that category of adults' children's books which has so far unaccountably eluded the trend-hounds (unless I have missed something, which I well may), and although the volume got a review in *Astounding Science Fiction*, rather puzzled in tone, I doubt if it has much circulation among ordinary readers of that journal.

To hark back now to my definition: its crucial point, clearly, lies in the mention of science and technology and their pseudo-forms. Many stories are based on, or incidentally involve, perfectly plausible extensions of existing theories and techniques. The use of robots, for instance, still a very popular subject, seems actually foreseeable, however unlikely, and even if the problem of fitting all that machinery into a container on the human scale would require the development of a kind of micro-electronics that for the time being, one would imagine, is at a rudimentary stage. Stories based on, or involving, space flight, again, which form probably the largest class, can rest on principles and processes that do no violence to what is already established. But those writers who feel constricted by a mere solar system face a certain inconvenience when they set about taking their characters to the farther parts of our galaxy or to other galaxies. The fact is—and I apologize to all those for whom it is an odiously familiar fact—that to reach any but the nearest stars would take several hundred years even if one travelled at the speed of light, in the course of doing which one would, if I understand Einstein's popularisers correctly, become infinite in mass and zero in volume, and this is felt to be undesirable. A few writers simply accept this difficulty and arrange for their travellers to put themselves into some sort of deep-freeze until just before planetfall, or allow them to breed in captivity for the requisite number of generations, in which case the plot will concern what happens when a couple of centuries have elapsed and nobody on board is any longer aware of the situation. But most commonly, the author will fabricate a way of getting around Einstein, or even of sailing straight through him: a device known typically as the space-warp or the hyper-drive will make its appearance, though without any more ceremony than "He applied the space-warp," or "He threw the ship into hyper-drive." Such reticence may baffle and annoy the neophyte, as unfamiliar conventions will, but one would not demand that every Western include an exposition of ranching theory, and the space-warp is an equally acceptable convention, resting as it does on the notion that while there is a theoretical limit to the speed at which matter can be moved through space, there is no such limit to the speed at which space can be moved through space. Therefore, if the space being moved contains a space-ship, this can be shifted from the neighbourhood of the Earth to the neighbourhood of the Dog Star in an afternoon or so without any glaring affront to Einstein.

So much for real or good-imitation science; a few words now on the flagrantly pseudo variety. If aliens are to be introduced—alien is the term applied in the trade to any intelligent creature orginating outside the Earth—the problem of communicating with them is likely to arise. Some excellent stories have been written about non-communicating aliens, from *The War of the Worlds* onwards, but their potentialities hardly extend beyond simple menace, and, as we shall see, recent science fiction has tended to lose interest in menace of this kind. Talking to an alien, however, presents difficulties that are literally insurmountable. One doesn't want to start too far back, but granted that communication, whatever it is, can be conceived of in other than human terms, and granted that it might involve something analogous to speech, one is still faced with a choice of infeasibilities. Direct learning of an alien language as one might under adverse conditions learn a human language, by ostensive definition and the like, entails presupposing an alien culture with human linguistic habits, which seems unlikely. The idea of a translation machine, recalling the space-warp in being usually introduced by phrases like "He set up the translation machine," differs from the space-warp in presenting a direct affront to common sense, for such a machine would clearly be foiled even by an utterance in Portuguese unless it had been "taught" Portuguese to start with. Telepathy—"The thought-forms of the alien flooded into his mind"—cannot exist. (Or can it? According to the director of its newly formed Astronautics Institute, the Westinghouse Electric Corporation is conducting research into telepathy as a means of long-distance communication.) My concern at the moment, however, is not that all these notions are, or may be, implausible, but that they are offered as plausible and that efforts are made to conceal their implausibility. The same is true of other traditional devices: time travel, for instance, is inconceivable, but if an apparatus of pseudo-logic is not actually set up to support it, the possibility of recourse to such an apparatus will not be explicitly ruled out. The science-fiction writer works by minimising what is self-contradictory.

Whether or not an individual story does justice to the laws of nature is a consideration that can affect our judgment of it, but my purpose here is to insist that such justice is always an aim—in the field of science fiction. The point of this is that immediately adjacent to this field, and in some instances to be distinguished from it only with difficulty, lies the field of fantasy. Fantasy of the kind I am going to discuss has developed into a self-contained form of writing in the same sense and over much the same period as science fiction: the two modes appeal to some of the same interests, share some of the same readership and unite in the name of a periodical, *The Magazine of Fantasy and Science Fiction.* It will be seen that I am using the term "fantasy" in a special and restricted sense, corresponding to a special kind of publication abutting upon my subject; I am aware of the existence of a body of work that can be called fantasy, from *Beowulf* to Kafka, which anticipates and parallels this kind of fantasy in a way that nothing quite anticipates or parallels science fiction, but my business is not with that. However, I acknowledge the fact that fantasy, in the special sense, gives, despite its much smaller volume, as valid a glimpse of contemporary attitudes as does science fiction. But I think it better to say straight out that I do not like fantasy, whether from *Beowulf* to Kafka, or in the specialised contemporary magazines, rather than take the trouble of devising reasons for my dislike, though I think I could do so if pressed. For now I merely intend to differentiate fantasy from science fiction, a task that involves little more than remarking that while science fiction, as I have been arguing, maintains a respect for fact or presumptive fact, fantasy makes a point of flouting these; for a furniture of robots, space-ships, techniques, and equations it substitutes elves, broomsticks, occult powers, and incantations. It may be to the purpose to quote an utterance by Fredric Brown, one of the most ingenious and inventive, though not one of the most self-questioning, writers of science fiction. In the introduction to his volume of short stories, *Star Shine,* we find Brown, who also writes fantasy on occasion, attempting to distinguish the two modes. After referring to the Midas myth—"remember it?" he asks, an apposite question when we try to imagine his readership, and goes on to give a summary—Brown says:

> Let's translate that into science fiction. Mr. Midas, who runs a Greek restaurant in the Bronx, happens to save the life of an extraterrestrial from a far planet who is living in New York anonymously as an observer for the Galactic Federation, to which Earth for obvious reasons is not yet ready to be admitted. . . . The extraterrestrial, who is a master of sciences far beyond ours, makes a machine which alters the molecular vibrations of Mr. Midas's body so his touch will have a transmuting effect upon other objects. And so on. It's a science fiction story, or could be made to be one.

It might be thought that, to push it to the limit, a fantasy story could be turned into a science-fiction story merely by inserting a few lines of pseudo-scientific patter, and I would accept this as an extreme theoretical case, although I cannot think of an actual one. Even so, a difference which makes the difference between abandoning verisimilitude and trying to preserve it seems to me to make all the difference, and in practice the arbitrary and whimsical development of nearly every story of fantasy soon puts it beyond recovery by any talk of galactic federations or molecular vibrations. One parenthetical note: it should not be thought that no story dealing with elves and such can be science fiction. There are pixies and four-leafed clovers and cromlechs and the land of heart's desire in Eric Frank Russell's story "Rainbow's End," but these are mere apparatus in a sinister hypnotic attack on a band of interstellar explorers. Similarly, although vampirism is one of the staples of nineteenth-century fantasy, Richard Matheson's novel *I Am Legend* makes brilliantly ingenious and incidentally horrifying use of the myth for science-fiction purposes, whereby every traditional detail is explained along rational lines: the wooden stake through the heart, for instance, which put paid to Dracula and so many of his playmates, is necessary in order to maintain the distension of the wound—bullets and knives are no good for that job, and the microbe which causes vampirism is aerophobic.

While perhaps seeming to have kept our definition only distantly in view, I have in fact been rather deftly filling out and limiting its various implications. All that remains in this section is to describe a couple of codicils, kinds of narrative to be included on the grounds that they appeal to the same set of interests as science fiction in the sense defined, or at least are written and read by the same writers and readers. The first of these, numerically unimportant and readily disposed of, consists of stories about prehistoric man. Their existence can perhaps be blamed, for blame seems called for, on the fact that Wells wrote something called "A Story of the Stone Age"; I also note, though without at the moment doing more than note, that the subject reappears in *The Inheritors*, the second novel of the contemporary British writer William Golding, who comes nearer than anybody so far to being a serious author working within science fiction. But more of him later. The second supplementary category includes stories based on some change or disturbance or local anomaly in physical conditions. This accommodates several very familiar types of story, mostly involving novelties that threaten mankind. These may originate outside the Earth, as in Conan Doyle's "The Poison Belt" and Fred Hoyle's recent *The Black Cloud*, or on the Earth itself, as in John Christopher's *The Death of Grass*, published in the United States as *No Blade of Grass*. Alternatively, the author will chronicle some monstrous emergence arising from existing science and technology, especially, of course, the hydrogen bomb. The film industry has fallen gleefully upon that one, serving up a succession of beasts produced by mutation via radiation—giant ants, for instance, in *Them*—or else liberated from some primeval underground cavity by test explosions— *Rodan*, a Japanese film, made great play with a brace of giant armour-plated radioactive supersonic pterodactyls finally despatched by guided missiles. Menaces of this kind naturally antedate the hydrogen bomb: an early and, I should guess, very influential example is Wells's unpleasantly vivid "The Empire of the Ants," in which the anomaly in question consists of an increase in intelligence, not in mere bulk. Although this is treated as having arisen in the course of evolution, not under artificial stimulus, the story has an obvious place in the development of its category. Finally, I should point out here, or hereabouts, that the last ten years have seen a perceptible decline in the role played in science fiction by actual science. The space-ship, for example, for a long time remained novel enough to be worth some description: nowadays it is often no more than a means of introducing characters into an alien environment, referred to as casually as an aeroplane or a taxi. Many stories of the future, again, and these commonly of the more interesting kind, take as their theme changes in the political or economic realm, with science and technology reduced to background detail: the hero will be served with Venusian flying-monkey steaks by a robot waiter, but the main business of his evening will be to persuade his fellow-members of the General Motors clan to take up the sword against the Chrysler clan. "*Science* fiction" is every day losing some of its appropriateness as a name for science fiction, and the kind of rearguard action that is being fought on its behalf by the commentators, on the plea that politics and economics and psychology and anthropology and even ethics are really or nearly as much sciences as atomic physics, is chiefly valuable as an indication of a state of mind. In any event, no alternative nomenclature so far suggested is applicable enough to justify the huge task of getting it accepted in place of a term so firmly established as the present one.

To restate matters, then: science fiction presents with verisimilitude the human effects of spectacular changes in our environment, changes either deliberately willed or involuntarily suffered. I turn now to a brief and selective account of the ancestry of the form. To do so is at any rate to follow an apparently unbreakable habit, except perhaps as regards brevity, of those who discuss science fiction from within the field. To be perpetually recounting its own history marks the attainment of a kind of puberty in the growth of a mode or a style, and here we have yet another parallel in development between science fiction and jazz. The year 1441 is, I think, the earliest date to which anybody has yet traced back the origins of jazz; historians of science fiction are likely to start off with Plato and the Atlantis bits in the *Timaeus* and the *Critias*. From there they will wander forward, usually lending their account increased bulk and impressiveness by subsuming fantasy as well as science fiction under the irritating heading of "imaginative fiction," and taking in on the way the *Dialogues* of Pope Gregory I, the *Niebelungenlied* and *Beowulf*, the Arthurian romances, Thomas More, Gulliver, *The Mysteries of Udolpho*, *Frankenstein*, a lot about Poe, *Dracula*, Verne and Wells, arriving finally at the really climactic event, the foundation of *Amazing Stories* in 1926. (All these names, and very many more, are conscientiously discussed in L. Sprague de Camp's representative *Science Fiction Handbook*, published in 1953.) These manoeuvres, which leave the jazz historian doing the best he can with Ravel and Milhaud and what an honour it was for everybody when Stravinsky wrote the *Ebony Concerto* for Woody Herman's band, perhaps recall the attempts of the Renaissance apologists to establish the respectability of poetry as something neither obscene nor trivial, and there may be more than a merely verbal resemblance between the boastfulness of much science-fiction propaganda and Scaliger's assertion that

> Poetry represents things that are not, as if they were, and as they ought to be or might be. The poet makes another nature, hence he turns himself into another god: he also will create worlds.

Histories of science fiction, as opposed to "imaginative literature," usually begin, not with Plato or *The Birds* of Aristophanes or the *Odyssey*, but with a work of the late Greek prose romancer Lucian of Samosata. The distinction of this, the so-called *True History*, is that it includes the first account of an interplanetary voyage that the researchers have managed to unearth, but it is hardly science fiction, since it deliberately piles extravagance upon extravagance for comic effect:

> Relinquishing the pursuit, we set up two trophies, one for the infantry engagement on the spiders' webs, and one on the clouds for the air-battle. It was while we were thus engaged that our scouts announced the approach of the Cloud-centaurs, whom Phaethon had expected in time for the battle. They were indeed close upon us, and a strange sight, being compounded of winged horses and men; the human part, from the middle upwards, was as tall as the Colossus of Rhodes, and the equine the size of a large merchantman. Their number I cannot bring myself to write down, for fear of exciting incredulity.

It is no more than appropriate that Lucian's trip to the moon should be preceded by an encounter with some women who are grape-vines from the waist down and followed by sea-battles inside a whale's mouth, nor in particular that it should be accomplished by the travellers' ship being snatched up in a waterspout. Leaving aside the question whether there was enough science around in the second century to make science fiction feasible, I will merely remark that the sprightliness and sophistication of the *True History* make it read like a joke at the expense of nearly all early-modern science fiction, that written between, say, 1910 and 1940. I note finally Lucian's discovery that the men in the moon are of fantastic appearance and habits, but certainly not menacing in any way. The notion of nasty aliens is a comparatively recent one, although it is dominant in the early-modern period I have just defined. The contemporary alien tends to be not only not menacing, but so much better than man— morally rather than technologically—as to put him to shame. I am not quite sure what kind of deduction to draw from that graph, but there must be some.

It is not for a millennium and a half that, according to the canon, further attempts at a moon voyage appear. There might be thought to have been a good deal of science around in the 1630's, what with Kepler's work just finished, Galileo still doing his stuff, and astronomical observation improved to the point where for the first time the planet Mercury was observed in transit across the sun. However, Kepler's *Somnium*— published in 1634, the same year as the first English translation of Lucian's *True History*—evidently describes a trip to the moon in which demons are used as the power source, or rather the hero dreams that this is what is taking place. I find all this of compelling interest, but the plea of the science-fiction historians, that at that time you had little hope of getting to the moon except by dreaming about demons, fails to convince me that the *Somnium*, like the *True History*, is anything but fantasy. The same applies to Bishop Godwin's pro-Copernican romance, *Man in the Moone, or a Discourse of a Voyage Thither by Domingo Gonsales*, which was published in 1638, though probably written a good deal earlier, and was reprinted half a dozen times before the end of the century. Gonsales gets to the moon on a raft drawn by wild swans, a device which John Wilkins, chairman of the body which later became the Royal Society, considered to be quite sound in theory. The only point of much concern to us, however, is that the inhabitants of the moon are found to be what they regularly are in the earlier examples, creatures of a superior morality, any who fall far short of the required standard being infallibly detected and deported to Earth: "the ordinary vent for them," Godwin explains, "is a certain high hill in the North of America, whose people I can easily believe to be wholly descended of them."

I have given enough, I think, of the traditional roll call to establish its tendency, a heavy reliance on accidental similarities. This judgment certainly applies to the next book on everyone's list, Cyrano de Bergerac's *Voyage dans la Lune* (1650). After an abortive experiment with bottles of dew—the sun sucks up dew, you see—Cyrano gets to the moon in a chariot powered by rockets. It is much worse than pointless to take this as an "anticipation" of the engine recently fired at the moon by the Russians or of anything in recent literature, and the same is true of the fact that in Voltaire's *Micromégas* we have the first visit to Earth by an alien. One awaits the revelation that Spenser's Talus is the first, or at any rate an early, robot in English literature. A work more oddly omitted from science-fiction annals is *The Tempest*, in which the very features which must have caused it to be passed over—the comparatively factual outline, the approach by ship, instead of in a waterspout or by demon-propulsion—are the ones which should have brought it to notice. Furthermore, whatever *The Tempest* may be currently agreed to be about, I cannot help thinking that one of the things it is about is specialised knowledge, and whatever may be the relation currently devised between Jacobean science and magic, it would be safe to say that contemporary attitudes towards what we now see as two things were partly inseparable. Even if one resists the temptation to designate Caliban as an early mutant—"a freckled whelp," you remember, "not gifted with a human shape," but human in most other ways—and Ariel as an anthropomorphised mobile scanner, Prospero's attitude to them, and indeed his entire role as an adept, seems to some degree experimental as well as simply thaumaturgical. These considerations, I suggest, while not making the play anything but a very dilute and indirect influence on science fiction, do make it a distant anticipation. On a cruder level, the eccentric scientist-recluse and his beautiful daughter are an almost woefully familiar pair of stereotypes in all but the most recent science fiction, and, incidentally, large areas of what I might call the *Tempest* myth reappear in one of the best of the science-fiction films. The title was *Forbidden Planet*, which induces the reflection that planets have only in the last hundred years or less become the natural setting for this kind of writing; if we want to find early forms of it in days when the Earth was still incompletely explored and space was utterly inaccessible, the obvious place to look is not on other planets but in remote regions of our own, in particular, of course, undiscovered islands.

To mention *Gulliver's Travels* next is not likely to cause any surprise, nor, I hope, alarm. This work is clearly an ancestor of science fiction, and not on the grounds that Laputa is an early powered satellite, either. The claim rests firstly on the notorious pains taken by Swift to counterfeit verisimilitude in the details of his story. Without attempting to draw an exact parallel, I submit that this is rather like the methods of science fiction, at any rate in that it serves to dispel that air of arbitrariness, of having no further aim than to be striking, which is characteristic of most fantasy: the surprising behaviour of Lilliputian candidates for preferment would lose its effect, I take it, in an anti-realistic context. All that businesslike thoroughness in description, with everything given its dimensions, reappears noticeably in the work of Jules Verne, where it constitutes the chief—often the only—method of keeping the reader's disbelief in some state of suspension. The other science-fiction thing about *Gulliver's Travels* is that it presents, clearly enough, a series of satirical utopias, these being chronicled with a great power of inventing details that are to be consistent with some basic assumption. This point, where invention and social criticism meet, is the point of departure for a great deal of contemporary science fiction, and no work is more relevant than *Gulliver's Travels* to this part of our investigation.

Some of these remarks apply to two other island utopias: More's work and Bacon's *New Atlantis*. Of these, the Bacon fragment more strongly recalls science fiction, in that some of its marvels are technological, with research in meteorology, medicine, horticulture, and methods of conjuring, plus aeroplanes, submarines, and microtonal music using echo-chambers. But neither *Utopia* nor *The New Atlantis* match the intent and satirical preoccupation with the social surface that we find both in the Swift and in, for instance, Pohl and Kornbluth's *The Space Merchants*, from which I quoted earlier. Both More and Bacon are, of course, darlings of the science-fiction academics, together with many another writer who falls short of grim documentary realism. Typical omissions of more or less unexpectedness include Chaucer, whose "Squire's Tale" surely includes an account of an early flying machine, and the *Mundus Alter et Idem* attributed to Bishop Hall (1607). The *Mundus*, traditionally taken as a source of *Gulliver's Travels*, is a string of comic-satiric utopias—the gluttons' paradise where staircases are banned as difficult for eaters and dangerous for drinkers, the feminist paradise where men do all the chores and parliament is in perpetual session with everyone talking at once— that anticipates with weird precision another Pohl and Kornbluth novel, *Search the Sky*. The Gothic novel and its successors do get into the canon, but, with one large exception, these, while all-important in the ancestry of modern fantasy, scarcely prefigure science fiction. The exception can hardly help being *Frankenstein*, which, albeit in a distorted form, has had a posthumous career of unparalleled vigour; even old Dracula has less often been exhumed in cinematic form and has never been mated or allowed to re-galvanise himself. (I had better explain at this point that the contemporary trade-term applying to the monster is "android," a synthetic being roughly resembling a man, as opposed to a robot, which is a mere peripatetic machine.) The notable thing about Frankenstein the character is that, far from being possessed of supernatural powers, he is a physiologist with academic training, a feature he has retained in his modern incarnations, while altogether losing the sentimental Shelleyan quality that marked his original appearance. Frankenstein, in the popular mind, when not confused with his monster, is easily the most outstanding representative of the generic mad scientist who plagued bad early-modern science fiction and has now been fined down† into the better-adjusted but still unsociable and eccentric scientist who, often with a Miranda-like daughter-secretary in attendance, continues to head an occasional reasearch project and figure in the hero's thoughts as the Old Man. More important science-fiction themes than this, however, have radiated from the original book. It is true that, as L. Sprague de Camp observes, "all the shambling horde of modern robots and androids are descendants of Frankenstein's sadly malevolent monster," but beyond this lies the whole notion of the artificial creation which turns and rends its master. Čapek's R.U.R. (1920) was perhaps the first modern treatment of this notion, which still regularly reappears, a recent instance being Robert Sheckley's story "Watchbird." Here an airborne device, programmed to detect and forestall aggressive intentions, ends by pro-hibiting most kinds of human action. This idea generalises into innumer-able fictionalised sermons on the dangers of overgrown technology which I shall be detailing later. Before leaving Frankenstein, it is worth observ-ing that a third aspect of the scientific character descends from it, that of the morally irresponsible researcher indifferent to the damage he may cause or render possible, a kind of person consciously described by Wells in The Island of Dr. Moreau, where animals are vivisected in an attempt to humanise them, and to all appearance unconsciously in The Food of the Gods, where Herakleophorbia IV, the growth-inducing compound, is thrown on to the rubbish dump and swilled down the drains and gener-ally scattered over the countryside in a fantastically light-hearted spirit. The irresponsible type of scientist is not altogether separable from a fourth type with a diverse ancestry, that to whom science is a route to personal power.

Some mention of Poe is sadly difficult to avoid in the present context: it has to be admitted that while he was much more important, perhaps to the point of being all-important, in the development of fantasy, he had in one sense a very direct influence on the development of science fiction. Before examining this, it may be just about worth while recalling that Poe seems to have invented the detective story, or so I remember being told at school. Without attempting to rival the complexity of my comparative analysis of jazz and science fiction, I should like to assert flatly that detective fiction and science fiction are akin. There is a closely

---

† The career of the mad scientist flourishes unchecked in the modern juvenile comic book. Those who see in this fact a conspiratorial attempt to undermine public confidence in scientists (which would be a praiseworthy attempt anyhow, I should have thought) may be reassured to find that these days the mad scientist tends to be deprived of his laboratory by other, saner scientists, rather than being overthrown by the two-fisted space rangers. His Einstein haircut should be taken as a tribute to the universality of that great figure.

similar exaltation of idea or plot over characterisation, and some modern science fiction, like most detective fiction, but unlike the thriller, invites the reader to solve a puzzle. It is no coincidence—how could it be?—that from Poe through Conan Doyle to Fredric Brown (the Midas expert) the writer of the one will often have some sort of concern with the other. Poe, at any rate, wrote a couple of stories involving balloon flight, at that time still a novelty, and another taking the destruction of the Earth as its point of departure. His unfinished novel, however, *The Narrative of A. Gordon Pym*, though sometimes cited, is a romance that wanders off into fantasy rather than having anything to do with science fiction. Such interest as it holds for us lies in the fact that Jules Verne's *An Antarctic Mystery* is a continuation, albeit an incoherent one, of the *Pym* narrative, and it is clear from innumerable resemblances, as well as from his own admission, that Verne learnt more from Poe than from any other writer.

With Verne we reach the first great progenitor of modern science fiction. In its literary aspect his work is, of course, of poor quality, a feature certainly reproduced with great fidelity by most of his successors. Although interspersed on occasion with fast and exciting narrative, for instance in the episode where Captain Nemo and his associates find their twenty-thousand-league voyage interrupted by the Antarctic ice pack, the story line is cluttered up again and again by long explanatory lectures and bald undramatised flashbacks. Even the more active passages are full of comically bad writing:

> What a scene! The unhappy man, seized by the tentacle and fastened to its blowholes, was balanced in the air according to the caprice of this enormous trunk. He was choking, and cried out, "*A moi! à moi!*" (Help! help!). Those French words caused in me a profound stupor. Then I had a countryman aboard, perhaps several! I shall hear that heartrending cry all my life!
>
> The unfortunate man was lost. Who would rescue him from that powerful grasp? Captain Nemo threw himself on the poulp, and with his hatchet cut off another arm. His first officer was fighting with rage against other monsters that were climbing the sides of the *Nautilus*. The crew were fighting with hatchets.
>
> The Canadian, Conseil, and I dug our arms into the fleshy masses. A violent smell of musk pervaded the atmosphere. It was horrible.

One would have to blame Verne's translator for some of those ineptitudes, but such was the form in which the novels reached English-speaking readers, none of whom, to my knowledge, has bothered to complain. The story and the ideas were the thing. These ideas, the scientific ones at least, have naturally got a bit dated: the helicopter with seventy-four horizontal screws, the tunnel to the centre of the Earth, the moon-ship shot out of a gun at a speed that would have pulped the travellers before they were clear of the barrel. But these errors hardly matter, any more than Swift's Brobdingnagians cease to be impressive when we reason that they would have broken most of their bones whenever they tried to stand up. It matters hardly more that Verne did successfully foretell the guided missile, nor that this extract from *Five Weeks in a Balloon* (1862) has a bearing on events of eighty years later:

> "Besides," said Kennedy, "the time when industry gets a grip on everything and uses it to its own advantage may not be particularly amusing. If men go on inventing machinery they'll end by being swallowed up by their own inventions. I've often thought that the last day will be brought about by some colossal boiler heated to three thousand atmospheres blowing up the world."
>
> "And I bet the Yankees will have a hand in it," said Joe.

The general prophecy about invention overreaching itself is clearly far more interesting than the particular glimpse of something like the nuclear bomb, or rather of its possible outcome. Verne's importance is that, while usually wrong or implausible or simply boring in detail, his themes foreshadow a great deal of contemporary thinking, both inside and outside science fiction.

As regards the mode itself, Verne developed the tradition of the technological utopia, presenting in *The Begum's Fortune* a rival pair of these, the one enlightened and paternalistic, the other totalitarian and warlike. This was published in 1879, so it is no surprise to find that the nice utopia is French and the nasty one German. There are also several novels virtually initiating what has become a basic category of science fiction, the satire that is also a warning, and it is here that Verne is of some general interest. Thus in *Round the Moon*, after the projectile has fallen back into the sea—at a speed of 115,200 miles an hour, incidentally, and without hurting anyone inside—we find a company being founded to "develop" the moon after a fashion that anticipates *The Space Merchants*. The sequel to *Round the Moon, The Purchase of the North Pole*, involves not only the said purchase on the part of the Baltimore Gun Club, the people who set up the cannon to fire the moon-projectile, but a scheme whereby a monstrous explosion shall alter the inclination of the Earth's axis and so bring the polar region into the temperate zone. Since parts of the civilised world would correspondingly be shifted into new polar regions, the response of officialdom is unfavourable. However, the explosion takes place, and only an error in the calculations preserves the *status quo*. The notion of an advancing technology increasing the destructive power of unscrupulousness reappears on a smaller scale in *The Floating Island*, where the huge artifact breaks up in mid-ocean as a result of rivalry between two financial cliques. The book closes with a straightforward Vernean sermon on the dangers of scientific progress considered as an embodiment of human arrogance. The heavy moral tone of this and many passages in the other books is among the less fortunate of Verne's legacies to modern science fiction, and some of his other anticipations, if they are properly that, give no cause for congratulation. In particular, his sexual interest is very thin: Phileas Fogg, the hero of *Around the World in Eighty Days*, does pick up an Indian princess in the course of his travels, but we discover almost nothing about her, and Fogg treats her with an inflexible courtesy which goes beyond mere Victorianism and which any girl of spirit might find subtly unflattering. Even the villains rarely do so much as aspire to lechery. It is in his political tone, which, however vague and eccentric, is nearly always progressive, and even more in his attitude to technology, fascinated but sceptical and at times tinged with pessimism, that Verne's heritage is most interesting and valuable: his last book, *The Eternal Adam*, is a kind of proleptic elegy for the collapse of Western civilisation. These are the considerations which go some way to override his ineptitude and pomposity, his nineteenth-century boys'-story stuffiness, and make him, not only in a science-fiction sense, recognisably modern.

Whatever else he may or may not have been, Jules Verne is certainly to be regarded as one of the two creators‡ of modern science fiction; the other, inevitably enough, is H. G. Wells. To treat Wells as such, rather than as the first important practitioner in an existing mode, is no denigration. Rather, it takes account of the fact that all his best and most influential stories appeared between 1895 and 1907, before science fiction had separated itself from the main stream of literature, and so were written, published, reviewed, and read as "romances" or even adventure stories. The expected comparison with Verne, made often enough at the time (though repudiated by both), now shows not only a huge disparity in literary merit but certain differences in the direction of interest. A main preoccupation of Verne's, as I said, was technology itself, "actual possibilities," as Wells put it, "of invention and discovery," and this holds true equally when what were possibilities to Verne are impossibil-

---

‡ There were, of course, innumerable other ancestors of secondary importance. The volume of utopian literature in the second half of the nineteenth century is huge, and its range stretches all the way from tract-like, plotless dogmatisms of politics, economics, or religion to adventure stories with a few ideas in them. Some of these works were of great and prolonged popularity: the classic instance is Edward Bellamy's *Looking Backward*, with its world-wide sale and its dozens of rejoinders. The vogue of this kind of writing was such that Gilbert and Sullivan, who had a sharp eye for fashions in taste if for nothing else, thought it worth a whole operetta, *Utopia Ltd.* (first performed in 1893), which I have so far been unable to see performed. Nor was this an interest confined to specialists or cranks, as is testified by the existence of utopian works by Bulwer Lytton, Samuel Butler, W. H. Hudson, William Morris, and William Dean Howells.

ities or grotesque improbabilities to us. The long scientific lectures inter-
polated in his stories—"If I created a temperature of 18°, the hydrogen
in the balloon will increase by 18/480s, or 1,614 cubic feet" and so on—
these lectures, however tedious, are highly germane to what Verne was
doing. Wells, on the other hand, is nearly always concerned only to fire
off a few phrases of pseudo-scientific patter and bundle his characters
away to the moon or the 803rd century with despatch. Verne himself saw
this point all right, and complained after reading (rather cursorily, it
seems) *The First Men in the Moon:*

> I make use of physics. He fabricates. I go to the moon in a cannon-ball
> discharged from a gun. There is no fabrication here. He goes to Mars
> [*sic*] in an airship [*sic*], which he constructs of a metal that does away
> with the law of gravitation. That's all very fine, but show me this metal.
> Let him produce it.

It is often said that Wells's main interest was not in scientific advance
as such but in its effect on human life. Although this is true of some of
his works, as we shall see in a moment, it is patently not true of the ones
which had the most immediate effect on the growth of science fiction.
Indeed, in this respect the Verne of *The Floating Island* or *The Purchase of the North Pole* seems distinctly more contemporary than the
Wells of *The Time Machine* or *The Invisible Man.* The real importance
of these stories is that they liberated the medium from dependence on
extrapolation and in so doing initiated some of its basic categories. The
time machine itself, the Martians and their strange irresistible weapons
in *The War of the Worlds,* the monsters in the first half of *The Food of
the Gods,* the other world coterminous with ours in "The Plattner
Story," the carnivorous plant in "The Flowering of the Strange Orchid,"
all these have had an innumerable progeny. What is noticeable about
them is that they are used to arouse wonder, terror, and excitement,
rather than for any allegorical or satirical end. When the Time Traveller
finds that mankind will have become separated into two races, the gentle
ineffectual Eloi and the savage Morlocks, the idea that these are descended respectively from our own leisured classes and manual workers
comes as a mere explanation, a solution to the puzzle; it is not trans-
formed, as it inevitably would be in a modern writer, into a warning
about some current trend in society. *The Invisible Man* is only very incidentally concerned with the notion that a scientific discovery may be
dangerously two-edged; the novel is about the problems, firstly of being,
secondly of catching, an invisible man. "The Country of the Blind,"
which is science fiction of the physical-change variety, is about what it
would be like for a sighted person in a country of the blind: the proverb
about the one-eyed man being king there doubtless inspired the story,
but its theme is a concretisation, not a daring imaginative statement, of

the untruthful aspect of that proverb. A contemporary writer, again, would have used the proposed blinding of the hero as a climactic point for the enfilading of our intolerance towards exceptional talents; Wells throws this away in an aside, giving us the hero of an adventure story in danger, not the representative of anything being threatened with anything representative. Dr. Moreau's beast-men are beast-men, not symbolic puppets enacting a view of beasts and men, or of men. *The First Men in the Moon* admittedly has some satirical discussions of war and human irrationality, together with one of several early anticipations of the conditioning-during-sleep idea Huxley developed in *Brave New World*, but Wells's main drive here is simple delight in invention, in working out an alien ecology, typical of what I might call primitive science fiction.

Despite the fluent imaginativeness of the stories mentioned, the most forceful of Wells's romances is the strongly Verne-like *The War in the Air* of 1907. This curious synthesis of World Wars I, II, and III, with Germany attacking the United States before both are overwhelmed by a Chinese-Japanese coalition, is certainly concerned with the effect of technology on mankind, since the one is made to reduce the other to barbarism, and being both satire and warning, it has, in the science-fiction context at any rate, an unmistakably modern ring. *The War in the Air*, however, rates comparatively little attention from the commentators, as do Wells's utopian romances and their not-so-remote ancestor of the early Fabian period, William Morris's *News From Nowhere*. *Men Like Gods*, with its nudism, or *In the Days of the Comet*, where a strange gas so fills humanity with loving-kindness that everyone gets started on companionate marriage, have none of the fire of the early Wells, and give a soporific whiff of left-wing crankiness, but their virtual exclusion from the modern science-fiction canon is surprising. This part of Wells's output anticipated, but evidently did not influence, later developments. Even "A Story of the Days to Come," an early and lively piece, never gets a mention, and yet it forecasts the modern satirical utopia with fantastic exactness: advertising matter is everywhere bawled out of loudspeakers, phonographs have replaced books, mankind is urbanized to the point where agriculturalists commute in reverse, huge trusts reign supreme, an army of unemployables is maintained by a kind of international poorhouse called the Labour Company, all children are brought up in State crèches, deviates get their antisocial traits removed by hypnosis, dreams can be obtained to order, and as a last detail, a prophecy so universal nowadays as to justify panic in razor-blade circles, men don't shave any more, they use depilatories. Quite likely Wells will soon get all, instead of part, of the recognition as pioneer he clearly deserves.

QUESTIONS

1. Explain further why Amis says science fiction is so "characteristically American."

2. Is Amis' comparison of science fiction with jazz a major aspect of the article?

3. Why is science fiction so hard to define?

4. Do you think it important for a genre of contemporary literature to have had a tradition and history?

5. For what sort of audience is "Starting Points" intended?

6. Is it necessary to have read the works Amis cites in order to follow his argument?

Social Science Fiction

Isaac Asimov

Science fiction is an undefined term in the sense that there is no generally agreed-upon definition of it. To be sure, there are probably hundreds of individual definitions but that is as bad as none at all. Worse, perhaps, since one's own definition gets in the way of an understanding of the next man's viewpoint. Under the circumstances, I think it best to make a personal definition. I should stress that my own definition is not necessarily better than the next man's or more valid or more inclusive or more precise. It simply expresses my way of thinking.

In 1952, I wrote an article for *The Writer* which I called "Other Worlds to Conquer." In it, I defined science fiction as follows: *Science fiction is that branch of literature which is concerned with the impact of scientific advance upon human beings.*

I intend to stick to that definition here, with a single slight modification which I will come to in a moment. I find intellectual satisfaction in the definition because it places the emphasis not upon science but upon human beings. After all, science (and everything else as well) is important to us only as it affects human beings.

The modification I wish to make in the definition is made necessary by the fact that it narrows the boundaries of science fiction to a greater extent than most people are willing to see it narrowed. For that reason, I would like to say that my definition applies not to "science fiction" but to a subdivision of the field which I find it convenient to speak of as "social science fiction."

It is my opinion that social science fiction is the only branch of science fiction that is sociologically significant, and that those stories, which are generally accepted as science fiction (at least to the point where skilled editors accept them for inclusion in their science-fiction magazines) but do not fall within the definition I have given above, are *not* significant, however amusing they may be and however excellent as pieces of fiction.

This is a broad statement and may even sound a bit snobbish. But then the general purpose of this essay is to give my opinions on the influence of society upon science fiction and science fiction upon society, so I am prepared to explain my stand at considerable length.

263

I

It is rather fashionable among some connoisseurs of science fiction to stress its age. This is partly the result of a thoroughly natural desire to lend an air of respectability to a class of literature that is often the target of laughter and sneers from those who picture it in terms of comic strips and horror movies.

August Derleth, for instance, one of the most able and indefatigable anthologists in the entire field of fantasy, has collected a volume called *Beyond Time and Space* (Pellegrini and Cudahy, 1950), which he has subtitled *A Compendium of Science-Fiction Through the Ages.* In it, he traces back his own conception of science fiction some 2400 years to Plato. The Platonic selection is, of course, the Atlantis story from the dialogue, "Critias." Selections are also included from More's *Utopia*, Rabelais' *Gargantua,* and Swift's *Gulliver's Travels.*

The anthology is one of the best and most fascinating in the field. Nevertheless, I think that Derleth is overzealous. The attraction of great names notwithstanding, science fiction, even at its broadest, cannot logically be traced further back in time than the period in which the western world became aware of the significance of the Industrial Revolution.

What about Plato's Atlantis, then? What about More's Utopia and Swift's Lilliput, Brobdingnag and Laputa? They represent superlative feats of imagination, but they do not have the *intent* of science fiction. They are social satires. The societies they describe are not intended to have meaning in themselves but are a reflection, usually a derogatory one, of the societies in which the authors lived.

Let's give this type of literature a name for convenience's sake. Let's call it *social fiction,* and define it in this way: *Social fiction is that branch of literature which moralizes about a current society through the device of dealing with a fictitious society.*

This is really an inevitable category of fiction if we consider that at most periods of human history, it was more than a little dangerous to analyze the then-prevalent society with too probing a finger and too curious an eye. It was far safer to show the reader his own image in a distorting mirror, hoping that sooner or later he would turn from the grotesque reflection to himself with the sobering thought that it *was* a reflection and, after all, not such an inaccurate one.

There is nothing in the definition of social fiction which limits the nature of the fictitious society. It can be a very realistic one, or it can be a fantastic one involving men on the moon, six-inch-high pygmies or intelligent horses. The presence of these *outré* overtones does not of itself convert social fiction into science fiction. It is, I repeat, a question of intent.

Social fiction, whatever the nature of its fictitious society, has its eye fixed on the current society. It pictures life not as it will be or as it might be or as it could be, but as it *should* be or as it *should not* be.

Science fiction, on the other hand, is really concerned with the fictitious society it pictures. It becomes not merely a lesson to us, a text from which to draw a moral, but something that bears the possibility of importance in its own right. When does science fiction become conceivable then? When the minds of mankind are so oriented by circumstance that it becomes reasonable to them that any society other than the one in which they live can be conceived of, if not in the present, then at least in the future.

This may sound startling. Surely it is obvious that more than one kind of society is possible. You have only to look about you to see India, China, the South Seas; only to look back in time to see pagan Rome and pharaonic Egypt.

But that is only because we live in an era of widespread education, rapid transportation and universal communication. Go back two hundred years and Earth expands into a tremendous, shadowy unknown while the horizon of the average individual shrinks to the village in which he is born, lives and dies.

Until the middle of the eighteenth century, the dominant factor in human history was stasis. Empires rose and empires fell. Conquerors flashed across the world stage. Barbarians thundered in from the steppes. To the peasant on his farm, generally speaking, it all meant nothing. The generations went on.

The "changes" that seem so impressive in the history books, the rise of this city or that, the fall of this empire or that, are really not changes to the average man. A given individual might have the current of his life turned awry if a war band clattered through his patch of farming ground, or if pestilence struck, or famine ground him. If he survived, however, he was back in the old place, and if in a large city a hundred miles away, a new king reigned, he heard it only by rumor and it meant nothing.

To a man who lived his life as his father had done and all his father's fathers as far back as his knowledge went, it would inevitably seem that there was a "natural order" of things. This natural order was prescribed either by the innate qualities of the human being and his world (if we listen to the Greek thinkers) or it was imposed by the greater wisdom of some supernatural being (if we listen to the Judean thinkers). In either case, it could neither be fought nor changed.

In such a world, science might exist, but its potentialities for social change would be understood only by a few, and that with difficulty. To the ancient Greeks, for instance, science was not the study of the blind laws that governed the motions of matter and its components. Instead, it was simply an aspect of beauty. Its final aim was purely and statically intellectual. By greater understanding, the educated Greek hoped to appreciate the design of the universe, almost as though it were a geometric figure conceived by a divine mathematician, rather than a handy device which impious man could seize and use to increase his own comfort.

Greek science was abstract geometry; Pythagorean studies of the mystical values of number; Platonic and Aristotelian speculations on the existence of "ideals," on the true nature of "virtue." Beautiful it was, but sterile, also.

To have viewed science as a means by which mankind could control his environment and deliberately change social structure would have made a marked man of one, a crackpot, a possible blasphemer. Plato, on being asked by an aspiring student as to the usefulness of geometry, gave him a coin that he might not feel he had gained nothing from the study, and ordered him to begone. A man who wanted practical applications was no true scientist.

It was the lack of social insight and not the lack of scientific ability that prevented Greece from initiating the Industrial Revolution two thousand years early. L. Sprague de Camp, in a brilliant commentary on the science of the Hellenistic age ("The Sea-King's Armored Division," *Astounding Science Fiction*, September–October, 1941) describes how close to it they were.

This is not to say that there was *no* change in human society until the mid-eighteenth century. Obviously mankind advanced continuously from the stone axe to gunpowder and from a hollowed-out tree trunk to the full-rigged ship. But the advance was slow in comparison to the passing of the generations.

Probably the first single event in history which affected the general population in a fundamental manner with sufficient quickness and intensity to be unmistakable to all was the French Revolution of 1789–1799. This phenomenon differed from previous rapid changes, such as Alexander's blitzkrieg against the Persian Empire, in that the alterations that resulted applied not to a thin Macedonian aristocracy, but to the entire French population from King Louis to Jacques Bonhomme.

It seemed like the end of the world to most of Europe. By the time the Revolution and its Napoleonic sequel had come to an end, the social structure of Europe had been changed radically in the space of *less than one generation*. The statesmen at the Congress of Vienna did their best to wipe out those changes, to restore the "natural order" of things, to replace the omelet within the eggshell. They failed, of course.

It is obvious then, that if science fiction is to deal with fictitious societies as possessing potential reality rather than as being nothing more than let's-pretend object lessons, it must be post-Napoleonic. Before 1789 human society didn't change as far as the average man was concerned and it was silly, even wicked, to suppose it could. After 1815, it was obvious to any educated man that human society not only could change but that it did.

Before passing on to the post-Napoleonic world, however, it might be well to forestall certain doubts that may exist in the reader's mind as to the true priority of the French Revolution as a recognizable rapid-fire social disintegrator. There have, for instance, been numerous religious revolutions in world history. Usually they are slow, but the Lutheran Reformation, two centuries before the French Revolution, was certainly rapid enough. In one generation, the religious map of Europe changed and was never the same again. Despite a series of wars, as vicious as any in history, the Reformation was another omelet that would not re-enter the egg.

Nevertheless, religious revolutions, important though they are, cannot be creators of nonstatic societies. Each new religion, however scornful of the claims to absolute knowledge and absolute authority on the part of the older faith, is firm in the belief that now, at least, the truth *has* been found, and that there is no ground for any further innovations.

Politico-economic revolutions are only slightly less emotion-ridden than are religious revolutions and there is little to choose in bitterness between them, but there is this important difference. A religious stasis is accepted by its devotees as having been ordained by a god or gods, and therefore not to be questioned by man. Not one jot or tittle of the law may be changed till all is fulfilled. Political stases, however, are ordained by men; none of their devotees can deny that. And it is easier to gainsay men, however great, than gods, however small.

Nevertheless, this difference does not seem sufficient to support my argument. Is there another difference between the time of Luther and Calvin and the times of Robespierre and Napoleon? The answer is, yes, the centuries involved—the sixteenth in one case and the eighteenth in the other.

Actually, the French Revolution itself was not primary. Underlying it lay centuries of slow changes in the fabric of society—changes of which most men were unaware. But from the nadir of western society—the tenth century—and through the Renaissance the *rate* of change had been steadily and continuously increasing. In the eighteenth century, the rate bounced forward tremendously. With the French Revolution, it became completely obvious.

To start the era of change with the French Revolution is therefore merely a handy way of pegging a date. The fundamental consideration is that about 1800, the tide of hastening change due to the scientific and industrial development of western society had become a colossal current that swept all other competing factors into discard.

In the eighteenth century, the Industrial Revolution began in England. It not only began, it was drastically stimulated by events on the Continent. The necessity of fighting France, then twice as populous, heavily militarized, and, eventually, the controller of all Europe from Madrid to Moscow, forced England's economy into hot-house growth. In 1815 after twenty years of continuous warfare, she was stronger and richer in relation to the rest of the world than ever before or since.

II

Even today it is not entirely plain to many people that scientific-economic change is the master and political change the servant. From 1789 to 1900, we changed from Louis XVI to the Third French Republic; from George III to Victoria; from George Washington to William McKinley; but we also changed from the stagecoach to the railroad; from the sailboat to the steamboat; from Buffon to Darwin and from Lavoisier's discovery of the nature of oxidation to Becquerel's discovery of the fact of radio-activity.

You may wonder how one can balance the Emancipation Proclamation against the electric light and the Bill of Rights against the X-ray tube, but we are not making moral judgments or comparisons here. We are trying to look the facts of social change in the face. Consider the political changes in our own generation. The rise and fall of Nazi Germany, with its World War II enclosure, took place in a round dozen years. Forty years ago the word "Fascism" did not exist. In less than forty years, Communism grew from a splinter group in the Socialist left to the predominant code of thinking of one third of the world. And today we live surrounded by a cold war of a type few could have anticipated ten years ago.

Tremendous! It seems more cosmic, more world-shaking than the scientific and technological changes in the same period of time: things like the rise and decline of radio, the growth of the automobile, the coming of television and sound movies, jet planes and radar. The only scientific innovation that perhaps really impresses us is the atomic bomb.

Yet consider! Imagine a world in which Communism suddenly ceased to be. It would be a different world, wouldn't it? Your life would be changed, perhaps drastically (if you were an aeronautical engineer, for instance). Now imagine a world in which the automobile ceased to be. I feel certain that your life would experience a greater *immediate* change in that case. In other words, while changes in political affairs often hit us at an abstract and rarefied level, technological changes always hit home, right in the bread basket.

Then, too, technological changes lie at the root of political change. It was the developing Industrial Revolution that placed western Europe so far ahead of the rest of the world, that it could control all of it from

China to Patagonia, either by outright political rule or by indirect economic mastery. Even the railroads of the United States were built as the result of the investments of European capitalists. And it is the Industrial Revolution spreading outward to America first, then to Russia, and now to China and India, that has shaken and is destroying European hegemony. Forty years ago, Russia couldn't build its own railroads without help. Today it is building jet planes we suspect of being better than ours. The world wags away, and these days the wagging is so rapid as to be a blur.

How did this new factor of social change enter western literature? In three ways, which we may list.

1) Through adoption in the field of social fiction. After all, the social satirists were describing fictitious societies. Why not one in which the obviously advancing technology advanced still further? Bellamy wrote *Looking Backward* and Wells wrote *The Shape of Things to Come*. But these were still social fiction. The writer's eye was still on the present. He was using science to help him point his moral, to shape his warning, or to help point the way. We might, if we wished to be whimsical about it, call this sort of thing enriched social fiction, since a moribund literary form was revitalized through the addition of a sprinkling of science, much as white flour is "enriched" with various vitamins. This type of literature is still with us today and the authors who engage in it are far from being unrespected. I point to Huxley's *Brave New World* and the quite recent 1984 of Orwell. But it is a blind alley. We cannot forever face the future only as the present's object lesson; we must look at it as the future, something as valid as the present. We may not like it, but there it is.

2) Through adoption in the field of Gothic horror fiction. The terrifying tale of the supernatural (or, usually, subnatural) is as old as literature, and to adopt the mysteries of science as an aid to horror was an inevitable development. *Frankenstein* is one of the first and certainly one of the most successful of its kind. That genre has lived through the decades also. Its recent representatives include the works of Merritt and Lovecraft.

3) Finally, around scientific advance there developed—there *had* to develop—a new and specialized literature, peculiar to itself. Let us now, therefore, make a new and very broad definition of science fiction. *Science fiction is that branch of literature which deals with a fictitious society, differing from our own chiefly in the nature or extent of its technological development.*

This is a very broad definition. Since nothing is said about whether or not this fictitious society is intended to be a possibly real one or is merely composed as a lesson to present humanity, it even includes "social fiction plus science." (My personal impulse is to add a clause to the definition to the effect that the fictitious society is not advanced for the purpose of conscious moralization—but such a limitation would conflict with the ideas of those science-fiction enthusiasts who consider the works of Stanton A. Coblentz, for instance, as science fiction.)

We have now reached the point of the foundation of science fiction. Before we pass on to a new section in which we consider the development and differentiation of science fiction, I would like to rephrase briefly the reason for its beginnings. I can do it in one sentence.

Technological advance, rapid with respect to the passing of the generations, is a new factor in human history, a factor that marks off the last few generations of mankind from all the generations that preceded, and science fiction is the literary response to that new factor.

III

The history of science fiction can be divided into four eras: 1) 1815–1926; 2) 1926–1938; 3) 1938–1945; and 4) 1945–present.

The first era, a long, amorphous one, may be termed "primitive." It was a primitive era because although the concept of science fiction had been born, the economic basis for the support of science-fiction writers did not yet exist. It may seem a detestably commercial attitude to take toward art, but before any extensive literature can exist, some method must be found for feeding, clothing, and sheltering the practitioners while they create the literature.

Until 1926, science fiction possessed no regular outlet. Individual science-fiction stories had to find a literary home in periodicals devoted to general literature. Such periodicals could absorb only a limited quantity of experimental material. Individuals of towering stature, a Jules Verne or an H. G. Wells, might publish these fantastic stories about trips to the moon but no young writer, still clumsy with his words, could think of specializing in science fiction unless he were quite content to make his living some other way while doing so. No large class of science-fiction specialists, such as exists today, could possibly have existed before 1926. The economic basis for it was lacking.

In 1926, Hugo Gernsback founded *Amazing Stories*. He had edited magazines previously which published science fiction among other things, but *Amazing Stories* was devoted exclusively to science fiction. What this meant, put in its baldest terms, was this: allowing six stories per issue, seventy-two science-fiction stories could be published each year. A corollary was that with the success of *Amazing Stories*, other publishers would take the risk. Within five years two more magazines, *Science Wonder Stories* and *Astounding Stories*, were out.

It is quite reasonable, therefore, to call the second era of science fiction from 1926 to 1938, the "Gernsback Era."

It is interesting that in the very early days of *Amazing Stories*, the poverty in the field was such that Gernsback devoted himself to reprinting H. G. Wells. It was only gradually that young authors developed to whom science fiction was the primary and, sometimes, exclusive means of literary expression; authors such as Edmond Hamilton and Jack Williamson, to name two who, a quarter of a century later, are still publishing.

But now we have a fundamental change. Social fiction (which may be considered a sort of ancestor of science fiction, as alchemy is to chemistry) was essentially an extremely mature fiction. Only men of mature thought would be expected to appreciate either the satire or the moralization (What does a youngster make of *Gulliver's Travels*? He considers it an English *Sindbad*.)

Science fiction, on the other hand, entered a domain that belonged almost exclusively to the young at that time, even to the adolescent. This *had* to be. A new literature, devoted to the principle that change was continuous, inevitable and even desirable, had to find its devotees among those to whom change was not something frightening; to the young, in other words.

To the youngster, born in the midst of this change, more change was only natural. They could hardly wait for it. The airplane had been invented; it was already old stuff; the next step is the rocket-ship; what are we waiting for? Well, we have radio; where's television; what's the delay?

This meant that science fiction had to lose most of its adult qualities, which were already well developed in the work of such a primitive master as Wells. (The word "primitive" is by no means to be taken as a derogatory term. I am merely placing Wells in time, setting him down as belonging to the "primitive era" because he wrote his science fiction before 1926.)

As most of the readers and many of the writers were in their teens, it was not reasonable to expect many stories containing social and economic complexities to be written, and even less reasonable to expect the few that were to be appreciated. In the place of such things there came again the epic individual who is the hallmark of primitive literature; the hero of infinite resource and daring, lacking completely the imaginative intellect that can conjure up horror and produce terror. The d'Artagnan sword and the Hickock six-shooter were thrown away and discarded and, in their place, there came the Hawk Carse-Richard Seaton hero with his ray gun and space ship.

The "adventure science fiction" dominated science fiction during the Gernsback Era. Please do not think that by this I imply that there are sharp boundaries in anything I discuss. Adventure science fiction existed before 1926 and it continued to exist after 1938. The point is that never has it dominated the field as it did between those two dates.

Among the connoisseurs of today, adventure science fiction is spoken of, with a certain flavor of disapproval, as "space opera"—the term being analogous to the contemptuous "horse opera" applied to the run-of-the-mill "western." There is perhaps a little unjust snobbery in this.

In the first place, space opera within the limitations of its own field can reach a high pitch of excellence. Edward E. Smith and John W. Campbell brought this type of story to its heights. With the entire cosmos as their field they streaked their heroes from star to star and from galaxy to galaxy. No homesickness intruded, no fear, no human weaknesses, no petty quarrels, no passion—only gigantic wars and conquests, tremendous victories and gargantuan dangers boldly disposed of.

Make no mistake. They were exciting reading.

Even today, many magazines specialize in adventure science fiction, and this is not an evil thing, or even particularly undesirable. The youngsters of today can't plunge head first into a complex adult story. They must begin with adventure, i.e., space opera. But space opera, unlike horse opera, is not a dead end. The youngster may grow out of the science-fiction habit altogether as he almost invariably grows away from Hopalong Cassidy, but he may also graduate into the more complex varieties of science fiction.

Another kind of science fiction that was important during the Gernsback era was the reverse of adventure science fiction. If the youngsters wanted their blood and thunder they also wanted their science, and so story after story came out in which that stock character, the irascible, eccentric (or even mad) scientist explained his inventions and discoveries in interminable double-talk.

We might call this "gadget science fiction," and dismiss further consideration of it here, since it becomes more important in the next era of science fiction.

IV

In 1938, John W. Campbell became editor of *Astounding Stories*. If Gernsback is the father of science fiction, Campbell is the father of "social science fiction"; that is, the branch of science fiction which really lives up to my original definition: *(Social) science fiction is that branch of literature which is concerned with the impact of scientific advance upon human beings.*

It would be wise to pause at this point. I have mentioned three varieties of science fiction now: adventure science fiction, gadget science fiction, and social science fiction. Definitions are all right but it won't hurt, and it would probably help considerably, if I come up with a few examples.

Let us suppose it is 1880 and we have a series of three writers who are each interested in writing a story of the future about an imaginary vehicle that can move without horses by some internal source of power; a horseless carriage, in other words. We might even make up a word and call it an automobile.

Writer X spends most of his time describing how the machine would run, explaining the workings of an internal-combustion engine, painting a word-picture of the struggles of the inventor, who after numerous failures, comes up with a successful model. The climax of the yarn is the drama of the machine, chugging its way along at the gigantic speed of twenty miles an hour between a double crowd of cheering admirers, possibly beating a horse and carriage which have been challenged to a race. This is gadget science fiction.

Writer Y invents the automobile in a hurry, but now there is a gang of ruthless crooks intent on stealing this valuable invention. First they steal the inventor's beautiful daughter, whom they threaten with every dire eventuality but rape (in these adventure stories, girls exist to be rescued and have no other uses). The inventor's young assistant goes to the rescue. He can accomplish his purpose only by the use of the newly perfected automobile. He dashes into the desert at an unheard of speed of twenty miles an hour to pick up the girl who otherwise would have died of thirst if he had relied on a horse, however rapid and sustained the horse's gallop. This is adventure science fiction.

Writer Z has the automobile already perfected. A society exists in which it is already a problem. Because of the automobile, a gigantic oil industry has grown up, highways have been paved across the nation, America has become a land of travelers, cities have spread out into suburbs and—what do we do about automobile accidents? Men, women, and children are being killed by automobiles faster than by artillery shells or airplane bombs. What can be done? What is the solution? This is social science fiction.

I leave it to the reader to decide which is the most mature and which (this is 1880, remember) is the most socially significant. Keep in mind the fact that social science fiction is not easy to write. It is easy to predict an automobile in 1880; it is very hard to predict a traffic problem. The former is really only an extrapolation of the railroad. The latter is something completely novel and unexpected.

In any case, it was this social science fiction that Campbell encouraged. A new group of writers grew up about him: Robert A. Heinlein, L. Sprague de Camp, A. E. van Vogt, Theodore Sturgeon and many others. Older writers such as Jack Williamson and Henry Kuttner changed their styles to suit the times. (I might mention as an aside that I sold my first story to Campbell only a few months after he became editor.)

What, specifically, did Campbell do? First and foremost, he de-emphasized the nonhuman and nonsocial in science fiction. Science fiction became more than a personal battle between an all-good hero and an all-bad villain. The mad scientist, the irascible old scientist, the beautiful daughter of the scientist, the cardboard menace from alien worlds, the robot who is a Frankenstein monster—all were discarded. In their place, Campbell wanted business men, space-ship crewmen, young engineers, housewives, robots that were logical machines.

He got them.

Again the dividing line is not sharp. Science fiction with real characters existed before Campbell, notably in the stories written by Stanley G. Weinbaum in his short, meteoric career. His first story, A Martian Odyssey is, in my own opinion, the first example of modern social science fiction. It dealt with an alien race not inferior to Earthmen; not superior; merely different. He got across that sense of difference. His environment was not merely grotesque or merely horrible. It was different, naturally different. The scene was Mars and it felt like Mars, not like a horror movie. Most of all, his people talked like people and acted and felt like people. A Martian Odyssey appeared in 1934 in Wonder Stories. The editor—give him credit—was Charles R. Hornig.

The importance of Campbell is that he was not content to let Weinbaums spring up accidentally. He looked for them. He encouraged them. It is that which makes the years 1938–1945 the "Campbell Era."

Campbell also brought to the field an increasing rigor as far as scientific background was concerned. In the cut, thrust, and slash style of adventure science fiction, science which was inaccurate or even ridiculous in terms of what was actually known at the time frequently found a place. The better writers of the type, the aforementioned E. E. Smith and Campbell himself, were too well-trained in science (Smith has a doctorate in chemistry and Campbell is a physics-major graduate of M.I.T.) to offend badly in this way, but hordes of lesser lights dealt with such things as a hollow Earth, inhabited within; atoms that were really miniature solar systems and inhabited; Mars that was pictured as having Earth gravity, atmosphere and temperature, with Earthlike inhabitants.

Although the stories written about such central ideas are often vastly entertaining, they remain completely fallacious. The Earth is not hollow. The atom is not a miniature solar system. Mars is very different from Earth and could not support Earth life.

The reader may seriously question my concern over such discrepancies. Does not all science fiction involve the fantastic? Yes, but there is a great difference between taking liberties with the unlikely and taking liberties with the impossible. The liberties allowed legitimate science fiction are so great that there is no need to drag in outright impossibilities, and there is an important social reason why it should not.

Science fiction aspires now to be more than a literature for youngsters. To appeal to adults, to gain serious consideration in our society, it must not offend reason. It must be coherent with the life we know in the sense that it does not contradict that which is known to be uncontradictable. A historical novel, to take an example from another field, might include a dozen thoroughly fictitious characters for the Civil War era, but it can't describe Stephen A. Douglas as president of the United States. It can make General Grant do many things he never did, but it can't make him surrender at Appomattox.

I will give my reasons later in this essay for thinking it important that science fiction be accepted with respect by society in general for the good not only of science fiction, but of society.

Two qualifications to my last argument must be made. It must not be thought that all writers of adventure science fiction are necessarily given to bad science. I have already mentioned Smith and Campbell. I want to emphasize the point and advance L. Sprague de Camp as an example. De Camp is one of the best, perhaps *the* best of the contemporary practitioners of the derring-do-and-sword-play school of science fiction. He is also one of the most meticulous men in the field when it comes to excluding known scientific impossibilities. Much more meticulous, for instance, than myself, though I do more preaching about it.

The second qualification has a name. That name is Ray Bradbury. Bradbury has written scores of stories about Mars. He gives Mars an Earthlike temperature, an Earthlike atmosphere and Earthlike people, sometimes down to tuxedoes and pocket-handkerchiefs. His stories reek with scientific incongruity. But he gets away with it. Not only does he get away with it, but, among the general population, he is by far the most popular science-fiction writer and regularly appears in such magazines as the *Saturday Evening Post*.

In my opinion, Bradbury gets away with it because he does not really write science fiction. He is a writer of social fiction. His "Mars" is but the mirror held up to Earth. His stories do not depict possible futures; they are warnings and moral lessons aimed at the present. Because Bradbury believes that our present society is headed for chaos and barbarism unless it changes its present course (he may well be right), his warnings are jeremiads. This has led some critics to the superficial belief that the man is simply "morbid" or that he has a "death wish." Nonsense! He is simply writing social fiction.

It is not my wish to imply that the creation of social science fiction was a complete tour de force on the part of Campbell. It was true that he had the wisdom to see and respond to a new demand, but the fact of fundamental importance is that the demand existed.

After all, twelve years had passed. The boy of fifteen who had read *Skylark of Space* in 1928 and was overwhelmed by it was now twenty-five and longing for the "good old days." He no longer enjoyed science fiction and remembered the past with nostalgia because he thought the stories were better. They weren't. He had merely been ten years younger. To satisfy the veterans of science fiction, to take into account the steadily increasing average age of the readers, to prevent the older enthusiasts from falling away as similar grownups fell away from Edgar Rice Burroughs and Zane Grey, science fiction had to mature with its readers. Fortunately, it did.

V

In 1945, the atom bomb was dropped on Hiroshima and a fourth stage of science fiction was ushered in.

Why? Primarily because the atom bomb put a new light on science fiction. Until 1945, it was only too easy to dismiss science fiction as "weird stuff," as "horror stories," as "comic-strip things."

"Do you read that stuff?" people would say.

The great popularity of such strips as *Buck Rogers*, *Flash Gordon* and *Superman* made it easy for people to categorize all science fiction as juvenile. The lurid covers of many of the science-fiction magazines did not help. As a result, many adults who would have enjoyed and appreciated science fiction did not, because it never occurred to them to try it.

And then a weapon right out of science fiction ends World War II and changes the balance of power on Earth. It is time for a sober look at the crackpots, so-called, who have been talking about atom bombs at a time when no one but a few specialists in nuclear physics even thought they were possible.

The result was that more people tasted science fiction and found they liked it. As the reading public suddenly grew larger, science fiction became "respectable." Publishing houses such as Doubleday and Simon & Schuster began putting out science-fiction books regularly and with no attempt at "diluting" them in any mistaken belief that the book-buying public was not yet ready for the straight stuff. In addition, science-fiction magazines other than Campbell's *Astounding Science Fiction* (both newcomers and old reliables) began shifting their story policy in the direction of Campbell's.

In 1950, Horace L. Gold brought out *Galaxy Science Fiction* which, from the very beginning, published only advanced social science fiction so that with the first issue it was accepted by most fans as sharing top honors with *Astounding*.

Campbell is still editor of *Astounding* and still a tremendous force in the field, but because he is no longer the lone champion of social science fiction, the era since 1945 cannot be tabbed with his name, or any name. It must simply be called the "atomic era."

VI

Now it is time to look closely at social science fiction. Having isolated it as one of three types of science fiction, and the *one* type with social significance, the question next comes up whether social science fiction is a precise term or whether within it there are also subdivisions.

Neither alternative, in my opinion, is quite correct. Social science fiction is not a precise term but neither is it old enough to have developed a clear-cut subdifferentiation. Instead it consists of a broad continuous spectrum. If we consider the two extremes of the spectrum, we will seem to be treating two widely different types of story, but we will have to keep it continuously in mind that one extreme shades imperceptibly into the other and no man can point and say, "Here is the dividing line." (To a lesser extent this is true of the broader categories of adventure, gadget, and social science fiction; also of the still broader categories of social fiction and science fiction.)

Despite what I have just said, I cannot resist the temptation to give the two extremes names. Names are dangerous because they imply neat categories. Nevertheless, I hope you will humor me in this respect. I could call the extremes conservative and radical; realistic and romantic; simple and complex. I'll use none of these. Instead, I'll use the terms "chess game" and "chess puzzle" which are more picturesque than any of these but, in my opinion, more accurate as well.

A chess game has the following important characteristics: 1) it begins with a fixed number of pieces in a fixed position, and 2) the pieces change their positions according to a fixed set of rules.

A chess puzzle differs from a game in that although the second point holds, the first breaks down. A chess puzzle begins with any number of pieces (up to and including the full amount used in a game) placed in any arrangement that does not break the fundamental rules of chess.

It is important to remember that in the case of the puzzle, the original position is not necessarily one that is likely to be arrived at in the ordinary course of a game. In fact, in the vast majority of cases, a pair of chess players would have to be most ingeniously insane to arrive at the sort of position that would make a good puzzle.

How is this analogous to the spectrum of social science fiction? Point 2, which is held in common by games and puzzles, i.e., the rules by which the pieces move, may be equated with the motions and impulses of humanity: hate, love, fear, suspicion, passion, hunger, lust and so on. Presumably, these will not change while mankind remains Homo sapiens. Stories can be written about "supermen" or intellectual mutants. They may even be written about alien species or robots that do not share these fundamental human drives. However, they must still be written by a very human author and addressed to a very human audience. If the characters are not recognizably human in these respects it is difficult or impossible to treat them adequately or to please the audience with them.

(One exception—and virtually any generalization about science fiction has a dozen exceptions—is Olaf Stapledon's *Odd John*. This is the story of a superman who is so skilfully drawn that he really seems both nonhuman and superhuman. Being only human myself, I didn't like Odd John

—the character, that is, not the story, which I thoroughly enjoyed—any more than a chimpanzee could like a human being if he were capable of really understanding the gulf of mental difference that separated himself from man.)

Point 1 of the chess-game–chess-puzzle dichotomy can be equated with the fundamental socio-economic environment of humanity. The type of story that corresponds to the chess game with its fixed starting position is that which assumes the socio-economic environment we now possess. That is: a city culture as opposed to a village culture; an agricultural economy as opposed to a nomadic or hunting economy; a family system as opposed to a tribal system. Add to these certain newer fashions which have become so ingrained in our own ways of thinking that any deviation has become abhorrent. For instance: heterosexual relationships as the sexual norm; monogamy; a mild, formal and passionless monotheism; taboos against cannibalism and incest; and so on.

With this starting position fixed, it is then only necessary to play the "chess game" according to the rules. The only modification from our own society is that certain technological innovations are allowed. Atomic power may have replaced coal and oil as these once replaced wood. Robots may have been developed. Interstellar travel may be commonplace. But people are still our kind of people with our way of thinking about things.

In the purest form of the chess-game type of social science fiction it is frequently found convenient to take advantage of the fact that "history repeats itself." Why shouldn't it? Given the same rules and the same starting position, the element of repetition must obtrude.

As a result, a whole class of "Galactic Empire" stories has arisen. The Galactic Empire, or its equivalent, is usually simply the Roman or British Empire written large, and the events that transpire can be equated without too much difficulty with analogous events that took place in past history.

I have a personal leaning toward this type of story and have written a few myself. My first novel, *Pebble in the Sky* (Doubleday, 1950), dealt with an Earth, ravaged by radioactivity, despised by its neighbors, but dreaming of its glorious past and certain of its special mission in the future. Most thoughtful readers had no difficulty in recognizing the fact that I was retelling the history of Rome and Judea. I even had Earth governed by an Imperial Procurator.

I wrote other stories, the germs of whose ideas I derived from the histories of Justinian and Belisarius, Tamerlane and Bajazet, John and Pope Innocent III. Naturally they were told in my own way and departed from their historical counterparts whenever it pleased me to have them depart. It was simply that I was following the chess-game theory in which all games start from the same point.

(I do not wish to imply that I am the only writer of such stories, or even the most important such writer. Robert A. Heinlein has specialized in this field and is widely considered to be the most proficient. Of the younger writers, one name which I pick at random is Poul Anderson who did an excellent job of chess-gaming in "The Helping Hand.")

Not everyone approves of this sort of thing. Damon Knight, one of the best and brightest of our postwar crop of social science fiction writers, and a devotee of the chess-puzzle variety, took particular issue with it in an article he wrote for an amateur science-fiction "fan magazine." His thesis was that history did *not* repeat itself.

Whether it does or does not repeat itself depends, of course, on what you mean by repetition. The same people never live twice, the same wars are never fought twice, the same conditions never occur *exactly* twice. Nevertheless, similar broad responses frequently occur under similar broad stimuli. If you stand far away from the great and variegated story of man and squint your eyes so that you drown out the details and see only the broad blocks of color, various repetitive patterns do appear.

We have, for instance, the alternation of city domination and nomad domination in the early days of Near-Eastern civilization; the pattern by which a dynasty or a nation or an empire establishes itself under a strong individual (usually destroying, in the process, a more aristocratic dynasty, a wealthier nation, a more civilized empire), maintains itself through a few harsh reigns or centuries, reaches a peak of luxury and magnificence and then declines to fall victim to another dynasty, nation, or empire.

However, I shall not try to repeat in detail what Toynbee has said in six volumes.

But, after all, how useful are these repetitions of extremely broad sweeps? Fiction to have a real interest must deal with specific happenings—and how specifically can history repeat? The answer is, in my opinion, that it can repeat with surprising specificity.

If you don't mind, now, I would like to present some examples. I have wanted to do this for years and now that the opportunity has come I do not intend to wait for a second knock. I will present, in bare outline, a certain passage of history, in which key words or phrases will be represented by dashes. I invite the reader to fill in the dashes before he looks at my own "solution" at the end of the passage.

VII

Sample: The Revolution

In the ——(1)—— Century, the European nation of ——(2)—— was in a shaky state. In the previous century, it had reached a peak of military glory under the monarch ——(3)——, under whose leadership the nation defeated the attempts of ——(4)—— to gain hegemony over Europe. Since then, the fortunes of the nation had declined, military defeats had been suffered and finances had grown nearly impossible.

The current king ——(5)—— was not noted for either firmness of character or brilliance of intellect. He was noted chiefly for the fact that, in a dissolute court, he maintained a spotlessly moral private life. He was well-meaning and amiable and had none of the sexuality and despotic instinct of his illustrious predecessor ——(6)—— who had a long and successful reign.

The king was, at least in the beginning, liked by the people who, however, bitterly distrusted Queen ——(7)—— who was of foreign extraction and, indeed, was of the ——(8)—— nation whom the people had thought of as enemies for generations. The queen was the stronger personality of the two, the less willing to compromise with the people and the more contemptuous of them.

Despite the resources of the nation, which were ample, and the taxes, which were ample, the government lacked money, partly because of waste and inefficiency and partly because of the ——(9)—— war.

Although the nation had been notoriously loyal to its sovereigns in previous centuries, it now rose in violent revolt. At first mildly radical policies prevailed under the influence of such personalities as ——(10)——. As the revolution proceeded, however, it grew more violent. Some of the original architects of the revolution were forced into exile, for example, ——(11)——. Others, as the revolution grew more violent, paid with their lives. Two of these, among numerous examples, are ——(12)—— and ——(13)——. Eventually, a strong government was formed under ——(14)——. The king was eventually executed, an act which shocked all of Europe.

What shocked some people even more were the measures taken against the established ——(15)—— church of the nation.

Although the rest of Europe would gladly have intervened to put down this dangerous new government and re-establish legitimacy and order, they were not in a position to do so efficiently. There was difficulty in coming to a common decision as to a means of action. In addition, much of Europe was disorganized because of the great ——(16)—— which was just coming to a conclusion.

Half-hearted attempts at intervention failed though they aroused the bitter resentment of the revolutionary government which was quick to respond. Its people became suddenly formidable. Against its foreign foes ——(17)—— it won unexpected victories that, for a time, established its government securely, and, in fact, made of it a menace to the rest of Europe. Eventually, however, the revolution came to an end and after an interlude of domination under General ——(18)—— the heir of the executed king returned to his kingdom as ——(19)——.

I doubt that any reader will not have definite ideas as to which nation and what period in its history I am talking about. Some, perhaps, are thinking that I may be talking of either of two nations. Actually, I am thinking of three. This is the way the blanks could be filled in:

	A	B	C
(1)	17th	18th	20th
(2)	England	France	Russia
(3)	Elizabeth I	Louis XIV	Alexander I
(4)	Philip II of Spain	(not applicable)	Napoleon I of France
(5)	Charles I	Louis XVI	Nicholas II
(6)	Henry VIII	Louis XIV	Peter I
(7)	Henrietta Maria	Marie Antoinette	Alexandra
(8)	French	Austrian	German
(9)	(not applicable)	American Revolution	World War I
(10)	Pym	Mirabeau	Kerensky
(11)	(not applicable)	Lafayette	Trotsky (later)
(12)	(not applicable)	Desmoulins	Zinoviev (later)
(13)	(not applicable)	Danton	Bukharin (later)
(14)	Cromwell	Robespierre	Lenin
(15)	Anglican	Roman Catholic	Orthodox
(16)	Thirty Years' War	(not applicable)	World War I
(17)	Holland	Austria	Germany
(18)	Monk	Bonaparte	(not applicable)
(19)	Charles II	Louis XVIII	(not applicable)

I maintain that this is not bad. To be sure the comparisons can only go so far. Lafayette and Trotsky are in no way comparable except that both went into exile and, more strongly still, General Monk and General Bonaparte are completely different except insofar as one succeeded Richard Cromwell and preceded Charles II, and the other succeeded the Directorate and preceded Louis XVIII.

Now does this prove that history always repeats itself? No, but it shows that it is legitimate to extrapolate from the past because sometimes such extrapolations are fairly close to what happens. Suppose that in 1910 a science-fiction writer wished to lay a story of the future in Russia and, after a shrewd consideration of the conditions then prevailing, decided to have its social background one of revolution. If he were a believer in the chess-game theory he would have used the French Revolution as a framework to keep himself from overstepping the rules of the game.

And he would have done pretty well, if he had done so. Of course, he might have had the Tsarevich Alexius returning to his throne in 1930, and he might have had the ragged Red Army *not* defeated at Warsaw in 1920, but advancing to the Seine before it could be stopped by combined Anglo-American forces (a contingency that may have been premature rather than entirely wrong). Otherwise, it would sound well.

Is this a freak case? Have I just picked out the one case of duplication (or rather triplication) in history, in order to back up my own argument? Not at all. I could find many others. This example could itself have been almost indefinitely extended with parallels all along the line. I might even have, as a particular tour de force, attempted a five-way correlation between Philip II of Spain, Louis XIV of France, Napoleon of France, William II of Germany and Hitler of Germany. But it is time to leave the chess-game variety of social science fiction and pass on to the chess puzzles.

VIII

In chess puzzles the starting position can be adjusted to the will of the puzzle composer. Analogously, in chess-puzzle social science fiction, the initial society in which the characters move can be as the author pleases. Ordinarily, the society is distinct from our own in one or more fundamental ways, though usually it can be viewed as possibly having originated from our society by some radical development or overgrowth of some aspect of our way of life. The heterogeneity of this type of literature is such that it can be explained satisfactorily only by examples.

Fritz Leiber, in an extraordinarily powerful story, "Coming Attraction," postulates an American society in which social disintegration is nearly complete. America is covered with patches of radioactive destruction as a result of a recently concluded atomic war. Women wear masks in public since sexual fixation has traveled from the breasts and hips to the face. Women wrestlers have become a recognized social caste and are more proficient than their male counterparts. The society reeks with a semi-accepted sado-masochism.

The reader is at once repelled by the story and strongly attracted. He is horrified at the society, moved by its reality and profoundly disturbed at the realization that it is an extrapolation of some of the worst features of our present way of life.

Another imagined society occurs in Wyman Guin's "Beyond Bedlam." Here we have a society in which schizoid personality is the accepted norm. It is, in fact, the compulsory norm. Each body is controlled by two minds and personalities, not simultaneously, but alternately for five-day periods. The two mind-controlled bodies bear no relationship to each other. A single person in alternate five-day periods may have two different occupations, two different wives, two different statuses in society and so on. The postulation states further that by forcing split personality on humanity, the eternal struggle between the half-formed personalities within men and women can no longer find its outlet in war and destruction. The two personalities are released, freed of one another, and may go their way in peace.

Guin goes further in this story than a mere statement of a schizoid society. He writes about a situation that is natural, perhaps inevitable, in such a society, but which is alien to us. He gives us an insight into life in a changed society that, in an abstract sense, is very valuable to those of us who expect inevitable change. The story deals with a man who has fallen in love with his wife's alter ego, who has in turn fallen in love with him. In the society of "Beyond Bedlam" this is evil, disgusting and immoral. The struggles and dilemmas of the two star-crossed lovers are followed to the inevitable tragic ending.

It is as though a Roman writer of the Augustan age told a story of a future society in which color distinctions were important, and in which a man found himself hopelessly in love with a girl whose skin tinge was slightly different.

Both "Beyond Bedlam" and "Coming Attraction" appeared in *Galaxy Science Fiction*. This is not to imply that chess-puzzle social science fiction does not appear in *Astounding Science Fiction*. In that magazine, I can cite William Tenn's "Firewater" as an excellent recent example. Nevertheless, due perhaps to the differing personalities of the two editors, the chess-game variety is slightly more prominent in *Astounding*, and the chess-puzzle variety in *Galaxy*.

Two more examples. (It is difficult to know where to stop.) Eric Frank Russell's story "—And Then There Were None" in *Astounding Science Fiction* dealt with a society in which individualism was carried to its logical extreme. Each man did exactly what he wished and no more. Efforts to persuade him to do otherwise were met with a grim, and effective, passive resistance. The other is *Rogue Queen* by L. Sprague de Camp, which has appeared in book form only (Doubleday), and which deals with a quasi-human society whose manner of living is akin to that of the bees, i.e., one functioning female per economic unit, a relatively small number of functioning males, and a large majority of nonfunctioning females.

I have now followed the divisions and subdivisions of science fiction as far as I can and I must pause to remind the reader of a statement I made at the very beginning of this chapter. All that you have read represents a strictly personal organization of the subject. I do not pretend that there is any objective truth in it or even that any sizable portion of science-fiction readers agree with me. It may well be that almost all disagree with me.

Even if we can suppose that in some way I can persuade most or all readers to accept my classification of the field, there would still be wide disagreement as to which story belongs where. To me, for instance, the stories of A. E. van Vogt are gadget science fiction since van Vogt uses Korzybskian semantics as a "mental-variety" gadget around which to build his story, much as George O. Smith used his "physical-variety" gadgets to build his Venus Equilateral stories. To others A. E. van Vogt is social science fiction.

Again, some readers are beginning to take the attitude that any story dealing in Galactic sweeps is automatically "space opera." They will include in the category such examples of adventure science fiction as *Galactic Patrol* by E. E. Smith, gadget science fiction such as *Weapon Shops of Isher* by A. E. van Vogt, and social science fiction of the chess-game variety, such as *The Stars, Like Dust* . . . by myself. To my own way of thinking that broadens the term, space opera, to the point where it is almost co-extensive with science fiction. I therefore disapprove of this tendency. To others this may seem very logical and right, on the other hand.

Since there is no way for any of us to establish absolute truth, if, indeed, such an animal exists, our only alternative is to consider the various classifications presented to us and make that decision among them which pleases us most. The one that pleases me most is the one I've presented here.

IX

Having until now considered the effect of society upon science fiction, its genesis and development, it remains to consider the reverse of the proposition: the effect, actual or potential, of science fiction upon society.

This may seem rather bumptious of me. Can a literary form such as science fiction seriously be considered to have any likely effect upon society? Is it not simply a form of escape literature, simply a kind of entertainment?

If it were, that would be no disgrace. Any human being has the right to relax and get his mind off his dreary surroundings, particularly today, when dreariness is a universal factor. As the tailor said, when reproached for taking a month to make a suit when God had created the world in only six days: "Feel the material of this suit and then come to the window and take a look at this phooey world."

The world today certainly does seem phooey, and it would be a harsh and self-righteous man indeed who could quarrel with the natural desire of an individual to look the other way. Unfortunately, the fact remains that we've got to face our problems at least part of the time. We have to live in the world and be part of it. Worse still, our children will have to also.

But *is* science fiction *only* escape literature? Is it similar in this respect to the western story which describes a world that has not existed these fifty years and probably never existed in the manner made familiar to our cap-pistol-toting children? Is it similar to the love story that lifts our typists and housewives into an imaginary world of synthetic passion purified by the Post-Office Department of any trace of true-to-life sex? Is it similar to the mystery story designed to present the *aficionado* with incredible amounts of make-believe danger and violence within the safe confines of an easy chair?

Superficially, science fiction is similar to these. In one way, however, it is vitally different. It treats not of a make-believe past or a make-believe present. It treats of a make-believe future.

The importance of this difference rests in the fact that a make-believe past or present must exist side-by-side with a known and actual past or present. A make-believe future has no known competitor. It can serve as a nucleus for serious thought without the distracting thought that it is a *known* falseness.

But is there a value in considering make-believe futures? I think so. For the first time in history, the future is a complete puzzle even in its most general aspects. There used to be the consolation, that even though we, as individuals, might die, life would continue, spring would come, flowers would bud. But now we have brought ourselves to such a pass that we wonder whether the planet itself might not die with us.

We've *got* to think about the future now. For the first time in history, the future cannot be left to take care of itself; it must be thought about.

But what can science fiction do about it? It can first, and most important, accustom the reader to the notion of change. The force of change is all about us, it is the essence of our society. Science fiction is the literature of social change, and it treats social change as the norm.

This is important. Resistance to change is, next to the desire for self-preservation, perhaps the most deeply ingrained behavior pattern in the human being. A child will not sleep in a strange crib. A man's digestion is upset if he eats at an unusual time.

In broader terms, you cannot reasonably expect any individual who has attained years of maturity and a place in society which seems natural to him (whether that place be stockbroker or dishwasher) to accept cheerfully any change that alters his place into a new and unaccustomed one.

I once did some library work for a sociology professor (in those days I had to work my way through college) who was writing a book on social resistance to technological change. It was a fascinating and frustrating experience. The priestly caste of primitive civilizations, for instance, fought any attempt to establish a system of writing. Once writing was established, they used all their influence to resist any simplification that would make writing more available to the general population. Naturally, that would weaken their own influence as the repositories of tribal wisdom. The introduction of the iron plow was met with the cry that iron would poison the soil. The use of coal for fuel purposes was opposed by the theory that the fumes would poison the air. Fulton's steamboat, the observers said, would never start. Once started, they knew it would never stop. The airplane, as Simon Newcombe (an eminent astronomer) proved mathematically, was an impossibility. No engine could be designed strong enough to lift a machine aloft which was capable of carrying a man. The Wright brothers flew at Kitty Hawk, and Newcombe changed his mind. All right, he said, *one* man. But no airplane, he insisted, would ever carry more than one man.

The dislike for technological innovations that upset the even comfort of a carefully-designed rut extends with even greater force to social customs. Even the skeleton of a custom of which the pith has long since rotted away remains untouchable.

But is change valuable? Is it even necessary?

In the study of evolution, it turns out that organisms which do not change to meet a changing environment become extinct. Organisms, on the other hand, which find themselves an unchanging environment, find themselves also in blind alleys with no possibility of future advancement.

Human societies, history shows, must also grow and develop or they will suffer. There is no standing still.

Examples can be presented. Two occur to me. In the eighteenth and nineteenth centuries, Europe was presented with the necessity of change. A new industrialism was upsetting the old peasant culture, bringing to the fore two new classes: the industrial employer and the industrial employee. The former became more important than the old landowning aristocracy; the latter, more important than the generally inarticulate peasantry.

Nowhere in Europe was this gathering change popular among those who were getting along perfectly well under the old system. On the Continent of Europe, the landowners resisted the change manfully. They would not and did not give in to change. They *fought* change.

Did they *stop* change? They did not. Resistance welled further and further up the dam formed by the unyielding breasts of the old aristocracy. Then when the dam buckled, the flood was infinitely worse than it would have been had it never been built. From 1789 to 1917 a series of revolutions shook and convulsed Europe.

In England, however, the landowning squirearchy retreated (often unwillingly, it is true) step by step, inch by inch, giving in here, giving in there. The result? Where in Europe, outside of England, is there such a secure throne, such a secure peerage?

Much the same may be said of the small Scandinavian countries and of Switzerland. Here, however, it is not so remarkable. Small countries may vegetate, unaffected by the stress of large world movements, except where it is forced upon them by invading armies. England, however, was subject at all times to the pressures and risks devolving upon a great power. (How much of her fortune is due to the twenty-two miles separating Dover and Calais?)

Another example! Our western culture hit the Far East with a thunderous roar one hundred years ago. The Far East, with a civilization of its own that was superior in many respects to ours, fought it bitterly and unsuccessfully, since our own civilization happened to possess one advantage worth all the rest—a superior technology. China rejected the technology along with all the rest of our culture. She would not compromise. She would not yield. She would not change.

The result? She lost anyway and what she would not give was taken by force.

Japan also retained her culture, but she had the wisdom to bow to the necessity of change. She accepted our technology. The result was that in fifty years she not only became a great power in her own right, respected by all the other great powers, but she was even able to join in the exploitation of China, and outdo all the rest.

Now a fictitious example! Suppose that in the 1840's, the American South had come to the conclusion that the world tide was against chattel slavery and had decided to make the best of a bad bargain by selling its slaves to the government and then rehiring them on the open labor market. Suppose that the North had decided that if matters went as they were, things would only end in a big catastrophe, and that they might as well contribute to the buying of the slaves and their subsequent liberation.

It might have cost money—but not 1 per cent of what the Civil War cost. The South would still have its labor supply, as it has now. Without the memory of a costly war and a costlier reconstruction, without the sense of a regional humiliation, without the sense of being picked on and kicked about, the South eventually might have come to feel less lordly about the color line.

What am I advocating? A doctrine of an irresistible *Wave of the Future, à la* Anne Morrow Lindbergh? Not at all.

I am saying this: it is useless to attempt to solve the tremendous problems of our times by adopting one of only two attitudes. Either to resist change, any change, and hold savagely to the status quo, or to advocate change, a certain change, and no other change. Neither of these views is flexible. Both are static. The result of a collision of such views is almost always disastrous.

I say there must be a third group, one which realizes that the status is not and cannot be quo forever, but which also realizes that the exact nature of the change which will best suit the currently changing social and economic forces may not be guessed at very far in advance.

Franklin Delano Roosevelt's New Deal represented such a third group. He broke with the brute capitalism of the 'twenties, yet did not accept a doctrinaire socialism. Roosevelt frankly and unashamedly experimented. He stated in one of his fireside chats that he liked to try *something*. If it worked, fine; if not, he tried something else.

I cannot help but wonder if a maturely developed sense of social experimentation may not some day bear as much fruit for society as physical experimentation has done for science.

Certainly, there is a good deal of this notion in science fiction. Its authors, as a matter of course, present their readers with new societies, with possible futures and consequences. It is social experimentation on paper; social guesses plucked out of air.

And this is the great service of science fiction. To accustom the reader to the possibility of change, to have him think along various lines—perhaps very daring lines. Why not? In the world, as it wags today, there is precious little to lose. We face the atom . . .

X

So far, the contribution of science fiction seems to be an entirely passive one. It says "Change!" but it doesn't say how. It says "Go!" but it doesn't say where.

As I have already pointed out, it is service enough merely to say "change" and "go." It would be nice, however, if science fiction could be said to point actively in a worthwhile direction. It would seem that it cannot. It presents a thousand possible futures and there is no way of telling which of these will resemble the real future or even whether any of them will resemble the real future.

Unless, that is, we can find any way in which most of the futures presented resemble one another. There is such a way. The large majority of the futures presented in science fiction involve a broader stage for the drama of life. The one world of Earth is expanded to a whole series of worlds, sometimes to millions of worlds. Other intelligences may exist or they may not, but at least the inanimate universe with which man struggles is stupendously expanded.

The result of that is that to science-fiction readers Earth becomes small and relatively unimportant. A subdivision smaller than Earth becomes even harder to focus upon.

There was some tendency, for instance, during World War II, to write science-fiction stories in which Nazis or Japanese were the villains. Such stories don't tend to be successful. They're too topical.

It is as though science fiction, dealing, as it does, with solar systems, cannot adjust itself conveniently down the scale to the villainies of a single country on this small world.

This is not because science-fiction writers are internationalists as a group, or because they have a more enlightened and all-inclusive outlook, are less patriotic or less given to sectional passions and race prejudice. They are human, as human as other people. I do not wish to imply that any effect science fiction has upon society is the result of conscious effort on the part of those who write it.

Using this present case as an example, writers ignore the subdivisions of mankind because the nature and scope of science fiction is such that anything less than the "Earthman" doesn't make much sense.

Whatever the reason for it, science fiction is serving a specific and important function. By ignoring "racial" divisions among men it is moving in a direction the rest of our culture must move in out of sheer self-defense.

There has always been hostility between the "us guys" and the "you guys." This hostility, however, need not flare into violence. I was brought up in Brooklyn, but for some reason I was a New York Giant fan. (I still am.) I hated the Dodger fans and they hated me, but it was a business hate. When we weren't discussing baseball, we were friends.

My state is better than your state, my city than your city, my block than your block, and my father can lick your father. It's all very normal. When your own group shines, you shine by reflected glory. When dear old Siwash wins a football game, all the Siwash alumni get drunk—although their only connection with their alma mater might have been a dismal four-year record of rejected education.

Where does this me-you rivalry stop being exhilarating and start being dangerous? When it coincides with a fixed belief that "you" are an inferior human being and "I" am a superior human being.

Just at the time that the western European powers began to expand across land and sea and to collide with societies other than their own, they also began to develop their superior material technology. Not only were the American Indians, the African Negroes, the Asiatic Indians and Chinese, the South Sea Malays and the Australian aborigines heathen and therefore inferior by divine fiat; they were unable to stand up to our gunfire and therefore inferior by natural law.

This division of mankind into whites (particularly Nordic whites) and everybody else was safe only as long as western Europe (and its cultural appendages in America and Australia) maintained their technological superiority.

But the superiority is no longer being maintained. In 1905, the Russians suffered the humiliation of being defeated by the yellow-skinned Japanese. But the rest of the white world took it calmly enough; after all, the Russians were half-Tartar and very backward for a theoretically white nation.

Then, in 1941 and 1942, Japan inflicted defeats upon British, French, Dutch, and American troops, the pick and cream of the white world. Even Japan's final defeat did not abolish the shock her initial victories communicated to the entire nonwhite world.

So times have changed and race prejudice is becoming a dangerous anachronism. We are treating with an outmoded emotional attitude a group of humans who outnumber us badly and who are drawing abreast of us technologically. For selfish reasons alone we should be wiser than we are. (And on moral grounds we never did have a leg to stand on.)

Science fiction, insofar as it tends to think of humanity as a unit and to face humanity, white, black, and yellow alike, with common dangers and common tasks, which must be pushed to a common victory, serves the world well, and America particularly well.

XI

I have written longer than I intended and more circuitously. I would like to make up for that by ending with a three-point summary:

1. For the first time in history mankind is faced with a rapidly changing society, due to the advent of modern technology.

2. Science fiction is a form of literature that has grown out of this fact.

3. The contribution science fiction can make to society is that of accustoming its readers to the thought of the inevitability of continuing change and the necessity of directing and shaping that change rather than opposing it blindly or blindly permitting it to overwhelm us.

QUESTIONS

1. Why does Asimov take such care to define science fiction and particularly "social science fiction"?

2. Find examples of "adventure science fiction" and "gadget science fiction" in this book.

3. Compare Asimov's concept of science fiction with that of Amis.

4. Both Asimov and Koestler (page 307) mention other types of literature. Explain why Asimov might disagree with aspects of Koestler's comments on the "historical novel."

5. Is the main function of science fiction predictive?

6. Discuss science fiction as a type of literature that can help change racial and religious prejudices.

Science Fiction, Morals, and Religion

Gerald Heard

Science fiction and morals-religion! Surely this is a grotesque assignment. Science fiction is escapism. Stalin, the puritan potentate, has said so. The Soviet has condemned these opium fantasies of a decadent capitalism. Fiction was never approved of by the moralist—it smacked of lying. Science was always making trouble for religion because it questioned theology.

And in science fiction's first phase it might have been admitted that ancient dogma and latest fantasy, moral rules and imaginary extravaganzas had nothing to do with each other. Science fiction was the extrapolation of science's wildest hopes and speculations. Science was then (as a corpus and a corporation) mainly an interest in the machine. It was the man in the machine (instead of the *deus ex machina*) that was to be "the master of things." And his answer to the Pascaline query, "May not the heart have reasons of which the mind is ignorant?" was the reply of the other French mathematician of a century later, "I have no need of such hypotheses." The universe is a vast machine and those therefore who would explore it will get furthest by and in machines.

Of course, H. G. Wells, who is a founding father of our fantasy, being a romantic socialist and for his "Fabian" years under G. B. Shaw's Emergent Evolution, was aware of Shaw's strange literary godfather, the Samuel Butler of Erewhon—Erewhon the inverted Utopia wherein man turned against the machines. Wells also once remarked that his own favorite story was "The Door in the Wall"—a tale both metaphysical and moral. But most readers decided that Jules Verne had a case when he claimed that Wells was a "deviationist," bringing into the purity of a world to be made manageable by instruments huge cloudy symbols of a high romance!

Romance, in the inhibited nineteenth century, could only find a place in science fiction as an effeminate desire for private petting which when thwarted spurred men "from all the littleness of love" out to real adventure. The most famous of all Verne's characters is Captain Nemo—the man who has chosen to call himself "no one"—the romantic who literally plunges into the abyss to drown his sorrow, where, in his super-submarine the *Nautilus*, he prowls the sunless deeps, not darker than his gloom, until, his rival unwittingly sailing over his lair, Nemo runs the rival's ship right through with his lancelike craft and sends his foe to the bottom.

Nor was there any change in the contemptuous indifference with which all serious-minded people regarded science fiction in the post-Verne period, when, extending the range but not adding to the variety, Mars became the target instead of the moon. With sub-adolescents (much keener on a car than on a mate) space-shooting in super-rockets, morality didn't arise and religion was decently escorted to rest beyond the limits of the space-time continuum. The young hero of course in the end killed the Martian monster, and married the maid from Venus. But that was the merely conventional epilogue of the ancient fairytale— "They married and lived happily ever after." The heart of the matter lay in the mortal risks run and the breath-taking, hair-raising hazards of steeplechasing among the stars and death-dodging with the aerolites. And when the young Twenties of the twentieth century emerged with its passport to freedom signed by Freud, that only rendered still colder than the abyss the disapproval with which conventional morals and traditional religion regarded science fiction. The hot rod, the hot boy and the hot girl were crudely extrapolated into the hotter space jet in which, in exhibitionistically hot space suits, the two perfervid kids skid, clamped together, through sub-zero space.

But the dawn phase of gadgetry is now long over. It faded with the rise of bio-fiction. A triple force has driven science fiction ahead; the quality of writing has improved; the genre has attracted writers of high competence. The public that reads such fiction is adult (having gone through the child and adolescent phases). And, thirdly, science itself has shifted the accent of its main interest. The mechanistic picture is no longer satisfying. In the past people might have supposed that mechanism was the main bone of contention between scientific humanism and religious moralism. But as a matter of fact this has not been so. Religious moralism finds it far easier to get on with mechanism than anyone expected. For a kind of concordat was devised whereby the invisible and the realm of values and ends were left to religion while the tangible and the realm of means were handed over to science. Both sides assumed (and in this they were mistaken) that they were agreed about morality. Whether you were in a machine or a shrine, a factory or a church, such vague generalizations as the Golden Rule were supposed to run and to be able to control all the issues of means and ends, of private behavior and public business.

The interest in the sciences of life brought out, however, acute points of dispute. Nor was the source of the trouble that western man's religious tradition had a description (Genesis) that was at variance with geology. As Carl Jung pointed out many years ago, humane and humanistic man has no quarrel with the traditional religious findings in regard to four out of the five questions of the Sphinx: How may you use force? How use wealth? How regard your word? And how your thought? The more the social sciences have advanced, the more psychological insight and mental hygiene have advanced, the more it has seemed clear that the individual cannot be sane and healthy unless he can regard himself as a highly responsible unit in an organic society. About how that may be done in regard to the four questions given above, science and religion are ready to confer, convinced that their aims are the same—a responsible, highly-controlled person serving his community. But about the fifth question, as Jung has said, as knowledge has grown opinions have diverged. Today in our extraverted society for the first time the term "an immoral man" is ceasing to have the special sense "one who does not conform with the current sexual rules." And it is science which has done this. Nor is it the speculations of scientists that have caused this upset. It is their research results, their actual findings and answers to the prime question: "What is human nature and how is it natural for a man to behave?" The great hypothesis of evolution, which in the nineteenth century won against the elder hypothesis of special creation, disturbed, it is true, the fundamentalists. We see now it had little effect on the ordinary man. Whether he had climbed up from an ape or fallen out from the Garden of Eden, here he was, far and away the wisest of all beasts and able to change his environment to suit his needs and wishes. Darwin and Thomas Henry Huxley had far more in common with the bishops with whom they disputed than either party knew. Evolutionary biology made, then, very little difference to social mores.

It is physiology that has brought us to a revolution. Even the simplest physiological research began to upset our rigid notions of the normal and the right. Genetic research showed that animals carrying high-grade genes could sire thousands of descendants. A little research, and artificial insemination became a hard-working fact. But what about man then? Wasn't he, as far as his reproductive body went, a mammal? Already the process, everyone knows who chooses to enquire, is in full play. But the Law is unready, because it is frightened of the moralists who talk of the unnatural but fear to study nature. Already in Great Britain a self-appointed influential committee of clergy and clerically minded lawyers has met and fulminated. Whosoever so practices or countenances such practices shall be punished. The matter is not open. Further, knowledge is not sought. The question is closed and the penalties are chosen which shall put an end to such depravity. It is certain they will not. They would not do so even were artificial insemination the only new physiological knowledge that we now have.

Of course, it is but the least of the new revolutionary discoveries that physiology has made in the last thirty years and which today are altering completely our notion as to what is human nature and what therefore is natural. Names as little known as Bayliss and Starling were to make more practical difference to our lives than any of the famous evolutionists. These men, working in the first two decades of the century, had the real dynamite that would test our prejudices. For firstly their work with hormones gave rise to the slogan "man is only his glands." Certainly as the glandular secretions were employed an unprecedented scientific magic appeared. When cretins by being given thyroid changed from idiots into normal persons, that seemed "nice" and not at all "unnatural." When in rarer, but not uncommon cases, acromegaly came on and the patient's head turned into something terrifyingly like a horse's, this was considered a freak of nature. When we were told this was due to a slight change in the small pituitary ductless gland just behind the root of the nose, we took some time to realize what that might mean. And as the ductless glands were explored, we came inevitably closer to head-on trouble with the conventional.

What was human nature? What was natural? Moralists had always claimed that the rules they imposed were to prevent deviations from the natural. Early societies were consistent about this. Any birth that was odd was killed. In many societies even twins were looked on as so unnatural as to be exterminated. Our society gave up infanticide for all but the most monstrous deformities and even that had to be done clandestinely. We had gone to the moral extreme (beyond that of the savage) of accepting anything that happened to us reproductively. As we have seen right back to birth control, anything that interfered with the simplest forms of reproduction was condemned as unnatural. But to hold that position consistently the puritan had to be ignorant of physiology. For nature—very slight inspection showed—refused to conform to conventional man's notion of the natural. The ductless glands were fantastically but factually involved with sex. A small tumor on the small kidney hump, which is the suprarenal gland, can and does off and on turn a woman into a man. The whole of the ductless glands, any and every one of them, can play the most carnival tricks with what seems most basic and polar, an individual human being's sex. Indeed it is now recognized that if the ductless gland balance tends toward manifestation of one sex, say the female, but the actual sexual organs belong to another, i.e., the male, then the behavior of such a person will be dictated by the ductless glands and not by the ducted. What is morality going to do about such finds? At present there is a hush-hush attempt to use science to make nature conform to the simplicities which uninformed moralists thought was all that was natural. Quite a number of physicians and surgeons are performing what the ordinary person still regards as science fiction, the favorite magic of the Arabian Nights—transforming a man into a woman or vice versa. This is permitted by official approval still in the name of the natural. For (the present argument runs) if nature is going to change a citizen's sex then, as we cannot destroy such a monster (as would the earlier traditionalists), we must insist that the change is complete, back or on. We cannot let nature, as she very well might, stop halfway.

Now all these are live issues, the liveliest issues for they are what science has found out about life. As long as the public thought science was simply money-making-power-giving gadgetry science fiction wasn't mature. But now it must decide—will it remain the boys' fairy book with a space-suited Prince Charming as the arrested idea, or will science fiction take its new assignment? If ever a choice was a moral one this is. For science fiction when it does its job (and it has been doing it increasingly) does not merely extrapolate inventions. If it is worthy of the name of the true novel it makes real persons and makes them develop psychological maturity under the pressure of unsuspected portentous events. Will science fiction have the nerve to tell the contemporary truth to the growing-up in this unforeseen situation (wherein nearly everyone, politicians, soldiers, executives, spend their time getting ready for the last crisis or the last war)? Will informed authors dare say what the cards, now in hand and on the table, actually are, what are in the pool ready for the next pick-up, and what is the game when such cards are held? Take two examples, the first negative and therefore, of course, safer: What is going to be the actual power war if the contest of the ideologies goes on? The atom bombs, going on inevitably past the helium to the lithium, etc., have made soldier war futile. The aim of mechanized scientific war was to improve weapons by making them into what are called "scientific instruments of precision." This ideal, of hitting that and only that which, in Clausewitz' classic phrase, would alter the will of the opposing commander, has been destroyed by the imprecise violence of atomic explosion. Such violence is as inept in our complex society as attempting to correct a chronometer with a sledge hammer. But apt violence is already past its experimental stage. The progress in the barbiturates, the study with sodium pentothal in making the unconscious patient speak out all his most inhibited secrets, these advances are toward a complete revolution in the struggle for power. The battle will go on in a world-wide frontierless underground. It will be scientific because it will be doubly precise: (a) precise in its aim, because instead of slaughtering millions of cannon fodder (good simple highly suggestible types which submit easily to propaganda and so make excellent slaves) it will only attack those cross-grained types who make trouble; (b) precise in its method because, even with these negative types, the process would be reconstructive, the mind would be unmade and remade according to the will of the dictator. Of course with hard-set types this would probably entail a psycho-physical modification by endocrine secretions. Indeed, as ridicule is the most powerful acid against heroism, it might be wise to transform the rugged rebel into a gay consenter—not degraded into a beast, that would be crude, but regarded and rejuvenated into an ephoebe, an Adonis elevated, apotheosized out of this dreary world by being made the latest "nova" in the heaven of the screen.

Such powers will be used if the struggle for political world dominance goes on. Science fiction in the hand of a character-draughtsman can create a new contemporary tension-of-choice, new moral decisions, and so indicate how they may be faced or flunked. These issues are not in a speculative tomorrow. Lobotomy is crude but already it is here and working. It is the new castration. The wild-beast paranoiac becomes the mild obedient animal. We can unbuild a rebel with a flick of a scalpel. The wizard's art is also offered us not merely to rebuild into fully human patterns of physique and behavior those who have given us trouble, but to make them into loyal supporters and truly thankful for our rejuvenating generosity.

The second example seems less sensational but in fact goes deeper and sets an even wider moral problem. Scientific research has from two directions converged on the problem: What will be the future society? And what its mores, its philosophy? We know from the history of the last seven thousand years that man has with increasing rapidity built up societies which in size and complexity are only equaled by the three great insect city-structures—the hive, the termitary and the ant hill. We know from the study of these three structures that though they are creations of three completely different insects they have certain striking characteristics in common. A social structure of such complexity (a complexity which goes beyond anything we have yet achieved though undoubtedly our process is directed to that goal), a civilization as perfectly integrated as is that of the bee, the termite and the ant, demands: (1) complete centralization (the individual finds its complete assumption in the society), and (2) such a completely organic society has successfully modified the original constituents—once simple male and female—into completely specialized parts of the whole. The force of the reproductive cycle, which, left to itself, will in the simple male and female relationship, be able to build up nothing larger than the family, is therefore canalized. No society, it is clear, can generate a loyalty as intense as that which the family generates. Hence in the communities that have been most successful in the social patterns of the three great insect groups, in order to make society come first, to make a unit of devoted loyalty larger than the family, a central reproductive unit provides a constant stream of embryonic life, and the servants of the state, the vast army of nurses and providers, rear these embryos. The facts are familiar; the implications extremely awkward and therefore repressed. Here is a sharp moral issue, as startling as, and indeed more unwelcome than, the apt violence of glandular operation and medication that can turn iron rebels into playboys or (if the statesman judges the joke would be more telling, the laugh more lasting) playgirls. The more complex the state is to be, the more it must have, between the simple extremes of male and female (that can only construct the family field loyalty), a series of stages. China more nearly and more long sustained a civilization able to embrace millions and transform in a generation barbarians into sophisticates. Every student of this amazing organism owns that its Achilles' heel was the fatal conflict between loyalty to the community and loyalty to the family. Conversely, it has been noted that every society (e.g., ancient Egypt and the medieval society of western Europe) when it becomes complex has to produce the clerk-priest type. In this administrative type two modifications are present: he is debarred from the usual male exercises such as war, and finally he is made celibate.

Today we demand ever higher specialization to give us the command of new elaborate violences in war, new techniques in surgery and drugs to prolong life and lessen discomfort, and new varieties of entertainment. These demands require a complex organic society. That society requires for its specialization of function that it be served by specialization of organism. Already, as Dr. William Sheldon (of *The Varieties of Human Temperament* and *The Varieties of Human Physique*) has pointed out, our society is sufficiently specialized that special physical types do tend to go toward and to fill special professions. It will be but one more step in "Scientific Management" when the psychophysical selectors of candidates and the trainers of the work teams give glandular treatments and/or operations to the members of each profession or "Shop" in order that, by psychophysical modification, they may become perfectly adjusted to their job. So the man and the machine would be brought into such symbiotic play as would fill Taylor (the father of scientific management) with ecstasy and Samuel Butler with "I told you so" despair.

Such themes, and there are many more, set character problems before the novelist beside which the old plots and play of temperament are rudimentary. It has been pointed out by E. M. Forster the novelist (and author of that lucid study of fiction's evolution, *Aspects of the Novel*) that Tolstoy is the first great novelist, and so established his psychological genius, because he can show his characters developing and changing— they are not static puppets. They are not mere stylized "humors" as for example are so many of Dickens' dramatis personae. Today we know that changes of character and indeed total modifications of the psychophysique are possible. Further we know that the power to make such changes will increase in a way and to a degree that Tolstoy would have thought utterly fantastic, utterly beyond any realism and only to be relegated to the absurdities of the Arabian Nights entertainment.

It is here where science fiction will be tested as to whether it is prepared to become fully adult and responsible. Will it be prepared to take, for instance, a theme which, starting with the basic situation boy-meets-girl (the source of the family pattern), faces the fact that each may be "drafted" (and so streamlined by the forced draft that they may be alienated and finally transmuted). Here is the material for a completely new drama, a fresh development of tragedy and an original extension of what the Greek poets called irony. Till now we have had in the moral-making forms of drama only two situations, one of comedy and the other of tragedy. In the first, things turn out well and after some surprises and contretemps everything ends in Laughter and Fun. Nature in the end turns out to have been friendly after all to our main design and desire. The master force in us, the desire to make love, is backed up by the life force. "Journeys end in lovers' meetings" and only old spoilsport, crabbed age, gets fooled and beaten up. In the second case nature does not co-operate; she does not care for man or his happiness even when he is a breeding animal seeking a mate. The universe is not friendly. It is hostile. But though it can and will smash man's body, it cannot bend his will or coerce his character. Here there is no possibility of a happy ending. But the audience gets its catharsis, its sense that you can let the cosmos do its damndest, because the individual protagonist "beneath the bludgeonings of Fate" has a head that is "bloody but unbowed."

Today however we have, in our morality and our drama, worked through stage two of tragedy and reached stage three. The character is altered by the crisis. And the "irony"—the onlooking "God's-eye view" of the audience—consists no longer in so simple a formula as being "purged of pity and of fear." We now face the fact that as the universe is in evolution so too is human character. The idea (basic to tragedy) that there is one thing unchangeable in the flux, and that it is man's "unconquerable soul" with its clutter of prejudices which it calls morality and its lack of humor which it calls dignity, goes overboard. So we come to the return of comedy—or rather meta-comedy. The first stage of drama (comedy) thought the universe was fun. The second (tragedy) thought man at least was dignified. The third sees man and the cosmos in play. If you can laugh at yourself and at the ever broader fun that the universe seems to be having at your expense, suddenly you will see the gigantic point of the joke. For the complete catharsis lies not in tears or in stoic repression but in laughter. The stoic tried to make himself invulnerable by his "apathy." But mind and body can't so be taken apart except by suicide—a course to which the stoic naturally resorted with increasing frequency. The only real freedom is by taking up a standpoint from which not only the body is seen as ridiculous but the personality also. The mind-body (not merely the body) is regarded with detachment and that detachment is not gravity (which is always full of self-focused concern) but laughter that is full of general amused insight. Comedy so seen is perceived as going far deeper than tragedy and so must be considered as the "real realism."

But where in this development of the human plot (whether in the novel, the stage or the screen) does science fiction come in? Right in the middle. For what is this blend of man and the universe (this the theme of meta-comedy) but the emergence into a complete art form of Taylor's dawn concept: that man and the machine must develop together as an integrated symbiot. Science fiction, in its attitude to morality, has today a double appositeness: (1) in its aim, and (2) in its method. In its aim it is bound, by its extrapolation of science and its use of dramatic plot, to view man and his machines and his environment as a threefold whole, the machine being the hyphen. It also views man's psyche, man's physique and the entire life process as also a threefold interacting unit. Science fiction is the prophetic (or to use a more exact special term) the apocalyptic literature of our particular and culminating epoch of crisis. It can shape our reactions to our destiny, it can show us how to react, how to adapt, how to endure. It can indicate by the convincingness of its stories how man's tensile strength of dynamic acceptance, his comprehending tolerance of new challenge can develop. So it will develop morality in the traditional sense—i.e., man's power to adjust to the demands of natural law. But further it can and must show how we can shape our destiny to our inherent demand, to our faith. For man is the one animal who profoundly modifies his environment. Science fiction must and can show man at last doing this intentionally and this is morality in the scientific sense. The aim of life, as far as man can see, is the increase of consciousness. A scientific morality (or a moralized science) is something more than the rather jejune formula "the pursuit of truth." That aim begins to look fuzzy and merely emotional when we consider Niels Bohr's summation of modern physics "the end of objectivity." The aim of science today is then to discover that super self-control whereby man learns to master, shift and expand the focal length of consciousness and so apprehends further alternative universes, as in the nineteenth century the rise of alternative geometries opened the way to new cosmogonies. It has been long said, and it is true, that those who write a people's songs forecast that people's history. Social psychologists today realize that the most important people in any community or nation or civilization are those who create its "patterns of prestige." That is the huge task of science fiction today, now that it has come so rapidly to adulthood. That and nothing less must be and can be its aim.

Its method too is apposite. The old comedy "laughed things off." And when things became too obviously grim and man too grimly set, then such fun was bundled off scene: that is to say such old broad undignified pantomime was regarded as obscene—what must not be shown on the stage. There were things to which the reaction of laughter was outrageous. Tragedy with its pretentious solemnity and puritanism with its repressions and censorship took over. Now science has shown that truth cannot be regarded as obscene and what actually takes place can't be called and banned as the unnatural. The method of science fiction is so to narrate the facts science has discovered that we may be presented with a new play of character. So we can view this, the immensely enlarged picture of what nature and human nature are and what their interplay is, with a new interest, a new humor, a new fun. "Laughter is the sound made by an exploding tabu." "Solemnity is the sign of an oncoming psychosis." For first you must not laugh off pain: you must be stoically tragic toward it. (This is an attitude which scientific progress with its advances in analgesics is making increasingly anachronistic. The invalid who exploits his spasms is becoming rightfully a figure for satire.) And next you must not laugh with pleasure. You must be secretive, whispering, ashamed, guilty. But laughter is not merely frankness; it is a necessary force for insight. This aspect of essential extravagance (one of the main characteristics of vigorous science fiction when it keeps in touch as it should with fantasy) is given classical expression in the shout of delight, the *"Eureka!"* of Archimedes as he capered in the street so self-forgetfully delighted in his find. In Hobbes' famous definition of laughter, "it is the sudden glory." The profoundest insights arise from making associations and correlations which at first seem absurd and can only be sustained by regarding them as humorous extravagances. For as Dr. Synge (*Science, Sense and Nonsense* by Dr. John L. Synge) has pointed out in his stimulating book, advanced physics can no longer be called sensible. Only the mind made flexible to accept absurdity can grasp the non-sensory significance of our present cosmological notions.

But though the dramatic form, the psychological atmosphere in which science fiction (and indeed all really contemporary fiction that deals with real character) must work, is meta-comic, that has nothing to do with the farcical or the burlesque. Indeed it and it alone can produce the situation in which the meta-tragic emerges. A person is noble who surrenders ordinary domestic happiness because he is intellectually convinced that he can serve civilization best in that way. But he is still possibly very human and may become melodramatically ridiculous in his self-admiration of the sacrifice he is making. And so the realistic novelist can and does debunk him. But science fiction, with its new psycho-physical challenges, with the endocrine choices now set human nature, can create decision-situations in which the central character, able to laugh at himself, can produce a super irony that leaves us unable to escape from the issue by mockery. Here then there is, in a sense even more penetrating than in Greek drama, the super irony which the Greek dramatist attempted as the acme of his art. His irony was the God's-eye view of the hero blinded by his own heroic *hubris*, the self-sufficient courage that will do everything but see itself as ridiculous. The super irony of science fiction can deal with the hero who does not bear off with a fine exit line "the pageant of his bleeding heart"—but who, undergoing endocrine change (because he thinks this is best for some cause he wishes to serve) watches his metamorphosis with increasing humor. He sees himself not merely altering in physique, not merely in a Nessus shirt of self-imposed suffering. He sees his psyche changing too. He sees his romantic attachment to home and family, and to the values which he considered to be eternal, fading away as an adolescent sees his taste for toys and candy yielding to a taste for girls.

Science fiction is therefore that creative myth-making which Toynbee sees as one of the most important of man's social and moral activities. But if it is to serve its distinctive purpose it must be courageously contemporary. Science fiction, because of its peculiar position, has a station as powerful and as influential as that seized upon and held by Jonathan Swift two and a half centuries ago. This terrific satirist saw how, with the new symbolism of science, he could frame parables that, under the guise of fairy tales, not only flayed the hypocrisies of his time but also (as in the voyage to Laputa in *Gulliver's Travels*) put the science of his day into an acid bath of contempt. There seems little doubt that Swift so protected himself against ecclesiastical attack and also lost the opportunity of founding a really creative science fiction.

That temptation again today is offered science-fiction writers. They can play for safety by keeping their eye fixed on two patrons, by writing stories that meet the demands of childish minds on the one hand and, on the other, minds that want to keep the public childish. If, however, they realize their opportunity they can take, one by one, all the rising issues wherein it is clear that within a few years scientific research and applied science must demand new interpretations of the traditional mores. This is certainly not an easy assignment. And indeed the man who, with a facile gift for exciting, picaresque narrative, takes to science fiction, may object to finding that he is being turned into a prophet and lawgiver. The fact remains that science fiction, partly because of the way in which science has produced new problems for morality and partly because of the many accurate forecasts science-fiction writers have made, has now the opportunity to be taken seriously. It can work out in "model form" what shape social behavior patterns will take. More than any other form of literature it can educate people as to what are the social situations in which they will soon find themselves. Further its responsibility and opportunity are immensely increased in that while it can make the public familiar with new conditions (which without preparation would prove highly shocking) it can also create the atmosphere, friendly or unfriendly, interested or indignantly disgusted, with which these new finds and forces will be confronted. It not only can show the new fact in an attractive guise. Even more important it can show ourselves behaving in an attractive, civilized, constructive, tolerant way toward the new knowledge and event.

Science-fiction writers are not merely introducing us to new scenes and new plots but to new characters. They can show us as rigid, intolerant, savagely repellent to new knowledge. They can play on old prejudices, making Martians monsters and any human variety which is new, a ghastly misbirth. Or they can show us of the next thirty years, surmounting each new wave of knowledge and pushing out with a new tolerance and fresh curiosity on wider seas of comprehension. There is a truth behind Oscar Wilde's absurdity, "Nature imitates Art," for it means that man having observed nature more fully than he knows produces forms and styles which afterwards he consciously perceives to be in nature and so to be natural. A more exact estimate of the social power of fiction has been given by Aldous Huxley, when he pointed out that character, ideals and patterns of prestige are today largely created by the novelist. Shelley's somewhat pretentious phrase that the poets are the unacknowledged legislators of mankind is given its share of truth when we recognize how the great fiction characters have influenced men and women in choosing the parts they would play. Homer idealized Achilles and in turn the actual Alexander played out the Achillean part in his historically theatrical campaigns. Meanwhile at this moment science fiction finds itself with two advantages. In the first place it can indicate a dynamic morality. There is no reason why morals should any longer be identified with reaction and conservatism. In the second place, science fiction, because it is rightly identified with adventure, can make its appeal to the young who want to find meaning in the future rather than the past.

Of course this is a tough proposition. This program however is not an extravagance of "realism," a temptation to shock still further the frightened reactionaries. It is an obligation forced today on all popularizers of science. Here are the facts. How are you going to make ordinary conventional people face up to them? It is possible to break news so as to produce an "elastic reaction" and not a fracture. It is possible to add to the tensile strength of the cylinder so as to allow higher explosive power to be used. It is possible to build up the "tolerance" of the organism which permits the body not to reject or be toxicated by an injection but to react into a higher health by producing dynamic antibodies. No one else is going to give this essential service if science fiction flunks it. The ordinary science news service that boasts it keeps the public up-to-date certainly shows grave symptoms of serious failure. Dr. Abbott, once head of the Smithsonian Institution, and Dr. Sinnott, head of the Sheffield School of Science at Yale, have both stated in print their disappointment and concern at the obscurantist attitude taken by rank and file scientists and most science news editors toward the researches carried on in six great universities in extra-sensory perception. The attitude toward the mysterious upper-atmosphere craft (saucers, disks, giant tubes) that are now authentically sighted in some part of the world several times a week, has been as gravely disappointing. Until *Life* broke the official "silence of sceptical contempt," American people who used to be the most empirically and open-minded public in the world were afraid even to report finds which they themselves had personally witnessed—so much did they dread being laughed at, so pathetically had they become dependent on authority as to whether they might believe the evidence of their own senses.

With people reduced to such a medieval frame of mind, science fiction has certainly a stiff assignment. But it is all the more worthwhile. And in this vital diplomatic mission between the pure researcher, who too often denies any evidence outside his speciality and who always researches in such detail that he cannot see the social consequences, and the public that has to take the consequences, science fiction has an unexpected ally. Up to this point only one part of this article's assignment has been dealt with—morals. We have seen science creating so many new social developments that conventional morality will be hard put to accept such changes and think out creative reactions. Indeed, do what the most informed, courageous and tactful science fiction may, many of the old-fashioned will not make a creative response. That is too much to hope. But especially among the young to whom science fiction fortunately most appeals, a decisive number of moderates may be won over if science fiction keeps in mind one important distinction: that though many moralists may be nothing more than blind adherents of the past, this is not so of all. The real strength of morality lies in those who, not afraid of new truth, do still demand that it should not take all worthy purpose out of life, all meaning out of existence. They do not say that truth must be made to yield to convenience or to goodness. What they urge is that both the researcher and the applier should meet in constant interpretive conference, wherein and whereby there may be worked out jointly the creative reactions that human conduct should and could make to and with the new information. Indeed here lies a good theme for a science-fiction history forecast, showing a Supreme Court of the World which sits and rules for this specific purpose. This bench would rule by deciding not whether some social activity were "constitutional" but (a far more basic finding) to what degree would a new discovery affect morals, and how the new freedom and the accepted code, the new force of the old frame of behavior, should be adjusted each to each. This shows that there are two sides to man's problem: one we usually call truth and the other goodness. And generally we have tried to hold one rigid and make the other to yield. Today however we see this is the grave mistake that leads to persecution and revolution. The conflict between science and religion is because religion which should really be enlarged to be a fulfilment and interpreter of science has been reduced to an aspect and defender of morality. This sounds like fantasy. It is true though. For when we see that religion is the cause and morality the consequence then we can perceive religion's co-operative relationship with science. Religion is basically a cosmology, an all-over hypothesis (a binding all together as the word means) of all observations of our entire environment. And any workable ethic is a rule of behavior deduced from the general natural principles (the universal law) that has been perceived. On the other hand science is that empiric exploration and experiment, whereby, using an all-over hypothesis, a frame of reference, a *religio*, a belief that there is pattern and the universe can be understood, man increases his comprehensible knowledge. This, through the interaction of science (empiric research) and religion (the frame of meaning), leads to the discovery of principles of meaning and these principles of meaning are then applied to make efficient and free modes of action (morality).

So we perceive the real difference between morals and religion. Morals are the worthy arrangements whereby individuals, who are on one side physiological organisms and on the other social units, may manage to get along with one another. In brief, religion—as we have seen the word actually means—is the binding force that, when it is alive, makes the individual an integrated triple whole (1) with himself, (2) with his society and (3) with nature. In this basic sense (that religion is the frame of meaning, the scheme of significance in which all findings are given purpose) there can be no dispute between science and religion. Science discovers and religion evaluates. Science produces facts; religion arranges them in a comprehensive frame and scale of meaning.

It is in this respect today that religion is coming alive, waking up again to its rightful place and vital importance. It is rousing itself after a long sleep during which it dreamed its duty was to defend the past and make the present conform with outgrown cosmogonies, inaccurate history and inapposite codes. The discovery of what Julian Huxley has called "the uniqueness of man"—that man is so richly various in the qualities of consciousness which he produces (the mathematician, the artist, the administrator, etc.), that he transcends any real comparison with animals in his mental power and indeed cannot rightly be called a species—has corrected the pessimism T. H. Huxley and many other moralists felt when they regarded the evolutionary picture. The discovery of the Brussels School, that open-ended systems (and living forms are such) are not subject to entropy, has made the vital process appear to be a far more formidable and initiatory power than nineteenth-century chemistry imagined. Von Frisch's astounding researches which now have convinced all zoologists that bees think, calculate, draw maps and by sign language talk to each other, have made us understand that instinct, instead of being automatism excluding intelligence, may rather be regarded as conscience advising understanding. President A. D. Adrian's work (see *Nature*, July 1951) in electroencephalogram study has (as Dr. Eccles has indicated) shown that whereas the brain is a three-dimensional detector, the mind shows evidence of being a four-dimensional field. Indeed today it appears that there is not a sector of the vast front of science wherein concepts are not appearing that (as Dr. Sinnott of Yale has pointed out) demote materialism as a basic hypothesis and make mechanism a notion convenient as a local generalization but inadequate as an all-over law. This, we must stress, will not mean the return of anthropomorphism. Many researchers still fear the public knowing how far materialism has vanished because they dread that might mean a return to superstition. It will mean an extension of meaning so vast that in this huge frame of reference man's adolescent anthropomorphism must go for good, must go with its companion piece of an out-lived science fiction—"mechanomorphism," the fantasy that the universe is a machine.

The return of meaning, the re-emergence of a contemporary religion is then what can give contemporary morality the courage to leave old tabus and construct an ethic deduced from a modern cosmology and producing rules of demonstrable psychiatric, hygienic and social value. This then is the second great task of science fiction today. No assignment could be of greater significance. It won't be an easier task than the first. What is called natural theology (i.e., the deduction that there is an all-over meaning from evidence obtained not from history but from science) is unpopular with the religious. The reason for that prejudice is however obvious: neither anthropomorphists nor mechanomorphists want to mention it. The anthropomorphists and mechanomorphists agree on one thing. And when they agree, it is so seldom and they are so strong that they are generally assumed to be right. They both assume in this case that any meaning that may be found in nature must be anthropomorphic—must support the old traditional picture as to meaning. Today it is clear there is a meaning and it is one so vast that to our geocentric religions it is even less welcome than mechanomorphism. It has no place for horizontal utopias which are seen to be no more than fanciful schemes for attempting to stabilize Homo sapiens in perpetual adaptation to that limited aspect of consciousness now apprehended as "the environment." So therefore neither has this new outlook much interest in our present notions of personality development or even of man's evolution. But it does point to an extension of conscious thought which indicates and will tend to explicate a vast directive, a concept that is more inspiring to the modern mind than any forecast of a concrete goal. Here, in fact, is the greatest revolution in man's thinking since he raised the first mastaba in proto-dynastic Egypt or the primal ziggurat after the Mesopotamian flood. Professional philosophy isn't going to help here nor is traditional religion. Science itself is too specialized. The job, thankless but immensely important, falls to the art which is as fresh and contemporary as the problem—the art of science fiction.

QUESTIONS

1. Do you agree with the duty of science fiction as it is outlined by Heard?

2. Compare Heard's article with Sisk's, particularly as both deal with the question of "choice."

3. Do you agree with the possibility of "character problems" which Heard anticipates in science fiction?

4. Discuss "A Rose for Ecclesiastes" in terms of the ideas about religion expressed in this essay.

5. Which stories in this book meet Heard's demands? Explain.

6. Do you agree that "the aim of life . . . is the increase of consciousness"?

7. Explain science fiction as myth-making and compare Heard's treatment of myth with that of Susan Sontag (page 312).

8. What new "ethic" do you see emerging from science fiction? Does it match what Heard sees?

The Boredom of Fantasy

Arthur Koestler

Once upon a time, more precisely on the 17th June, A.D. 4784, Captain Kayle Clark stepped into a public telescreen box to call up his fiancée, secret agent Lucy Rall. He was told that Lucy was not available as she had got married a week before. "To whom?" cried the exasperated Captain. "To me," said the man to whom he was talking. Taking a closer look at the telescreen, the Captain discovered with a mild surprise that the man he was talking to was himself.

The startling mystery was solved by Mr. Robert Headrock, the first immortal man on earth. Headrock, using his electronic super-brain computer, discovered that Captain Clark had taken a trip in a time-machine; that he had made a loop into the past, and married Lucy Rall without his unlooped present self knowing about it. Through this little frolic, he also became the richest man on earth as he knew the movements of the Stock Exchange in advance. When the point in time was reached where Clark had looped off in the time-machine, the past Clark and the present Clark became again one, and lived happily ever after. Meanwhile, Robert Headrock, the immortal man, sent a journalist called MacAllister several million trillion years back into the past and made him cause a cosmic explosion, which gave rise to our planetary system as we know it.

The book from which I was quoting is called *The Weapon Shops of Isher* by A. E. van Vogt. Mr. van Vogt is probably the most popular of contemporary American science-fiction writers. The book was recently published in England in a science-fiction series which signals, together with the founding of the British Science-Fiction Club, that the new craze, a kind of cosmic jitterbug, has crossed the Atlantic.

I had better confess at this point that while I lived in the United States I was a science-fiction addict myself and am still liable to occasional relapses. Reading about space travel, time travel, Martian maidens, robot civilizations and extra-galactic supermen is habit-forming like opium, murder thrillers and yoghourt diets. Few people in this country realise the extent and virulence of this addiction in the United States. According to a recent survey, the average sale of a detective story or a Western thriller in America is four thousand copies; the average sale of a science-fiction novel is six thousand copies, or fifty per cent higher. Every month, six new novels of this type are published in the U.S.A. and three large publishing firms specialise exclusively in science-fiction. There is a flood of science-fiction magazines, science-fiction clubs, science-fiction films, television programmes and so on. The addicts are called "fen", which is the plural of fan. Fen gather in clubhouses called slanshacks, "slan" meaning a biologically mutated superman, and hold conferences, called fenferences. The characters in science-fiction speak a kind of cosmic R.A.F. slang (it ought to be called, evidently, "cosmilingo"). Young space cadets, for instance, dislike meeting Bems—for bug-eyed Monsters —in alien galaxies unless armed with paraguns—paralysis-causing rayguns. They swear "By space," "By the seven rings of Saturn," or "By the gas-pits of Venus."

If grown-ups betray these strange symptoms, one can imagine how the kiddies react. Your friends' children no longer plug you with six-shooters; they atomise you with nuclear blasters. They wear plastic bubbles around their heads which look like divers' helmets and enable them to breathe while floating in gravity-free interstellar space. These are sold by the thousand in department stores together with other cosmic paraphernalia, and are steadily replacing cowboy equipment, just as on the television screen Tom Corbett, Space Cadet, is in the process of replacing Hopalong Cassidy as the children's national hero. Even the housewife, listening in to the radio while on her domestic chores, is becoming cosmic-minded. The soap opera has branched out into the space opera. Imagine the opposite number of Mrs. Dale in Texas or Minnesota: "I am so worried about Richard not being back from his luncheon date on Jupiter. Maybe he's got space-happy and gone on to Venus. Or one of those nasty meteors may have deflected him from his orbit."

So much for the grotesque side of science-fiction. But a craze of such vast dimensions is never entirely crazy. It always expresses, in a distorted way, some unconscious need of the time. Science-fiction is a typical product of the atomic age. The discoveries of that age weigh like an undigested lump on the stomach of mankind. Electronic brains which predict election results, lie-detectors which make you confess the truth, new drugs which make you testify to lies, radiations which produce biological monsters—all these developments of the last fifty years have created new vistas and new nightmares, which art and literature have not yet assimilated. In a crude and fumbling fashion, science-fiction is trying to fill this gap. But there is perhaps another and more hidden reason for this sudden hunger for other ages and other worlds. Perhaps, when they read about the latest hydrogen bomb tests, people are more aware than they admit to themselves, of the possibility that human civilisation may be approaching its end. And together with this may go a dim, inarticulate suspicion that the cause lies deeper than Communism or Fascism, that it may lie in the nature itself of *homo sapiens*; in other words, that the human race may be a biological misfit doomed to extinction like the giant reptiles of an earlier age. I believe that some apocalyptic intuition of this kind may be one of the reasons for the sudden interest in life on other stars.

As a branch of literature, science-fiction is, of course, not new. As early as the second century Lucian, a Greek writer, wrote a story of a journey to the moon. Swift wrote science-fiction; so did Samuel Butler, Jules Verne, H. G. Wells, Aldous Huxley, George Orwell. But while in the past such exercises were isolated literary extravaganzas, they are now mass-produced for a mass audience. Moreover, modern science-fiction takes itself very seriously. There are certain rules of the game which every practitioner must observe, otherwise he will be torn to shreds by the critics. The basic rule is that the author may only operate with future inventions, gadgets and machines which are extrapolations (that is, logical extensions) of present discoveries, and do not go against the laws of nature. A number of physicists, doctors and biologists are employed by the film and television industries to make sure that, even in the children's science-fiction show, every detail is correct. Some of the best-known science-fiction authors in America are actually scientists, several of international repute, who write under pen-names. The most recent and distinguished recruit to their ranks is Lord Russell. All this is a guarantee of scientific accuracy, but unfortunately not of artistic quality.

Mr. Gerald Heard has recently expressed the opinion that science-fiction is "the mark of the dawn of a new vision, and the rise of a new art", and simply *the* future form of the novel. Other well-known critics overseas also believe, in all seriousness, that science-fiction, now in its infancy, will grow up and one day become the literature of the future.

I do not share their opinion. I believe that science-fiction is good entertainment, and that it will never become good art. It is reasonably certain that within the next hundred years we shall have space-travel, but at that stage the description of a trip to the moon will no longer be science-fiction but simple reportage. It will be fact, not fantasy, and the science-fiction of that time will have to go even further to startle the reader. What Mr. Heard's claim really amounts to is the replacement of the artist's disciplined imagination by the schoolboy's unbridled fantasy. But day-dreaming is not poetry, and fantasy is not art.

At first sight one would of course expect that imaginative descriptions of non-human societies on alien planets would open new vistas for the somewhat stagnant novel of our time. But most disappointingly this is not the case, and for a simple reason. Our imagination is limited; we cannot project ourselves into the distant future any more than into the distant past. This is the reason why the historical novel is practically dead to-day. The life of an Egyptian civil servant under the Eighteenth Dynasty, or even of a soldier in Cromwell's army, is only imaginable to us in dim outline; we are unable to identify ourselves with the strange figure moving through such a strange world. Few Englishmen can really under-stand the feelings and habits of Frenchmen, much less of Russians, much less of Martians. And without this act of identification, of intimate un-derstanding, there is no art, only a thrill of curiosity which soon yields to boredom. The Martian heroes of science-fiction may have four eyes, a green skin and an accent stranger than mine—we just couldn't care less. We are tickled by them for a few pages; but because they are too strange to be true, we soon get bored.

For every culture is an island. It communicates with other islands but it is only familiar with itself. And art means seeing the familiar in a new light, seeing tragedy in the trivial event; it means in the last resort broad-ening and deepening our understanding of ourselves. Swift's *Gulliver*, Huxley's *Brave New World*, Orwell's *Nineteen-Eighty-Four*, are great works of literature because in them the gadgets of the future and the od-dities of alien worlds serve merely as a background or pretext for a social message. In other words, they are literature precisely to the extent to which they are not science-fiction, to which they are works of disciplined imagination and not of unlimited fantasy. A similar rule holds for the de-tective story. Georges Simenon is probably the greatest master in that field, yet his novels become works of art precisely at the point where character and atmosphere become more important than the plot, where imagination triumphs over invention.

Thus the paradoxical lesson of science-fiction is to teach us modesty. When we reach out for the stars, our limitations become grotesquely ap-parent. The heroes of science-fiction have unlimited power and fantastic possibilities, but their feelings and thoughts are limited within the nar-row human range. Tom Corbett, Space Cadet, behaves on the third planet of Orion exactly in the same way as he does in a drugstore in Min-nesota, and one is tempted to ask him: "Was your journey really neces-sary?" The Milky Way has become simply an extension of Main Street.

Travel is no cure for melancholia; space-ships and time-machines are no escape from the human condition. Let Othello subject Desdemona to a lie-detector test; his jealousy will still blind him to the evidence. Let Oedipus triumph over gravity; he won't triumph over his fate.

Some twenty years ago the German writer, Alfred Döblin, wrote a novel in which humanity discovers the secret of biological self-transfor-mation: by a click of their fingers people can change themselves into giants, tigers, demons, or fish—much like Flook in the *DailyMail* car-toon. At the end of the book the last specimens of this happy race sit, each on a solitary rock, in the shape of black ravens, in eternal silence. They have tried, experienced, seen and said everything under the sun, and all that is left for them to do is to die of boredom—the boredom of fantasy.

QUESTIONS

1. How do the first five paragraphs of this essay prove that science fiction of the kind Koestler first discusses is "the grotesque side"?

2. Compare Koestler's sense that science fiction "always expresses, in a distorted way, some unconscious need of the time" with Susan Sontag's ideas about SF film in the next essay.

3. How fair is Koestler to the views of Gerald Heard?

4. Explain what Koestler means when he says Martian heroes "are too strange to be true." Do you agree?

5. Discuss Koestler's comment that the "lesson of science-fiction is to teach us modesty."

6. How would Koestler define boredom?

The Imagination of Disaster

Susan Sontag

The typical science fiction film has a form as predictable as a Western, and is made up of elements which, to a practiced eye, are as classic as the saloon brawl, the blonde schoolteacher from the East, and the gun duel on the deserted main street.

One model scenario proceeds through five phases.

(1) The arrival of the thing. (Emergence of the monsters, landing of the alien spaceship, etc.) This is usually witnessed or suspected by just one person, a young scientist on a field trip. Nobody, neither his neighbors nor his colleagues, will believe him for some time. The hero is not married, but has a sympathetic though also incredulous girl friend.

(2) Confirmation of the hero's report by a host of witnesses to a great act of destruction. (If the invaders are beings from another planet, a fruitless attempt to parley with them and get them to leave peacefully.) The local police are summoned to deal with the situation and massacred.

(3) In the capital of the country, conferences between scientists and the military take place, with the hero lecturing before a chart, map, or blackboard. A national emergency is declared. Reports of further destruction. Authorities from other countries arrive in black limousines. All international tensions are suspended in view of the planetary emergency. This stage often includes a rapid montage of news broadcasts in various languages, a meeting at the UN, and more conferences between the military and the scientists. Plans are made for destroying the enemy.

(4) Further atrocities. At some point the hero's girl friend is in grave danger. Massive counter-attacks by international forces, with brilliant displays of rocketry, rays, and other advanced weapons, are all unsuccessful. Enormous military casualties, usually by incineraton. Cities are destroyed and/or evacuated. There is an obligatory scene here of panicked crowds stampeding along a highway or a big bridge, being waved on by numerous policemen who, if the film is Japanese, are immaculately white-gloved, preternaturally calm, and call out in dubbed English, "Keep moving. There is no need to be alarmed."

(5) More conferences, whose motif is: "They must be vulnerable to something." Throughout the hero has been working in his lab to this

end. The final strategy, upon which all hopes depend, is drawn up; the ultimate weapon—often a super-powerful, as yet untested, nuclear device—is mounted. Countdown. Final repulse of the monster or invaders. Mutual congratulations, while the hero and girl friend embrace cheek to cheek and scan the skies sturdily. "But have we seen the last of them?"

The film I have just described should be in Technicolor and on a wide screen. Another typical scenario, which follows, is simpler and suited to black-and-white films with a lower budget. It has four phases.

(1) The hero (usually, but not always, a scientist) and his girl friend, or his wife and two children, are disporting themselves in some innocent ultra-normal middle-class surroundings—their house in a small town, or on vacation (camping, boating). Suddenly, someone starts behaving strangely; or some innocent form of vegetation becomes monstrously enlarged and ambulatory. If a character is pictured driving an automobile, something gruesome looms up in the middle of the road. If it is night, strange lights hurtle across the sky.

(2) After following the thing's tracks, or determining that It is radioactive, or poking around a huge crater—in short, conducting some sort of crude investigation—the hero tries to warn the local authorities, without effect; nobody believes anything is amiss. The hero knows better. If the thing is tangible, the house is elaborately barricaded. If the invading alien is an invisible parasite, a doctor or friend is called in, who is himself rather quickly killed or "taken possession of" by the thing.

(3) The advice of whoever further is consulted proves useless. Meanwhile, It continues to claim other victims in the town, which remains implausibly isolated from the rest of the world. General helplessness.

(4) One of two possibilities. Either the hero prepares to do battle alone, accidentally discovers the thing's one vulnerable point, and destroys it. Or, he somehow manages to get out of town and succeeds in laying his case before competent authorities. They, along the lines of the first script but abridged, deploy a complex technology which (after initial setbacks) finally prevails against the invaders.

Another version of the second script opens with the scientist-hero in his laboratory, which is located in the basement or on the grounds of his tasteful, prosperous house. Through his experiments, he unwittingly causes a frightful metamorphosis in some class of plants or animals which turn carnivorous and go on a rampage. Or else, his experiments have caused him to be injured (sometimes irrevocably) or "invaded" himself. Perhaps he has been experimenting with radiation, or has built a machine to communicate with beings from other planets or transport him to other places or times.

Another version of the first script involves the discovery of some fundamental alteration in the conditions of existence of our planet, brought about by nuclear testing, which will lead to the extinction in a few months of all human life. For example: the temperature of the earth is becoming too high or too low to support life, or the earth is cracking in two, or it is gradually being blanketed by lethal fallout.

A third script, somewhat but not altogether different from the first two, concerns a journey through space—to the moon, or some other planet. What the space-voyagers discover commonly is that the alien terrain is in a state of dire emergency, itself threatened by extra-planetary invaders or nearing extinction through the practice of nuclear warfare. The terminal dramas of the first and second scripts are played out there, to which is added the problem of getting away from the doomed and/or hostile planet and back to Earth.

I am aware, of course, that there are thousands of science fiction novels (their heyday was the late 1940s), not to mention the transcriptions of science fiction themes which, more and more, provide the principal subject-matter of comic books. But I propose to discuss science fiction films (the present period began in 1950 and continues, considerably abated, to this day) as an independent sub-genre, without reference to other media—and, most particularly, without reference to the novels from which, in many cases, they were adapted. For, while novel and film may share the same plot, the fundamental difference between the resources of the novel and the film makes them quite dissimilar.

Certainly, compared with the science fiction novels, their film counterparts have unique strengths, one of which is the immediate representation of the extraordinary: physical deformity and mutation, missile and rocket combat, toppling skyscrapers. The movies are, naturally, weak just where the science fiction novels (some of them) are strong—on science. But in place of an intellectual work-out, they can supply something the novels can never provide—sensuous elaboration. In the films it is by means of images and sounds, not words that have to be translated by the imagination, that one can participate in the fantasy of living through one's own death and more, the death of cities, the destruction of humanity itself.

Science fiction films are not about science. They are about disaster, which is one of the oldest subjects of art. In science fiction films disaster is rarely viewed intensively; it is always extensive. It is a matter of quantity and ingenuity. If you will, it is a question of scale. But the scale, particularly in the wide-screen Technicolor films (of which the ones by the Japanese director Inoshiro Honda and the American director George Pal are technically the most convincing and visually the most exciting), does raise the matter to another level.

Thus, the science fiction film (like that of a very different contemporary genre, the Happening) is concerned with the aesthetics of destruction, with the peculiar beauties to be found in wreaking havoc, making a mess. And it is in the imagery of destruction that the core of a good science fiction film lies. Hence, the disadvantage of the cheap film—in which the monster appears or the rocket lands in a small dull-looking town. (Hollywood budget needs usually dictate that the town be in the Arizona or California desert. In *The Thing From Another World* [1951] the rather sleazy and confined set is supposed to be an encampment near the North Pole.) Still, good black-and-white science fiction films have been made. But a bigger budget, which usually means Technicolor, allows a much greater play back and forth among several model environments. There is the populous city. There is the lavish but ascetic interior of the spaceship—either the invaders' or ours—replete with streamlined chromium fixtures and dials and machines whose complexity is indicated by the number of colored lights they flash and strange noises they emit. There is the laboratory crowded with formidable boxes and scientific apparatus. There is a comparatively old-fashioned-looking conference room, where the scientists unfurl charts to explain the desperate state of things to the military. And each of these standard locales or backgrounds is subject to two modalities—intact and destroyed. We may, if we are lucky, be treated to a panorama of melting tanks, flying bodies, crashing walls, awesome craters and fissures in the earth, plummeting spacecraft, colorful deadly rays; and to a symphony of screams, weird electronic signals, the noisiest military hardware going, and the leaden tones of the laconic denizens of alien planets and their subjugated earthlings.

Certain of the primitive gratifications of science fiction films—for instance, the depiction of urban disaster on a colossally magnified scale—are shared with other types of films. Visually there is little difference between mass havoc as represented in the old horror and monster films and what we find in science fiction films, except (again) scale. In the old monster films, the monster always headed for the great city, where he had to do a fair bit of rampaging, hurling busses off bridges, crumpling trains in his bare hands, toppling buildings, and so forth. The archetype is King Kong, in Schoedsack's great film of 1933, running amok, first in the African village (trampling babies, a bit of footage excised from most prints), then in New York. This is really no different in spirit from the scene in Inoshiro Honda's *Rodan* (1957) in which two giant reptiles—with a wingspan of 500 feet and supersonic speeds—by flapping their wings whip up a cyclone that blows most of Tokyo to smithereens. Or the destruction of half of Japan by the gigantic robot with the great incinerating ray that shoots forth from his eyes, at the beginning of Honda's *The Mysterians* (1959). Or, the devastation by the rays from a fleet of flying saucers of New York, Paris, and Tokyo, in *Battle in Outer Space* (1960). Or, the inundation of New York in *When Worlds Collide* (1951). Or, the end of London in 1966 depicted in George Pal's *The Time Machine* (1960). Neither do these sequences differ in aesthetic intention from the destruction scenes in the big sword, sandal, and orgy color spectaculars set in

Biblical and Roman times—the end of Sodom in Aldrich's *Sodom and Gomorrah*, of Gaza in De Mille's *Samson and Delilah*, of Rhodes in *The Collossus of Rhodes*, and of Rome in a dozen Nero movies. Griffith began it with the Babylon sequence in *Intolerance*, and to this day there is nothing like the thrill of watching all those expensive sets come tumbling down.

In other respects as well, the science fiction films of the 1950s take up familiar themes. The famous 1930s movie serials and comics of the adventures of Flash Gordon and Buck Rogers, as well as the more recent spate of comic book super-heroes with extraterrestrial origins (the most famous is Superman, a foundling from the planet Krypton, currently described as having been exploded by a nuclear blast), share motifs with more recent science fiction movies. But there is an important difference. The old science fiction films, and most of the comics, still have an essentially innocent relation to disaster. Mainly they offer new versions of the oldest romance of all—of the strong invulnerable hero with a mysterious lineage come to do battle on behalf of good and against evil. Recent science fiction films have a decided grimness, bolstered by their much greater degree of visual credibility, which contrasts strongly with the older films. Modern historical reality has greatly enlarged the imagination of disaster, and the protagonists—perhaps by the very nature of what is visited upon them—no longer seem wholly innocent.

The lure of such generalized disaster as a fantasy is that it releases one from normal obligations. The trump card of the end-of-the-world movies—like *The Day the Earth Caught Fire* (1962)—is that great scene with New York or London or Tokyo discovered empty, its entire population annihilated. Or, as in *The World, The Flesh, and The Devil* (1957), the whole movie can be devoted to the fantasy of occupying the deserted metropolis and starting all over again, a world Robinson Crusoe.

Another kind of satisfaction these films supply is extreme moral simplification—that is to say, a morally acceptable fantasy where one can give outlet to cruel or at least amoral feelings. In this respect, science fiction films partly overlap with horror films. This is the undeniable pleasure we derive from looking at freaks, beings excluded from the category of the human. The sense of superiority over the freak conjoined in varying proportions with the titillation of fear and aversion makes it possible for moral scruples to be lifted, for cruelty to be enjoyed. The same thing happens in science fiction films. In the figure of the monster from outer space, the freakish, the ugly, and the predatory all converge—and provide a fantasy target for righteous bellicosity to discharge itself, and for the aesthetic enjoyment of suffering and disaster. Science fiction films are one of the purest forms of spectacle; that is, we are rarely inside anyone's feelings. (An exception is Jack Arnold's *The Incredible Shrinking Man* [1957].) We are merely spectators; we watch.

But in science fiction films, unlike horror films, there is not much horror. Suspense, shocks, surprises are mostly abjured in favor of a steady, inexorable plot. Science fiction films invite a dispassionate, aesthetic view of destruction and violence—a *technological* view. Things, objects, machinery play a major role in these films. A greater range of ethical values is embodied in the décor of these films than in the people. Things, rather than the helpless humans, are the locus of values because we experience them, rather than people, as the sources of power. According to science fiction films, man is naked without his artifacts. *They* stand for different values, they are potent, they are what get destroyed, and they are the indispensable tools for the repulse of the alien invaders or the repair of the damaged environment.

The science fiction films are strongly moralistic. The standard message is the one about the proper, or humane, use of science, versus the mad, obsessional use of science. This message the science fiction films share in common with the classic horror films of the 1930s, like *Frankenstein, The Mummy, Island of Lost Souls, Dr. Jekyll and Mr. Hyde.* (George Franju's brilliant *Les Yeux Sans Visage* [1959], called here *The Horror Chamber of Doctor Faustus*, is a more recent example.) In the horror films, we have the mad or obsessed or misguided scientist who pursues his experiments against good advice to the contrary, creates a monster or monsters, and is himself destroyed—often recognizing his folly himself, and dying in the successful effort to destroy his own creation. One science fiction equivalent of this is the scientist, usually a member of a team, who defects to the planetary invaders because "their" science is more advanced than "ours."

This is the case in *The Mysterians*, and, true to form, the renegade sees his error in the end, and from within the Mysterian space ship destroys it and himself. In *This Island Earth* (1955), the inhabitants of the beleaguered planet Metaluna propose to conquer earth, but their project is foiled by a Metalunan scientist named Exeter who, having lived on earth a while and learned to love Mozart, cannot abide such viciousness. Exeter plunges his spaceship into the ocean after returning a glamorous pair (male and female) of American physicists to earth. Metaluna dies. In *The Fly* (1958), the hero, engrossed in his basement-laboratory experiments on a matter-transmitting machine, uses himself as a subject, exchanges head and one arm with a housefly which had accidentally gotten into the machine, becomes a monster, and with his last shred of human will destroys his laboratory and orders his wife to kill him. His discovery, for the good of mankind, is lost.

Being a clearly labeled species of intellectual, scientists in science fiction films are always liable to crack up or go off the deep end. In *Conquest of Space* (1955), the scientist-commander of an international expedition to Mars suddenly acquires scruples about the blasphemy involved in the undertaking, and begins reading the Bible mid-journey instead of attending to his duties. The commander's son, who is his junior officer and always addresses his father as "General," is forced to kill the old man when he tries to prevent the ship from landing on Mars. In this film, both sides of the ambivalence toward scientists are given voice. Generally, for a scientific enterprise to be treated entirely sympathetically in these films, it needs the certificate of utility. Science, viewed without ambivalence, means an efficacious response to danger. Disinterested intellectual curiosity rarely appears in any form other than caricature, as a maniacal dementia that cuts one off from normal human relations. But this suspicion is usually directed at the scientist rather than his work. The creative scientist may become a martyr to his own discovery, through an accident or by pushing things too far. But the implication remains that other men, less imaginative—in short, technicians—could have administered the same discovery better and more safely. The most ingrained contemporary mistrust of the intellect is visited, in these movies, upon the scientist-as-intellectual.

The message that the scientist is one who releases forces which, if not controlled for good, could destroy man himself seems innocuous enough. One of the oldest images of the scientist is Shakespeare's Prospero, the overdetached scholar forcibly retired from society to a desert island, only partly in control of the magic forces in which he dabbles. Equally classic is the figure of the scientist as satanist (*Doctor Faustus*, and stories of Poe and Hawthorne). Science is magic, and man has always known that there is black magic as well as white. But it is not enough to remark that contemporary attitudes—as reflected in science fiction films—remain ambivalent, that the scientist is treated as both satanist and savior. The proportions have changed, because of the new context in which the old admiration and fear of the scientist are located. For his sphere of influence is no longer local, himself or his immediate community. It is planetary, cosmic.

One gets the feeling, particularly in the Japanese films but not only there, that a mass trauma exists over the use of nuclear weapons and the possibility of future nuclear wars. Most of the science fiction films bear witness to this trauma, and, in a way, attempt to exorcise it.

The accidental awakening of the super-destructive monster who has slept in the earth since prehistory is, often, an obvious metaphor for the Bomb. But there are many explicit references as well. In *The Mysterians*, a probe ship from the planet Mysteroid has landed on earth, near Tokyo. Nuclear warfare having been practiced on Mysteroid for centuries (their civilization is "more advanced than ours"), ninety percent of those now born on the planet have to be destroyed at birth, because of defects caused by the huge amounts of Strontium 90 in their diet. The Mysterians have come to earth to marry earth women, and possibly to take over our relatively uncontaminated planet . . . In *The Incredible Shrinking*

Man, the John Doe hero is the victim of a gust of radiation which blows over the water, while he is out boating with his wife; the radiation causes him to grow smaller and smaller, until at the end of the movie he steps through the fine mesh of a window screen to become "the infinitely small." . . . In *Rodan,* a horde of monstrous carnivorous prehistoric insects, and finally a pair of giant flying reptiles (the prehistoric Archeopteryx), are hatched from dormant eggs in the depths of a mine shaft by the impact of nuclear test explosions, and go on to destroy a good part of the world before they are felled by the molten lava of a volcanic eruption. . . . In the English film, *The Day the Earth Caught Fire,* two simultaneous hydrogen bomb tests by the United States and Russia change by 11 degrees the tilt of the earth on its axis and alter the earth's orbit so that it begins to approach the sun.

Radiation casualties—ultimately, the conception of the whole world as a casualty of nuclear testing and nuclear warfare—is the most ominous of all the notions with which science fiction films deal. Universes become expendable. Worlds become contaminated, burnt out, exhausted, obsolete. In *Rocketship X-M* (1950) explorers from the earth land on Mars, where they learn that atomic warfare has destroyed Martian civilization. In George Pal's *The War of the Worlds* (1953), reddish spindly alligator-skinned creatures from Mars invade the earth because their planet is becoming too cold to be inhabitable. In *This Island Earth,* also American, the planet Metaluna, whose population has long ago been driven underground by warfare, is dying under the missile attacks of an enemy planet. Stocks of uranium, which power the force field shielding Metaluna, have been used up; and an unsuccessful expedition is sent to earth to enlist earth scientists to devise new sources for nuclear power. In Joseph Losey's *The Damned* (1961), nine icy-cold radioactive children are being reared by a fanatical scientist in a dark cave on the English coast to be the only survivors of the inevitable nuclear Armageddon.

There is a vast amount of wishful thinking in science fiction films, some of it touching, some of it depressing. Again and again, one detects the hunger for a "good war," which poses no moral problems, admits of no moral qualifications. The imagery of science fiction films will satisfy the most bellicose addict of war films, for a lot of the satisfactions of war films pass, untransformed, into science fiction films. Examples: the dogfights between earth "fighter rockets" and alien spacecraft in the *Battle of Outer Space* (1959); the escalating firepower in the successive assaults upon the invaders in *The Mysterians,* which Dan Talbot correctly described as a non-stop holocaust; the spectacular bombardment of the underground fortress of Metaluna in *This Island Earth.*

Yet at the same time the bellicosity of science fiction films is neatly channeled into the yearning for peace, or for at least peaceful coexistence. Some scientist generally takes sententious note of the fact that it took the planetary invasion to make the warring nations of the earth come to their senses and suspend their own conflicts. One of the main themes of many science fiction films—the color ones usually, because they have the budget and resources to develop the military spectacle—is this UN fantasy, a fantasy of united warfare. (The same wishful UN theme cropped up in a recent spectacular which is not science fiction, *Fifty-Five Days in Peking* [1963]. There, topically enough, the Chinese, the Boxers, play the role of Martian invaders who unite the earthmen, in this case the United States, England, Russia, France, Germany, Italy, and Japan.) A great enough disaster cancels all enmities and calls upon the utmost concentration of earth resources.

Science—technology—is conceived of as the great unifier. Thus the science fiction films also project a Utopian fantasy. In the classic models of Utopian thinking—Plato's Republic, Campanella's City of the Sun, More's Utopia, Swift's land of the Houyhnhnms, Voltaire's Eldorado—society had worked out a perfect consensus. In these societies reasonableness had achieved an unbreakable supremacy over the emotions. Since no disagreement or social conflict was intellectually plausible, none was possible. As in Melville's *Typee*, "they all think the same." The universal rule of reason meant universal agreement. It is interesting, too, that societies in which reason was pictured as totally ascendant were also traditionally pictured as having an ascetic or materially frugal and economically simple mode of life. But in the Utopian world community projected by science fiction films, totally pacified and ruled by scientific consensus, the demand for simplicity of material existence would be absurd.

Yet alongside the hopeful fantasy of moral simplification and international unity embodied in the science fiction films lurk the deepest anxieties about contemporary existence. I don't mean only the very real trauma of the Bomb—that it has been used, that there are enough now to kill everyone on earth many times over, that those new bombs may very well be used. Besides these new anxieties about physical disaster, the prospect of universal mutilation and even annihilation, the science fiction films reflect powerful anxieties about the condition of the individual psyche.

For science fiction films may also be described as a popular mythology for the contemporary *negative* imagination about the impersonal. The other-world creatures that seek to take "us" over are an "it," not a "they." The planetary invaders are usually zombie-like. Their movements are either cool, mechanical, or lumbering, blobby. But it amounts to the same thing. If they are non-human in form, they proceed with an absolutely regular, unalterable movement (unalterable save by destruction). If they are human in form—dressed in space suits, etc.—then they obey the most rigid military discipline, and display no personal characteristics whatsoever. And it is this regime of emotionlessness, of impersonality, of regimentation, which they will impose on the earth if they are successful. "No more love, no more beauty, no more pain," boasts a converted earthling in *The Invasion of the Body Snatchers* (1956). The half-earthling, half-alien children in *The Children of the Damned* (1960) are absolutely emotionless, move as a group and understand each others' thoughts, and are all prodigious intellects. They are the wave of the future, man in his next stage of development.

These alien invaders practice a crime which is worse than murder. They do not simply kill the person. They obliterate him. In *The War of the Worlds*, the ray which issues from the rocket ship disintegrates all persons and objects in its path, leaving no trace of them but a light ash. In Honda's *The H-Man* (1959), the creeping blob melts all flesh with which it comes in contact. If the blob, which looks like a huge hunk of red Jello and can crawl across floors and up and down walls, so much as touches your bare foot, all that is left of you is a heap of clothes on the floor. (A more articulated, size-multiplying blob is the villain in the English film *The Creeping Unknown* [1956].) In another version of this fantasy, the body is preserved but the person is entirely reconstituted as the automatized servant or agent of the alien powers. This is, of course, the vampire fantasy in new dress. The person is really dead, but he doesn't know it. He is "undead," he has become an "unperson." It happens to a whole California town in *The Invasion of the Body Snatchers*, to several earth scientists in *This Island Earth*, and to assorted innocents in *It Came From Outer Space, Attack of the Puppet People* (1958), and *The Brain Eaters* (1958). As the victim always backs away from the vampire's horrifying embrace, so in science fiction films the person always fights being "taken over"; he wants to retain his humanity. But once the deed has been done, the victim is eminently satisfied with his condition. He has not been converted from human amiability to monstrous "animal" bloodlust (a metaphoric exaggeration of sexual desire), as in the old vampire fantasy. No, he has simply become far more efficient—the very model of technocratic man, purged of emotions, volitionless, tranquil, obedient to all orders. (The dark secret behind human nature used to be the upsurge of the animal—as in *King Kong*. The threat to man, his availability to dehumanization, lay in his own animality. Now the danger is understood as residing in man's ability to be turned into a machine.)

The rule, of course, is that this horrible and irremediable form of murder can strike anyone in the film except the hero. The hero and his family, while greatly threatened, always escape this fate and by the end of the film the invaders have been repulsed or destroyed. I know of only one exception, *The Day That Mars Invaded Earth* (1963), in which after all the standard struggles the scientist-hero, his wife, and their two children are "taken over" by the alien invaders—and that's that. (The last minutes of the film show them being incinerated by the Martians' rays and their ash silhouettes flushed down their empty swimming pool, while their simulacra drive off in the family car.) Another variant but upbeat switch on the rule occurs in *The Creation of the Humanoids* (1964), where the hero discovers at the end of the film that he, too, has been turned into a metal robot, complete with highly efficient and virtually indestructible mechanical insides, although he didn't know it and detected no difference in himself. He learns, however, that he will shortly be upgraded into a "humanoid" having all the properties of a real man.

Of all the standard motifs of science fiction films, this theme of dehumanization is perhaps the most fascinating. For, as I have indicated, it is scarcely a black-and-white situation, as in the old vampire films. The attitude of the science fiction films toward depersonalization is mixed. On the one hand, they deplore it as the ultimate horror. On the other hand, certain characteristics of the dehumanized invaders, modulated and disguised—such as the ascendancy of reason over feelings, the idealization of teamwork and the consensus-creating activities of science, a marked degree of moral simplification—are precisely traits of the savior-scientist. It is interesting that when the scientist in these films is treated negatively, it is usually done through the portrayal of an individual scientist who holes up in his laboratory and neglects his fiancée or his loving wife and children, obsessed by his daring and dangerous experiments. The scientist as a loyal member of a team, and therefore considerably less individualized, is treated quite respectfully.

There is absolutely no social criticism, of even the most implicit kind, in science fiction films. No criticism, for example, of the conditions of our society which create the impersonality and dehumanization which science fiction fantasies displace onto the influence of an alien It. Also, the notion of science as a social activity, interlocking with social and political interests, is unacknowledged. Science is simply either adventure (for good or evil) or a technical response to danger. And, typically, when the fear of science is paramount—when science is conceived of as black magic rather than white—the evil has no attribution beyond that of the perverse will of an individual scientist. In science fiction films the antithesis of black magic and white is drawn as a split between technology, which is beneficent, and the errant individual will of a lone intellectual.

Thus, science fiction films can be looked at as thematically central allegory, replete with standard modern attitudes. The theme of depersonalization (being "taken over") which I have been talking about is a new allegory reflecting the age-old awareness of man that, sane, he is always perilously close to insanity and unreason. But there is something more here than just a recent, popular image which expresses man's perennial, but largely unconscious, anxiety about his sanity. The image derives most of its power from a supplementary and historical anxiety, also not experienced *consciously* by most people, about the depersonalizing conditions of modern urban life. Similarly, it is not enough to note that science fiction allegories are one of the new myths about—that is, one of the ways of accommodating to and negating—the perennial human anxiety about death. (Myths of heaven and hell, and of ghosts, had the same function.) For, again, there is a historically specifiable twist which intensifies the anxiety. I mean, the trauma suffered by everyone in the middle of the 20th century when it became clear that, from now on to the end of human history, every person would spend his individual life under the threat not only of individual death, which is certain, but of something almost insupportable psychologically—collective incineration and extinction which could come at any time, virtually without warning.

From a psychological point of view, the imagination of disaster does not greatly differ from one period in history to another. But from a political and moral point of view, it does. The expectation of the apocalypse may be the occasion for a radical disaffiliation from society, as when thousands of Eastern European Jews in the 17th century, hearing that Sabbatai Zevi had been proclaimed the Messiah and that the end of the world was imminent, gave up their homes and businesses and began the trek to Palestine. But people take the news of their doom in diverse ways. It is reported that in 1945 the populace of Berlin received without great agitation the news that Hitler had decided to kill them all, before the Allies arrived, because they had not been worthy enough to win the war. We are, alas, more in the position of the Berliners of 1945 than of the Jews of 17th century Eastern Europe; and our response is closer to theirs, too. What I am suggesting is that the imagery of disaster in science fiction is above all the emblem of an *inadequate response.* I don't mean to bear down on the films for this. They themselves are only a sampling, stripped of sophistication, of the inadequacy of most people's response to the unassimilable terrors that infect their consciousness. The interest of the films, aside from their considerable amount of cinematic charm, consists in this intersection between a naïve and largely debased commercial art product and the most profound dilemmas of the contemporary situation.

Ours is indeed an age of extremity. For we live under continual threat of two equally fearful, but seemingly opposed, destinies: unremitting banality and inconceivable terror. It is fantasy, served out in large rations by the popular arts, which allows most people to cope with these twin specters. For one job that fantasy can do is to lift us out of the unbearably humdrum and to distract us from terrors—real or anticipated—by an escape into exotic, dangerous situations which have last-minute happy endings. But another of the things that fantasy can do is to normalize what is psychologically unbearable, thereby inuring us to it. In one case, fantasy beautifies the world. In the other, it neutralizes it.

The fantasy in science fiction films does both jobs. The films reflect world-wide anxieties, and they serve to allay them. They inculcate a strange apathy concerning the processes of radiation, contamination, and destruction which I for one find haunting and depressing. The naïve level of the films neatly tempers the sense of otherness, of alien-ness, with the grossly familiar. In particular, the dialogue of most science fiction films, which is of a monumental but often touching banality, makes them wonderfully, unintentionally funny. Lines like "Come quickly, there's a monster in my bathtub," "We must do something about this," "Wait, Professor. There's someone on the telephone," "But that's incredible," and the old American stand-by, "I hope it works!" are hilarious in the context of picturesque and deafening holocaust. Yet the films also contain something that is painful and in deadly earnest.

There is a sense in which all these movies are in complicity with the abhorrent. They neutralize it, as I have said. It is no more, perhaps, than the way all art draws its audience into a circle of complicity with the thing represented. But in these films we have to do with things which are (quite literally) unthinkable. Here, "thinking about the unthinkable"— not in the way of Herman Kahn, as a subject for calculation, but as a subject for fantasy—becomes, however inadvertently, itself a somewhat questionable act from a moral point of view. The films perpetuate clichés about identity, volition, power, knowledge, happiness, social consensus, guilt, responsibility which are, to say the least, not serviceable in our present extremity. But collective nightmares cannot be banished by demonstrating that they are, intellectually and morally, fallacious. This nightmare—the one reflected, in various registers, in the science fiction films—is too close to our reality.

QUESTIONS

1. Discuss the predictability of the typical SF film by checking the basic elements of any recent one you have seen against Miss Sontag's lists of characteristics.

2. Do the SF films discussed here resemble any particular stories found elsewhere in this book?

3. Explain what Miss Sontag means when she writes that in SF films "we are rarely inside anyone's feelings."

4. Discuss Miss Sontag's statement that "the notion of science as a social activity, interlocking with social and political interests, is unacknowledged."

5. Do you think all science fiction is necessarily heavily allegorical and moralistic?

6. Explain the "inadequate responses" of the SF film, and also of its usual audience.

7. Do you agree that science fiction can provide us with a vision of our "collective nightmare"?

The Future of Prediction

John P. Sisk

Despite the fact that a sizable portion of the under-thirty crowd is trying to make its preoccupation with NOW the special mark of the late 60's and early 70's, most of us of whatever age appear to be more concerned with the future. The futures business is big business, according to a feature article in the August *Chemical and Engineering News*; there is even a World Futures Society with three thousand members and its own journal—the *Futurist*. Some of the most respectable people are staring into crystal balls, reading palms, consulting the numbers, or dropping hot wax into bowls of water; astrology is experiencing a renaissance (there is even an astrological company that uses a computer to cast its horoscopes); the pentecostal movement, whether Catholic or Protestant, has revived interest in the charismatic gift of prophecy; biologists, picking up where science fiction left off, foresee the genetic engineering of slave animals and cybernetic organisms, as well as the control of mutation by genetic surgery or artificial wombs. Meanwhile, think-tanks such as the Rand Corporation, General Electric's TEMPO, the National Industrial Conference Board, the Institute for the Future, the Stanford Research Institute, and Herman Kahn's Hudson Institute continue to sophisticate their extrapolations and refine their scenarios in an effort to make the 21st century endurable, or at least possible—despite the fact that a man named Criswell has announced that the world as we know it will come to an end on August 18, 1999.

Criswell, who can be as grim about the future as French sociologist Jacques Ellul or Birchite Robert Welch, demonstrates that a prophet need not be an optimist to be successful. Indeed, there are times when it seems that George Orwell and Aldous Huxley (not to mention William Golding and Konrad Lorenz) have set the tone for modern prediction, especially among those humanists whose natural bias is for the catastrophic. The bias is understandable when one reads the list of the hundred likely technical innovations in Herman Kahn and Anthony Wiener's *The Year 2000*, or is confronted with the highly rational and technological future in Gerald Feinberg's *The Prometheus Project*. Such forecasts might have passed for visions of paradise at the turn of the century; now, with their emphasis on control, manipulation, and transformation they strike many of us as previews of disaster.

However, for the hopeful there are more promising signs: McLuhanites still anticipate the electronic global village; R. Buckminster Fuller has great hopes for non-specialized man; Herbert Marcuse has not given up on the conquest of surplus repression; the disciples of Norman O. Brown still dream of the ultimate triumph of the polymorphous perverse; some highly regarded astrologers are convinced we are due for a two-thousand-year Aquarian reign of enlightenment and peace; Bob Dylan in his prophetic poem "When the Ship Comes In" foresees the hour when "They'll raise their hands/Sayin' we'll meet all your demands"; and Jean Dixon, whose autobiographies *A Gift of Prophecy* and *My Life and Prophecies* have been best-sellers, is sure that America "will be divinely protected during the difficult years ahead."

All of this is to be expected. Men being time-bound and therefore compelled to bind up time are constitutionally prediction-prone. In order to make sense out of their allotted time, Frank Kermode writes in *A Sense of an Ending*, "they need fictive concords with origins and ends, such as give meaning to lives and poems." Predictions supply these concords, especially, as T. S. Eliot puts it in "The Dry Salvages," "When there is distress of nations and perplexity/Whether on the shores of Asia, or in the Edgware Road." It is this perplexity, this lack of a sense of an ending, that is intolerable. Aristotle reports that the playwright Agathon operated on the principle that it is likely that the unlikely will happen. No doubt, a history of prediction would bear him out, and Lloyd's of London, who recently announced that unlimited liability must go because of the riskiness of the future, would probably agree with him. As a matter of fact, Kahn and Wiener themselves, after almost four hundred pages, admit quite soberly that "the future is an area of great uncertainty." But if this is the truth of the matter, for most of us it is unacceptable; we want what the Hudson Institute strives to give us, and what Lloyd's of London would sell its soul for: surprise-free projections. The direst prediction, if it extends the familiar, at least makes an intelligible connection between present and future. To "know" that it will all end on August 18, 1999, makes some kind of sense, however appallingly, in terms of the world in which we currently live. It gives one an end to plan toward.

Smart predictors have no doubt always known that Agathon is right—that in fact they have a great professional dependence on the unpredictability of the future. They rely on a public in which a hunger for prediction is combined with a living awareness of what might be called the Agathon factor in the human condition. Like political candidates (or like charismatic totalitarians, for that matter) they know that it can be more important to predict than to predict accurately, and that there are times when it is even safer to predict catastrophes categorically than triumphs subjunctively. Perhaps this is why Criswell and Jean Dixon have a larger following than Kahn and Wiener. The latter deal in alternate futures and so place too great a burden on man's capacity to plan. The early Church's not too successful efforts to demythologize the Apocalypse imposed a similar burden. It was easier to plan apocalyptically, suffer disconfirmation (to which, Kermode observes, people tend to be remarkably indifferent), and then invent a new end-fiction, perhaps no less naive than the old.

The relative immunity of predictors from the consequences of inaccurate prediction suggest some general, if implicit, awareness of the predictor's utility for the present. Kahn and Wiener appear to have this "present" function of prediction in mind when they speak of the prediction fictions of Orwell and Huxley as "passionately aimed at changing the future." The adverb recognizes, if only indirectly, the fact that 1984 and *Brave New World* are satiric anatomies of the worlds in which they were written more than they are efforts to present surprise-free scenarios of the future. Insofar as they are effective, such fictions counter undesirable futures by directing attention to trends or potentialities "passionately" present to their creators. In fact, to the extent that it is a criticism of the present, all fiction tends to counter possible futures which it considers objectionable. This is one reason why great fictions continue to be meaningful: they continue to function as counters to futures that continue to be undesirable—resembling in this respect the utterances of Old Testament prophets, who were less concerned with predicting particular events in time than with revealing what history was all about at any time. *Macbeth*, one of the greatest of these fictions, and itself a play about prediction, continues to counter the dehumanizing aspiration to confine the future to the expansion of one's own ego.

Popular prediction is no less present-serving, however literally future-anticipating. Indeed, the two aspects of prediction cannot be separated, probably because it is impossible for most of us to live with any comfort in a present in which we cannot sense that some appreciable effort is being exerted to prevent quite possible but unwanted futures. Even the passionate commitment to momentary experience that characterizes so many of the young implies a future in which it will be possible to continue so to commit oneself (and implies too a theology in which some transcendent power guarantees continuing protection for a kind of heroic fecklessness). Popular prediction also indicates the need of prediction fictions (in effect, dramatized ideologies) in order to evaluate and come to some kind of terms with the present. If it does nothing else, it gives the illusion of countering one of the worst possible futures in our kind of society: an utterly unpredictable one. For without prediction most of us are in the predicament Pascal imagines in his *Pensées*: "like a man who should be carried in his sleep to a dreadful desert island, and should awake without knowing where he is, and without means of escape."

Daniel Bell, chairman of the Commission on the Year 2000, observed in *Daedalus* (Summer 1964) that one of the "hallmarks of modernity is the awareness of change and the struggling effort to control the direction and pace of change." It is such an awareness that leads Kahn and Wiener to conclude that the prediction fictions of Orwell and Huxley are likely to prove more influential than more systematic and scientific projections. This surely has something to do with the fact that these fictions are predictions of disaster. Such predictions give hyperbolic expression to present fears about quite possible futures and so focus attention on their probable causes in the present. They have the effect of morale-building devices, as if they were the horror stories people quite deliberately tell themselves in an effort to marshal their energies for counteraction. Thus for some years now we have had the John Birch Society predicting an almost certain Communist takeover on the one hand, and acting vigorously as if to prove that prediction false on the other. Such a paradox calls attention to an easily overlooked aspect of prediction: that it is, among other things, a dramatic device directed against the human capacity for complacency and inattention, and hence has many of the marks of the advertisement and of rabbinic midrash.

Predictions of disaster are dialectically related to those promoters of complacency and inattention, our daydreams. Daydreams are the most naive and least surprise-free forms of prediction we know; if they are not countered they can lure us into a future in which we will be disillusioned and demoralized. Daydreams have exponential growth patterns (they increase geometrically and reach for the stars) as against the logistic patterns of actual experience. The gap between the two is one measure of the human condition. Predictions of disaster, then, can be panicky overreactions to the discovery of this gap; hence they are the frightening but conceivably sobering underside to an either/or. This is why popular predictions of disaster are so often dreamlike in their naiveté: the weird little men descend from their space ships prepared to devastate the earth; the megalomaniac super-scientist threatens to push the button that will unleash the doomsday machine; the totalitarian Big Brother and his cynical elite lock the human race in spirit-destroying servitude. Such fantasy horrors cannot be separated from those visions of a godlike capacity for consumption and satisfaction with which modern man is bedazzled, and by the immoderation of which he senses himself to be threatened. One might, in other words, consider the possibility that the human race possesses a certain protective awareness that to hope for a future in which things do not get worse is really to hope for a great deal.

Myths, those marvelously economic processors and organizers of information, bring past, present, and future into a magic continuity and are thus highly predictive. They counter possible futures by restricting choices, and most of them build morale by ignoring the Agathon factor —both important features in a period when, because of the accelerating rate of flow of time and information, too many futures appear possible. The 19th century's myth of progress was such a predictive morale builder, but, as we have learned painfully, its predictions turned out to be highly inaccurate. As it seems now, the myth of progress was countering the wrong future all along: hence in the 20th century those who had been entranced by it were demoralized when the unpredicted future became the appalling present. The 19th century lived in and projected a cultural daydream from which we are still trying to recover.

Americans are still trying to recover from their entrancement by the highly predictive myths that structure the national experience: the myth of the city on the hill, the myth of the journey toward the east, the myth of the garden, the myth of a salvational relation with wilderness. The fact that America was for so long, and so successfully, a concatenation of optimistic predictions helps to explain why Fitzgerald's *The Great Gatsby* had to wait so long before being widely accepted as a major American novel. It was necessary first that we experience as a nation Jay Gatsby's profound, if only briefly endured, disillusion with the predictions of the American Dream.

The magic predictive world of American myth helps to explain too the religious heat with which conservatives have tended to react to liberal advocacy of federal planning as a profane rejection of the old predictions, which by having come true not only made America great but validated themselves as standing predictions. American conservatives (except when radicals are too noisy) naturally tend to be optimistic and to see the future in exponential terms, and yet there has always been a static quality in their predictions: they have promised more of the same and so have tended to ignore the possibility of a future in which economic and technological progress produces profound sociological, psychological, and biological problems. The American Right, having dreamt non-ecological dreams, has woken to ecological nightmares. Meanwhile, the New Left devotes a good deal of its energy to proving, or at least asserting by way of counter-prediction, that the ecology of the Old Left was really a failure of nerve.

In the "Phaedrus" Plato has Socrates distinguish between the divine madness of prophecy and the more rational but inferior art of divination. In this scheme Criswell and Miss Dixon would rank higher than Kahn and Wiener, who are mere diviners. The latter, however, have a very real advantage in a time when too many futures appear to be possible: they hedge their bets by considering alternate futures and canonical variations on standard worlds. Thus they might be called ironic predictors. Most prediction in America, whether Right or Left, has tended to fall in the

Criswell-Dixon category: prophetically extremist and non-ironic. Whitman, a predictive poet if there ever was one, is typical at the end of "A Passage to India" when he urges us to

> steer for the deep water only,
> Reckless O soul exploring, I with thee and thou with me.
> For we are bound where mariner has not yet dared to go.
> And we will risk the ship, ourselves and all.

And yet, he promises, this is a "daring joy, but safe! are they not all the seas of God?" Whitman's confident openness to the future (remember that he was a believer in phrenology and took great comfort from the predictions yielded by the measurement of his skull) is a kind of laissez faire that has its profane parallel in the post–Civil War establishment world, in which also men were sailing forth with all the energy and intrepidity of those to whom the future had been guaranteed by the Great Phrenologist Himself.

In America as elsewhere the predictions of the Right and Left tend to be mutually determining. The closer they come to a state of polarization the more they resemble each other: law-and-order libertarianism on the Right is matched by anarchic egalitarianism on the Left. Right and Left use predictions of disaster as threats, the tactical hyperbole of the one determining that of the other, so that in effect George Wallace and Jerry Rubin attempt to immobilize each other in a dilemma that involves a choice between an unacceptable goal and an unthinkable catastrophe. One can of course conceive a future in which the real catastrophe will be not the triumph of either extreme but the consequences of the violent dialectic itself.

However, it is conceivable too that the violent dialectic will inspire a more ironic attitude toward all prediction and toward the impatience that non-ironic prediction both expresses and induces. Such an attitude would have to anticipate accusations of indifference or backlashing failure of nerve, particularly if it did not itself become the informing tone for a program of constructive action. Those who pursue such a program would be aware that goals turn into predictions out of a need to give them sanction and validity and to improve operational morale. They would have learned the extent to which rapid change induces in many people (not all of them under thirty) the expectation of a quantum leap that will deliver them at last from the whole burden of the past. They would also recognize the extent to which most prediction is at bottom the expression of a conservative impulse: the desire to achieve in some future present a state of affairs so satisfactory and so solidly established that time and change are no threat to it.

Lewis Mumford has shown in an important *Daedalus* essay (Spring 1965) how ingrained in our culture this impulse is, how involved with the history of the city and the machine. What strikes him, as it has indeed struck many, is the impoverishment of imagination revealed in our utopian speculations. Contemplating the compulsion and regimentation that mark "these supposedly ideal commonwealths," and comparing them "with even the simplest manifestations of spontaneous life within the teeming environment of nature," he is forced to conclude that "every utopia is, almost by definition, a sterile desert, unfit for human occupation." The same thing might be said of Gerald Feinberg's Prometheus Project, despite its high-minded concern for a future grounded on a worldwide democratic consensus.

Feinberg, a theoretical physicist, envisages a future in which a symbiosis of man and machine will be achieved—one in which machines, having become in some real sense both intelligent and creative, will even afford a degree of spiritual companionship to man. To him biologic engineering holds out the possibility of extending human life indefinitely, of transforming human personality so that the gap between desire and fulfillment will be eliminated or sharply reduced, and of moving all men toward "the level of the best-endowed normal man." Here, mixed with a genuine concern for grave human problems, and a commendable suspicion of goal-setting elites, is that abstract intelligence which Mumford sees as "operating with its own conceptual apparatus, in its own restrictive field . . . determined to make the world over in its own over-simplified terms, willfully rejecting interests and values incompatible with its own assumptions."

Feinberg's Prometheus Project demonstrates not only the inseparability of prediction and technological planning but the fundamentally restrictive nature of most prediction: the extent to which it is a conservative and protective recoil from the mysterious complexity of human nature and the bewildering variety of alternatives built into the human condition. One can see this recoil at work in the condescension with which some scientists react to what seems to them to be the conceptual ambiguity, structural open-endedness, and thematic triviality of literature. To the Columbia physicist I. I. Rabi, for instance, poems, even the works of Shakespeare, are only "wonderful glorified gossip," and poets, who talk about everyday things, are inferior to scientists, the only ones who deal with the grand themes and display imagination in its most profound reaches.

There is no shortage of grand themes in our predictive scenarios, which have gathered to themselves much of the impulse that once went into epic. How hypnotically restrictive they are too likely to be in their grandness can be seen in that great piece of gossip, *Macbeth*. Macbeth is compelled by the grandest of themes—"the imperial theme," as he terms it. Enthralled by the witches' prediction, he attempts to transform his nature in the interest of closing the gap between desire and fulfillment: he attempts to remove that troubling and complicating part of himself which his wife calls the "milk of human kindness." But the impatient effort to transform himself in pursuit of the grand theme displays the same impoverishment of imagination that the acceptance of the prediction did in the first place. To pursue grand themes in such a constricted and dehumanizing perspective, Shakespeare and Lewis Mumford agree, is to create, and risk ultimate demoralization by, grand and unanticipated problems, for the pursuer is haunted by the once possible future he chose to ignore. Analogically, then, *Macbeth* is a play about technology: its hero is both agent and victim of an inexorable man-consuming process.

The best prediction is ecological in that it tries to take into account the interrelationship of all relevant factors, which is to say that it is a highly imaginative act. At the same time it is ironic, which is to say that it is prepared to discover that some factor or factors were not taken into account. Most prediction in America is non-ecological as well as non-ironic, and far too much of it is not even recognized as predictive since prediction is a built-in function of our myths and dreams. An ironic attitude toward our predictions would tend to moderate the hubristic and Faustean impulses which they give shape to, in however disguised a manner. Kahn and Wiener recognize that these impulses are responsible for some of the nightmares in their scenarios. Daniel Bell would seem to agree with them. "For in the preoccupation with prediction," he says at the end of his *Daedalus* essay, "one risks the hubris of the historicist mode of thought which sees the future as 'pre-viewed' in some 'cunning of reason' or other determinist vision of human affairs."

Our Faustean impulses imply a scenario somewhat different from that of the pre-romantic Faust story, in which the central figure must suffer the consequences of his immoderate aspiration to live like a god. They embody our modern confidence that, as Bell puts it, "there are no inherent secrets in the universe, and that all is open." As John McDermott has pointed out in "Technology: the Opiate of the Intellectuals" (the *New York Review of Books*, July 31, 1969), this confidence is most conspicuously located in a scientific and technological elite convinced that technological innovation "exhibits a distinct tendency to work for the general welfare in the long run." It depends upon the conviction, crucial to both Macbeth and Feinberg, that the gap between the knowable and the known has been reduced to the point where long-range planning is possible for the first time in the history of man, and that "through our scientific knowledge and technological ability," as Feinberg puts it, "we can be fairly confident that there will be no technical barriers to the accomplishment of our goals."

The proper reaction of the ironist to such a conviction is that of St. Paul. The latter rated prophecy high among the gifts of the spirit, but this did not keep him from reminding the Corinthians that since our knowledge is partial, since "we see now in a mirror, in a confused sort of way," therefore our prophesying is incomplete. In St. Paul, as in Aga-thon, there is a warning for all future Macbeths—the warning implied in Bell's remark that "the function of prediction is not, as often stated, to aid social control, but to widen the spheres of moral choice." Unfortu-nately, most of our predictions, expressive as they are of the various tyrannies that contend for dominion in our world, aim at an opposite state of affairs: one in which the only available choice is an orthodoxy.

QUESTIONS

1. Explain what Sisk means by "it is this perplexity, this lack of a sense of an ending, that is intolerable."

2. Compare the ideas in Sisk's essay to the concepts mentioned at the end of Asimov's essay.

3. Do you feel that any particular one of the selections in this book, if widely read, could change the future?

4. How does "popular prediction" differ from other kinds of prediction?

5. What does Sisk mean by "the magic predictive world of American myth"?

6. Why does Sisk say that prediction in America is generally "non-ecological"?

7. Discuss the relationship between the function of prediction and the conception of freedom.

Topics for Writing and Research

Short Papers

1. Although many definitions of science fiction are given in this book, none quite agree. By reference to the criticism and to at least four of the short stories, decide which definition you find most accurate; or derive your own definition.

2. Isaac Singer, Nathaniel Hawthorne, Donald Barthleme, and E. M. Forster would generally be called "mainstream" writers by SF fans. When their work is compared to that of writers whose reputation centers in the SF field (Robert Heinlein, Ray Bradbury, or Arthur Clarke, for example) what major differences might be noted?

3. The articles in *Science Fiction: The Future* carry us into the future, as do many of the fictional selections. Does the "truth seem stranger than fiction"? Which way of writing about the future seems more effective? What is gained or lost by one form, as opposed to the other?

4. The nature of time is very important in science fiction. Most SF writers throw themselves forward, imagining beyond their own lifetimes. Write a paper in which you discuss how the conception of the nature of time in science fiction differs from that in stories written about the past or present.

5. Write a paper on what you imagine the role of women will be in the future.

6. Many of the selections in this book deal with the end of mankind. Write an essay in which you compare and contrast several of these selections and their various implications for the present.

7. Science fiction has been called "space fiction," "science fantasy," "science fiction," and "speculative fiction." Each term denotes a value judgment of the literature. Is there a significant difference between "science fiction" and "speculative fiction"? Further, is there a difference between "science fiction" and "fantasy"? Using the materials in this book, write a paper in which you classify the various forms.

8. Critics have charged that in much of science fiction characterization is weak, that many of the characters are stereotyped. Discuss characterization in science fiction, perhaps with particular reference to "They," "The Machine Stops," and "A Rose for Ecclesiastes."

9. If most of science fiction is "escapist" literature, how does it significantly differ from such other forms as the mystery and the western? Is the "escape from reality" function of literature as necessary as the learning and feeling experiences?

10. Susan Sontag has shown how a popular art form can reveal important contours of belief and fear among people. Using a similar approach, write about the significance of one "type" of SF story. You might choose, for instance, the "alien encounter" story or the "overpopulation" story or the "new medical technique" story.

11. Almost everyone is familiar with pictures of Earth taken from deep in outer space, and from the moon. Write a paper about the "feeling" of space, and how it can affect one's sense of perspective concerning earthly problems.

12. Science fiction is often a vehicle for social satire. Discuss the use of humor and message in such works as "Jachid and Jachidah," "Crab-Apple Crisis," "Harrison Bergeron," "History Lesson," and "The Artist."

13. Just how different will the morality of the future be? Write a paper in which you venture some predictions. The essays by Asimov, Heard, and Sisk might be helpful in providing a basis.

14. Is there any kind of meaningful relationship between a need to believe in magic and the hope for existence in the future?

15. Imagine that you are an SF writer. Take one or two of the stories in this book and try to decide what is or is not probable about them; for instance, in two hundred years will the speech patterns not be considerably different from ours today?

16. Ecology stresses the interrelatedness of all things. Write a paper in which you show the relationships between the techniques used for ecological studies and for studies of the future, both in fiction and in nonfiction.

17. Three of the poems here ("Crab-Apple Crisis," "The Artist," and "Tithonus") are narrative and dramatic. Would they have been as effective had they been written as short stories? Do they anywhere approach the usual intensity of lyric poetry?

18. After reading through many of these selections, does science fiction strike you as more a progressive or a reactionary form of literature? That is, are not many of these stories "warnings" designed to convince readers that it is desirable to maintain a status quo?

19. In what sense can "The Country of the Blind" be considered an allegory dealing with questions concerning personal happiness versus group happiness in utopia?

20. Write a paper concerning the possible and probable politics of the near or far future.

21. Do you think that the proximity of the year 2000 A.D. has created an abnormal degree of interest in the future?

22. Who is the real hero of most science fiction? What are some characteristics of the hero in this genre of literature?

23. Do a study of the vocabulary used in science fiction and in articles relating to the future. What does it reveal about the imagination?

24. "The Balloon" is a story that uses a great deal of symbolism. What other uses of symbolism are made in these selections? How, for instance, would you compare Barthelme's story and Hawthorne's "Earth's Holocaust"?

Longer Papers Requiring Research

1. How have SF elements been used by contemporary "mainstream" writers?

2. Write a paper in which you study the probable results of overpopulation as seen by various SF writers.

3. The word "robot" was popularized by Karel Čapek in his play *R.U.R.* Read this play and some SF stories dealing with robots and write a paper on your observations.

4. The computer is frightening to many humans. But it is often said that the computer will never be able to feel, that it will forever be the slave of man. Discuss the future role of the computer as seen in SF stories and in articles about the future.

5. Science fiction, like other forms of literature, often deals with the problem of man's aggressive heritage and tendencies. Many SF writers have offered solutions to war. Do a research paper in which you compile and analyze some of these proposed solutions.

6. Write a paper in which you compare "first men on the moon" stories with what actually happened.

7. After reading Jonathan Swift's *Gulliver's Travels*, write a careful analysis in which you maintain that Swift can or cannot really be called the first SF writer. The same kind of paper could be done on *The Odyssey*.

8. Write a study of Soviet science fiction, perhaps as compared to American and British science fiction.

9. Can a good case be made for the idea of the SF writer as prophet?

10. Read several novels and a number of short stories by a selected SF writer and write a paper in which you analyze his work, as well as attempt to judge its lasting merits.

11. What are the basic similarities and differences between the SF novel and the historical novel?

12. Can prediction of the future ever become a legitimate science?

13. Write a paper on SF elements in contemporary music.

14. Will there be drastic mutations in love in the near and far future?

15. SF movies have changed considerably since "The Imagination of Disaster," most notably with Stanley Kubrick's and Arthur Clarke's 2001: *A Space Odyssey.* An interesting paper might be written on contemporary SF movies.

16. Science fiction is a mainstay of juvenile literature. Write a paper on what you think accounts for this phenomenon.

Further Topics

The 35 paper titles listed here suggest the range of possible papers that can be written with this book as a basis. Most of the titles deal with topics that can be adequately studied using this book alone; many can also be used for both critical and research papers. A number of the titles definitely require your working with material beyond this book. Be certain, before you begin to write, that you have a clear understanding of which type of paper your instructor prefers.

1. The Human Race Has a Lot More than Thirty Years Left
2. Truth Is Always Stranger than Fiction
3. Science Fiction: A Literature of Planned Obsolescence
4. The Alien Encounter: In America Right Now?
5. This Is the Way the World Ends; This Is What It Means
6. Science Fiction and Propaganda
7. The Metaphor of Space
8. Fantasy and the Persistence of a Belief in Magic
9. Our World Is a Blue Marble
10. The Race's Utopia Versus the Individual's Utopia
11. Making the Unseen Real: Use of Description and Imagery in Science Fiction
12. A Literature of Gadgets Is No Literature
13. Surprise Endings: Cheap Tricks?
14. Medical Science Fiction: Brainwashing to Prepare for Brainwashing?
15. The "Superior" Tone of Much Science Fiction—What Accounts for It
16. Politics of the Near and Far Future
17. Younger and Older SF Writers: Age *Does* Make a Difference
18. Pictures of the Scientist in Power
19. The Future As Now
20. How to Adjust to "Future Shock"
21. The Willing Suspension of Disbelief: An SF Necessity
22. Why the SF Story Usually Will Mean, Rather Than Be

23. The SF Writer Has Always Been an Ecologist
24. How We Look from a Martian's Point of View
25. The World Is Actually Flat
26. The Need for Flying Saucers
27. In Science Fiction, Function Follows Form
28. Point of View in Stories About the Future
29. Life or Death—Which Is the Stranger?
30. In Science Fiction, the Message Is the Medium
31. Popular SF Magazines: A Survey, with Observations
32. Who Reads Science Fiction, Anyway?
33. Fantasy Stories and Surrealistic Paintings
34. Juvenile Science Fiction: The Comic Book, the TV Program
35. Ten SF Poems: A Critical Evaluation

Suggestions for Further Reading

The fields of science fiction and future studies have, like so many other fields, recently experienced an "information explosion." The following brief lists will indicate some of the materials available. Almost all the works can be obtained in paperback. The sampling of SF writers and SF works at the end is by no means exhaustive, nor is the inclusion of an author or work necessarily a comment on its merit. In this list book publishers are not given as many of these works are continually being reissued by various companies. Any SF fan would be able to make up his own, quite different listing.

I. GENERAL ANTHOLOGIES

Asimov, Isaac, and Groff Conklin, eds. *50 Short Science Fiction Tales.* Collier, 1963.

Conklin, Groff, ed. *Omnibus of Science Fiction.* Crown, 1952.

Ellison, Harlan, ed. *Dangerous Visions* (3 vols.). Berkley (Medallion), 1969.

Heinlein, Robert A., ed. *Tomorrow, the Stars.* Berkley (Medallion), 1952.

Knight, Damon, ed. *A Century of Science Fiction.* Simon & Schuster, 1962.

Merril, Judith, ed. *SF: The Best of the Best.* Dell, 1967.

Silverberg, Robert, ed., *The Mirror of Infinity: A Critics' Anthology of Science Fiction.* Harper & Row, 1970.

Silverberg, Robert, ed. *The Science Fiction Hall of Fame, Volume One.* Doubleday, 1970.

Stern, Philip Van Doren, ed., *Great Tales of Fantasy and Imagination.* Pocket, 1954.

II. YEARLY ANTHOLOGIES

Analog. John W. Campbell, ed. Pocket.
Annual of the Year's Best Science Fiction. Judith Merril, ed. Dell.

The Best from Fantasy and Science Fiction. Various editors. Ace.
Best SF. Harry Harrison and Brian W. Aldiss, eds. Berkley (Medallion).
The Best SF Stories from New Worlds. Michael Moorcock, ed. Berkley (Medallion).
The Galaxy Reader. Frederik Pohl, ed. Pocket.
Nebula Award Stories. Various editors. Pocket.
New Writings in SF. John Carnell, ed. Bantam.
Orbit, Damon Knight, ed. Berkley (Medallion).
Spectrum, Kingsley Amis and Robert Conquest, eds. Berkley (Medallion).
World's Best Science Fiction. Donald A. Wollheim and Terry Carr, eds. Ace.

III. SPECIALIZED ANTHOLOGIES

Blish, James, ed. *New Dreams This Morning: A Science Fiction Anthology About the Future of the Arts.* Ballantine, 1966.
Carr, Terry, ed. *The Others.* Fawcett World, 1969.
Carr, Terry, ed. *Science Fiction for People Who Hate Science Fiction.* Paperbooks, 1968.
Clarke, Arthur C. *Time Probe: The Sciences in Science Fiction.* Dell, 1966.
Conklin, Groff, ed. *Great Stories of Space Travel.* Grosset & Dunlap, 1970.
Davenport, Basil, ed. *Invisible Men.* Ballantine, 1960.
Elder, Joseph. *The Farthest Reaches.* Trident, 1968.
Elwood, Roger, ed. *Invasion of the Robots.* Paperback Library, 1965.
Harrison, Harry, ed. *The Year 2000.* Doubleday, 1970.
Knight, Damon, ed. *Cities of Wonder.* Macfadden, 1967.
Lucie-Smith, Edward, ed. *Holding Your Eight Hands: An Anthology of Science Fiction Verse.* Doubleday, 1969.
Pohl, Frederik, ed. *The Expert Dreamers: 16 Stories by Scientists.* Avon, 1962.
Silverberg, Robert, ed. *Earthmen and Strangers.* Dell, 1966.
———. *Voyagers in Time.* Grosset & Dunlap, 1970.

Science Fiction from the Soviet Union

Asimov, Isaac, ed. *Soviet Science Fiction* and *More Soviet Science Fiction.* Collier, 1962.
Ginsburg, Mirra, ed. and tr. *The Ultimate Threshold.* Holt, Rinehart and Winston, 1970.

Merril, Judith, ed. *Path into the Unknown: The Best of Soviet Science Fiction.* Dell, 1968.
Suvin, Darco, ed. *Other Worlds, Other Seas.* Random House, 1970.

IV. CRITICAL WORKS

Bailey, J. O. *Pilgrims Through Space and Time: Trends and Patterns in Scientific and Utopian Fiction.* Argus, 1947.
Bretnor, Reginald, ed. *Modern Science Fiction—Its Meaning and Its Future.* Coward-McCann, 1953.
Clareson, Thomas, ed. *Extrapolation: A Science Fiction Newsletter.* (The newsletter of the MLA conference on science fiction. For copies write to the Department of English, Box 2515, College of Wooster, Wooster, Ohio 44691.)
Franklin, H. Bruce. *Future Perfect: American Science Fiction of the 19th Century.* Oxford, 1966.
Hillegas, Mark R. *The Future as Nightmare: H. G. Wells and the Anti-Utopians.* Oxford, 1967.
Huxley, Aldous. *Literature and Science.* Harper & Row, 1963.
Knight, Damon. *In Search of Wonder.* Advent, 1967.
Lerner, Fred. *An Annotated Checklist of Science Fiction Bibliographical Works.* Privately printed, 1969.
Moskowitz, Sam. *Explorers of the Infinite.* Meridian, 1963.
———. *Seekers of Tomorrow: Masters of Modern Science Fiction.* Ballantine, 1967.
Philmus, Robert M. *Into the Unknown: The Evolution of Science Fiction from Francis Godwin to H. G. Wells.* University of California, 1970.

V. WORKS ON THE FUTURE

Amalrik, Andrei. *Will the Soviet Union Survive until 1984?* Harper & Row, 1970.
Baade, Fritz. *The Race to the Year 2000.* Doubleday, 1962.
Calder, Nigel, ed. *Unless Peace Comes: A Scientific Forecast of the New Weapons.* Viking, 1968.
Calder, Nigel, ed. *The World in 1984* (2 vols.). Pelican, 1964.
Clarke, Arthur C. *Profiles of the Future.* Bantam, 1964.
Darwin, Charles Galton. *The Next Million Years.* Doubleday, 1953.
De Bell, Garrett, ed. *The Environmental Handbook.* Ballantine, 1970.
De Chardin, Pierre Teilhard. *The Future of Man.* Harper (Torchbooks), 1969.
De Vries, Egbert. *Man in Rapid Social Change.* Doubleday, 1961.

Ehrlich, Paul A. *The Population Bomb*. Ballantine, 1968.

Eurich, Alvin C., ed. *Campus 1980: The Shape of the Future in American Higher Education*. Delacorte, 1968.

Fairbrother, Nan. *New Lives, New Landscapes: Planning for the 21st Century*. Knopf, 1970.

Feinberg, Gerald. *The Prometheus Project: Mankind's Search for Long Range Goals*. Doubleday, 1969.

Ferkiss, Victor C. *Technological Man*. Braziller, 1969.

Fuller, R. Buckminster. *Utopia or Oblivion: The Prospects for Humanity*. Bantam, 1969.

Glass, Justine. *They Foresaw the Future*. Berkley (Medallion), 1970.

Greeley, Andrew M. *Religion in the Year 2000*. Sheed & Ward, 1969.

Gutkind, Erwin A. *The Twilight of Cities*. Free, 1962.

Hoffer, Eric. *The Ordeal of Change*. Harper & Row, 1963.

Kahn, Herman. *Thinking about the Unthinkable*. Avon, 1969.

Kahn, Herman and Anthony J. Wiener. *The Year 2000: A Framework for Speculation on the Next Thirty-Three Years*. Macmillan, 1967.

McHale, John. *The Future of the Future*. Braziller, 1969.

McLuhan, Marshall. *Understanding Media: The Extensions of Man*. McGraw-Hill, 1965.

Osborn, Fairfield, ed. *Our Crowded Planet: Essays on the Pressures of Population*. Doubleday, 1962.

Pell, Claiborne. *Megalopolis Unbound: The Supercity and the Transportation of Tomorrow*. Praeger, 1966.

Ramo, Simon. *Cure for Chaos: Fresh Solutions to Social Problems Through the Systems Approach*. McKay, 1969.

Ritner, Peter, *The Society of Space*. Macmillan, 1961.

Russell, Bertrand. *Has Man a Future?* Penguin, 1962.

Snow, C. P. *The State of Siege*. Scribner's, 1969.

Stent, Gunther S. *The Coming of the Golden Age: A View of the End of Progress*. Doubleday, 1969.

Toffler, Alvin. *Future Shock*. Random House, 1970.

"Toward the Year 2000: Work in Progress" *Daedalus* (Summer 1967).

Van Doren, Charles. *The Idea of Progress*. Praeger, 1967.

World Future Society. *The Futurist: A Journal of Forecasts, Trends, and Ideas About the Future* (P.O. Box 19285, Twentieth Street Station, Washington, D.C. 20036).

VI. SCIENCE AND TIME

Asimov, Isaac. *Is Anyone There?* Ace, 1970.

———. *The Solar System and Back*. Doubleday, 1970.

———. *View from a Height*. Lancer, 1969.

Barnett, Lincoln. *The Universe and Dr. Einstein*. Mentor, 1950.

Berkeley, Edmund C. *The Computer Revolution.* Doubleday, 1962.
Coleman, James A. *Modern Theories of the Universe.* Signet Science Library, 1963.
Gamow, George. *One, Two, Three, Infinity: Facts and Speculations of Science.* Bantam, 1967.
Hall, Edward T. *The Hidden Dimension.* Doubleday, 1969.
Priestley, J. B. *Man and Time.* Dell, 1968.
Rosenberg, Jerry M. *The Computer Prophets.* Macmillan, 1969.
Sullivan, Walter. *We Are Not Alone: The Search for Intelligent Life on Other Worlds.* Signet, 1966.
Velikovsky, Immanuel. *Worlds in Collision.* Dell, 1967.
Wilford, John N. *We Reach the Moon.* Bantam, 1969.

VII. A SAMPLING OF SCIENCE FICTION

Brian W. Aldiss. *Earthworks.*
Pohl Anderson. *Beyond the Beyond, The Horn of Time, Vault of the Ages.*
Isaac Asimov. *The Currents of Space; The End of Eternity; Fantastic Voyage; Foundation; Foundation and Empire; I, Robot; Pebble in the Sky; Second Foundation.*
J. G. Ballard. *Billenium, The Crystal World, The Drowned World, The Voices of Time, The Wind from Nowhere.*
Alfred Bester. *The Demolished Man.*
James Blish. *A Case of Conscience, Cities in Flight, Vor, The Warriors of Day.*
Ray Bradbury. *Fahrenheit 451, The Illustrated Man, The Martian Chronicles, A Medicine for Melancholy, The October Country, R Is for Rocket.*
John Brunner. *Bedlam Planet, Stand on Zanzibar.*
Anthony Burgess. *A Clockwork Orange, The Wanting Seed.*
Edgar Rice Burroughs. *The Gods of Mars, The Land that Time Forgot, Llana of Gathol, Under the Moons of Mars.*
John Campbell. *Islands in Space, The Mightiest Machine.*
Karel Capek. *R.U.R., War with the Newts.*
John Christopher, *The Long Winter, No Blade of Grass.*
Arthur C. Clarke. *Against the Fall of Night, Childhood's End, The City and the Stars, The Deep Range, A Fall of Moondust, Prelude to Space, 2001: A Space Odyssey.*
John Collier. *Fancies and Goodnights.*
Cyrano De Bergerac Savinien. *A Voyage to the Moon.*
Samuel R. Delany. *Babel-17, The Einstein Intersection, Empire Star, The Jewels of Aptor, Nova.*

Philip K. Dick. *Counter-Clock World, Do Androids Dream of Electric Sheep? Eye in the Sky, Galactic Pot-Healer, The Man in the High Castle, Ubik.*

Thomas M. Disch. *Echo Round His Bones, The Genocides.*

Arthur Conan Doyle. *The Lost World, The Poison Belt.*

Harlan Ellison. *Doomsman, I Have No Mouth and I Must Scream, From the Land of Fear.*

Hugo Gernsback. *Ralph 124C41+.*

H. Rider Haggard. *She.*

Robert A. Heinlein. *The Door into Summer, Double Star, Farnham's Freehold, Glory Road, The Green Hills of Earth, The Man Who Sold the Moon, Methuselah's Children, Sixth Column, Starship Troopers, Stranger in a Strange Land, Waldo and Magic, Inc.*

Frank Herbert. *Dune.*

John Hersey. *The Child Buyer, White Lotus.*

Aldous Huxley. *Brave New World, Brave New World Revisited, Island.*

Daniel Keyes. *Flowers for Algernon.*

Damon Knight. *Analogue Men; In Deep, Far Out.*

Fritz Leiber. *The Big Time; Destiny Times Three; Gather, Darkness; The Silver Eggheads; The Wanderer.*

C. S. Lewis. *Out of the Silent Planet, Perelandra, That Hideous Streugth.*

H. P. Lovecraft. *Beyond the Wall of Sleep, The Colour out of Space, At the Mountains of Madness, The Season out of Time, The Whisperer in Darkness.*

Judith Merril. *Out of Bounds, The Tomorrow People.*

Walter M. Miller, Jr. *A Canticle for Leibowitz.*

Michael Moorcock. *Behold the Man.*

Ward Moore. *Bring the Jubilee.*

Philip F. Nowlan. *Armageddon 2419 A.D.*

George Orwell. *Animal Farm, 1984.*

Edgar Allan Poe. *The Narrative of Arthur Gordon Pym.*

Frederik Pohl (with Cyril M. Kornbluth). *Gladiator-at-Law, The Space Merchants.*

Robert H. Rimmer. *The Harrad Experiment, Proposition 31.*

Joanna Russ. *And Chaos Died, Picnic on Paradise.*

Robert Sheckley. *Dimension of Miracles, Journey Beyond Tomorrow.*

Mary Wollstonecraft Shelley. *Frankenstein, The Last Man.*

Robert Silverberg. *Conquerors from the Darkness, The Man in the Maze, Nightwings, Those Who Watch.*

Clifford D. Simak. *The Big Front Yard, Cosmic Engineers, The Goblin Reservation, Ring Around the Sun, Strangers in the Universe, They Walked like Men, Time and Again, Way Station, The Worlds of Clifford Simak.*

E. E. (Doc) Smith. *Children of the Lens, Galactic Patrol, The Gray Lensman, Second Stage Lensman, The Skylark of Duquesne, The Sky-*

lark of Space, The Skylark of Valeron, Skylark Three, The Space-hounds of IPC, Triplanetary.

Olaf Stapledon. *The Flames, Last and First Men, Odd John, The Star-Maker.*

Theodore Sturgeon. *Caviar, E Pluribus Unicorn, More than Human, The Synthetic Man, A Touch of Strange, Venus Plus X, A Way Home, Without Sorcery.*

William Tenn. *Of All Possible Worlds, The Human Angle, Of Men and Monsters, The Seven Sexes, The Square Root of Man, The Wooden Star.*

J. R. R. Tolkien. *The Lord of the Rings.*

Mark Twain. *A Connecticut Yankee in King Arthur's Court.*

A. E. Van Vogt. *The Book of Ptath, Empire of the Atom, The Far-out Worlds of A. E. Van Vogt, The Silkie, Slan, The Weapon Shops of Isher, The World of Null-A.*

Jules Verne. *From the Earth to the Moon; Five Weeks in a Balloon; Hector Survadac, or Off on a Comet; A Journey to the Centre of the Earth; The Master of the World; Robur the Conqueror; Twenty Thousand Leagues Under the Sea.*

Kurt Vonnegut, Jr. *Cat's Cradle; God Bless You, Mr. Rosewater; Mother Night; Player Piano; The Sirens of Titan; Slaughterhouse-Five; Welcome to the Monkey House.*

Stanley G. Weinbaum. *The Black Flame, The Mad Brain, A Martian Odyssey, The New Adam, The Worlds of If.*

H. G. Wells. *In the Days of the Comet, The First Men in the Moon, The Food of the Gods, The Invisible Man, The Island of Doctor Moreau, The Time Machine, The War in the Air, The War of the Worlds.*

Jack Williamson. *Bright New Universe, The Cometeers, The Legion of Space, The Legion of Time, One Against the Legion.*

Philip Wylie. *The Disappearance, Gladiator, Opus 21, Tomorrow;* (with Edwin Balmer) *When Worlds Collide, After Worlds Collide.*

John Wyndham. *The Day of the Triffids, Out of the Deeps, Village of the Damned.*

Roger Zelazny. *Damnation Alley, The Dream Master, Four for Tomorrow, Lord of Light, This Immortal.*